COLD CASE HEAT

Visit us at www.boldstrokesbooks.com

By the Author

Forging a Desire Line

Suspecting Her

Cold Case Heat

COLD CASE HEAT

by

Mary P. Burns

2023

COLD CASE HEAT
© 2023 By Mary P. Burns. All Rights Reserved.

ISBN 13: 978-1-63679-374-0

This Trade Paperback Original Is Published By
Bold Strokes Books, Inc.
P.O. Box 249
Valley Falls, NY 12185

First Edition: September 2023

Credits
Editor: Cindy Cresap
Production Design: Susan Ramundo
Cover Design By Inkspiral Design

Acknowledgments

Based on a real event in my life, this story was a difficult labor of love and redemption to write. I needed to capture as much of what happened as I could in order to be true to how it happened and to what should have happened and didn't.

Quite a number of people helped me reach back in time to re-create things. A heartfelt thanks to my cousin Martha Joumas and her husband Ray, former accountants, for their financial insight and advice when it came to the 1980s. My sister Sarah Blume was an enormous help not only with my fundraising and donor questions, but she's there for every text question I send in the middle of the day on all kinds of oddities, and if she doesn't know the answer, she always calls on a friend who does.

And one of those friends, Maryrose Preisel, lent me her golf expertise. Unfortunately, most of those scenes ended up on the cutting room floor—but I've saved them for a future novel!

Thanks to Tony Weiner for walking me through computer and phone hacking, and for dubbing Sydney Hansen's bug "banana creampie.exe."

Thanks to my wife Andrea for listening to everything, encouraging me, and cooking dinner (and doing SO much more) so I can continue to write into the evening and the morning and the afternoon.

And there is always the Monday Night Brilliant Writers Group: Paulette Callen, Jon Fried, Gary Reed, and Suzanne Schuckel Heath. This time, they kept me from going off the tracks with character names, clues, plot devices, and some less-than-stellar writing. I also have to thank Lewis Heath, Suzanne's daughter, for coming to my rescue when I called Suzanne about aspects of my thirteen-year-old creation, Isabella Reid.

And finally, an enormous thanks to Paulette Callen and Linda Doll, two of the most dedicated beta readers. They went above and beyond, reading the manuscript multiple times, rooting out problems from legalities to red herrings, character flaws to dropped emotions.

Especially helpful were the Zoom sessions, Paulette—being able to toss ideas around was an invaluable gift. Because of both of you, my editor, Cindy Cresap, deemed this novel the best I've written yet.

Many, many thanks to Cindy for letting me continue to work on the manuscript through numerous deadlines because I knew I could iron out the flaws and make it so much better.

And to Inkspiral Design, thank you for a cover that is unparalleled.

Dedication

For Gary Ruth

CHAPTER ONE

Sydney Hansen's hands shook, making it impossible to control the eyeliner pencil. She put it down and braced her hands on the bathroom counter. The old, yellowing "Page Six" column she'd torn out of the *New York Post* that was on top of a stack of dated newspapers in the recycling room before Christmas stared up at her, a few splotches of water marking it. It was nothing short of a miracle that she'd even come across it. The empty Tide bottle could've waited until morning. Or the person who'd obviously been cleaning out their apartment might've put the papers out tomorrow afternoon instead. But there sat the sensational rag. The cover story blared something about federal agents beginning to crack open a decades-old multimillion dollar money laundering scandal tied to the current city administration that involved the mob, labor unions, Wall Street, and a high-end prostitution ring. But Syd only saw the little banner above the headline. She'd tossed the bottle into the plastics bin and picked up the paper, thumbing it open to the page. It had been years since there was anything about him in the press. And decades since she'd gotten that first threat she was so sure had come from him—she thought he'd finally decided he'd silenced her. Going to see him now could be a grave risk.

She reread the "Page Six" headline. "Hedge Fund Gazillionaire Dumped into Gold-Plated Home, Ne'er-Do-Well Son Battles Board for Company." The *New York Times* would surely have covered this story; she must've missed it. *I might've reached an age where I forget why I walked into a particular room, but I would've remembered seeing this.* She looked up into the mirror. Her deeply felt fear wasn't reflected in her eyes, but it was there. She knew it was still there. After Drew's surprise visit yesterday, she'd finally had to face it. She'd never let him down before, keeping her promise to Wyatt to make sure his son was taken care of if anything happened to him.

Far from simply "making sure," Syd became an integral part of Drew's life after Wyatt's death, spending many holidays in Nebraska where he lived with Wyatt's parents. She'd carried on the tradition of the boy's summer visits to the city, Fire Island, and the summer camp in the Adirondacks, too. That was why Wyatt had given her the beach house and legal guardianship of Drew for most of July and August every year until his eighteenth birthday. Those carefree summer weeks had been among the best times in her life. She and the boy would spend a few days in the city going to museums and Broadway shows. Then would come lazy days on the beach and nights on the deck under the stars before he went off to camp. New memories took root and blossomed where the sadness surrounding Wyatt's death had been. Drew was so different from his father, yet he had so many of Wyatt's mannerisms; it was like having a bit of Wyatt for a few weeks each year.

Grown and married, Drew now sent his daughter Isabella for those same magical summers. It was as though the clock turned back to days of idyll, this time with a child who was a cookie-cutter version of Wyatt, but who embraced life with a fierce passion. The little ball of blond energy had been a constant surprise to Syd, even as she morphed into a tween recently—she couldn't imagine life without Izzy.

Syd hung her head for a moment. No, she had never let Drew down. Until now. He'd made that very clear as he sat in her living room yesterday afternoon with his grandfather's notebook in his hands. He was so angry that he'd flown over thirteen hundred miles to confront her with it. Hadn't told her he was coming, simply showed up in her lobby. He'd found the little notebook while cleaning out Joe's house after losing him to Covid in November. The shock of discovering his father was murdered propelled him blindly onto the plane.

Dismantling Joe's house had been a difficult task for Drew. Almost every night she'd spoken to him as he worked his way through his grandfather's belongings amid the surroundings of the boyhood he'd spent in the shadow of his own father's youth. It took an emotional toll on him, trying to decide what to do with certain family heirlooms. Those conversations had also included what to do with his own broken heart.

When he finally tackled the attic, he came across the notebook in a small box marked "PERSONAL." And he couldn't believe what he read when he opened it. He wanted to know why she and his grandfather had kept the details of his father's death from him, details that Joe obviously wanted him to know one day or he never would've written them down. Syd tried to pacify him. She had no idea that Joe kept this recollection of everything surrounding Wyatt's death, and their many conversations about it afterward. Would she have told Joe what her fears were if she'd known he was recording them like that?

It had been hard to explain to Drew, now fifty, that it would've been too much for Joe to share any of this with him. And harder even to admit that his grandfather's theories were built on her fears and prejudices, and some guesses and rumors that she couldn't prove then. The look of anguish on Drew's face had hurt. He left for the airport a mere hour later and Syd went right to her closet, to the banker's box she kept there, the box that had moved everywhere with her since the fallout from Wyatt's murder. For the first time in years, she combed through it—the photos, legal documents, police notes, financial documents and all those notes Ned Rossiter had made in the margins of them. Everything was there, and it added up, just as she'd always suspected.

Which was why twenty hours later, she stood in her bathroom, galvanized to do what she should have done years ago. She never should have let herself be bullied into silence when Wyatt was killed.

There would be no room for forty years of dread in this equation today, either.

Trusting her hands again, she finished her makeup and brushed her hair, twisting the up-curls around the brush to get the contours exactly right. She wanted to make certain he recognized her. As she worked, she went over everything in her head one more time—what she wanted to say to him, how she wanted to say it, and how she wanted to leave afterward. A deep-seated anger slowly took the place of the fear. It settled in her spine, reaching hot fingers in every direction. Father Moore would have warned her that she wasn't exemplifying good Christian behavior, that it was better to live in the grace of forgiveness. Syd had lived her life by that tenet, but today, she felt neither forgiveness nor the grace that came with it, and she wondered who was forsaking whom. Father would probably say He was carrying her because she was too blind to see. If anything, her eyes were fully open for the first time in years.

An hour later, she was driving up the local road that paralleled the Long Island Sound in Sagaponack. The day was becoming unusually warm for March. Daffodils dotted the roadside, and fat premature leaf buds on many of the trees were challenging winter for dominance. Each rise in the road afforded her a view of the choppy waters, dazzling morning sunlight casting flashes of white and yellow across the ripples of blue. She put the window partway down so she could smell the salt water and the scents the sun coaxed from the waking earth.

The GPS system announced that she was less than a mile from the exclusive long-term care facility that was nestled on the border of this gilt-edged hamlet. The stone wall on her right and the perfectly squared hedges rising above it had already announced it, though. She turned into the gates and eased into a parking space.

For a moment, she paused in the front seat to gather herself, astonished by the splendor that greeted her. Manicured lawns were golf-course precise. Among the dense oaks and the tall stark plane trees that would soon enough create great canopies of shade, dogwoods bloomed. Lilac bushes throughout the grounds were budding, and forsythias, their branches already heavy with yellow flowers, bowed to greet the purple tulips beginning to rise about them. In the distance, at various junctures along the stone wall, berms of fir trees protected the grounds from nor'easters, whether of snow or rain, the last of February's snowdrops tucked in among them.

She stepped out of the car and took in the graceful three-story white Colonial Revival mansion with its spartanly contrasting black shutters. Single-story wings stretched in either direction, curving out of sight. A portico of columns protected a deep porch.

There was a flagstone sidewalk leading up to the front door. A cement ramp running beside it reminded Syd who lived here. Several green slat-backed rockers and some small tables sat about the porch. She eyed the front doors. Knowing she was closer to her quarry, her own inner fire flickered hotter than the sun that burned down brightly on this corner of Eden.

Syd smoothed the front of her navy blue suit jacket, straightened herself and squared her shoulders. It was a trick Wyatt had taught her, a quick way to project cool control before you walked into a room, even if you didn't remotely feel it. She made her way to the front doors which automatically opened. Certain that masks were required, she donned the one in her pocket.

"Good morning!" A cheerful, perfectly coiffed bleach-blonde chirped at her from behind the front desk, her arms weighed down with a stack of Easter-egg-green file folders. "Welcome to White Willows. How may I help you?"

The woman was older—Syd guessed she was in her seventies, which surprised her. Did the facility's owners want their residents to feel comfortable with a staff closer to their own age? Obviously they wanted residents to feel the staff was close to their financial median because the woman's mauve tweed suit was as expensive as her hair and makeup. Syd noticed the nametag pinned to her lapel and then she met the woman's direct gaze. "Good morning, Miriam. How are you this morning?" Behind Miriam was a wall of message cubbyholes, each box labeled with a resident's name and condo number. Syd surreptitiously scanned them as she continued chatting amiably. "Spring's coming a little early this year—it's so nice out today! It's a shame no one's on the porch." Having found what she was looking for, she smiled at Miriam. "I'm here to see the gentleman in one-oh-five."

Miriam stopped sorting through the files in the crook of her left arm and blinked at Syd. Her eyes above her mask seemed troubled. "He's had so few visitors since his son moved him in here. That was two years ago."

"Oh." Syd wasn't sure how to react or where that left her.

"His son hasn't even come since then."

Syd searched the countertop for an answer. Her gaze swept over a tall glass jar of mints individually wrapped in a kaleidoscope of reds, blues, greens, and golds, and settled on the studiously arranged potted plants on the right side of the counter, but only one thing came to mind. "I'm not sure he and his son were ever close." She was relieved to see Miriam nodding, her brow creasing. "I only recently found out he was here, and someone else told me." Syd paused, measuring her words. "I used to work with him."

Miriam's eyes darted over Syd approvingly. "Well, I'm sure he'll welcome your visit. His aide left a few minutes ago. She won't be back until she takes him to lunch in an hour or so." Miriam put the folders down on a desk. "I'll need to see some identification, dear."

Syd took out her wallet and extracted her driver's license. Miriam scanned it and returned it to Syd along with an adhesive nametag. She hated those sticky tags, but she made a show of beginning to peel it.

"He's right down that hall," Miriam pointed behind Syd. "Five doors down on the right. It's an efficiency but he has the view of the Sound."

Of course he does.

"His door's unlocked, you can knock and yoo-hoo."

She made her way across the cream-colored lobby that was carpeted in a rich Williamsburg blue. Her chest was thrumming with panic as she passed a rosewood Art Deco table with ebony inlay, the Brilliant-era cut-glass vase on it holding bright yellow winter jasmine and broad-leafed greens. Numbers based on the lobby décor alone clicked through her brain, a habit of years of accountant's training which had taught her to measure and weigh the value of everything from stock offerings to new office furniture to human lives. She quickly shut it down, though, when she got to the brightly lit hallway. She slipped the nametag into her pocket and seeing no one else around, removed her mask. A moment later she rapped on the door of 105 and opened it.

The room was dark. Syd needed a moment to adjust, realizing all the curtains were closed. Then she saw him in the wing-back chair. Little about him seemed to have changed except that the curly puffs of dark hair had gone white. He still bore that peculiar tilt of the head. Those big square, black-framed glasses he'd long favored were present. The way they magnified his dark eyes had always made them seem like two giant TV cameras following her around whenever he'd been near her. She slowly walked around the room opening the curtains. The radio was on, his beloved opera music playing at a low volume. Syd reached for the knob and turned it off as he blinked up at her, fighting the sunlight that filled the room. It revealed that he was an old man. And frail, a fragile lanky doll tucked beneath the plaid wool blanket that bound his legs. Those long legs, that tall frame. Once upon a time he'd menaced her with his size. She shook a little at the memory as she looked into the eyes that had pinned her so coldly back then. Now they were confused, rheumy.

She sat on a beige button chair and regarded him for a long moment. A bit of spittle oozed out the corner of his mouth. "You don't know who I am, do you?"

His gaze was blank.

"Look at me. They say our eyes never change. Neither does our voice."

He searched her face.

"My hair may be white now but forty years ago, it was blond."

Light dawned in his eyes.

"And I worked at the Academy of the Divine Heart." Syd wasn't sure, but she thought the recognition might have turned to fear. "That's right. Wyatt Reid's junior accountant. Sydney Hansen."

His hands moved beneath the blanket.

"I haven't forgotten any of it. And neither have you."

He opened and closed his mouth, a fish out of water, no sound coming out.

"You made my life a living hell after Wyatt's death," she said quietly.

The old man strained to hear her.

"You terrified me with your veiled threat, made me feel you'd always be watching me. That you might kill his son, Drew. Or me."

He shook his head, his face draining of color, becoming an ashen mask.

"I couldn't sleep, I couldn't eat, I thought I might go mad." She'd balled her hands into fists and slowly opened them, putting them palms-down on her thighs. "I had no one to talk to but Marie and Nicholas, and Marie—finally left me because I couldn't function. Nicholas committed suicide a year later. But you knew that, didn't you?"

He slumped in his chair.

"Well, I didn't go mad. I just—lived. Quietly. But now I'm angry. Because last November, Wyatt's father died. Complications from Covid. You remember Joe, don't you? He certainly remembered you all these years. The loss of a son and the people involved in that loss are not something you forget."

The old man raised his eyes to her imploringly.

"I kept in touch with Joe." She leaned forward. "I went to Nebraska to see Drew quite often. And he came to New York every summer like he did when Wyatt was alive. We'd spend time at the house on Fire Island. Wyatt gave it to me for just that purpose. But you knew all that, too, because it was in the will that you and Ben Ford tried unsuccessfully to change."

He closed his eyes for a moment.

"I kept looking over my shoulder for you, but you never came. You were confident that you'd gotten away with it, weren't you?"

The old man blinked, and his mouth opened again.

"You know what? You did. And your threat, it stayed with me. So did Joe's advice not to go to the police. We didn't dare challenge that you might hurt Drew. But guess what happened? Drew grew up. And he found out about you. That's why I'm here. We never told him that Wyatt was murdered, but he came across a notebook Joe kept all through the police investigation. Such as it was." Syd looked out at the Sound. "Joe never got over Wyatt's death, you know." Her voice softened. Joe had been more of a father to her than her own cold Nordic parent, and she missed him terribly.

One of the old man's hands crept above the blanket, coming to rest on the arm of the chair, and gripped the carved wooden handle. Syd stared him down.

"Drew confronted me with that notebook. He was angry with me, rightfully so, beyond upset to find out his father was murdered. And that brought everything up again. The loss, the pain, all of it. How could I tell him someone had threatened him through me so that I wouldn't talk? *That* made *me* angry. At you. I should have been smart enough to know you didn't have anything to back up your threat. You were never anything more than a paper tiger." Syd stood and began pacing. "I was too young to see that though." She wanted to sit still and keep him in her crosshairs, but her anger was getting the best of her. And she refused to let him see that. "There's no one left in your life, is there? And you're on Death's doorstep." She stopped in front of him. "Why you didn't succumb to Covid I'll never know. You should have, you bastard."

For a second, he cringed, but then he looked up at her as if he knew he shouldn't take his eyes off her.

"So I'm finally going to do what I think Wyatt was about to do all those years ago. What I should have done in the first place. Because I don't want you threatening me or anyone else I love ever again. I'm going to the police with every last shred of evidence I have. There may be a statute of limitations on embezzlement, but there isn't on murder. So I'm going to see to it that you're ruined before you die, that all of this"—she gestured around the little apartment and out the big picture window to the sun-splashed Sound—"is gone, that you have nothing left when they lower you into the ground, not even your sterling reputation. And we both know how tarnished that should be."

Syd wanted to feel bad for making a ninety-five-year-old man cry, but he'd been the root of so many of her tears forty years ago that this payback was just for her. She handed him a tissue so he could catch the snot running out of his nose.

"What happened to all those pretty, lost boys who used to flock to you? Where are they now?" Syd snorted. "I understand no one visits you here. You might as well be dead already. But I'll bury you before you are." Syd leaned down, her hands on either arm of the chair, her face inches from his. "And you can take that to the bank."

His little mewling sounds stirred something deep within her, and for a moment it was herself she heard as she lay in Marie's arms after finding Wyatt dead in his apartment that morning, blood everywhere, wondering who could possibly want to harm him so, trying to make sense of it all. And then the memory faded, taking Marie with it. It always ended that way, Marie gone from her life.

Syd picked up her purse and turned on her heel. She strode through the lobby, her mask back on, not acknowledging Miriam's questions or breaking stride as the front doors opened at her approach. If she stopped, she'd cry, but she didn't know if the tears would be for Wyatt, for her younger self, or for finally doing what that younger self couldn't. When she drove through the gate, a lightness of being enveloped her. The Sound seemed bluer, the daffodils yellower, and the sky brighter as she sped down the road.

When she got home, she'd call Drew and tell him that the noose was slipping around the neck of his father's murderer. Then she'd go to the police with her evidence, like she'd promised the old man a minute ago.

As for forgiveness and grace, she'd seek Father Moore's counsel in the confessional.

❖

Syd's phone rang. The bright LED screen glowed in the dark of the bedroom. Unknown caller. Ordinarily she wouldn't answer, but eleven thirty at night was a very odd time to call someone unless you really knew them. She reached for the phone.

"Hello?"

"Sydney? It's Lucas Rose."

She was instantly awake. "Lucas." The sound of his voice unnerved her.

"Yes. You remember me."

"Of—of course."

"Oh—good—I was afraid you might've forgotten."

"No." Syd could never forget the lost boys. What she'd never understood was that Wyatt had ever counted them among his friends. They couldn't be trusted. "How did you find me?" An uneasiness stole beneath the quilt and up her spine. She sat up.

"The registry book at White Willows. I'm up here now. I'm calling because I saw you visited today. And I thought you should know—he died late this afternoon, Syd."

The shock was like a wasp's sting.

"Are you still there?" Lucas's voice was icy.

"Yes, I am…but how…"

"Heart attack."

"No. I mean—why are *you* there?" Miriam had said no one visited him.

"I'm his emergency contact. I've always been his emergency contact. I was on my way to have dinner with him when I got the call."

Syd was stunned. She hadn't known that about Lucas, that he was Ned's emergency contact. That meant Lucas had been in touch with him all these years. Of that whole circle of young men, she'd liked him the least. Everything rolled off him because he had no conscience.

Lucas's sigh was audible. "I'm sorry to disturb you and break it to you this way but, well, I thought you'd want to know since you came to see him."

Syd ran her hand over the exposed sheet, now gone cold. "Yes. Thank you."

"Why did you come to see him today? Can I ask?"

Syd hesitated. "I—found out he was there, and I wanted to make amends for some things I said to him that I shouldn't have so long ago."

"I see."

"Well, thank you for calling, Lucas." Syd hit "end call" and tossed the phone onto the quilt. The second hand ticked around the white face of her alarm clock several times before she threw back the covers. The chill in the dark apartment matched the emotional one gripping her as she wrapped herself in her oversized white terrycloth robe and walked down the hall. She went right to her liquor cabinet and reached for one of the bottles of single malt she kept in the back, a dark green bottle with a gold-banded yellow label. That was how they came from the Single Malt Society, simply numbered, no name. Her lifetime membership had been one of many gifts from Wyatt. The memory of his impish smile as he presented her with her first personal bottle brought back the dull ache, buried as it was, of still missing him. *"Happy birthday, kiddo. Welcome to adulthood."* She ran her fingers over the embossed "one-twenty-six" before opening the bottle.

Pouring a snifter was bittersweet. Ned's death meant that it was over. There was no need to go to the police now with a box of evidence that pointed at him as Wyatt's murderer. She settled onto the upholstered chaise by the French windows and gazed out onto the lights of the buildings across the East River. It brought her comfort that Wyatt had a hand in her finding this most perfect apartment, even if he never knew it.

The hints of peaty smoke, vanilla, and caramel that her nose detected as she held the glass to her lips turned to embers and blowtorched chocolate on the way down, and she closed her eyes as it warmed her insides.

Ned was gone.

She wanted to cry, but nothing came.

CHAPTER TWO

C hurch bells.

That was the first sound that made its way through the fog of Sydney's nascent wakefulness on this early April Sunday morning. She lay on her side, half of her face planted into her firm down pillow. The arm underneath her was tingling. She moved the tiniest bit, enough to increase blood flow to the arm. The movement caused a mild roiling everywhere. With a great deal of effort, she opened the one free eye against the brightness that bathed her bedroom, gasped, and scrunched it shut. Way too bright! Was that a shot of scotch on her nightstand? A buzzing commenced in her head.

Syd hazarded moving again, slightly, trying to turn over by tiny degrees, and was stopped by rolling waves. It was not a waterbed and should not be feeling like the Atlantic Ocean pitching beneath her.

I usually hold my liquor much better than this.

She rested on her journey to turning over and wondered exactly how many drinks she'd had at her retirement/birthday party last night. Someone handed her a Johnnie Walker Blue when she'd walked in the door of the restaurant. At least one other made its way to her before her best friend, Elisa Morales, quieted the room for her toast, Dom Pérignon all around. Armed with more than thirty years of anecdotes, she had the room roaring with laughter in short order and Syd blushing. Everyone had always thought Elisa was nicknamed "the Cuban Missile" because of her deadly sense of humor, but Syd knew the childhood moniker marked a then ten-year-old Elisa as part of the Cuban boatlift in 1965. When Elisa finally told her the story,

Syd had hugged her close. *"Your nightmare became my gift. I hope I've given some of that gift back to you."*

Champagne glasses were refilled. Then there were the single malts after dinner. Two, maybe? Did she drink them both? She wasn't one to waste a good scotch.

An accountant who can't keep track of figures. She breathed in, meaning to exhale a sigh somewhere between misery and defeat but it came out a groan. *Correction: a retired accountant. Who is going to miss eight thirty Mass if she doesn't get moving.*

Syd threw back the covers. The action depleted her. She lay there for a few minutes. At least now her bed only felt like it was rocking on middling swells, banging on the dock where it was moored.

But then Gene Krupa's "Sing Sing Sing" drum solo invaded her head. She eyed the bottle of Advil on her nightstand. Too far away. The bottle of eye drops was within reach, though, so she grabbed it and squeezed a drop into each eye. They stung and she blinked against the pain. She hated them, but they would keep the glaucoma her ophthalmologist had recently diagnosed from stealing her eyesight down the road.

She inched her way up the bed, stretched her arm as far as it would go, and was rewarded with the smooth plastic of the pill bottle against her hand. Sitting up was a task she'd rather have left to Sisyphus, but once there, she used the scotch to down four Advil. When the cap proved too difficult to get back on the bottle, Syd thought about calling the fire department for help but didn't think they'd appreciate it. Or send a truck. So she slid the nightstand drawer open and dropped the whole mess in there: she couldn't hazard the cats finding the open bottle. They wouldn't eat the pills—Lord knows it was impossible to get any down their throats when medically necessary. But she didn't want them playing Nok Hockey with a couple hundred little orange pucks, either. Gingerly, she put both feet on the ground. Everything ceased moving. Looking down at her mesh shorts and T-shirt and pondering how she'd gotten into them last night, Syd wondered if Father Moore would care if she showed up to mass in them. Before she could make that call, a grouchy "meow" came from the bedroom door. She looked up to see her two tabbies in their matching banker's gray sitting at the edge of the light blue

Oriental carpet. Price thumped his tail on the floor, obviously mad at her for breakfast's delay. Waterhouse stalked over to her, a scowl on his face, lowered his head, and butted her leg like a bull who was phoning in his half of the fight.

"Well, good morning, gentlemen." She leaned down just enough to rub Waterhouse's head—nothing swirled. He settled against her leg, purring, all sins forgiven. After a moment of this, Price coughed.

Obviously, they had to be fed. She looked at the clock to recalibrate the time needed to get ready for church and was appalled to see it was twenty after twelve. Those bells hadn't been for eight thirty Mass—they'd been the noon bells. Even if she wasn't behind the eight ball, she'd barely make it in time for communion.

"All right, guys, I concede defeat. We will talk to God on our celestial ham radio after breakfast. Father Moore will understand." Syd made her way to the kitchen, cats in tow. The thought of "ham" and "breakfast" had simultaneously awoken hunger pangs and repulsed her *and* called to mind the trays of hors d'oeuvres floating around the party last night. Mushroom caps with chopped asparagus and toasted parmesan, little shrimp toasts, chicken satay kebabs, bruschetta, mini quiches, and those pigs in blankets that everyone claims are passé but then gobble up. And then the sumptuous dinner, a choice of beef Wellington, chicken Kiev, or blackened herbed salmon. Syd didn't even want to think about the birthday cake from renowned baker William Greenberg—it had been a work of art.

The evening was a sparkling dreamland that she'd floated through, chatting with friends Elisa had pulled from every corner of her life for her sixty-fifth birthday to join long-time work colleagues saying good-bye to her, everyone coming together to surprise her for these two momentous occasions. Elisa knew how much this particular birthday and her retirement were bothering her, so she'd thrown the best party Syd had been to in years. How she'd managed to do it, and right under her nose, she didn't know. No one had hinted at anything in the months it must have taken her to do it, including her battle-worn assistant—he'd followed her through three companies over fifteen years earning the nickname Confidence Man for keeping all hers, telling her everyone else's, and protecting her from everything. Syd had to admit that Elisa Morales was a sterling best friend.

She fed the cats, put the kettle on for tea, and slowly settled at the table. Finally, steam blew from the spout. A generous dollop of honey went into the tea, and the ice pack from the freezer around the back of her neck for the return journey to the bedroom. She wanted to get out on this beautiful spring day and take a walk, even if the hangover protested, but the fact that she made it only as far as the sofa had her rethinking her goal.

The morning sun was hitting the bookcases, sending a painful glare off the glass of a certain photo. A familiar sadness crept over her, lingering a moment. She reached for the photo. It had paled sitting on that shelf in the passing sun every day. But no amount of light or passage of time would diminish Wyatt Reid, the cocky blond in the photo with her. Arms draped around each other's shoulders, they stood in the middle of the 1982 San Gennaro Festival, triumphant smiles on their faces. Wyatt's unusual emerald eyes blazed as he toasted the camera, no, the world, with a bottle of 1962 Château Lafite Rothschild. He'd found it in one of the tiny restaurants they'd ducked into, and of course bought it right off the shelf, had the owner open it. Back in the street, he'd lifted it to his lips before giving it to Syd. He didn't care that they were breaking the law in the process because that's what Wyatt did. *"Glitter and be gay,"* he used to say. *"Do what makes you happy because life can be short."* Had he lived, Wyatt would be seventy-five this year. Syd sipped the hot tea. It threaded its way through her in warm rivulets.

Wyatt's life had been shorter than any of their circle of friends then could have imagined. For years, whenever she looked at this photo, it was the aftermath of his murder in his apartment less than a week later that she really saw. The bloody disarray was imprinted on her mind like a lurid Weegee photo. Wyatt had picked up some guy in a leather bar not far from where he lived on the Upper East Side and brought him home. Odd, she'd thought at the time—a leather bar in that tony neighborhood. But there were all kinds of jewels and forbidden delights tucked all over the city in those days. Far more absurd, she'd thought a second later, surreal, even—that Wyatt was dead. And that he'd been so irresponsible as to bring Death home with him that night. God knows, he was as wanton as they came. But he'd never been stupid. Sydney winced, knowing that on occasion she'd indulged that same stupidity herself.

The police back then concluded that the beginning and the end of the case lay with the missing stranger. Sydney hadn't believed that. But Wyatt was just another faggot killing to them. And in the early eighties, that sort of outlook was only beginning to be challenged, the gay community only starting to push back. She should have pushed back.

Syd drew her thumb over the glass on the photo. Only recently could she look at it and see him, the beautiful young man who'd changed her life, the manifestation of violence that had greeted her that awful morning taking a back seat in her memory. In his face, now, she saw the day she'd walked into the intimidating private Catholic girls' school on Fifth Avenue at 93rd Street for her interview with a Mr. Reid, comptroller.

The building was a butter yellow in the sun, all at once inviting, gracefully stunning, and imposing. She'd stopped to read the Landmarks Preservation Commission's historical plaque: the Academy of the Divine Heart had started life as the mansion of one of New York's legendary German immigrant bankers, among the largest of the private homes in Manhattan in 1918. The French limestone gave it its yellowish hue, and its size rivaled the Whitney and Vanderbilt mansions, embodying the magnificent Gilded Age.

She'd felt less than magnificent herself, small against the great carved oak double doors she pushed against that morning. The receptionist directed her to take a seat on the long low bench against the wall of the cold stone lobby to wait for Mr. Reid. The bench was a Tudor design, not one of her favorite eras—she'd fallen in love with Art Deco when she'd studied art history and furniture design in college. This, she thought, couldn't possibly be the real thing, though, any more than the Constable painting above the receptionist's desk. She would come to find out, when Wyatt gave her a tour through the great oak and marble rooms after hiring her, that everything in the building was authentic, from the Byzantine, Flemish and Italian Renaissance art on the walls to the Tudor, Neoclassic, and Queen Anne furnishings in many of the administrative offices. Almost everything she laid her eyes on had a history of at least a century to it, and an iron-clad provenance.

The tea had cooled enough for Syd to take long draughts of it, the honey soothing her. She turned the icepack on her neck to the colder side.

Mr. Reid had been her last resort after sending out hundreds of résumés in answer to ads in the *New York Times* and going on dozens of interviews. No accounting firm had wanted her straight out of college because she lacked experience. And no small business would take a chance on her because she'd never worked at an accounting firm. It was the worst kind of catch-22. So when she'd gotten the call from him, she'd gone to the main public library at Fifth Avenue to research the school. The librarian in the enormous newspaper file room brought her back issues of the *Times* that had articles about the school's recent fundraising activities. She'd scanned wedding announcements and the society pages for information on alumnae. Then she'd stumbled across the picture of Wyatt Reid at a summer fundraiser held at an alumna's grand Westchester home. She sat back and marveled at his youthful beauty. The article said he was thirty-two, but the shadows high on his cheekbones indicated a ruddiness, and the smirk on his full lips, made her think of all those boys she'd known in high school who thought they had the world by the tail before life showed them otherwise. Somehow, he looked like he still had it by the tail.

She wasn't prepared for his presence, though, when she'd walked into his expansive office. Her shoulders straight, she hid the defeat she'd been carrying around for weeks. She couldn't let that give her away and risk losing the job before she even had the chance at it. The space, so bright and sunny, lifted her spirits, and she looked up to see the source of the light pouring in from above. For a moment, the Catholic in her thought it might be a sign from God. The geometrically-shaped panes of glass that made up the roof light were held by wrought iron window stays that came together like the pitched roof of a church. The window had stolen her breath with its odd beauty.

Mr. Reid followed her gaze and laughed. "It's hell in here when it rains. Sounds like a locomotive, or, worse yet, wild horses rampaging. But you get used to it."

In the swath of sunlight, his blond hair ablaze, green eyes bright with glee, Syd thought he might be a wayward angel. The interview soon took on the breezy air of a conversation between two old friends; it was clear that they had an affinity for each other, and "Mr. Reid" was "Wyatt" by the time she left.

A week later, she'd tucked herself behind the Hepplewhite writing table he'd moved into the corner of his office for her. It was maple, replete with inlaid seashells, and she ran her fingers over the delicately carved ridges. During the interview, they'd talked about beaches and seashores, his favorite being Fire Island and hers Cape Cod, and she couldn't help wondering, looking at this table, if he'd known it was among the furnishings he'd told her were stored in the basement of the convent that was attached to the school, or if he'd waded through them looking for something special for her, the seashells a touch of kismet.

She looked out the window now at the buildings in Long Island City shimmering in the late morning sun. So many memories of Wyatt had been stirred up since Joe's death in November. Hardest to reconcile was that she was celebrating things Wyatt never got the chance to—another landmark birthday, retirement. It reminded her that his killer had never been brought to justice. Approaching the NYPD to ask the cold case squad for help now that Ned Rossiter was dead seemed futile, and it would certainly be painful. She had told Drew as much when she'd finally called him a few days after Ned's demise. He had disagreed vehemently, told her he wanted to come to New York again after he took care of his grandfather's estate, and this time, he wanted to see all the things she'd shared with Joe when the investigation was first unfolding. Reluctantly, she'd agreed. She knew she owed him that much. The banker's box had stayed on the shelf in the corner of the closet, though.

She closed her eyes against the pain she knew would be dredged up yet again. It was going to be so difficult looking at everything in that box with him, explaining it, stringing the story together with each article and document. And the photos. She'd never wanted him to see the photos. Suddenly, she felt exhausted.

Instinctively, she knew she needed to get out, go sit in the sun in the park for a bit and let it restore her. She went to the bedroom and carefully put on a pair of khaki shorts and a polo shirt. Her sunglasses helped blot out the light that still hurt her eyes.

At the front door, she pocketed her keys, flipped the locks, opened the door—and a blue envelope dropped onto the floor. It must've been lodged in the jamb. There was nothing written on the front of it. Maybe a neighbor was throwing a party now that Covid restrictions were lifting. She slit it open. Inside was a folded piece of paper. When she took it out, a photograph tumbled to the floor. She picked it up.

It took her a moment to process what she was seeing. It wasn't making sense because her head still hurt and it was a picture of Wyatt's thirteen-year-old granddaughter, Isabella, Drew's daughter. She was in front of the public school in her little town in Nebraska with a group of friends, the familiar yellow buses with bold black lettering lined up to take them home. Syd recognized her immediately, used to the nu-Goth look by now that she'd adopted right before the pandemic hit. Her hair was black, short, and spiky, her eyes ringed in black makeup.

It had horrified Syd when she'd first seen the look on a Zoom chat almost two years ago—she'd been expecting the angelic face of the blond preteen. Instead she'd gotten the excited girl moon-eyed over a boy who had the same black spiky haircut and makeup in the picture Izzy held up to the screen. In fact, he was standing near her in this photo. Her backpack was slung over her shoulder, a black hoodie and vest zipped up against the cold afternoon, and her face was turned toward a camera she didn't know was there. Any hope that it wasn't Izzy was wiped away by that remarkable emerald gaze that had belonged to Wyatt staring back at her. She touched the photo. Her hands shook. She opened the piece of paper and froze. It was the obituary she'd been looking for every day in the *Times* since Lucas Rose's call: "Edward Rossiter, Hedge Fund Genius, Dead at 95." But it wasn't the fact of the obituary itself that stopped her. Scrawled across it in black felt tip pen were the words "It's not over."

Bits of the black ink had seeped through the paper, dotting the other side. Fear bled into Syd like the ink, dot by dot, until the dots began to run together into blotches and those grew into a stain that spread everywhere inside her.

She dropped into the ladderback chair next to the door. The obituary and photograph fell to the floor. With every ounce of strength she had left, she willed her foot to push the door shut.

CHAPTER THREE

S yd had no idea how long she sat there before pulling her cell
phone out of her pocket and calling Marcus at the front desk.
He told her there had been one visitor to the building this morning, a
repairman from the telephone company.

"Which one?" Syd asked.

"AT&T," he said. "He showed me his ID, and he was wearing an
orange mesh vest with the logo on it. They got calls yesterday from
people in the building. He said their computers showed a problem
with our main fiber optic line. I signed him in, showed him down to
the basement, and twenty minutes later, I signed him out. Why? Is
there a problem?"

"I'm coming downstairs," she said. Syd wanted a photo of that
signature. She didn't know why, she just knew she needed it.

Back upstairs a few minutes later, she sat at her dining room table
and smoothed out Ned's obituary, trying to stave off the oncoming
panic attack. If she could come up with a plan to deal with this, her
heart rate would stop spiraling, but it was hard to come up with a plan
when there was a locomotive in her chest. She took a deep breath
summoned her great-aunt Ingrid's voice, calm, steady, slow, urging
her to breathe as she'd done when a seven-year-old Syd was blindsided
by her first panic attack. *Breathe, Sydney. You're panicking. I do it,
too. Three deep breaths will kill it.* Sometimes it took more. The calm
came by degrees, and what she had to do was clear: she had to call
Drew and warn him, and she had to go to the police.

Staring at the picture of Izzy again, a nauseous feeling overtook
her. It was so familiar. That same feeling had haunted her in the months

after Wyatt's murder as she tried to pick up the pieces, go on with life, and keep things together with Marie. The difficulty of those tasks was compounded by the violent tear in the fabric of life at Divine Heart. Faculty and staff were numb, yet there was Ned Rossiter, and Syd had to deal with him. Each day became an exercise in terror as he sat at Wyatt's desk taking his business life apart. In his capacity as treasurer, Ned owed the board of trustees the equivalent of an annual report on the state of the school's finances in the wake of Wyatt's murder. He was furtive and angry, alternately explosive and solicitous. At first she assumed he was as upset as everyone else by Wyatt's death. He'd been so close to him, spending a great deal of time with him beyond school functions. And then there were the Friday lunches. Wyatt couched them as business meetings, but Syd overheard conversations, knew he and Ned were making plans for their weekend prowling through the gay bars even though Ned was married and had two children. That was what had propelled Syd to Wyatt's apartment that morning: he hadn't shown up at the office, which happened on occasion—he was known to oversleep or to be too hung over to call her, or to call Ned, so she'd gone to his apartment with her set of keys.

As angry as Ned was in those weeks, as much as he ordered her around and treated her like a maid, she tried to empathize—until Mother Adeline pulled her into her office and asked her if she was aware of Wyatt's embezzlement scheme. Ned sat on the couch with Mother Adeline, a respected nun who still commanded the honorific since the conferring of the more egalitarian "Sister." His eyes were trained on her, his face reflecting hatred. It frightened her. Everything ceased in that moment. No sounds of traffic filtered up into the great office from Fifth Avenue. The grandfather clock disappeared from her line of view. No air filled her lungs. She'd suddenly understood: all the documents she'd collected for Ned hadn't been for the board, not yet. He was going to use them to hang both her and Wyatt out to dry.

Wyatt taught her one thing early on: *"Either keep a 'cover your ass' file to prove your innocence, or don't keep a single piece of paper so they can't pin anything on you."* Syd had instinctively made copies of everything she'd given to Ned since her fingerprints were on some of the transactions—Wyatt hadn't kept much of anything on paper, so she'd made it her job to organize the files and reconstruct things following donor meetings and fundraisers. That included bank transactions.

Slowly, the clock's swinging pendulum came back into her sight line, a taxi horn blared, and she managed to tell Mother Adeline she'd had no idea after surreptitiously taking a breath of much-needed air. She had not looked at Ned. Mother Adeline accepted her answer. But she knew it was time to get those copies and other things she'd extracted out of the school, and to leave before anything befell her.

The irony of Ned threatening her from beyond the grave now wasn't lost on her after the years she'd spent watching and waiting for him. But the contents of this blue envelope—this wasn't Ned. This was someone here and now, and that terrified her as much as the first threat she'd found.

It was folded up like a miniature piece of origami and tucked into the corner of the framed photograph of a seven-year-old Drew that sat on Wyatt's desk. She didn't know how long it had been there because after the difficult clean-up of his apartment, the seemingly easy job of dismantling his very neat office had been hard to face, and it was weeks before she could touch even one thing.

His father had asked for everything to be sent to him in Nebraska. Wyatt was so proud of that photo, and of the son who'd been the biggest surprise in his life, who was by then ten and embarrassed already by the picture. She'd opened the note carefully so as not to tear it. "Keep quiet or it won't only be Wyatt." She'd stood for a long time with it in her hand trying to comprehend it. The author was smart enough to know that menacing Drew would have a deeper effect on Syd than marking Syd herself. And now they were doing it again.

Syd had been so sure Ned was behind the threat, bullying her daily and then turning on the sardonic charm as he completed the audit. Who, then, had picked up the banner? Lucas Rose? He'd been on his way to have dinner with Ned the night he died. She'd never trusted him, but she'd certainly never thought he was aware of the embezzlement; he was too busy selling drugs to all the lost boys in those days, a "business" everyone knew was backed by Ned's deep pockets. Of course that history would play into it: Lucas had always done Ned's bidding, and even with one foot in the grave, Ned would protect the anonymity of Wyatt's killer, taking it with him. Who better than Lucas to take his place?

Syd went to her computer to scan the photo and the note and text Drew, urging him to go to the Alma police immediately, heavy with an emotional weight of what this would do to him. *I'm on my way to the police here,* she wrote.

Before folding the obit back into the envelope, she took one more look at the photograph. Wyatt would have been as taken with this child as he'd been with his own son. She wished she could put her arms around an unsuspecting Izzy right now. She picked up her keys again and put the envelope into her jacket pocket. Before she reached the door, her phone rang.

"I'm coming to New York tomorrow, Aunt Syd." Drew's voice held a resolve she knew was useless to fight. "I'm gonna keep Izzy home for a while. Her mom is pretty good with the home schooling since the pandemic. I want to know everything now. And I want to go to the police with you."

Syd leaned wearily against the wall. This morning's hangover headache was coming back, compounded by the ache of the arthritis in her neck. "This is too serious, Drew. I'm going now. I'll call you tonight to let you know what happens. You're going to the Alma police, right?"

"Yes, but I don't know what to tell them."

"Show them the note. Tell them about Izzy's grandfather's cold case murder here. We need to take every precaution."

"I don't know if that's going to help. Can the Alma police do anything?"

"I don't know but it's all we've got."

Syd slipped her phone into her pocket and headed to the elevator. As she stood there waiting, lists began automatically forming in her mind, a lifelong habit of organization and a further tool from Aunt Ingrid. *"Order will help the panic. It will give you a road to stay on when you think you can't move."* Clean the guest room. And the kitchen—Drew liked to cook. When she stepped into the elevator, she was still calculating. Drew cooking meant she had to bring in groceries. There was a supermarket she could stop into on the way back home to pick up some things before bringing in a full delivery. She didn't know how long Drew intended to stay.

By the time she finally mentally listed exploring the banker's box of evidence with him, including what to remove before she did, she was on the block of the 17th Precinct. The blue-and-white NYPD cars were angled out from the sidewalk in their tight parking spaces, crowding traffic on the street. The precinct house itself was a nondescript black marble-fronted affair tucked into the ground floor of one of the city's blander glass and marble monoliths. The blinds in its two large front windows were always drawn no matter what time of day or night Syd had ever walked by, and she'd walked by for years on her way to and from work.

"Help you?" A young cop held the door of the station open.

Syd didn't realize she'd stopped right in front of it and was staring at it. "Thank you," she said, and walked into the glare of the fluorescent lobby.

Half an hour later, Syd walked out of the precinct. She didn't know whether to be angry or to laugh. Talking with the two young detectives had felt like conversing with Tweedledum and Tweedledee. In point/counterpoint, they'd enumerated that the murder hadn't taken place in this precinct, Isabella didn't live in New York City, she wasn't family, the threat was obtuse, and threats weren't the homicide department's domain.

"If the girl turns up dead, then it becomes our concern," the first young detective had said. He was very clean-cut and spit-polished.

"No, then it becomes Nebraska's concern," his partner said, folding a stick of gum into his mouth. "No matter how you cut it, it'll never be our concern."

Their responses only served to heighten Syd's mounting sense of panic.

"You need to go to the Nineteenth. Their murder to begin with."

His partner nodded. "You know how to get there?"

That was the moment at which Syd almost laughed. However, the mere mention of the 19th Precinct also sent a shiver through her. So much was dredged up in the short time she'd talked with these two men—she hadn't expected it to hit her so deeply. At one point, one of them handed her a tissue when tears threatened. The detectives were sympathetic, but that was as far as it went. The police station that had held such sorrow for her so long ago was thirty blocks north. Needing air and a clear head, she decided to walk.

Usually an inveterate window shopper, she passed by stores now, their windows empty unseeing eyes that reflected what had breached the surface as she talked to those detectives, what was breaking through barriers she'd hammered into place after Marie left her. *"You're a mess, Syd,"* Marie said before walking out the door. *"You've slipped beneath the muck of this police investigation, and I can't reach you anymore. And you have nothing left to give me."*

No. I'm crushed by the loss of my best friend. But if she'd admitted that, Marie would've known she held Wyatt close in a way that she could never hold Marie because she could unburden herself to him without risking a lover's recrimination. That was a gift Marie never could have offered. Nor did Marie understand how unmoored Syd felt, how at sea without the means to reach land she was. Years later, while having dinner one night with Father Moore, she told him the story of Wyatt's murder, about her relationship with Marie, and what had happened to it in the wake of that awful morning. Jim Moore, that rare priest who didn't judge, who believed the Church should be all-encompassing, listened attentively. It was why Syd had sought him out, chosen his masses and eventually his friendship, when she ventured back to church after a thirty-year hiatus, knowing the diocese didn't necessarily approve of his outlook. She knew it was what she needed. That evening he told her she was seeking absolution for a guilt that was never hers. That was when she realized that Marie's accusation that she'd had nothing left to give was astonishing in its brazen narcissism and outright selfishness. And yet she'd carried the belief that she had nothing to give into every relationship after that, even though she knew it wasn't true, so no relationship lasted long. Father's advice to look within had left her in a difficult place. "Within" was a place Syd rarely went.

In the months of desolate solitude that followed Marie's desertion, Syd somehow put one foot in front of the other. She'd gone to work every day, kept her head down and done what Mother Adeline expected of her until the comptroller who replaced Wyatt was hired. But she put her résumé together. And she continued attending classes toward her MBA at Columbia. They, too, had been a gift from Wyatt, underwritten by his munificence. It was all rote at first, all Things That Must Be Done. Then one day she realized she'd laughed at Sister Elizabeth's joke at lunch, and it became clear to her that each passing day had been a nail hammered into pieces of wood that were becoming a fence containing her emotions. She didn't want to feel, didn't want to bleed anymore. She simply wanted to get through. She'd left the Academy as soon as she could, landing a position at one of the Big Five insurance companies, the experience Wyatt had given her finally opening the door that had been shut to her. In turn, she shut the door on all of it. On all of them.

Walking up Lexington Avenue in the afternoon sun, she was bleeding again. When she made the trip to Connecticut to confront Ned she knew that opening that never-fully-healed wound could be a distinct possibility, that things would again ooze out. But it hadn't happened. She'd been mentally ready for it, already trying to think of it, if it happened, as a purification and not a loss, a wound opening to exude toxins. A new beginning.

But she didn't want a new beginning that day. She'd needed the pain that old wound caused her, needed the anger and bile it pushed out to face Ned. After she left, an exhilaration consumed her, and perhaps with it, a healing. And then Lucas Rose called to tell her that Ned was gone. She'd managed to keep the barriers in place. Or so she'd thought. But years of quietly missing Wyatt had worn and splintered the wood. A sadness she hid from everyone had eroded the nails. Now every step she took toward those heavy oak doors of the 19th Precinct pulled at the fencing and stressed the nails, and it all felt like it was coming loose. She knew that whichever way it went uptown, the old scars would tear a little bit more. She would no longer be able to stop what had been so securely contained. *And maybe I shouldn't stop it.* Maybe…the very act of those barricades coming down and the outpouring that would likely follow *would* be the cleansing she'd needed so many years ago.

CHAPTER FOUR

The Renaissance Revival building that housed the 19th Precinct still looked invincible. It was only four stories tall, but the brick facade's granite frontispiece columns gave it a commanding presence. Even now it made Syd feel insignificant and forlorn. Except for the tall arched casement window frames painted a marine blue, it appeared exactly as it had forty years ago. Exactly as it had a hundred and fifty years ago.

She stood up straighter, as if bracing for an old foe, and crossed the street. Her right knee groused with each step she climbed toward the front doors. A ramp would be nice right about now, she thought.

The afternoon sun reflected off the brass plaque affixed to the building announcing completion of the precinct house in 1887 by Nathaniel D. Bush, architect to the New York City Police Department. She remembered walking into the building for the first time three days after the murder, seeing that plaque then, and thinking that was so "New York" for the police department to have had its own architect once upon a time. The plaque had blazed in her dreams for years. Syd stood before the huge carved oak doors that had felt as heavy as the loss of Wyatt the first time she'd pushed against them, when the police brought her in to question her. It was a long night, and it left a mark on her, different from Marie's, but as deep. She opened them now. They weren't as heavy as she remembered. The lighting in the quaint anteroom was still overly bright, though. No one was wearing a mask. The governor had vacated that Covid policy, so Syd left hers in her pocket. Glancing around, everything seemed the same, a page out of time. She walked toward the high counter, but before she could even clear her throat, the sergeant, brown hair in a firm bun, the gear on her belt making her appear stockier than she was, looked up.

"Yes?"

Syd hesitated and then took a deep breath. "I received a threat this morning that's related to the murder of a friend of mine forty years ago."

The sergeant regarded her, nonplussed. "This morning? Forty years ago? In this precinct?"

"Yes. It happened at Eighty-Ninth and Lex. October thirtieth, nineteen eighty-two."

"Sweet Jesus," the sergeant said quietly. "Are you a relative?"

"He was a friend."

The sergeant examined her, picked up her phone, and hit three buttons. As close as she was, Syd couldn't hear what she said. When she hung up, she nodded at the benches against the wall.

"Have a seat. Detective's on the way."

Syd sat down. She was nervous. The detective would probably be young, in his thirties, and likely blasé in the face of such an old case. Or worse, dismissive. Mentally bracing herself, she looked around. Oak paneling that gleamed with years of buffing rose halfway up the walls giving the room a warmth most other police stations lacked. Institutional white covered the rest of the space. A large photo of Teddy Roosevelt held center stage on the opposite wall. From somewhere in her knowledge bank, AP History in high school, she thought, she recalled that he'd been commissioner in the 1880s. Photos of the current commissioner, the precinct captain, mounted units, and shots of the NYPD Emerald Society Pipe and Drum Corps at parades dressed the rest of the pristine space.

"Sydney Hansen?"

The question broke her study. She looked up to see a tall, handsome woman standing under the archway that led into the rest of the building. Syd was struck by the short dove-gray hair perfectly feathered around a face at once chiseled and worry-worn. Her eyes were a hazel flecked with so much gold that they almost seemed to glitter. She wore a sharp banker's gray pinstripe suit. Beneath the jacket was a collarless white shirt that followed the lapel lines down to the hint of her cleavage. Syd thought she might be fifty-five.

"I'm Sydney Hansen, yes." She stood and almost extended her hand. While masks were finally less prevalent everywhere, absolutely no one had returned to shaking hands, which Syd missed very much. A handshake had been her doorway to many a deal at the office, and many rambunctious nights in bed with women she met over drinks or at friends' apartments. She missed the solid unspoken agreement it signaled.

"And you just received a threat related to a cold homicide?"

Syd nodded. The detective's eyes intrigued her. They were alert, questioning, and trained on her, taking in everything about her and weighing and measuring. Syd understood such assessments.

Like the desk sergeant had, she raised her eyebrows, then held her right hand out toward the hallway behind her. "I'm Detective Gale Sterling."

This part of the building carried the unmistakable smells of floor wax and old polished wood. It was comforting and helped to calm her down, bringing her back to elementary school, a converted Gothic mansion full of uniformed girls skittering across the same kind of polished floors, their laughter absorbed by wood paneled walls exactly like these. Life had been safe and orderly there. Walking behind Detective Sterling, Syd caught the trail of her perfume—a mix of citrus, jasmine, and thyme. And was that a trace of—leather? It was a captivating scent.

"This was a friend of yours? The victim?"

"Yes." Syd hated that word, "victim."

"And the threat came this morning?"

Syd was now abreast of the detective. "Yes."

"Do you have it with you?"

Syd pulled the envelope from her jacket pocket and handed it to the detective. They had arrived at a large airy room that contained six gray metal desks. Three men and two women of varying ages sat at all but one of them. Syd scanned the room: sleek black filing cabinets, wood planking floor, shelves of books and notebooks, corkboards covered with papers. There was even a white board on wheels like the ones she saw on TV shows, with faded and smudged black streaks from hasty erasures.

All three large archway windows raised to let in the spring air rested on worn wood-framed screens. Sterling walked to the only empty desk. It was next to one of the windows. Syd followed, feeling five pairs of eyes on her. The detective nodded at the chair next to her desk, a regulation steel-framed thing with a blue-gray padded seat and back that looked like those all her teachers had at their desks back in the 1960s. Syd sat down. Sterling picked up a yellow legal pad and took a pen from the NYPD mug on her desk. Perching on the edge of her chair, she opened the envelope and studied the contents.

Syd watched her, thinking how chic she looked at the gray desk in her dark gray suit, the black filing cabinets providing a dramatic backdrop. Those radiant eyes sparked with an intelligence Syd always looked for in a woman.

"Tell me about this," the detective said matter-of-factly. "Who is the child?"

"My friend Wyatt Reid's granddaughter, Isabella."

"So the threat is for you but aimed at her. That's a serious scare tactic. Tell me about the murder and what 'It's not over' refers to."

Syd hesitated. It was a story that was painful to tell. That's why none of her friends knew about it, not even Elisa.

"Not sure where to begin?"

"I think I need to begin with Friday, October thirtieth, nineteen eighty-two."

Gale wrote it down. "Everyone always remembers the date," she said quietly.

Syd took her small black leather wallet out of her shorts pocket and retrieved a photo of Wyatt that was tucked in among her insurance cards. She didn't even carry any photos of her parents, but Wyatt had been with her for forty years now. She handed it to Detective Sterling. "Wyatt was the chief controller at the Academy of the Divine Heart School on East Ninety-Third Street."

"The one in the old Otto Schiff mansion on Fifth Avenue."

"Yes." Syd was a little surprised that the detective knew the school and the building's past. She also noticed the mix of pride and amusement that flashed across the detective's face.

"I love this city's history. I've studied it back to the sale of the island for twenty-four dollars."

Somewhere behind her, a detective groaned. A wadded-up piece of paper hit Sterling's desk. "And she's insufferable about it some days, a self-appointed WikiNYC."

Several detectives stifled guffaws when Syd turned around to look at them, puzzled. One thirty-ish man rolled his eyes at Sterling. Syd figured he was the catapult engineer.

"Shut up, Miller. You don't even know when the city was founded." Sterling tossed the wad of paper back across the room and into Miller's trash can with an expert flick of her wrist. The shot was met with several admiring whistles. "And I doubt you could find DUMBO on a map."

"What, he's an elephant! City was founded in sixteen twenty-four."

"Well, I'll be. You *do* know something."

Syd looked at her, bewildered.

"I apologize for some *very* ill-timed but good-natured poking at the boss." She turned to address the room. "If you all want more cases, I can find 'em."

"No, we're good," another detective said. "Shut up, Miller."

Three wads of paper hit Miller's desk.

"So," Sterling said to Syd, "please, go ahead."

Syd was aware of the gentleness in her voice. It was probably a professional trait, but she sensed something more there and wondered what it was. "He picked someone up at a bar called Bareback that Thursday night and brought him home."

Sterling raised an eyebrow again and nodded. "The leather bar. Used to be on Eightieth at Third." This time, no wad of paper came her way. "Go on."

Syd thought it interesting that the detective knew about the leather bar. Maybe it was a point of police work? The place had closed its doors more than twenty years ago. "He didn't come in to work on Friday morning, so I went to his apartment. And found him."

"How did you get in?"

"I had a set of keys. Wyatt could be a twenty-four-seven kind of boss, calling me at almost any hour. Sometimes he needed last-minute help at a black-tie fund raiser or prepping for an out-of-state alumnae event meant to shake the trees for big money." Syd shrugged. "He overslept sometimes, so I'd go get him up and get him to work."

"I see." Sterling tapped her pen on the pad. The page was half full of notes. "So you were his assistant."

"No. Junior accountant. But it was only the two of us, so I did whatever he needed done."

"Okay, so you let yourself into his apartment. And then?"

"I called nine-one-one." Syd was already feeling drained. But she told the detective everything, from the horrifyingly disarrayed state of the apartment to the arrival of the police and the two detectives who handled the scene, the little evidence collection that took place, and the derogatory remarks.

"They let you stay while they worked?"

The incredulity in Sterling's voice registered on her face; Syd couldn't have missed it if she'd tried. "I insisted. I told them I was his sister. But I think I was in shock."

"You probably were. They should have made you leave."

"But if they had—they did a shoddy job, Detective. I watched them."

Sterling pursed her lips and took in a breath. "You said you had evidence they didn't want to hear."

"Afterward. There were things I came across afterward. Documents pertaining to the embezzlement that was discovered at the school. Wyatt was taking money, but I don't think he was working alone, and I don't think it was even his idea. I think he was killed because of it." Syd looked at her hands, aware that Detective Sterling's face had become an impassive mask. She hated it when she couldn't read a person. Calculating numbers, budgets and bottom lines had been Syd's career bread and butter, but calculating people's reactions had been the skill that set her apart, leading to a corner suite on the executive floor. "I think the guy who did it was possibly hired to kill him. The police never found him."

"Hired by whom?"

"I've always thought it was Ned Rossiter, the board treasurer. He and Wyatt were very close." Syd took in a deep breath and let it out, aware that what she was about to say could sound preposterous. "I had no way to prove it. In fact, I wasn't even aware of the embezzlement until Ned uncovered it after Wyatt's death. But it was the way he discovered it, the way he carried out his forensic audit, like he already knew about it." She kept her eyes on Detective Sterling's face, wanting to make sure she understood the implication.

"If he was the treasurer, he must've been well connected in the community and had a solid financial background. What did he do for a living?"

"He had his own hedge fund."

Sterling made a note. "Rossiter Enterprises?"

"Yes." Syd figured everyone knew Ned's firm after some of the brutal national corporate takeover wars of the nineties.

"And he and Wyatt were close—how?"

"I think they might've been—involved. Although Ned was married and had children. And Wyatt had a boyfriend."

"So there could've been some jealousy there."

"I suppose. Although I never saw it."

"But you think the murder had to do with the embezzlement?"

"Yes. Ned was so angry after the murder, and I became aware that he was using the documents I was collecting for him to blame it all on Wyatt, and maybe me as well. But the Wyatt I knew wouldn't have done it." Syd began to think Sterling's line of questioning meant she didn't believe her.

"Maybe Ned was as angry as you that some stranger killed his good friend who was also possibly his lover." Sterling sat back and folded her hands. "You know, there were a fair number of murders back then. Of gay men. In the eighties, low-level Mafia guys who decided the bar scene was a good shake-down opportunity. If a guy protested or fought back, he was knifed or shot."

Syd, momentarily shocked by Sterling's explanation, and her change of tone and demeanor, got angry—for the dismissal and for all the gay men who'd lost their wallets and their lives. "No, I didn't know about that," she said sharply. "But if the cops knew, why did it go on? And where were these men killed?"

"Usually near the bar they were in, often in their own apartments."

A sigh of frustration escaped Syd. Why she'd thought this detective would be different she didn't know. "So you're going to tell me that's likely what happened to Wyatt, and I should live with what the detectives found back then."

Sterling sucked in her bottom lip and looked at Syd thoughtfully. "Building out a case this cold involving embezzlement is tricky at best. Records are gone, bank accounts long closed, money trails dead. How much are we talking about here?"

"Ten million dollars."

Sterling looked out the window. "That is considerable. On the other hand, if your friend picked up a stranger that night…"

Syd couldn't believe what she was hearing. "But I got a threat."

"And that's, quite frankly, my main concern."

"But you'll tell me you can't do anything anyway unless someone actually harms me." Syd picked up her bag.

"That wasn't where I was going."

"You know, not for nothin'," the cop sitting at the next desk said. "But some o' those guys back in the day could be assholes."

Syd turned to look at him.

"Your detectives. I don't usually butt in, but small office and all. That generation wasn't very understanding, shall we say." He put air quotes around the word "understanding."

"This is my partner, Tommy D'Angelo," Sterling said.

Obviously, D'Angelo *did* butt in, and had been listening, waiting, biding his time. Syd assessed him. He was a block of granite possibly in his late fifties, dark hair slicked back, coal-black eyes, clean-shaved, an inscrutable gaze. His tie was a skinny black one, his gray suit pinstriped, like Detective Sterling's, but off-the-rack worlds apart from hers in make and cost. Syd didn't like stereotyping, but he could've passed for a member of the Mafia himself. "And you've been listening to this conversation the whole time, haven't you?" Syd cocked her head in the "I see you" moment.

The detective leaned forward. "O' course. We tag team. She looks, I listen." He shifted in his chair to face Syd. "I worked that gig undercover right outta the academy. The gay bars. They needed guys looked like me, young thugs. A lot of those murders *were* Mafia Turks making their mark and some bank, knowin' these guys couldn't afford to be outed. But a fair amount weren't Mafia." Tommy counted off on his fingers. "You had your psychos, your fag baiters and some just plain robberies, wrong place, wrong time, like any New Yorker. You also had your lovers' quarrels. Though why anybody'd wanna knife a lover in an alley I don't get. I mean, who argues in an alley?"

"Men who couldn't be seen doing it in public," Syd said. She knew all too well the precautions they'd had to take back then, when she was unable to even touch Marie out on the sidewalk the way she longed to do.

"I'd still take the argument home. Point is, Gale," he said, turning toward his partner, "we know what went on back then. You worked that stuff, too. I'm not pointin' fingers, but some gold shields coulda cared less, right?" He looked back at Syd. "You're sayin' this Rossiter fellow was maybe involved in the embezzlement, involved with your friend, and then suddenly your friend is gone after he picks up a stranger in a bar. Kind of a coincidence, don't you think, Gale?"

"And I know what you think about coincidences, yes," she said quietly.

"No such thing in a murder case. If she's got stuff, why don't we at least look at it? And maybe pull a file or two, see who the guys back then liked for it. We both know from sittin' at these desks that they got some cases wrong. Besides, now she's got the active threat."

Syd cleared her throat. "I got a threat back then, too."

"Well, that was quite a lede to bury," Detective Sterling said, a trace of concern in her voice.

Syd put her bag back down. "I'm sorry, I should've brought it with me, but I don't think I was thinking too clearly this morning. My only concern is protecting Izzy."

"And that's a good call. Do you by any chance still have the original threat?" Tommy asked.

"Or remember what it said?" Sterling asked.

"Wyatt kept a photo of his seven-year-old son, Drew, on his desk. It was tucked into the corner. It said 'Keep quiet or it won't only be Wyatt.'"

"So they threatened his kid then—"

Sterling handed the contents of the blue envelope to Tommy. "And now his granddaughter. Spreading the love down the ages."

"So out of nowhere, although it's a month after the Rossiter fellow kicks the bucket, you get this."

"Not—out of nowhere. About a month ago, I went to see Ned. He was in a facility in Connecticut. White Willows." She told them about Drew, Joe, the notebook, and Drew's heartbreak and anger at finding out how Wyatt died. "Drew wanted to go to the police. Which I would have done with him. But I knew where Ned was, and I wanted him to know all of this—that Joe was dead, that Drew found out—I wanted him to know what it felt like, to be as afraid as he'd made me all those years ago, so I drove to Connecticut to confront him. But I think I opened Pandora's box. And quite frankly, it's terrified me. I can't let anything happen to Izzy. Losing Wyatt was hard enough. Please—you have to reopen this case. And solve it."

"That's where I was going before," Sterling said, "what I was thinking. The threat to the child, and therefore to you, are very real." Gale ran a hand through her hair. "All right, well, we know probably nothing will be in the databases, Tommy, but why don't we do a quick search anyway? Then we can go out to Brooklyn and see if there are files or boxes of evidence out there."

"What was Wyatt's address?" Tommy asked.

When Syd got home an hour later, she unpacked the groceries she'd picked up on the walk back, and then opened the French doors in the living room. There were three sets of them overlooking the building's back yard, with the FDR Drive and the East River beyond. Each one had a tiny decorative balcony. Those doors were the reason Syd had fallen in love with the apartment she could barely afford at the time. Because her cats then, Scrooge and Marley, always wanted to curl up in the sun on those little balconies, she'd had sturdy screen doors made. It turned out to be a wise foresight. She could keep the outer doors open day or night without fear of birds or bugs flying in, or cats flying out as they chased them. She and five other neighbors were the only people she knew in Manhattan who had such screen doors.

That fresh scent she could only call sunshine rode in on the spring breeze. From across the river, which was a bright blue in the afternoon sun, the enormous red Pepsi-Cola sign stared back at her. She waited; a moment later, she was rewarded with the smell of the wild pink roses that someone had planted long ago on the strips of city property that paralleled the FDR Drive behind all the buildings on

Syd's street, continuing for many blocks uptown. Because they were wild, they'd proliferated—she could see them from her windows. The City of New York seemed not to mind the roses on its property because they remained untouched, a bit of Heaven beside the constant ebb and flow.

She leaned against the door frame, breathed in the cool air and gazed at the river. All the way home she'd thought about the banker's box in the back of her closet. Sterling and D'Angelo wanted the contents. It would feel odd handing it over, finally putting the encumbrance down. Trusting someone else with it. Syd wasn't sure she could do that. She'd told Sterling she wanted to know as much as they could tell her as they worked, wanted to help them if they ran into dead ends where her firsthand knowledge could shed light. Then she'd watched as they began the first steps, jotting things down, trading ideas in shorthand, fascinated by their relationship.

"Let me get the physical evidence," Tommy had said to Sterling, "and I'll work with it in the warehouse in case it's in bad shape. I know how much you hate mold and crud. You chase down the paper files and then sit with Syd and get names, addresses." He'd turned back to Syd. "Everything you can remember about everyone involved. And I want the photos you mentioned of your friend's apartment afterward right away."

Syd shuddered. They were buried at the bottom of the box in manila envelopes. She hadn't seen them since the day her friend Nicholas St. John dropped them off several weeks after taking them for her. She'd called him a few days after the murder, asking if he'd take on the difficult task of the photos. Something told her she'd need them. Nicholas had developed them in a friend's dark room to avoid questions at the lab he usually took his rolls of film to on the Upper West Side. It had been a somber moment, a changing of the guard, Nicholas entrusting her with his burden. That night she'd looked at them all, reliving the shock, the pain and the heartache, working her way through a box of tissues, and then she'd put them away. A year later, Nicholas was gone. The note he left was brief, but Syd hadn't needed to read it to know what it held. She'd shared Nicholas's grief with every photo he snapped, with every bucket of bloodied cleaning water they poured down the bathtub drain as they scrubbed Wyatt's apartment—neither one of them had wanted a faceless company coming in to do that. When they pushed Wyatt's blood-soaked mattress out the bedroom window to the super waiting in the courtyard below, they'd sat on the fire escape afterward, Nicholas sobbing; Syd was, by that point, empty, and questioning their pact to clean up Wyatt's apartment as one last act of preserving his memory. It had, instead, been insanity.

She knew about Nicholas and Wyatt's affair, knew it ended when Theo swept Wyatt off his feet. Anyone could see that Nicholas was crushed. Syd had tried to help him move on. When the call came from his roommate, she was devastated. Memories of Nicholas would always be with her, shadowing those of Wyatt.

It would be a relief to get the photos out of her apartment before Drew arrived—she couldn't let him see them.

She'd told Tommy that the other information he wanted could result in a lot of dead ends. "I know I won't remember a lot of the names of those boys who hung around Ned and Wyatt." She thought of Lucas Rose. He would remember. But she had no desire to contact him. "I lost track of so many of them. And I'm certain AIDS took its toll."

"Be that as it may," he'd said. "Anything, everything. Board members who served with this Ned fellow, parents who parted with truckloads of donations, nuns, friends, enemies."

The irony that one could be both a friend and an enemy hadn't been lost on her. "You think the nuns…?"

Tommy had wagged his finger. "Lotta stuff can get tangled up in a pair o' rosary beads, you know what I mean."

Syd shook her head—obviously, Tommy was Catholic. Divine Heart nuns could be savvy, and they were certainly cunning businesswomen, but thieves? "Anyway," she'd said, "they're all dead now."

"Don't care," Tommy replied. "Gimme anything you have— old addresses, old phone numbers, old employers, grad schools." He explained that he wanted to see the cross-pollination on all the lists. "There could be a thread somewhere, but if I don't have all the players, I can't see the thread to yank on it. I want to know who is on your lists that wasn't on those detectives' lists."

"If there *was* a list of suspects," Sterling had added quietly.

On the walk home, Syd thought about the lost boys, too. Tommy was very interested in those beautiful young men who'd hung around Ned Rossiter like he was the pied piper. She'd never liked any of them. They couldn't be trusted. They were the kind of boys who'd step over their dying mothers to get to her favorite feather boa. Syd could see their faces even if she couldn't remember their names. The urge to call Lucas Rose to find out who among them might still be alive nibbled at her, but it left her cold, and then shaking with the same kind of angry heat that had burned within her when she went to see Ned that day. His last day. But Lucas would know it wasn't a social call. Disturbing the wasp's nest of Wyatt's murder now that she was certain someone somewhere had been enraged by her visit to Ned was going to have consequences. Or more consequences than the one it had already had. Lucas would surely be one of those threads Tommy wanted to yank. She'd find a reason to call him.

And as much as she hated thinking about Lucas, she'd had to focus on Ned Rossiter again, too. Wyatt knew exactly who Ned was, and still he'd not been immune to his charms. The strike against Syd with Ned was that she was a woman among those particular men. Because of her burgeoning relationship with Wyatt, and their mutual need to be in Wyatt's orbit, she and Ned had created a delicate dance. That seemed to come easily to Ned, who made immediate connections to everyone. Those connections were all about need and usury, but Ned cloaked them so well in camaraderie, intimacy, even: the dark eyes behind imposing black glasses frames, a hand gently placed on the small of the back, the unrepressed laughter, the shared secret. She'd watched him at work countless times with everyone in his sphere, always astonished at how it transformed a person, as if Ned had waved a wand. But she wasn't fooled. She saw through it all, and because she knew Wyatt was better than that, she'd never understood his need to be with Ned and those boys.

"They're low-class," she said quietly when they were talking one morning after he came in hung over and Syd got him up and running with enough coffee to wipe out a small plantation in Brazil. She didn't care that he shared the antics of what had gone on the night before. She cared that these young men dragged him down into the muck.

"Darling," he said with a wave of his hand. "What do you think I am?"

She'd opened her mouth to protest until she'd caught the cold glint in his eye.

"I'm a low-class farm boy from Nebraska who figured out how to negotiate the big city, wear bespoke threads, and find a few like-minded men."

"They're not like you, Wyatt."

"No, I'm like them. And so is Ned. We are all pigs rutting in the mud."

Syd hated when he stared her down.

"In the mud," he'd repeated. "You have a lot to learn, kiddo, and I promise to teach you everything."

"I will never rut in the mud."

"Never say never, darling."

And then one night, Ned turned his charm on her. She'd gone out to dinner with Wyatt and Ned soon after that conversation. Had Wyatt told Ned about her remarks? Or was it a peremptory peace-keeping mission? It didn't matter, for Ned figured out what Syd secretly wanted and needed, had never had, and that night he fulfilled the wish. His paternal demeanor set her at ease, his benevolent questions drew her out, her answers finding safe landing in his encompassing gaze. Afterward, they'd gone to a club, and as if by magic, hers was the conversation that sparkled all night, drinks were delivered right when they were needed, pretty girls arriving the same way, one of them sure to take her home. All of it from a wand Ned held that no one ever saw, the simple trick of paying exclusive attention. And the boys, the beautiful boys—they fluttered around Ned, his pockets full of Ecstasy, and they floated on the dance floor, and it was hard to look away from any of it, or to leave it when the clock struck midnight. Wyatt had joked once that Ned was like the last lifeboat leaving the *Titanic*, all the boys wanting to be aboard it. But Syd had always suspected it was the other way around, that the boys were the ship glittering on the water in the night, and Ned had needed to board it, no one aware that it was going to sink. With his expensive suits, Patek Philippe watches, Louboutin loafers, and a wallet that rained money, he was the epitome of what the boys wanted, or wanted to be. And he used it.

She'd stayed away from Ned as much as she could after that night. It wasn't enough to see through him, she had to keep clear of his alchemy as well. She had a father, and she didn't like him, either.

She settled on the chaise by the window and reached for a notepad on the table. The sun warmed her, and she lay back for a moment thinking about all the ways her life was about to drastically change, praying she was ready for it. It wasn't what she'd envisioned at this juncture. She thought she'd be planning her summer on Fire Island, going out to the house weeks earlier now that she could spend the next five or six months there. She wanted to be making a chart of all the friends she intended to have to the house, and what weekend they'd come, not lists of people who might've been involved in Wyatt's murder forty years ago. She ran her hand comfortingly over the chaise's maroon material, the raised diamond brocade pattern resonating on her skin. It was beginning to feel worn in places. She'd have to have it reupholstered soon.

With a dejected sigh, she began to write the names of all those young men she'd recalled on her walk home, and bits of information about the ones whose faces were the only thing she could remember. After a few minutes, it occurred to her that she'd kept old address books in the bottom of a drawer in her desk. She dug them out. Miraculously, there was a tatty purple vinyl thing from 1983. Flipping through the pages, she found familiar names, sat back down, and transcribed them onto the pad. Waterhouse jumped up, stepped into her lap, and kneaded her thighs. When he was satisfied that they were the right consistency, he turned in a pin-tight circle and curled up. She ran her hand over his back, and he burred twice, fixing narrowed eyes on her.

"It's not dinner time. And you can't guilt me into snacks, either."

He didn't budge.

"No, you can't."

His head popped up and he unfurled a paw, put it on her arm.

"Thank you, sweetie." She scratched him between the ears, and he purred. "Yes, it was a very hard day, and I love you, too, but none of that translates to treats. You're too portly as it is."

She did love Waterhouse. And Price. As she'd loved Scrooge and Marley, and Astor and Vanderbilt before them. They were easy to love. They didn't wonder where she was or when she was coming home. They didn't accuse her of not loving them. They didn't need her attention—at least not much of it. And they didn't judge her and find her lacking. Nor did they walk out on her. They were the perfect companions.

And right now, Waterhouse was doing what he did best, comforting her. He always knew when she needed it. Drew's arrival tomorrow was weighing on her. She worried about the impact the contents of the evidence box would have on him. It had been so easy to protect a little boy, but she couldn't protect the man. She wasn't sure she'd be able to protect her own emotions, either.

The change that she'd thought was about to happen—in truth, it had already come in the form of that blue envelope she'd left on Detective Sterling's desk. Now she'd have to make good on her promise to Ned Rossiter: she wouldn't let him hurt anyone else in her life.

She couldn't let anything happen to Isabella.

CHAPTER FIVE

G ale Sterling stared out the window. She held Ned Rossiter's obituary, the threat printed across the bottom. Tommy was already on the phone with the evidence warehouse in Brooklyn that retained such old cases among its inventory.

She turned her attention to the photo of Isabella Reid. Syd's voice held an inherent love and her face had visibly softened when she'd described a still-angelic kid who'd impulsively turned to Goth recently because of a boy she liked. Gale wondered how Syd dealt with that so easily. She didn't have that maternal gene. Children mostly confused her. But it was evident that Wyatt's family meant the world to Syd and that they adored her. Why else would a thirteen-year-old still spend an hour on Zoom with her?

Sydney Hansen. She was certainly a striking woman. There was an elegance to her bearing, and the ice blue eyes against the shoulder-length white hair created a startling effect. Gale had been aware of her perfume from the moment they'd walked toward her office. She couldn't put her finger on it, but it smelled expensive. Everything about Syd was expensive, from her Prada loafers to the Jimmy Choo woven canvas bag she carried. Gale was well acquainted with "expensive." It was her Kryptonite. She loved high-end tailored clothing, and that couldn't be found off the rack. Sharp classic cuts in soft materials were a particular weakness, as were shoes made in a custom shop that kept clients' shoe lasts in labeled boxes on a shelf in the back room. All her shirts, crisply folded and stacked on built-in shelves in her closet, were tailor-made as well.

It had been the only bone of contention between her and Kate. In the thirty years they'd been together, it accounted for most of the arguments they'd had. Not that they'd argued a lot. Kate compared her to a drug addict. She wasn't wrong. To afford her clotheshorse ways, Gale learned how to fix anything mechanical, from cars to blenders, so they'd never need to lay out money for repairs. She'd even made a name for herself in the department, picking up repair jobs on the side. The resultant cash mollified Kate until the next time a box arrived from a British shirt maker.

Gale ran a hand through her hair. Not a day went by that she didn't miss Kate. Getting out of bed every morning in the weeks after she died had been nearly impossible. It was like swimming up from the bottom of the ocean, the pool of light on that surface stagnant, unreachable. And no Kate there when she finally clawed through the water and reached precious air. She didn't see the point of even moving many mornings. But she *had* moved. Sometimes with her father's gentle prodding. Some days, on her own. And then she'd walk through all her cases wishing for the shift to be over so she could go home and crawl into bed, not think, not feel. Tommy quietly carried her. Seasons passed; friends gave her plenty of room to grieve. Even her father maintained a stoic ex-cop silence. And then one day, she found herself smirking and shaking her head at one of Tommy's bad puns and it became clear to her that for months, she'd walled herself off from the world, which was exactly what Kate had made her promise not to do. In that moment she knew that she couldn't bleed anymore. And that she'd have to get in touch with feelings she'd stuffed far away, stop taking the sleeping pills that helped her get through the night. She found a therapist and began the climb back. That included recent conversations on opening to the possibility of a relationship.

She would doubtless get to know Sydney Hansen as she and Tommy worked the case. Beautiful, expensive, startling Sydney Hansen. But that would be as far as it went.

Gale carefully stapled Isabella's photo to a sheet of paper, wrote her name and the Nebraska address Syd had given her on it, stapled the blue envelope to the back of the obit, and made a new file for the case. This one she was going to keep on her desk for now. Syd would email her tonight with the list of all those young men who'd been in Ned's and Wyatt's orbits. Gale sat back and thought about Syd arguing to be an active part of their investigation just before she left the precinct. She and Tommy rarely allowed that—relatives could get in the way and muck things up. She always kept them informed, but Syd was right, they were going to need her. There would be things that were too old, or that only she would know. Gale had responded to Syd's quicksilver analysis—she was a smart woman and Gale found herself looking forward to working with her. There was something else about Syd that had caught her attention, something she couldn't quantify. The moment when she'd walked Syd out of the station house and Syd had stopped Gale in the lobby played back in her mind. It had been—almost intimate.

"Thank you for taking me seriously. You have no idea how this makes me feel."

"It's my job." In truth, it was, but Gale knew from years of listening to her father's stories and from many of her own cases how diminishing it could be to someone when the police turned their backs on a case.

"That may be, but you've already treated me so differently than the cops back then. It's night and day." Syd looked at the floor. Gale felt her discomfort, but when she met her gaze again, there was a new light in her eyes. "I let them erase Wyatt and you're restoring him to me."

Gale nodded. "Well, let's see if we can get anywhere."

"I have faith in you." Syd touched her arm.

That touch had gone right to Gale's core, even though she hated when people put their faith in her. Especially if they didn't solve an old case. She couldn't carry that burden of faith. But somehow, Syd's touch infused her, turned her into a talisman.

She'd noticed that Syd wore only one ring, a school ring, perhaps, on her left pinkie finger. She added "possibly not married" to an inventory that already included "expensive clothing," "Sutton Place address," and "dedicated friend." None of these attributes meant that Syd was gay. Gale wanted her to be because she was taken with her. And feeling guilty about it. Kate had been adamant that her life should go on. They'd had plenty of time to talk about it while the cancer claimed her in pieces and parts. But Gale still keenly felt the hole in her existence, still felt like she was cheating on some level when she appreciated a beautiful woman. And the sight of a lesbian couple walking hand in hand left her wistful and wanting. Despite time spent with friends, and even with her father one floor below in his apartment in the townhouse, his team of home health aides becoming family in the last three years, she felt the loss of Kate. The bed seemed vast when she settled in at night. There were always books and magazines piled on Kate's half now, but it was still empty.

"What did Brooklyn have to say?" Gale asked when Tommy finally hung up.

"That it'll be a pain in the ass to locate the barrels because they'll be out in pre-computerized boondocks. Like I care. You wanna do the score card?" he asked. "Somethin' tells me our killer is on Syd's list and she has no idea. Probably someone everyone knew, close to this Rossiter fellow, and easily taken for granted."

Gale narrowed her eyes. "I was thinking more along the lines of *he* was dispatched a long time ago, and the guy who did *that* is your someone who everyone knew."

Tommy considered this idea. "Because the killer theoretically disappeared. So you think there was a clean-up man."

Gale raised an eyebrow.

"Interesting theory. So—outside killer for hire gets whacked himself. You wanna tell me how you arrived at that?"

"I didn't say outside killer."

Tommy hadn't wanted the new chairs on wheels that the department had ordered some time ago because, as he'd said, he couldn't think on wheels. Now he tipped back on his chair legs. "Wow, you been goin' places."

Gale pulled the photo of Isabella Reid out of the file. "I'm not the only one." She handed the photo to him.

"Yeah, I was worried about that. Long range lens."

"Long range from New York. That photographer was there. And he knew who she was."

"Which is troublesome. And he was far enough away that the kid never saw him. Like, half a football field away. I bet this is a standard zoom lens." He flicked a finger at the photo.

"That's what I think, too."

Tommy rubbed his chin. A five o'clock shadow was beginning to show. "So?"

"I think someone's in Syd's electronics."

"So she shouldn't email us the list."

Gale picked up her phone. "No, she shouldn't." She looked inside Syd's file and punched her number on the keypad. "Nothing by computer. Everything by hand. But I doubt the captain's going to let us requisition time from the tech guys to verify it."

"Ugly redheaded stepchild, we are." Tommy drummed his pencil on the desk, waiting. He'd once told Gale how much he loved listening to her on the phone. *"United Nations diplomats got nothin' on you."* Gale had laughed.

"It's an imposition, I know, and I'm so sorry," Gale said to Syd. Syd was nobody's fool, and her cryptic response told Gale that Syd already knew something was amiss. "I'd rather tell you why when I see you tomorrow. Trust me that there's a reason." Gale ended the conversation quickly—even this much discussion could tip off anyone tapping Syd's phone.

"Photo taken in Nebraska doesn't mean it was someone from here went out there," Tommy said when Gale hung up, flapping the photo. "Coulda hired someone there. Still…" He nodded at the picture. "She's in his crosshairs. Literally."

"I think we'd better bring the Alma police into this. At the very least to keep an eye on her."

"You think someone would do this kid?"

"No, but if this gets messy and another threat comes through, if they shoot more pictures down the road…"

"But this guy coulda been a block and half away from the school."

"They don't have blocks in Alma. I already looked at a map."

Tommy scowled. "Whatever they got, this guy could be so far away no one would know what he was taking a picture of, and I'm sorry, no cop even in a patrol car could see that."

"He doesn't need to see that. Alma's a small town. I think they'd notice a stranger."

"Said the city girl."

Gale chuckled. "Growing up, I spent part of my summers with cousins who lived in a tiny town in apple territory way upstate. My dad thought it would be like summer camp. Believe me, in these small towns, they know." She pulled a package of M&Ms out of her desk drawer. "What are you thinking so far?"

Tommy tipped back in his chair and studied the ceiling. "I'm goin' with the money this time. You take jealousy."

"Good. I wanted it." Gale loved these fencing matches with Tommy—they fed her soul and kept those nagging thoughts of retirement away. She wasn't ready to leave the game yet.

"Really? Why?"

"He was involved with a married board member *and* he had a boyfriend?"

"Good point. But the embezzlement and the affair happened with the same guy. Money's an aphrodisiac, and a more powerful motive."

"We don't know if Rossiter was involved with the embezzlement. This is going to be a deep dig. Too much time has passed on the money aspect."

"I'll find something."

"You always do. But I think this has jealousy written all over it."

"The usual ten bucks?"

Sterling reached across the divide between their desks and they shook hands.

❖

Syd was disturbed by Detective Sterling's call. When the phone rang, she was in the middle of preparing a roast chicken for dinner. The carrot, celery, quartered onion, and bay leaf were already inside the seasoned bird, and she was sliding slivers of butter and sprigs of sage under the breast skin. Recognizing the number from Sterling's business card, she'd quickly swiped her hands with the soapy dish sponge and picked up.

The detective's request was unsettling. In the corporate world, when you turned from email to personal delivery, it was because you didn't want to leave a traceable footprint. Or let someone in your division know there was business going on that you didn't want them privy to.

Gale's response to Syd's question for the reason behind the request had been cagey. The blue envelope left Syd feeling vulnerable and scared, not something she could tell the detectives. She wanted to present a strong persona, someone they'd have confidence in sharing information with because she wanted it. Anyway, they couldn't provide her with protection. Not until someone harmed her. Who was Sterling trying to shut out this early in the investigation?

She stood in front of the oven watching the chicken quietly sizzle after the call. A burst of fat spattered in the pan. Coupled with the aroma of the roast, it gave Syd a sense of comfort. She mentally pulled it around herself like a protective cloak against the fear she was fighting. Finally, she set the timer for basting and went to the closet in her bedroom, and the banker's box.

She'd wanted to look at the papers and articles in it thinking there might be more names she might've forgotten among them. Well, she didn't want to, but she had to, with Drew coming tomorrow. And she was contemplating looking at the photographs Nicholas St. John had taken of Wyatt's apartment in the aftermath before handing them over to Tommy.

So it was a relief, that phone call, for in those few minutes, Syd had lost the nerve, taking the envelope of photos to the kitchen where she grabbed a bag from the supply she kept in her broom closet and slipped them into it. She stopped to baste the chicken. Price watched from the doorway, hunkered down and sniffing the air. When she set the bag down by the front door, she saw the logo for Mr. Wright Fine Wines & Spirits. She smiled to herself, if not sadly—there was a certain morbid humor in carrying these photos to the police station in a bag in which she would have toted a bottle of the best wine to Wyatt when he was alive.

Sitting on the bed, Syd began excavating the box. She needed to look at everything anyway before laying it all out for Drew. If she did it right, it would tell the story for her from start to finish. Or, she thought ruefully, unfinished.

She lifted the first handful of things out and the scent of musty old newsprint hit her. Sepia-colored confetti littered her bedspread as she carefully opened each newspaper article. She didn't need to read them. She was still able to recall almost every word that had been written. What had been sensationalized.

The *Daily News* got its hands on the story first, probably monitoring police radios in its building that was on 42nd Street then. It aggrandized the murder for a few days and then moved on to what became the Hudson River Killer. He was drowning blond prostitutes before dawn off the Twelfth Avenue piers where the Circle Line tour boats were moored.

Next, she read the *New York Post* articles. It followed the story a few days longer. That salacious coverage disappeared after a week, traded for the greener pastures of a local NFL wife beater.

The *New York Times's* only article was short, concise, and buried in what was then the daily Metropolitan section. She'd always suspected Ned Rossiter, with his many friends at the Gray Lady, had stopped any investigation by the *Times*.

Syd folded the articles back up and stacked them in date order, making a list of what they were and slipping them into a clear plastic baggie to preserve their edges. She took a yellowing envelope out next, opened it, gently unfolded a set of age-tinged papers, and perused them. *The Last Will and Testament of Wyatt Copeland Reid.* All the black letters had miniscule voids in them where the typewriter keys, lacking ink from the worn ribbon, had struck the paper. She'd thought it odd, then, that anyone in a law office would use a ribbon that worn. Then a trace of the guilt and shame she'd felt that long-ago afternoon she'd stood in Ben Ford's office came back to her in a rush.

He'd called her in to talk to her about Wyatt's will. While she waited for him, she'd poked around his desk. She knew it wasn't right, and wasn't even sure what possessed her to do it. But she'd come across Wyatt's signed and dated will. Beneath it was this second will, unsigned, but dated two days later. And they were different. Almost everything in this will went to Ben and Ned. Including the house on Fire Island that Wyatt had promised her. There was a note attached on Wyatt's signature line: *"Have Ned sign."* How could Ned sign this? And it was already witnessed—by Lucas Rose and Ben's secretary, Edna. She didn't want to believe they were absconding with Wyatt's worldly goods—and the house he'd promised her—but before she could figure out what to say to Ben that didn't have her looking like a common thief herself, she'd heard Ben talking to Edna in the outer office, impulsively folded the will up and shoved it into her jacket pocket.

She was pretty sure that, all these years later, she was the only other person who knew that Ben and Ned had meant to take everything of Wyatt's. Ben had certainly done that when she and Nicholas cleaned Wyatt's apartment. He'd come by every day, leaving with artwork that had hung on the walls, including an original Erté, his beaver stadium coat, expensive kitchen appliances, extensive record collection—and much more. She and Nicholas didn't confront him or say anything. After all, he was Wyatt's attorney, and they were just a couple of twenty-somethings. Ben never said anything to her about that will. She wasn't sure he knew she'd been the one who'd taken it. Now she put it back in the envelope.

The next set of papers, the detectives' police notes, Syd had sweet-talked out of an adorable patrol officer at the station house. She would meet her at Peaches, the lesbian bar near Wyatt's apartment, and for the price of a few drinks and dances, the notes were hers. These were still in good condition. She'd forgotten she had them. Sterling would want them. She wondered if the same notes would show up in the files from those old detectives who'd treated her like so much pocket lint. Perusing them, she saw that she was right in her assessment to Sterling—little to nothing had been done once the cops left the scene. The word "fag" was even written in the report, just like she remembered.

Stuffed gray interoffice envelopes came next. The financial documents. Listed on the many "To/From" lines on the fronts of the envelopes was what was inside each one. She turned the first envelope over and untwined the red string from around the rivets. This one contained the original notes and pages of the 1981 annual report that Wyatt had put her to work on right after hiring her. She spread them out on the bed. So many envelopes had come from Ned Rossiter's secretary that fall with pages already typed for the report. Wyatt claimed they contained in-depth financial information, charts he didn't think she'd understand well enough to be able to create and drop into the report, so he'd had Ned's much more experienced girl do it. Wyatt substituted the pages himself before she took it to the printer.

She'd kept copies of both the old and the new charts hoping that she could study them and learn how to do them. They were more complicated than the assignments she'd gotten in school. Right away she noticed an enormous difference between funds listed in the capital campaign in the original pages versus what was listed in the substituted pages. She'd hesitated asking Wyatt about that because she'd more or less stolen them. For a moment, her hands shook. She'd likely committed a crime, removing evidence that proved the embezzlement, but at the time she couldn't face Wyatt being hung out to dry for something she thought Ned had perpetrated. He'd been hung out anyway. Easy to do to a dead person.

The next big envelope held donor notes from that spring and summer. Wyatt had courted three heavy hitters among the parents then, landing enormous donations that would form the basis of an endowment fund to anchor a new capital campaign meant to see the school through to the next century and well beyond. Wyatt gave the pledges to her, along with the first checks to take to the bank, and then come looking for them in a panic hours later. She knew there was something wrong with those checks before his rattled state indicated it because they were for far more than the pledges. She meant to talk to him about it before sending official thank you letters. Dutifully, she'd kept copies of the pledges and mistaken checks. When Ned showed up after the funeral, she quietly removed them, too. She'd already watched him shred correspondence from the triumvirate, so she knew something was amiss. After that, every time she watched police procedural shows and "obstructing an investigation" came up, she felt horribly guilty. Then she remembered that it was Ned's investigation first, and he'd likely done the same thing. When Mother Adeline finally brought in financial forensics people, all Syd could think of was the threat: "Keep quiet…" Since her last day at the school before departing for her new job happened to be two days after the auditors arrived, she'd had no trouble abiding by the note.

The third envelope contained photocopies of Wyatt's date book. She was earmarking certain pages one afternoon at the photocopier when Ned came searching for her. She pushed the slim book into the trash. Later, she'd retrieved it and finished copying the pages that were missing key donor meetings. She discovered the mistakes months before when she phoned parents following up on some of Wyatt's "ask" visits logged in her master schedule. Those parents said Ned had called instead and asked them to send their checks to his office to save time since he was investing some of it on behalf of the school. She hadn't thought anything of it. Wyatt occasionally skipped meetings with donor parents and spent the afternoons shopping with Ned, one of them calling the parents later. When Ned began combing through Wyatt's old date books, she knew she had to preserve that information, too.

And then there were the other photocopies: cancelled checks and accompanying bank statements from a bank the school didn't do business with; charts and graphs from other annual reports that hadn't matched up; notes to vendors explaining why they hadn't been paid in full. And the red ledger Ned had found at the bottom of a drawer in Wyatt's desk that Syd knew wasn't there in the weeks before his death. When she saw it in Ned's briefcase that day, she slipped it out before he left. She hadn't known what it was, but it had to be important if Ned wanted it. She ran her fingers over the leather-bound cover. It was the kind of handsome book that would've caught Wyatt's eye in one of the better stationers on Madison Avenue. She still didn't understand the figures Wyatt had written inside it.

Recollections were swirling through her head. She reached for the pad on her nightstand to scribble them down so she could bring them to Sterling.

The timer sounded from the kitchen; the chicken was done. She methodically put the things back in the box and set it on a chair. Something heavier than sadness settled within her. But so did hope. Maybe these two detectives would help her put right the terrible wrong that had been done to Wyatt. There weren't many people she could say she loved, but Wyatt she carried in her heart.

Waterhouse padded into the room and looked at her. She was as grateful for his need now as she had been for his comfort earlier.

"Yes, darling, there's roast chicken for dinner."

The cat immediately trotted to the kitchen.

CHAPTER SIX

D rew was dazed and looked like he was going to cry as he
sat at Syd's dining room table when they'd finished going
through the things in the banker's box. She wanted to put her arms
around him and hug him like she did when he was a boy and had
skinned his knee. But this was so much deeper than that. He might
be fifty, but that little boy Joe taught to fish and hunt and build things
still existed in her heart. Syd was doubly glad she'd dropped off the
photos at the station house before picking him up at the airport. She
knew now that he could never see those.

"I'm sorry," she said quietly. "We didn't want you to have to
know any of this."

Drew lifted his head to look at her. "That's what hurts the most."

His facial expression hit that maternal center that she'd always
reserved for him. It nearly gutted her.

"If I hadn't discovered Opa's notebook, I never would have
known. You were never going to tell me."

He was right. The summer vacations they'd spent at Wyatt's Fire
Island house had been oases of shelter and as insulated as Joe had kept
him after he took the boy in to raise on the farm. What would have
been the reason to tell him, even when he reached an age that he might
have understood? Syd could still hear Joe's voice the only time they'd
talked about it on the phone, right before Drew went off to college,
right before his last summer visit.

I know you think it's important that he know the truth," Joe
said. *"But it could crush him."*

Syd wondered if Joe really meant it would crush *him*.

"I don't want him to understand this sadness he knows I carry with me. He's been such a light in my life, Syd. Don't take that from us."

"Your grandfather felt there was no purpose to your knowing," Syd said. "He never wanted you to see that notebook." Pulling her chair close to his, Syd stroked his back like she'd done when he was young and had awoken from bad dreams.

"Then he should have destroyed it. He had to know I'd come across it when I cleaned out the house."

Syd sighed. How could she explain that the notebook was a vestige of Wyatt for Joe, a memory to hang on to? He must have some understanding now, with the loss of his grandfather, that when someone you love goes forever from your life, you're lucky if something of theirs comes your way. If nothing does, you're left with letters, maybe, photographs, a Christmas card you might've thought to keep one year. After her own mother died, the only thing she'd taken from her parents' house was the tall Brilliant-era cut glass vase that had belonged to her great-aunt Ingrid, her mother's aunt. It stood on her coffee table, always filled with fresh flowers, and on sunny days, it filtered spectacular prisms of light. In them she saw the beloved white-haired woman who recognized the lonely child and took care of her in ways her parents didn't, who encouraged her in all her undertakings, who made her laugh and feel loved when she hugged her. So different from her austere mother and remote father. Syd had retained a single photo of them from among her mother's things. It was in a drawer. Unframed.

Syd gently ruffled Drew's hair. "He couldn't destroy that notebook. It was all he had."

"No." A thoughtful look settled on Drew's face, followed by a little smile. "There were boxes of dad's things in the attic, right near the Christmas decorations. Opa said I should leave them be, that Nana didn't want them opened. But I'd sneak up there and look at the things—posters of Cary Grant and Lana Turner, books, clothes, a drama club trophy." He smiled. "When I was in seventh grade, I found an old jean jacket he'd had in high school, and it fit me then. I knew I'd get into trouble, but I brought it to Opa. He talked to Nana and they let me have it."

Syd couldn't help her own answering smile—imagining first a skinny Wyatt in the jacket, mustering all the "bad boy" attitude that he could at sixteen, and then his burly son inhabiting the same coat at a much younger age, looking every inch the wholesome Nebraska farm boy.

"Izzy has it now."

"Then you had a gift, didn't you?"

Drew looked at her quizzically.

"A real piece of your father, and not"—Syd indicated the things spread out on the table—"this story. Because he was so much more than this."

"And that's what I need from you, now."

Syd wasn't sure she understood.

"Tell me about my father. The way you knew him."

Tommy had pinned the photos Syd brought in earlier in the day to the whiteboard. Both sides. And still there were photos left over. He moved them around now as he looked at the rudimentary floor plan Syd had drawn of Wyatt Reid's apartment so that all the detectives could see the progression the camera had taken from the front door to the door in the bedroom that led to a back hall and the service elevator. He'd asked them to look at the photos because sometimes, a second—or fourth—set of eyes uninvolved in your case caught something that you didn't. It was the kind of quid pro quo they all engaged in for each other.

"Closer together," Gale said, "Fit them all in."

Tommy nodded. No one spoke as they watched him work with the old three-and-a-half-by-five-inch photos. They were too busy studying the images. Occasionally one of the detectives would lean forward, shake his head, another would mutter, "Wow."

Gale had seen hundreds of shots like this in her time, but somehow, these affected her more deeply. They were horrific, to be sure. But it was imagining a young Syd walking into this, seeing the overwhelming mess, perhaps not understanding at first, that made her a little sick. Among her notes was one to contact a forensic spatter specialist to see if, from these photos, it could be determined where the attack had actually started. Had it been in the kitchen, where there were swipes of blood on the counter, cupboards, and drawers? It looked like the trails in the hall led both ways. In the living room, there were dried pools on the rug, splatters on the walls, and Syd told them that one of the piano legs bore large traces as though maybe Wyatt had grabbed it as he slid down. The bedroom—Gale could not even put together a scenario that made any sense for what they saw there. The bed covers Syd had thrown back when she found Wyatt tucked beneath them revealed a mattress so soaked that she wondered what was left inside him. Blood on the walls brought to mind a Pollock drip painting. The rugs were matted and black. And the dark handprints all over the back door, the gold handle itself mostly black, had given her pause. It became obvious as Tommy tacked the photos up that Wyatt Reid had fought desperately to escape the attack. Gale wondered if he knew he wasn't going to survive it. When Tommy got to the photos of the bathroom, the black water in the toilet bowl where Syd told them the seven-inch knife had been tossed was splashed everywhere. Someone had defecated on the floor. Miller got up and left the room. She didn't blame him. When he got back, she decided she needed a cup of coffee and a breather herself and was a little perturbed to see Tommy hand the photos to another detective and follow her.

In the breakroom, he stood beside her at the counter. His thick fingers curled around the handle of his coffee mug, and he stared at the coffee pot. She poured the now-pungent coffee into their mugs and followed it with healthy splashes of still-cold milk from a carton sitting on the counter.

"You want I should make the next pot?"

"I got it," Gale said. Neither one of them looked at the other.

Tommy reached for the filters and the five-pound container of coffee in the cupboard. As Gale rinsed out the pot, he put a filter into the basket and heaped spoons of coffee into it.

"We haven't seen one like this in a while."

"No." Gale filled the empty pot with cold water and poured it into the top of the coffee maker. "The preferred method of mayhem these days is guns. Knives are almost relics of the past." She braced her hands on the counter, her stomach roiling. Tommy put a hand on her shoulder.

"Why don't we go walk around the block? Nice spring day and all."

"Good idea." They walked out of the breakroom leaving everything on the counter.

When they reached Lexington Avenue, they turned left, a long-practiced habit in the many walks they'd taken over the years while puzzling out cases. At the end of that block, they made another left.

"This was personal," Gale said. She crossed her arms over her chest, hugging herself against the solid spring breeze.

"I was thinkin' the same." Tommy picked a leaf from a bush next to an apartment building door as they passed and shredded it, tossing each piece to the sidewalk as they continued up the street.

"Anger *and* passion." Gale kicked at a pebble.

"Yeah. A hired gun woulda been more efficient—one and done."

"That's what I was thinking."

"So, Syd's theory is wrong? Nothin' says this had to do with the embezzlement."

"The threat to Syd—we have to take it seriously."

"Yeah, of course. Absolutely. But I also think we answer the question, do all roads lead back to Rome, to Ned Rossiter? Or did Wyatt cross someone he'd been having a fling with? And here's what I see." Tommy held up his left hand in a fist, fingers popping up as he spoke. "Coulda been Ned or someone he hired or who was involved, and he instructed him to go to town." Three fingers rose. "Coulda been random, coulda been a guy Wyatt knew." The last two fingers came up and all five went down again. "Coulda been the guy left and the boyfriend came home. Or the boyfriend came home when the guy was still there. Could even have been the boyfriend." He looked at Gale, his hand open.

"That's a lot of fingers."

At Third Avenue, the light was green, and in silent agreement, they crossed and continued east.

"All doors open, we see where whatever evidence we dig up leads us," Tommy said.

"So we begin with what we absolutely know," Gale said, starting a review process they'd refined over the years. "He picked up someone at Bareback that night. Stranger or known entity? If we can, that should be the first piece of the puzzle we solve. Because the crime scene of a guy out to kill gay men for kicks can present as a lover's quarrel, too. We've seen it before."

"We have."

"Next, was the murderer looking for something or was he instructed to make it look like he was to throw the investigation off?"

"We'll need one of your charts with all the 'if-then' columns once we get Sydney's list of those boys involved with Wyatt and Ned, cross-reference the names and the 'why' possibilities." Tommy rubbed the back of his neck. "This is gonna take time."

"It always does."

"Oh—the notes from the detectives came in this morning, I gave 'em a quick glance before Sydney got here. They concluded Wyatt picked up a john because a neighbor saw him bring in an unknown male."

"How did the neighbor know he was unknown?"

"Apparently, this guy was a nosy parker, told the detectives Wyatt was bringin' in johns all the time."

Gale snorted. "Maybe he was jealous. Too bad he didn't also see the guy leave. Might've solved the crime if the guy was covered in blood."

"Never that easy, is it?"

"It wouldn't be a cold case if it was."

"So it's Sydney's say-so that this guy came from Bareback because she knew Wyatt went there that night."

"Maybe he wasn't from there. Wyatt could've gone to the piers, picked someone up there. I was mulling the theory that if Ned hired someone, the guy would've made sure Wyatt picked him up at Bareback since Ned knew he went there so often," Gale said.

"Okay, so why go the hiring route?"

"I get the sense that Ned Rossiter was a gloves-on kind of guy who didn't want to leave any traces of himself. But if we depart from Syd's theory, and I think we have to, maybe he wasn't hired. Maybe he wasn't even a stranger."

"So we set up two columns, 'known' and 'stranger.'"

"Let's concentrate on 'known' for the time being and see who we can rule out. We'll divvy up Syd's list and see where those people are today, go question them to start."

"I love these walks," Tommy said as they turned onto Second Avenue.

"If it was someone who knew him," Gale said, oblivious to Tommy's remark, "that would account for the passion. Or at least the degree of difficulty in killing him. And if that guy also knew what was going on, if he was in on the embezzlement, that accounts for the anger. That ties Syd's theory to it."

"And if it's a stranger?"

"Wouldn't you tell someone you hired to kill someone that they should make the place look like it was tossed?"

"Except that apartment looked like a war zone."

Gale stopped. "Someone *was* looking for something, weren't they? Those swipes on the kitchen counter weren't marks of a fight—they were from pulling open drawers and cabinets. Somebody was in such a hurry to find something that they didn't stop to clean their hands."

"So, what were they lookin' for? It makes sense that it would be somethin' tied to the embezzlement, which would make Syd correct in her assessment."

They continued walking.

"That should become apparent when we dig into Wyatt's life," Gale said. "Especially who he was sleeping with. Plural. I wonder what the boyfriend thought about that. Because if Wyatt was picking up guys in bars, he was likely sleeping with those—what did Syd call them? The lost boys. He'd be sleeping with them, too."

"Do we want to put the boyfriend at the top of the interview list?"

"Let's build a picture first."

"Which one of us should sit down with Syd to go over her list of who was who in Reid's life?" Tommy asked. They turned back onto East 67th Street.

"Why don't we go through all those old detectives' notes together and isolate the names. Then let's go to Brooklyn, see who might show up in the boxes of evidence. We can assign them value according to how often they come up. I'll make the chart from there."

"Please, give me a heads up if you're gonna do a Venn diagram when we get closer to figuring it out."

"Sorry to trigger high school algebra nightmares."

"No you're not."

Gale chuckled. They were a block away from the station house.

Tommy stopped and shoved his hands in his pockets. "You think she knew who he was intimate with, in this group of friends?"

"Maybe. But that's not going to show up in any evidence box. And you know those detectives didn't ask anyone. But I think she can handle the question. And for the record? No, I don't. I researched her career last night at home. She was a hayseed from a small town in Minnesota when she stepped off the train here. I hardly think she had a handle on the gay community in the city even after living here for two years."

"I got a lot of questions to get down on paper after this session. And maybe we should have a lightning round of questions, see what shakes out. I like those even better than our walks. I need a good cup of coffee first, though," Tommy said, poking his chin at the bodega across the street. "You want your M&M's?"

Gale handed him a five-dollar bill. "Coffee's on me. I'll get my top ten questions down on paper."

Tommy jogged across the street.

"I should write you up for jaywalking," she called after him.

Without looking back, Tommy held up his middle finger.

Gale laughed.

CHAPTER SEVEN

All the windows in the apartment were open to the cool cross breeze, that smell of evening dew as a sunny spring day waned toward dusk pervading the dining room. Syd sat at the table enjoying the last of a woody-toned cabernet. Drew had chosen to pair it with the steak he'd seared perfectly in her cast iron pan along with caramelized onions and heaps of diced mushrooms. He was in the kitchen washing the dinner dishes, the sound of running water mingling with that of the distant steady flow of traffic floating up from the FDR Drive. The moment was reminiscent of the last summer Drew had come to see her, before starting his construction job in June and then going off to college in August. Every morning they'd make the rounds of various markets, and he'd pick up ingredients for the epicurean delights he'd become interested in making after taking a cooking class at school. The final stop was always the wine shop where she'd teach him about regions, vintages, and growing years like Wyatt had taught her, and they'd buy a bottle for that night's dinner.

"Do you want coffee, Aunt Syd?" Drew called from the kitchen.

"No, thanks, but you make it if you want it."

Diana Krall's voice quietly crooned through the stereo speakers. Exhaustion was creeping up on Syd. It had been a long day, facing the banker's box and its contents with Drew. He'd had all kinds of questions. She'd anticipated some, but others surprised her. She told Drew everything she knew about Wyatt; his need to know about his own mother had been a curveball. His pain cut her in a thousand different ways as she watched him process, no, struggle with everything. "It's like losing my parents all over again," he'd said. There was little she could do for him except listen.

Drew was astonished at the information she'd collected and appalled that the police hadn't been interested in any of it even a few weeks later when Syd began piecing together that the murder and the missing money might be linked. But as she pointed out to him, the police were in the murder business, and she was, at best, an amateur sleuth.

Drew joined her with his coffee. "I've hesitated to ask, but are we going to the police station tomorrow?"

"No. I left Detective Sterling a message that you're here. They have a lot to dig through, wherever it is they keep old evidence pertaining to cases like this, so we'll wait until she calls."

"There must be something we can do in the meantime." Drew put his head in his hands and scrubbed at his eyes. "I'm so freaked out about the photo of Izzy, you have no idea. And I haven't come all this way to do nothing." He put his hands behind his neck and stretched to dissipate the tension. "Who the hell took that picture!"

He'd been antsy as Syd walked him through the mountain of information. She was all too familiar with his anguish, paralyzed with fear herself by the meaning behind the photo of Izzy, afraid whoever snapped it might harm her. She hadn't told Drew that she was communicating everything either in person or on her cell phone to the police since Detective Sterling's call yesterday intimating that her phone and computer might be bugged. She still hadn't had the chance to talk to Sterling about it, and she didn't want that bit of info to send him spiraling. It had been a little over twenty-four hours since she'd opened that blue envelope, and she was trying not to panic herself.

"I know you don't want to hear this, but I think we're faced with a waiting game. I gave the detectives everything they asked for this morning. But they want to look at what the department has in evidence before they see the rest." She nodded toward the bedroom and the box full of documents. "Patience. In the meantime, Izzy is safe. They called the Alma police yesterday."

Drew nodded. "Yes. Jeri told me patrol cars roll by the house all the time now. Izzy hates us."

"Why don't we call her later? It might help if I talk to her."

Drew nodded again.

Syd tapped a nail on her wineglass. "There might be something we can do." It occurred to Syd that Drew's "get it done" attitude could help her carry off a visit to Lucas Rose. Even as a kid, Drew had been focused and driven, preferring to putter around Wyatt's garden deadheading the flowers than wasting time lolling on the deck after swimming. No other six-year-old she knew cleared the dishes without being asked, crumbed the table and set it for the next meal. That ethic had been instilled in him by his mother with her strict German upbringing.

Wyatt had finally told her all about Georgia one night when they were well on their way to getting drunk after a successful fundraiser. It was the usual story of pretty gay boy hides behind pretty straight girl in college so no one suspects him. When she showed up in New York after graduation, it became the same old story of a one-night stand, Wyatt's single foray into sex with a woman resulting in a surprise pregnancy. Georgia left soon after their dalliance, moving to San Francisco to follow her bliss as a photographer over the objections of her unyielding parents. She didn't tell him about Drew at first, until success caught up with her and she needed Wyatt's help.

"She began landing major magazine covers, but it was hard for her to take long-range assignments with a kid. That's when she called. You coulda knocked me over! When I recovered, we brokered the deal for Drew's summers with me so she could travel." Syd emptied the second bottle of wine into Wyatt's glass as he recounted the dreadful call he'd received from Georgia's father in November of nineteen seventy-nine. *"She took a quick assignment to Tehran to do a shoot for a fashion magazine, didn't even tell me she was going. She thought she'd only be gone for five days so a friend watched Drew. Somehow she ended up outside the American embassy in the middle of that insane takeover with the hostages and she was killed. It was so surreal."* Wyatt finished the glass of wine and laid his head back on the couch. *"It was bad enough that he was calling to tell me Georgia was dead, but then he said that they didn't want the boy. I was so shocked I didn't know what to say. So I called my dad."* Two days later, a four-year-old Drew took his paternal grandmother's hand at the little airport in Nebraska and walked into a new life.

Syd had connected with the lonely boy the first time they met, recognizing a kindred spirit. The rapport caught Wyatt's eye. She never told Wyatt of her solitary and desolate childhood that had left her feeling unloved and unwanted. She made sure Drew never felt like that when he was with her.

"I need to go see an old friend of your father's," Syd said. "He'll remember people we knew back then, information I need for Detective Sterling. But he has no idea I've gone to the police, and I don't want him to know."

"Why wouldn't you want to tell an old friend of my dad's about the investigation?"

"I don't trust him, Drew. I didn't trust many of your father's friends. They were shallow and insipid and selfish."

Drew took in a breath. "Wow. I hope that's not an indictment of my father."

"No." Syd put a hand on his arm. "Wyatt was the kindest and most generous person I knew. He could be an ass, make no mistake about that. But he was very good to me. It would be a great help if you came to see Lucas Rose with me, though. I could use the moral support. The last time I spoke with him was when he told me Ned Rossiter died." Syd sighed. "I'm afraid I was short with him."

Drew blew on his coffee and took a sip, but Syd noticed that he never took his eyes off her. "The Ned Rossiter behind all the documents in your box."

"Yes." Syd tried to remain inscrutable. She didn't want Drew to draw conclusions she couldn't prove about Lucas and wasn't even sure were in the right ballpark. One thing was certain, though: she'd be able to get information from Lucas that the detectives wouldn't when they questioned him. Drew's presence might keep anything from resonating on Lucas's radar.

"You think Lucas knows something about what's going on now?"

"Honestly, I have no idea, but I'll only be able to figure that out if I poke a little, see what his reaction is."

"I don't know, Aunt Syd. Is that such a good idea?" He took another sip of coffee, his gaze leveling her. "If he was involved then, he might be now. We'd be walking into the lion's den. And I'd want to kill him. I think you should leave that to your detectives."

He was right. And yet she was being pulled to it like tidal waves drawn by the moon. Lucas was the only source of what she wanted. Syd knew who Lucas was then; the detectives didn't. She could reach back through time for things they'd never see. If she waited for Sterling and D'Angelo, she might never get this chance to be with him on his turf, to sense if he was behind the photo of Isabella. The minute they called him, sat down with him, put questions in front of him, the level playing field would be gone.

"And you know, I was thinking last night," Drew said, tugging Syd back, "Why did this threat come? After all these years?"

"Because I went to see Ned. And he died that night. Someone thinks I know something. They tried to silence me forty years ago, and they're trying to do it again."

The cup of coffee was barely visible in Drew's large hands. His mouth was a thin line of concentration. "Jesus, Aunt Syd. If that someone is Lucas, then this *is* all my fault."

"No, it isn't."

"Yes, it is. My anger sent you to see Ned." He drained the coffee. "But you're going to go see Lucas whether I agree to this or not, aren't you? Whether I think this is a bad idea or not."

Syd simply looked at him.

"What makes you think he'll tell you anything?"

"Because he was always a cocky son-of-a-bitch and a snake in the grass. He wanted you to know that he had power, and what he was capable of doing with it." The drop of venom in her voice hit home, Drew sitting a little straighter to listen. "He was manipulative, bitchy, holier-than-thou, and he was a bully on top of everything else. I couldn't stand being around him unless your father was there."

"Why? What would he do?"

"Lucas was out of control whenever we went out, using Ned's credit cards like they were his own personal bank account, dealing drugs right out in the open, even dealing the boys. And I'm not talking about to just anybody. There were some very prominent people at these clubs, and money exchanged hands right in the open. He was brazen—he thought the world was his. It was dangerous, and Ned let it happen."

"But you were friends with him."

"No, your father was. So I had to tolerate him. But now I need him. Lucas knew everything and everyone." Syd hugged herself tightly, as if she could shut out Lucas's very existence. Then, apologetically, she said, "I need to know who among those lost boys might still be alive. Lucas will have the answer. And if you're along as my foil, maybe he won't suspect anything." *Although I have my doubts.* She gazed out the window. Corals and oranges shot across the dusky western sky lighting up the dark blue bottoms of the clouds in the east. "So many of those boys could've died of AIDS and I wouldn't have known."

Drew didn't respond. When she looked back at him, she saw the concern on his face.

"I know you lost a lot of friends."

Syd's gaze returned to the window. Red was overtaking everything, tinges of purple bleeding into it from behind. Memories of young men long gone and funeral upon memorial service that she'd attended still haunted her if she allowed herself to think about those years. How many of those friends didn't get the decades she'd had for enjoying something as simple as this, watching the sun set, and thinking about what the night might bring. Sometimes her mind played snippets of that past like an old black-and-white movie echoing in a half-filled cinema, the screen featuring the young men who'd become her friends beyond dance floors, offices, and cabarets, who'd stayed after boyfriends left them and girlfriends left her, and then were themselves gone in a flurry of powerful cancers and pneumonias. "Too many to count," she replied. By the time she looked at Drew again, she'd won the battle for her composure. But he was fighting his.

"I'm so worried about Izzy. I don't want you to do this, but I sure as hell don't want you to do this alone." He ran his thumb and forefinger over his eyes, the face emerging behind their path looking older, worn. "I'll come with you, but if there's any indication this guy was involved, or has anything to do with the threat to Izzy, I'll take him apart right there. You understand?"

Syd took her cell phone out of her pocket and looked up Lucas Rose's number.

❖

Gale was confused by the smell of standing rib roast permeating the house as she dropped her briefcase and coat on the couch. It wasn't Sunday, and it certainly wasn't autumn or winter. She went to the kitchen in search of her father or Celia, the home health aide who'd be on duty now. She found them deep in concentration over a game of Scrabble, he with his usual scotch on the rocks and her with a cup of tea.

"Who's coming to dinner tonight, the queen?"

Sullivan Sterling, still every inch the gruff cop despite his ninety-one years, waved his hand at her without looking up. "Cleaning out the freezer. We got that roast for Christmas and then never used it, remember? It's about to expire."

Gale almost snorted at him but checked herself. "Remember? What I 'remember' is that you ended up in the hospital. You scared the crap out of me!"

"It was merely a fall." He ran his hand over the back of his head, his white hair military short. "How did I know they were going to keep me for four days? And then try to put me in this wheelchair permanently?"

"You did a pretty good job of fighting your way out, but it still comes in handy when you're done in, doesn't it?

He scowled at her, his white brush mustache twitching.

Celia's call to her as Gale was leaving the precinct on that snowy evening had sent her into a tailspin. She'd used her lights and siren to get to the hospital, not caring that department policy frowned on that sort of thing, arriving in her father's curtained ER cubicle as the first battery of doctors went over his vital signs. They asked him dozens of questions and put him through myriad tests before deciding that beyond a broken wrist and a banged-up hip, the header he'd taken had caused no other damage. In the ensuing weeks, however, Sullivan had felt like nothing more than toast, eggs, soups, and baked potatoes while he complained to the aides and the PTs who worked with him. It had been touch-and-go keeping him at a sustainable weight—Gale didn't want him packed off to a rehab facility. The roast, and a lot of other things, sat in the freezer waiting for better days.

"But look," he said, flopping his hand and wrist around. "Good as new. I still know how to roll when I hit the ground. So tonight, roast beef with Yorkshire pudding." He rubbed a thumb over his moustache. "And I'm sorry I ruined Christmas."

"If I don't get to work on the rest of the dinner, we won't be eating anything a'tall," Celia said, her soft Jamaican accent flowing into a chuckle. "You take over my tiles and finish the game. But I'm warning you, he's on a tear. Last game, he used a blank tile he'd been sittin' on to make 'syzygy' and beat me."

"Damn right I did. After she screwed me the game before with 'waqf.'"

"And you didn't question the legality of it?"

"It's in the UK Scrabble dictionary," Sullivan said, the hint of a growl in his voice.

"And you're playing on US territory. Good Lord, how long have you two been sitting here?"

"We did our stretches first. *And* took a walk between games. Water's still hot if you want a cup of tea." Celia picked up her china cup to take over to the sink.

Gale glanced at the teapot, the delicate hand-painted Victorian roses climbing up the sides. The cup in Celia's hand matched it. The first time she'd seen it on the kitchen table after it had been buried in a cupboard for years, along with the memory of her mother, she'd stopped in her tracks. Celia was snapping fresh green beans for dinner, the cup and pot sitting next to the colander full of them. Gale's knee-jerk instinct to warn her to be careful with her mother's most prized possession passed quickly when it occurred to her that the teapot was a sign that perhaps she was watching over them. After that, Gale had welcomed the teapot's every use.

"Thanks, Celia, but I need what he's having." She took a glass from one of the cupboards, pressed the icemaker in the refrigerator door until the glass was half full of cubes, and opened the cupboard where Sullivan kept his liquor.

He politely waited until they'd both laid out several words on the board before clearing his throat. That was always a prelude to his venturing into territory Gale didn't necessarily want him.

"So. What's got you so cross lately?"

Gale contemplated her rack of tiles—one consonant and six vowels. She was going to lose. She shook her head. Sullivan, a former chief with a wealth of policing knowledge and the kind of mind that could still untangle any problem, was still her father. She'd always thought of him as "Sullivan," though, the authoritative cop whom she happened to call "Dad" by dint of birth, and he could be overbearing. "I'm doomed here, Dad. I have the worst set of tiles. And a cold case from nineteen eighty-two that's proving to be convoluted after only forty-eight hours."

"Really? Why'd you take it?"

"It came with a brand-new threat."

He idly moved his glass in a small circle. "And? But?"

Gale laid two 'o' tiles next to a 't,' and Sullivan wrote down her score as she told him everything she and Tommy knew. The original detectives' notes were proving to be of little help, and the paperwork they'd filed for all the old evidence was going to take days to retrieve. The online search for the people whose names Syd had given them who might know something or might've been involved was slow going. And the embezzlement discovered after Wyatt's death was a conundrum. What she left out, what she couldn't admit to her father, was Sydney Hansen. The seed of attraction had sprouted almost immediately, and that wasn't professional on her part. She wouldn't let him see that.

"Why don't you look at everything this woman has while you're waiting on Brooklyn to turn the old stuff up? Wealth of clues might be there."

"I didn't want to muddy the waters until we'd seen the old NYPD evidence first." Gale tapped the top of a tile on the rack as she looked over the board. "But you're right." She'd known it when she and Tommy left the evidence warehouse in Brooklyn after talking with the property clerk there who had all but laughed at them when she'd looked at their request form. When Officer Bevins asked them why they hadn't filed it electronically, Tommy shrugged and said it was a nice day for a drive. But what he'd really wanted was to get a look at who he'd be dealing with in the property division. Plus something told him, and Gale concurred, that the less computerized they were on this case, the better off they'd be. If Syd's phone and computer were compromised, that meant their investigation might be as well, if somebody wanted something that badly. What that was they hadn't gleaned yet.

Officer Bevins shook her head. "The stuff from the year you're looking for's in a different warehouse and that's gonna take me a while to get hold of. Plus there was a flood in that one a while back. Stuff's not necessarily in date order after it got dried out. It's gonna be a fucking headache."

Bevins was pissed off about this request. But it wasn't as though this short pudgy blonde had to get up on ladders and retrieve the boxes herself, Gale thought.

"Happy to help," Tommy said. He took his card out of his pocket. "We've pulled stuff for cases before."

"Might take you up on it. I'll call and let you know."

"What makes you two think anyone would be interested in such an old case?" Sullivan asked.

"I think the woman who brought it to us is being hacked, phone and computer."

"Proof?"

"Not yet. Just something innate. Not sure I can get the captain to sign off on lending us the tech division to find out, either. They're stretched thin on current homicides and Homeland Security stuff."

"Well, if this murder had been that important, they'd have solved it up front back then."

"Not if Ned Rossiter didn't want it solved."

The name got Sullivan's attention. "Rossiter Enterprises? That thief is involved in this?"

"On the school's board. Treasurer. I didn't realize he was that bad."

"All of those corporate raiders were. If you ask me, they ruined capitalism, and he was one of the worst." Sullivan's disgust was clear as he shifted in his chair. "There's enough on him that you could dump his life upside down and figure out if he quashed that investigation. I'd get that gal back into the station house and look at everything she has, anyway. Might be more on him there if she's got anything on the embezzlement." Sullivan picked up the last tile on his rack and laid it next to the "o" in Gale's previous word. "I win."

"No way! 'Jo' is a proper name."

"It's also a Scottish word for sweetheart." He reached across the table and rubbed her cheek with his knuckle. "And you're still mine."

"Oh, for God's sake, Dad." Gale swatted at his hand.

He chuckled and rose to get ice from the refrigerator, careful to lock the wheelchair and as careful to stretch his six-foot-five frame to its fullest height before taking a step. "And of course you've thought of who has anything to lose that they need to silence this woman who brought you the case after all these years."

"Been bothering me from the get-go. I'm building that list slowly. There were a lot of possible players in Wyatt Reid's death. We have to find out who's living and who's dead. And if they're dead, exactly how they were involved in both Reid's and Rossiter's lives."

"I'm not so sure I'd bother with the dead."

Gale furrowed her eyebrows.

"Dead men don't make threats." Sullivan walked out of the kitchen.

Gale sat back. Her father's observation came with a sense of exhilaration and that feeling of the chase that she used to love. Quick on its heels, fear snuck in. There was too much about this case that she didn't like; too many variables were becoming apparent in the chart she was building. And too much didn't add up or make sense. She hated when she couldn't get a handle on a case. The threat after forty years had made her uneasy immediately, something she'd not shared with Tommy. It meant someone had been watching Syd for decades. What kind of person did that? Obviously, someone who knew there was no statute of limitations on murder. And Gale didn't like that at all. It meant Syd wasn't safe, and her cold case wasn't so cold. She wanted another scotch. Instead, she went to her briefcase, pulled out her laptop, the chart of suspects and the file of notes she'd brought home, and settled onto the couch to begin researching obituaries for every name on the list.

If Syd wasn't safe, Gale wasn't going to take a night off.

CHAPTER EIGHT

"Come in, come in!" Lucas stepped aside from the open doorway of his apartment. Syd had been surprised when he gave her his Park Avenue address. The last time she'd seen him, he was in a tiny fourth floor walk-up studio in the West Village. That was in 1983. She thought he'd never leave the Village. Or do this well. She kicked herself for not looking him up online last night when she'd thought about it, but she was in the middle of a really good book, so she made a mental note. By the time she put the book down, all thoughts of Lucas had vanished.

"My God, Sydney, you look the same, except for the white hair." He hugged her and she tried not to stiffen. His voice still carried that note of insincerity it always had. "Time comes for us all, though, doesn't it?" He pointed to his own crew cut, his blond hair having gone white, too, and he smiled. Syd had always categorized his smile more as a baring of the fangs. Those blue eyes that had entrapped so many young men back in the day were still lit with intelligence and the promise of something she could never put her finger on. It was a promise that had never been meant for her, though.

"And this must be Drew." Lucas held out his hand, and when Drew clasped it, he slapped him jovially on the shoulder. Even though Lucas was still well-muscled and stood straight as a rod at seventy, the motion was akin to David trying to make nice to Goliath the way Drew outweighed him and stood a head taller.

Drew's smile in return was cold, but he switched gears immediately. "Nice to meet you, and thanks for seeing us. I'm not here that long and we got to talking last night, Aunt Syd and I, about my father, and when she told me there might still be people here who knew him, well, I wanted to meet them."

Syd's own insincerity as she watched Drew's "aw, shucks" performance nearly got the better of her. But she'd come for information, vowing to do whatever it took to get it.

"Yes, sorry to hear about the loss of your grandfather. Those events tend to make us think of what we don't know or thought we'd have all the time in the world to find out." Then he paused, almost dramatically, making Syd think of those heightened moments on Broadway stages when the leading man appears to think of something weighty he needs to impart to the audience in the next bit of dialogue. "Oh—" He put his hand on the small of Syd's back. "That reminds me. Ned's service was quite beautiful. I'm sorry you couldn't make it."

"I'm sure it was lovely." Lucas's hand on her back nauseated her, so reminiscent of the way Ned used to touch her when he was trying to include her because he needed her.

"Many old friends came out of the woodwork."

Probably to make sure he was dead.

"His son and daughter were there, of course."

Syd hadn't thought about them in years because they'd been the brattiest children she'd ever met. And it would seem that "Edward Junior," as he'd been called since he was in a bassinette, had become the kind of bratty adult who stole Daddy's company when he couldn't wait for him to die. "Of course."

"Arlene's married and lives in California, couple of kids. And Edward Junior is on Park and Eighty-seventh, a block away."

The superior tone made Syd want to roll her eyes.

"Come on." Lucas swept his hand in the direction of the living room. "I thought we could sit on the terrace and enjoy the view. With Bloody Marys. I know it's early, but it would be a marvelous way to celebrate Wyatt."

Syd was torn between revulsion for Lucas and his blithe comment, and a curiosity about his apartment and the attendant wealth that it signaled as she and Drew made their way through the large living room. It was spacious enough to accommodate quite a number of people for parties, and Syd had no doubt that Lucas threw them. Hand-knotted rugs in hues of blue underpinned elegantly upholstered couches. Chairs and ottomans were gathered around a vast marble fireplace. Highly polished end tables, coffee tables, and bookcases completed the room, with ornate lamps and sconces strategically placed. Artwork from several different modern periods hung on the wall, along with tasteful groupings of photographs that Syd wanted to examine when she spotted some of the lost boys in them, but Lucas wasn't allowing for any kind of tour. There wasn't a television in sight. Syd recognized Vivaldi's "Four Seasons" coming from speakers mounted in the upper corners of the room. That meant there was a music system somewhere else in the apartment. The dining room they passed was wallpapered in a delicate spring green and white stripe. Ficus trees graced the corners of the room, a rustic oak Craftsman-style table and chairs at the center. There must be a den somewhere, too, she thought, with a television and the source of the music. They stepped out onto the roomy cement terrace that Lucas had overlaid with the kind of planking floor that was reminiscent of a beach boardwalk. It had weathered like the walkways of Cherry Grove on Fire Island where they'd all partied at Wyatt's summer house when they were young. She wondered if it was a nod to those halcyon days. He'd been so angry when he'd found out Wyatt had left his house on Lewis Walk to her. Wyatt had done it for Drew, which Lucas had neither understood nor cared about. He'd wanted the house, plain and simple, wanted to buy it from the estate. With what money, she couldn't figure out, since he had none then. She'd heard he'd taken up with a wealthy sugar daddy from the Pines the following spring and spent all his summers there after that.

The view of Central Park to the west was stunning. Syd sat at the large teak table in the center of the terrace. Protected from the sun by a great canvas umbrella, it was already set with a fruit plate and a cutting board laid with slices of a dark heavily grained bread and cheeses. The service trolley on the side held dishes, a pitcher of Bloody Marys, glasses, an ice bucket, and a small tray of leafy celery sticks. Lucas held up the pitcher.

"Oh, not for me," Drew said.

"I have freshly made lemonade in the fridge. Would you rather that? Sydney?" He tipped the mouth of the pitcher over a sturdy pint glass and looked at Syd expectantly.

It was eleven in the morning, but Syd thought of Wyatt, the whole reason she was here. He would've jumped at the offer. "Yes, actually, a drink sounds good."

Lucas poured two glasses and slid celery stalks into each one. Syd could smell the Worcestershire sauce from where she sat. Lucas's drinks had always been on the pungent side, and strong. He set the drinks on big round tile coasters. "Let me get the lemonade, Drew. I'll be right back. Please, make yourselves at home, have some fruit." He set a stack of three white Bauhaus bowls and plates on the table and disappeared through the glass doors.

Syd looked at Drew and shook her head.

"He's a piece of work," Drew said sotto voce "I think 'supercilious' is the word I'm looking for."

"I need to get a look at the photos on his walls before we leave." Drew nodded.

Once they were all settled at the table, Lucas asked Drew about life in Nebraska. He kept his answer short, giving Lucas enough background to keep him from being bored, but emphasizing that he'd grown up on the same farm as his father, and that he now owned and worked it.

Lucas nodded. "A good life then."

The sheer breeziness of the comment stuck in Syd's craw.

"And, Syd, catch me up. Tell me, why did we ever lose touch? You disappeared from our lives so soon after…well, after Wyatt's passing."

Syd had popped a cherry into her mouth from her bowl of fruit salad and almost choked on it. She wanted to scream at him that he hadn't "passed." He'd been murdered. Instead, she collected herself and gave him a thumbnail sketch of her career.

"I'll be darned. Dale and Terry were at that firm. Do you remember them? I think it was the same time you were. They're both gone, now. Terry died from AIDS in ninety-four and Dale had a heart attack two years ago." Lucas rubbed his chin. "So many gone…"

Syd did remember Dale and Terry. They'd been the type of class clowns she had no patience for, and when she found out they were working in a division two floors below her, she'd stayed as far away from them as she could.

"How about you, Lucas? What have you been up to all these years?

"Mergers and acquisitions. I went to work for Ned."

Had a pigeon feather floated down, Syd was sure it would've knocked her over.

"Well, you've certainly done well. This place is lovely." She waited the requisite moment while Lucas all but crowed his "thank you" before her next question, hoping he wouldn't hear it for the fishing expedition that it was. "Tell me, where is everyone now?"

She kept her voice on a gentle spectrum as Lucas dredged up names, the litany turning into one of careers half-finished, lives cut short, some caught up in drugs, most caught up by AIDS. Many names were on the list she'd given to Detective D'Angelo. Lucas's roster supplied her with the ones she hadn't been able to recall.

Of the dozen plus boys they reminisced about, only three were still alive. When Syd asked Lucas if he knew where they were, he took out his cell phone.

"Let's see...Zach Feinberg is in Connecticut, of course. Big need for plastic surgeons there." He chuckled.

"He became a doctor? That surprises me."

"How do you mean?"

"He didn't seem ambitious or even inclined toward school at all."

"Oh, he was. But he didn't know how to get there. Ned took care of him."

Syd looked at him, unsure of what he was intimating even as she suspected she knew the answer. "Took care of him?" Before Lucas answered, it dawned on her that the generous gift Wyatt had given her to pursue her studies at Columbia's B School was resonating with a whole new meaning.

"Got him a scholarship to NYU. And a partial to med school there as well. Ned paid for the rest."

Even with her suspicions, the information surprised Syd. "Wow." College *and* med school were quite a chunk of change. She grappled with her astonishment. It was coupled with an accountant's awareness of what such generosity would have amounted to.

Lucas nodded. "He did that for a number of us." There was a note of reverence in his voice.

"Really." Syd recalculated the finances.

"They were loans, of course. We paid him back. Well, at least I did."

Syd regarded Lucas a little apprehensively now. "And how did he help *you*?"

"MBA. NYU."

"Oh." Syd kept her reactions low-key so she didn't raise suspicions. "That was—incredibly big of him." It suddenly occurred to her why Ned might have chosen Lucas as executor of his rather large estate over his son. "I guess it made sense, then, Ned making you executor. You knew the boys so well, you had a bond with him, and you were, well, always the one in charge." Syd meant it tongue-in-cheek, but Lucas preened; she wanted to gag.

"There was really no one else except for his wife, and he didn't want to burden her once she was diagnosed with MS. Actually, Wyatt was his executor until…well, yes, I guess it did make sense. Like you said, I knew the boys so well. Ned was kind of like his own personal foundation for at-risk youth. I think he thought about transferring executorship to his son, but by then, I knew everything and, well, passing all that info on to Edward Junior would've been a nearly insurmountable task. He was never all that smart *or* good with numbers."

Syd barely heard anything Lucas said after he mentioned that Wyatt had been Ned's executor first. Processing that information was proving difficult through the buzzing in her ears.

"He wanted to help us, you know," Lucas continued, "give us a start. Those of us that wanted to get out of that rut then, anyway."

Syd forced herself back to the present. "That rut."

"Partying and drugs and tricking."

She picked at the napkin in her lap. She'd spent enough time at clubs with the lost boys to know that they didn't think of their lives as "a rut." And it had long been whispered that the deep pockets for everything they did were Ned's, that he footed the bill for all the "partying" as well. "I see." Looking at Lucas, she thought she saw a cruel amusement on his face. "How many—I mean, who all did he help?"

"Almost everyone, Syd. Let me put it to you this way. Duane Valchek, Hugh Morrison and Billy Highsmith didn't want what Ned was offering. That's why they moved on from our circle. The rest of us, we took the leg up."

Syd registered that Billy's name wasn't among the dead. "So Ned did this out of the goodness of his heart."

"All he asked was that we keep him company."

Syd almost laughed at Lucas's innocent phrasing for Ned's ruse. But then she had a clear vision of the red ledger she'd found in Wyatt's desk, the one in which the numbers made no sense. "Can I ask—how did you all pay Ned back?"

Lucas's eyebrows rose quizzically.

"From a purely accounting point of view, I mean, we both know Ned wouldn't have kept track of all that."

Lucas chuckled. "Wyatt told me you were always about the books and the organization. No, not Ned. His secretary. Edna. Remember her? All payments were sent to her."

Syd did remember Edna, mostly for the charts and graphs she sent Wyatt for the school's annual reports that didn't necessarily match what she knew to be the truth. "I haven't thought about her in years."

"She was Ned's bedrock. Finally retired to Florida. She passed about a year ago."

"Oh." She looked out at the park. She wanted to steer the conversation back to her original fishing expedition. "Billy Highsmith was such a nice guy. Where is he these days?"

"I don't know. I lost touch with him. But let me give you Mike Avery's address. I'm sure he'd love to see Drew. Mike was close to Wyatt." Lucas leaned over his phone to block out the sunlight now infiltrating the shade on his side of the table so he could see the screen.

"And what's he been doing?"

"Funeral director. Over on the West Side."

"And Ned put him through mortuary school."

"Mm-hm. Mike saw what was coming with the AIDS crisis. At least we had one funeral home we could count on. I'll call him, tell him you'll be in contact."

Syd typed the information Lucas dictated to her into the notes app on her phone. "Lucas, this has been wonderful. Thanks so much." Syd rose. She'd stayed long enough to be polite. Taking his cue from her, Drew pushed back his chair, picked his cell phone up from under his crumpled napkin, and pocketed it. "You've been so generous with your time, but I don't want to keep you, and Drew and I have some things to attend to this afternoon."

"Of course. Well, now that we're back in touch, don't be a stranger."

There was no warmth behind his request, but this time, Syd hugged Lucas. Not, however, for the reason he thought.

In the elevator, Syd leaned back against the wall, depleted. "Did you get it all?"

Drew pulled his phone out of his pocket. "The app shows a two-hour recording."

"I was afraid he was going to see it under the lip of your plate."

"That's why I ate so quickly and dropped my napkin next to it."

Syd nodded. "Thank you for doing this with me. And for asking for the tour of his apartment before we left."

"You saw what you needed to see?"

Syd nodded.

"Good. You should know I wanted to grab his scrawny little neck the whole time and force him to tell me if he was behind the threat and the photo of Izzy."

"Well, thank you for your restraint. I can't add bailing you out of jail to this mess, too."

"What's next?"

"We go to Home Depot for the hardware you need for the shower bars. I'll call Mike when I know what I need from him."

In the cab back to the apartment later that afternoon, Syd slumped in her seat with a groan and let her head loll back.

"Are you okay?" Drew asked.

"My knee is killing me. This day has taken a lot out of me."

"The Home Depot or the visit with Lucas?"

Syd gave him a gimlet eye.

"He didn't buy your story about me wanting to meet old friends of my father's, you know. I mean, he seemed the perfect host, but it was like he was watching and listening between the lines."

"Yes, I was aware. But I got some very valuable information."

"Such as?"

"One of the boys I knew from back then was in a photo taken in nineteen eighty-five. But he died in nineteen eighty-two."

Drew furrowed his eyebrows. "Are you sure? That he died?"

"He went home to his parents not long after Wyatt died. Someone said he was sick but that the doctors didn't know what it was. We heard he passed away right after the new year. Of course, later on, we figured it had to be AIDS, a very early case."

"No one went to his funeral?"

"We were in our early twenties. No one had the money to travel to a small town up near the Canadian border. The news came to us afterwards. I think I remember Billy Highsmith going. They were best friends, Billy and Duane." All the more reason, Syd thought, that she needed to find Billy, to find out why Duane Valchek was in a photo on Lucas's wall after he was supposed to be dead.

"I'm sure your detectives are going to want this bit of info."

Fear slid down Syd's gut. "It scares me, Drew."

"Then let's call them when we get back to your apartment."

She looked at him. "You know, I couldn't help wondering, walking around that apartment—was all Lucas's money rooted in his career? Or was some of it embezzlement money? What did Ned do with all that money?"

The cab pulled up in front of her apartment building and all Syd could think of was that she needed a cold glass of something that wasn't water, and the calm steady influence of Detective Sterling. She handed Drew the keys to the apartment, sat on the wrought iron bench by the revolving door, and pulled her phone out as Drew paid the driver—she had a missed call from Elisa. They hadn't spoken in several days, and now she couldn't decide whether to share what was going on in her life.

Elisa could wait. Syd needed to talk to Sterling about that photograph in Lucas Rose's apartment, and the fact that the visit she probably shouldn't have made might have put her on his radar in a way that wasn't good. She was certain Sterling wouldn't be happy about this. But she'd had to do it. When the detectives visited him, they wouldn't know who was in those old photographs, wouldn't have known a dead boy stood right in the middle of a tight circle of young men who were still very much alive that year. Only Syd knew that face, and that that party had taken place more than three years after his supposed death. Only Syd, and Lucas.

The small kernel of fear inside her was replaced by one that hoped Detective Sterling would ask her to come into the station house tomorrow to talk. She'd begun to realize she liked being fixed in that hazel gaze whenever they spoke in person. It was warm and focused, like there was no one else in the world when Sterling looked at her. Of course, she would remain as professional as she'd been from the start.

Syd massaged both sides of her knee, finding momentary relief. Billy Highsmith had not been in that photo. What happened to Billy? She needed to track him down. He had once mentioned that he and Duane Valchek grew up together in a small town upstate and had come to the city together to seek their fortunes. Duane was a graceful boy who'd wanted to dance on Broadway. Find his obituary, find the town. Or Google "Highsmith, upstate New York." It wasn't such a common name. She could begin the online search while Drew prepared dinner, an Asian recipe he was excited for her to taste. With a groan, she stood. Her back hurt and she was tired. It was easier to lean on the revolving door and hope it moved than to push it outright.

CHAPTER NINE

Syd called Sterling from the relative cool of a bench on the far side of the building's lobby, keeping her voice low enough that the doorman paid no attention. Two things occurred to her after Detective Sterling answered her phone and she'd briefly spilled everything about her visit with Lucas Rose: she was doing all the talking, and Sterling was in a car.

"I'm sorry," Syd interrupted herself. "I didn't even ask you if you could take this call right now. You're on the road, aren't you?"

"Yes. And you're a little wound up, aren't you?"

Syd heard the concern in her voice. It unsettled her, confirming what she hadn't wanted to admit to herself: the visit to Lucas was a step over the line. "Lucas Rose sets me off. You have no idea."

"Oh, I think I do."

The touch of steeliness in Sterling's voice was crystal clear. Syd hadn't bargained on that.

"Then you know what it cost me to go see him and get the information that I did."

Sterling laughed out loud, a short bark of a thing. Syd knew it wasn't a laugh of amusement.

"What I think is that it was a very dangerous move and I'm certain you knew it. Don't make me worry about you, Syd. I have too many other things to do. But since you got something out of him that could be of value, we should meet."

"I was hoping you'd say that." Even though there were miles of fiber optics between them, Syd blushed in the moment of silence that followed. What, she wondered, was Sterling thinking about in that same silence?

"Come in to see us at nine. And bring that box of yours."

"I thought you didn't want any of that yet."

"Well, it may take a while to get the evidence from this case. So we might as well see what you have, see what pops out."

Syd knew they'd come to the end of the call, but she wasn't ready to let Sterling go—she could be terse, but she was never disingenuous. Each time they spoke, her calm voice steadied Syd. "Where are you, by the way? I hear a lot of traffic." Not that it was any of Syd's business, although she wanted it to be, if it had anything to do with the case.

"Brooklyn, on the BQE. Tommy and I went to file paperwork for the evidence. Listen, no more going to see anyone. Leave that to us. We'll do the talking to anyone from your list who's still alive and in New York. When the time is right."

"But—"

"Syd, investigating is literally our job. You don't have our training or experience and you could be putting yourself in harm's way." Sterling's sigh was audible over the traffic in the background. "I don't want anything happening to you. We have no idea what these men are capable of—but I'll remind you that you came to us with a photo someone took of a thirteen-year-old girl who is very dear to you who lives halfway across the country. We are not taking the threat lightly. And you might already have compromised our investigation."

That was a reality check. Syd had done the one thing she promised herself she wouldn't: she'd lost sight of the fact that it was Izzy in their crosshairs. "I'm sorry—that was never my intention." Syd slumped against the bench.

"Well, keep in mind that the road to hell is paved with those. We'll talk more tomorrow morning."

Sterling ended the call and Syd sat quietly, contemplating the slate stones of the lobby floor. Detective Sterling had confirmed how risky her visit to Lucas was. But she'd found the photo of a not-so-dead Duane Valchek on Lucas's wall. *That* was an entry in the credit column, worth all the debits that accompanied it.

A feeling of fatigue set in, something that had been happening more often in the last few years. She didn't like it. She pushed up off the bench and made her way to the apartment, research on Billy Highsmith on her mind.

Drew's voice reached her when she entered—he was obviously on a Zoom call with a petulant Izzy and seemed to be on the losing end of the conversation and running out of ammunition. She pulled a chair next to his at her dining room table so that they could both be seen in the laptop's camera.

"So, what round is this and who's winning?"

Izzy raised her fists, danced around like a miniature boxer in the ring, and comically lowered her voice, adopting her idea of a New York accent. "And in this cohnah, weighing eighty-two pounds and wearin' black jeans and an AC/DC T-shoit is Isabominable Reid!"

Syd laughed. She wanted to reach through the computer and pinch one of those ruddy cheeks, but she realized she'd made a mistake when the smile disappeared and Izzy transformed into a heavy-lidded stone-faced thirteen-year-old. She guessed Drew was trying to reason with her, and she was having none of her father's excuses for what had turned her world upside down again just when the pandemic restrictions were lifting and she could be with her friends. Syd was sometimes surprised by Izzy's emergent beauty: the big doe eyes that glimmered green; the complexion that could only be described, clichéd as it was, as peaches and cream; the smile that could melt you on your worst day. Now, however, Izzy affected that sultry bored stare, probably to piss off Drew, her eyelids slowly sinking by degrees until they reached "I'm not listening anymore."

"I'm under house arrest, yo," Izzy huffed, and then folded her arms across her chest. "Police cars be rollin' by the house every fifteen minutes."

Syd contained her amusement at Izzy's drama and use of the vernacular. "I think that's an exaggeration, sweetie."

"No-oo. They do-oo." Izzy looked away again but glanced sideways at them. Syd recalled the move from her own youth, trying to measure the effect she was having on her mother whenever they argued. She stifled another laugh.

"You know there's only one reason we're doing this, don't you?" Syd finally asked her.

"It's because you hate me," Izzy replied sullenly.

Syd nodded sagely. "Exactly."

Expressions of astonishment, disbelief, and self-doubt passed across Izzy's face in quick succession. Even Drew looked at her in surprise.

Syd smirked, and then Izzy sat back and laughed that hiccuping laugh she'd had since childhood that delighted Syd. Those green eyes lit up like Wyatt's used to, and with them the room, that peculiar feeling of missing someone mirrored in the person right in front of you hitting Syd like a poke in the chest.

"You could never hate me, Aunt Syd!"

She chuckled. "Don't push your luck, kid."

The laughter stopped unexpectedly. "How long, Dad? Really?"

Drew looked down at his arms folded in front of him on the table. "Answer's not going to change, sweetie. You'll know when I know. And promise me you won't sneak out of the house. There *is* a reason this is happening."

Izzy used her right hand to make that universal duck-billed "blah blah blah" sign and looked away. "I can't promise."

Syd felt Drew tense up and stepped into the fray. "Izzy, I'm going to bottom-line this for you."

Izzy narrowed her eyes, the black Goth makeup around them becoming like smudge pots. "Accountant-speak, Aunt Syd."

Izzy's arrow hurt. Whenever Syd had visited during Izzy's not-so-long-ago childhood, she took over the bedtime stories, and substituted accounting phrases strung into nonsensical sentences for the words in the book that Izzy knew so well, and Izzy would laugh uproariously, breathlessly trying to say the right words, covering Syd's mouth to stop her. The girl gazing back at her reminded her that those days were long gone. "Teenaged insolence, darling," Syd taunted her back gently.

Izzy lowered her chin to her chest. "'K. We're even."

"This is my fault. Someone sent me a threat and it included my family. Which is you, among others. Now, we don't know how serious this is. So until the police help me sort this out, you will please do as your father asks. No sneaking out." Syd and Drew had decided it was best not to tell Izzy about the photo. Better to simply make it seem like a pestering threat to Aunt Syd that still had to be taken seriously. Syd tried to gauge Izzy's reaction, and then decided to sweeten the pot. "I'll tell you what. Dad, if she can have any friends over for dinner that she wants, whenever she wants, I'll foot the bill for that Chinese restaurant to deliver the dinners." That caught Izzy's attention, she sat up straight, and Syd nearly laughed. Izzy became obsessed with Chinese restaurants when she first visited New York five years earlier. They were everywhere, each one an exotic outpost in Izzy's eyes since Alma had none. So Syd took her to Chinatown, which charmed and enchanted Izzy in its otherness. They'd walked around all day looking at things, Izzy absorbing like the proverbial sponge everything Syd imparted about the neighborhood, its history in New York, and whatever Syd knew about China itself, and they tasted everything she was curious about. When Pearl's Lotus Blossom opened in Alma a few years later, Izzy called Syd to tell her about it. *Now I can be like you and order takeout all the time!* Syd had heard the excitement in her voice and feared for Drew's wallet.

"Or pizza? Can I have a pizza party, Dad?"

So much for favorites.

"Your mother has guest list approval."

Izzy rolled her eyes. "Fine. How long are you staying?"

"Did you think if you asked the question differently, the answer would change?"

"It does when Mom does that," Izzy aimed, fired, and hit Drew, who shifted uncomfortably.

Syd chuckled. "Oops."

"When Aunt Syd is safe, I'll be home."

"We'll talk to you every couple of nights, okay?" Syd counted on her soothing tone to appease Izzy. "Meantime, I'll send the money through Zelle." That brought another smile to Izzy's face.

"I love you, Aunt Syd."

"You love the pizza my money can buy." Syd winked at her.

Izzy scrunched up her face, kissed her fingertips, and touched the screen. Syd did the same, and then Izzy cut the connection.

Drew sighed. "Of course you get the love. I'm just her dad. And every couple of days? How long do you think you can keep tap-dancing before she gets antsy?"

Syd rubbed her face with the palms of both hands. "I wish I had an answer to that."

"I need a drink. That child seriously tries my patience. And maybe I should get started on dinner a little early since we didn't have lunch."

"I won't fight you on that. I'll make the drinks—what are you having?"

"Gin and tonic?"

"Ooh, that sounds good."

Drew followed Syd into the kitchen and took the ingredients he'd prepped earlier for a chicken-broccoli-red pepper sauce stir-fry out of the refrigerator. He put Syd's steamer on the stove and dropped a foil-wrapped packet of rice he'd made last night into it as Syd mixed their drinks.

"For someone who doesn't cook, you have a really well-stocked kitchen." Drew took a long-handled tong from the utensil drawer.

"All of it amassed girlfriend by girlfriend. No better way to attract a good cook than with the kitchen of her dreams." Syd grinned.

"You're a sly fox, Aunt Syd. So what did your detectives have to say?" Drew worked the chicken chunks along with diced orange bell and cayenne peppers around a smoking sauté pan. The aroma of the peppers filtered through the heavier scent of the chicken, and she realized how hungry she was.

"Detective Sterling was concerned."

"I bet she was."

Syd rolled a lime on her cutting board and then carefully inserted a paring knife under the skin. "And I have to apologize to you." She turned it in her hand as she worked, forming a long, curly strip that dropped to the board.

Drew stopped chopping mushrooms and looked at her. But she found she couldn't meet his gaze so she busied herself twisting the lime strip, dropping it into the glass, and pouring the shot glass of gin and the splash of tonic in after it.

"I should have listened to you about going to see Lucas. I put my need for information in front of Izzy's safety." She placed the drink next to Drew on the counter, finally facing him.

"I'll admit I was mad, and I should have said so." Drew sprinkled the mushrooms into the sauté pan and stirred them as they began to release their liquid.

"Why didn't you?"

"Would that have stopped you?"

"Yes."

"I honestly didn't think it would, and I was afraid that if I argued with you, it could get ugly. You and I don't need that right now."

"I'm truly sorry. But next time—" At Drew's look of alarm, Syd held her hand up. "Not that there will be a next time—there won't. Tell me it's not all about me. That will get my attention."

"Deal." Drew julienned a red pepper on Syd's mandoline slicer and scattered the pieces into the pan. Their scent as they sizzled and curled up mingled with the already savory smell of the other peppers, mushrooms and chicken, seduced Syd's olfactory senses. She grabbed a can of cashews, opened them and coaxed handfuls into two small bowls. She slid one over to Drew. "Detective Sterling did the 'angry' for you, said I endangered Izzy. And myself. And might've thrown a wrench into the investigation."

"Huh. I'm liking her more and more." Drew ate a handful of cashews and dropped broccoli florets into the sauté mix. Then he tossed a generous handful of red pepper chunks and several roasted red peppers into the blender with a drop of olive oil, slivers of garlic, and a splash of chicken broth. "I should have brought up Izzy. Lord knows, she's all I think about now. But something also told me your instinct was right, so I crossed my fingers. And look, you saw the photo of the guy who should've been dead. What did Sterling say about that?"

Syd's mouth began to water anticipating the red pepper sauce before it even hit the pan, so she grabbed several cashews, shaking them in her hand like dice. "We didn't have time to get into it." She popped the cashews into her mouth and pulled a second strip from the lime, twisted it, and dropped it into her drink. "Good news, though— Sterling wants us to bring the box to her tomorrow."

"Great."

"They want to hear about Lucas in detail."

Drew began ladling out the Chinese stew, tipping the pan to scrape all the sauce onto the rice. "Well, we have a whole recording for them, if they want it."

"Yes, we do." Syd leaned over her plate, inhaled, and dipped a finger into it to taste. "This is heaven. Thank goodness your grandmother taught you how to cook, or we'd have been ordering out while you're here. But I know she didn't teach you any recipes like this."

He swept his hand over the plates, "Courtesy of Izzy. That Chinese restaurant's not cheap, so I taught myself some basic dishes for her."

"You're a good dad."

"I had good grandparents. C'mon." He picked up the plates. "Aunt Syd, I love your jazz collection, but do you have any Garth Brooks? I need me a little country tonight."

After dinner, Drew opted for a New York Yankees game on TV. Syd sat in the dining room with her laptop. She'd listen to the game as she searched for Billy Highsmith. First, however, she called Elisa back.

"How *are* you, sweetiedahling? Are you hitting the museums and the movie theaters and the golf course?"

Syd laughed. "It's been less than a week, you goofball! I haven't even looked at the folder HR sent me with my retirement package." In truth, Syd had sat down with the VP of HR months prior and knew exactly what was in the folder.

"Ahhh, I'm jealous, that's all." Elisa sighed. "I'm stuck here for three more years. All of them without you on a day-to-day basis. I'm going through withdrawal—no one around here has your biting sense of humor with its deep vein of sarcasm."

"Then we need to get together."

"We do. What did you have in mind?"

Syd hesitated. But then she realized that after more than thirty years, there was literally nothing she couldn't tell Elisa. "How about right now. Are you up for a walk?" Syd was met with a moment of silence from Elisa's end.

"Is everything okay, Syd?"

"Can you meet me in the north park? We can walk along the river."

"I'll be there in twenty minutes."

Syd heard the disquietude in Elisa's voice but was glad Elisa heard the need in hers and was willing to drop everything. She went to the hall closet for a jacket.

"Hey, sorry to interrupt the game, but I'm going to meet Elisa Morales for a walk."

Drew smiled. "I haven't seen the Cuban Missile since I was a kid. Tell her I send my love. Or do you need me to come along?" Drew sat up. "Will you be okay at this hour?"

Syd waved him off. "We'll be fine—we do this all the time."

"Okay. And listen, I'll do the grab bars in your bathroom tomorrow. I wanted to do them tonight, but it's getting late for that kind of noise and I'm done in."

Syd blew him a kiss. "Don't wait up for me."

It was a short walk to the park, but it gave Syd time to think about how she was going to tell Elisa about the cold case investigation. That meant telling her about an entire segment of her life she'd never shared with her. Elisa would listen without judgment. She always did. It was one of the reasons Syd loved her.

She turned her attention to Drew's insistence on installing those grab bars in her bathroom. "I don't want you to slip and fall in here and be unable to summon help," he said earlier in the day when he'd assessed the layout of the room. So they'd gone to Home Depot after leaving Lucas's apartment so he could get the proper hardware. She felt old, the second time she'd been reminded since her retirement party that time was gaining on her. But Drew's decision to install them himself was an act of love she could certainly live with.

Elisa stood at the railing overlooking the East River.

"Hey," Syd called, and nudged Elisa's shoulder when she didn't turn around. Something was wrong so she waited and watched the river roil past.

"You have cancer, don't you?"

"What? No! I'd definitely tell you *that* over the phone."

"Then what is it, Syd?" She took Syd's hand. "I'm worried sick. You hardly ever call for night walks like this."

Syd led her to a stone bench and told her about 1982, the blue envelope, and everything that had been going on in the last few days.

After the initial shock, Elisa finally let out a big breath. "And here I was joking about you going to the movies and golfing and you were dealing with this! Oh, sweetiedahling, I don't even know what to say. Except that I'm frightened for you." Elisa took her hand again. "You say you're okay, but are you really?"

Elisa put the question quietly. And for that reason, and because Elisa knew her so well, it almost broke Syd.

"I'm so aware now that I have no control over anything. My visit to Lucas was like putting an oar in the water. For a minute, I had direction. I feel like I'm drifting at sea and I'm not sure how to deal with that. And I'm scared."

"I think you need to tell those detectives how you feel."

"They're cops, not shrinks."

"Don't underestimate them. And you've got me. I can't actually do anything, but I can listen."

Syd hugged her. "I don't know what I'd do without you."

Even though opening up to Elisa had been like turning a steam valve, it had only siphoned off some of the pressure. Syd's thoughts on the walk home ran rampant like a toy car being driven by a toddler who had no concept of direction: Lucas—what had she done; Sterling—would she trust Syd again; Drew—how would she manage him; the blue envelope; Izzy; she needed groceries; Gale Sterling; Wyatt; her life had been drop-kicked in the wrong direction and it wasn't going to let up, was it; Fire Island—she needed to open the house; the banker's box; Gale Sterling; Gale Sterling. Gale Sterling.

Thoughts of her were beginning to vault all Syd's walls. And because her adult life had been about numbers, stats and the truths they told, she couldn't deny how this was charting for her. *My life is a mess. Even if I thought I* could *handle a woman right now, it certainly wouldn't be the handsome lead detective on this case.* That didn't mean she didn't think about her. A lot.

She'd been keeping at bay how unmoored and helpless she felt. Admitting it to Elisa unleashed it. The last time she'd felt this way was when Wyatt was murdered. And now here she was again. It wasn't a place she wanted to be.

But this time, she thought, time might be to her advantage. She had a foundation that came with age and experience, and her faith. This was one of the trials she and Father Moore often spoke about that show up in one's life; she could ask for his guidance. She could also lean on his insight that Wyatt had been a gift, but she'd always known that. These things would tether her this time. As would Drew. And this time, detectives were taking her seriously. Now Elisa would be there for her, too. So she wasn't alone.

When she got back to the apartment, Drew was asleep in front of a West Coast game. Syd turned down the sound and settled in front of her laptop. She typed "Duane Valchek obituary" into the search engine. Twenty minutes later, totally frustrated at finding nothing, she typed in "Billy Highsmith, Malone, New York." It didn't take her long to piece together his life. She was astounded to find out he'd lived fifteen blocks east of her for almost thirty years.

CHAPTER TEN

Tommy stopped short of his desk when he spotted the overstuffed cranberry muffin sitting on his blotter. He knew the sign.

"All good. Really." Gale flashed a smile and went right back to the computer.

Tommy waited, as he always did.

Gale looked up at the ceiling. "Fine. You win. I talked to Sullivan about the case last night. All it took was one sentence for him to render my chart nearly irrelevant."

Tommy chuckled. "Ah, the mighty Sullivan Sterling. Well, that accounts for the black suit and the black shirt you're wearing today—I almost thought there was a memorial service I'd forgotten about." He whistled a note of relief. "And what was that sentence?"

Gale fixed Tommy with a glare of defeat and frustration. "Dead men don't make threats."

Tommy let out a big sigh. "I been thinkin' about that myself."

"Uccch!" Gale put her head in her hands. "That's, like, policing one-oh-one."

"Okay, but this case is a little different. A lot different." Tommy sat at his desk, peeled the ribbed paper from the bottom of the muffin, and bit into it. He put his head back to savor the tangy flavor. Gale grinned. "It's the orange zest—gets me every time." A short, satisfied moan emanated from somewhere low in his body. "So, how many other batches did you turn out after the old man pissed on our parade?"

"Blueberry and chocolate chip. He's right, you know."

"I'm gonna disagree with him. We got a lotta dead guys on our hands on this case. And we both know it's the living that make them talk. Somebody dead coulda killed Wyatt, and someone alive is gonna make that dead man talk from beyond the grave—mark my words."

"Operative word dead. So we can't question him."

"We won't need to question him. Our ten years on this squad proves dead men *do* tell tales when live ones use them to save their skins. So old Sullivan can go dance the tarantella."

"Highland jig."

"Same thing, different boat at Ellis Island. So listen, I started working up a list during the ball game last night, the main players and the order we oughtta maybe take them on, dead or alive."

"Mets were losing, I take it."

"Moving on." Tommy smoothed his club tie.

Gale chuckled. "Yeah, I heard Sullivan swearing at the TV downstairs at one point. And I had the same thought you did last night, only on a different vector of the clock, so I started searching obituaries of the guys on Syd's list. Came in at six this morning to continue."

"Ouch! I'm sorry your old man has that effect on you. On the other hand." Tommy raised his muffin to toast Gale. "We get these when he does."

Gale grunted. "I'm sure he's going to drive me mad with his insights on this one, so there will be muffins. And Syd's coming in this morning. By the way, she texted me last night."

"About?"

"Billy Highsmith. Turns out they've lived fifteen blocks away from each other most of their adult lives. And didn't know it."

"Does not surprise me. My cousin Rocky? Sublettin' three avenues from me for two years and I didn't know until I ran into him in church on Easter Sunday. *My* church, not his."

Several of the other detectives walked in, some with two of the muffins in hand that Gale had left on trays in the break room.

Miller bowed down, then held up a chocolate chip muffin. "I am lighting candles at your altar, boss. I worship your muffin."

"Shut up, Miller," Gale and Tommy said in unison.

The other detectives saluted Gale before sitting down at their desks.

Tommy turned back to their conversation. "So, what's our take-away about Highsmith?"

"I don't know yet. Syd researched his background, said he's also in finance, like Lucas, but apparently no love lost there."

"Think we can believe that?"

"I've decided I don't know anything until we begin shaking the trees."

"I love interviewing people in these cold cases. When we show up and they get that look on their faces like the four horsemen of the apocalypse are ridin' into town—warms my heart." Tommy sat back and put his feet up on his desk. "I'm particularly interested that she found a guy in a photograph years after his death. You wanna revisit Sullivan's advice?"

"I do not. That photo is what prompted my obituary search."

"And?"

"Slow going, but so far, so dead." She held the list up, several checkmarks on it.

"Let's split it up, move this faster. Miller, you eating that whole chocolate chip muffin *and* the blueberry Frank just gave you?"

"I made Syd stand down from also visiting the funeral director who used to run with the lost boys, as she calls them. Not that it would happen, but we don't need her dead, too." Gale was beginning to get the feeling that Syd wasn't the passive type, and that it might be a little troublesome corralling her. Sometimes when they began poking into these cold cases, things heated up. And with this one, depending on how it went, ten million missing dollars could prove to be incendiary no matter how many people around it were dead.

Tommy caught the half muffin that Miller lobbed to him. "Yeah, well, more than that, we don't want her screwing up our plans for approaching this." He rubbed his eyes, leaving a trace of chocolate near his right eyebrow. "Already I'm afraid we're gonna have to step things up in terms of talking to the living."

"I gave that some thought last night—"

"Let me guess—over the blueberry. They're so killer with the cinnamon tops."

Gale smiled. "Yeah, I had one or two with my midnight coffee."

"Jesus, how are you even standing this morning?"

"Chocolate smudge." Gale pointed to her eyebrow.

"Crap." Tommy grabbed a tissue and wiped it off. "So, what did you come up with?"

"If Syd's forced our hand? Why don't we use that to our advantage? Go in and interview Lucas, blow up his world a little. Maybe we end up not needing to do the research we think we need."

"See if a rat deserts the sinking ship?"

"Exactly. Bring a little heat, see if this Billy Highsmith or the funeral director make a move."

"Oh, crap, I hate stakeouts."

"We'll get better food this time."

Tommy snorted. "It ain't the food."

"Well, it certainly can't be the company." She turned in her chair to face him. "Okay, maybe at this juncture, we just get footage from security cameras near their homes. Here's what else I was thinking. What if that guy Syd saw in the photo *isn't* dead? Lucas *told* her these young men had died."

"Well, ya gotta figure, AIDS *was* a major sword that cut through that generation. Then you got your old age, and now your Covid."

"Tommy, a plague is a perfect place to hide."

Tommy tipped back on his chair legs. "You are evil, Sterling. It gives me the willies sometimes the way you think like the criminals."

"It's a big crossword puzzle to me, the mind of a criminal."

"Yeah, I don't get that."

"Sudoku, then."

"That I get."

"Look, I did some other figuring last night while I tried not to eat the chocolate chips. There were fifteen guys on Syd's list. Most of them intersected with both Wyatt and Ned. But there were 'only Ned's and 'only Wyatt's.'" She held up a piece of paper.

"Oh, crap, the Venn diagram."

"Settle down, you knew it was coming. And there will be more. Now, in addition, Sullivan suggested we turn Ned Rossiter's life upside down. It'll be easy to find out who he did business with—I've already done a preliminary look-see online, but I'll end up at the library for a deeper dive. Old society columns. Business reference data, everything on his hedge fund. Actually, you should take the money side."

"I don't know—you think that kind of info is necessary? I mean, forty years ago, that'll definitely be a list of dead guys."

"I know. But as Dad pointed out, if Ned killed the embezzlement story in the press, he didn't do it alone. He had help from someone with power. And that made me wonder: were any of those money types involved in other aspects of Ned's life? His hedge fund? Were any of them into the lost boys?" She held up the diagram again. "If so, involvement equals motive. Because something tells me Wyatt and the boys were familiar with Ned's moneyed crowd."

"My train arrived at that junction last night, too."

"And—and." Gale held up a finger. "There were powerful people among the parents at that school, and they were money with a capital M. Secrets and money, Tommy, deadly combination."

"All right, so you cover Ned's social and personal life. I'll follow the money trail. I *do* love that chase. And let's give Lucas Rose a call, but let's see Syd's stuff and finish the background check on him before we rattle his cage."

Like a perfectly timed stage entrance, Syd and Drew appeared in the doorway. Gale and Tommy rose to greet them. Miller quickly threw a large black bed sheet they kept for such occasions over the white board that still held the photos of Wyatt's apartment. Gale nodded her thanks, pretty sure Syd hadn't noticed.

Syd was carrying two muffins on a plate. Drew held the banker's box.

"I hear you're an expert baker, Detective. I'm intrigued."

"It's a sideline. Keeps me out of trouble." Gale admired Syd's burgundy suit, and the casual route she'd taken pairing it with a simple white button-down and black pumps. A gold cross sat right above her cleavage.

"They smell divine. I was hoping you wouldn't mind if we tried them while we talked?"

"Of course not."

Tommy pulled up three chairs and Drew set the box on one of them.

"This is Wyatt's son, Drew. His daughter is Isabella, the girl in the photo."

Tommy took the box from Drew and set it on Sterling's desk. He shook Drew's hand. "Sorry this is happening, man."

Drew nodded his thanks.

Gale turned on her phone's recorder, stated the case number and date, and Tommy got a digital camera out of his desk.

Syd removed the box lid and began taking out one item at a time. As Syd explained each thing, Tommy shot photos.

"That's smart," Drew observed.

"Sometimes, evidence walks. Or gets misplaced, too. This way, we have a record." Tommy's phone rang. He picked it up, turning away from the conversation. When he hung up, Gale caught his glance.

Syd carefully pulled the brittle and torn will out of its yellowed envelope. She related the story of finding it buried beneath the original signed will on Ben Ford's desk and taking it. "I realize what I did could be construed as robbery, but it was instinctive—there was something very wrong with this will. Wyatt was already dead." She pointed at the faded note. "Was Ben doing what I think he was doing?"

Syd's anger and a sad frustration were clashing on her face, and Gale chose to shrug noncommittally. "If Ned and Wyatt were embezzling, that would be the first thing they'd learn. Each other's signatures." As soon as she'd done it, though, she wished she could take it back—not the fact of the statement because Syd needed to hear that—but the callous tone of it. Gale didn't usually let anyone's emotions affect her as she worked a case, but Syd's obvious momentary descent into sorrow touched her. She sensed Sydney Hansen was not afraid of the truth, though, and in fact sought it out. Time would tell, and Gale vowed to learn how best to impart information to her more compassionately.

An hour later, Syd pulled out the last piece of evidence. It was a small white envelope. Gale opened it. The smaller square of paper inside still bore the ghosts of many crease marks. Gale studied it and handed it to Tommy. "The first threat."

Tommy showed it to Drew. "You should probably see this."

"I didn't show this to you yesterday," Syd said to Drew by way of apology, "because I wanted to wait and do it here today."

"My God, they threatened me." Drew's voice held anger and bewilderment. "And now they're threatening my daughter."

"That makes this a less than cold case, and we're going to solve it," Gale said.

"You have to," Drew said. "I can't lose my only child."

"They want something from Syd. I think whoever this is is smart enough to know that another murder isn't a good idea."

Drew didn't look convinced.

Gale put the note back into the envelope, placed it in the box, replaced all the other items in it, and lifted it into an evidence locker behind her desk. As she sat back down and put the key to the locker in her desk drawer, she thought she caught a look of relief on Syd's face. She slid the pages of notes she'd taken into the file folder on her desk. She'd transcribe them later, after she and Tommy had time to sift through them.

Gale had seen Syd looking at the sheet-covered white board a few times as they went through the evidence but decided that sometimes the elephant got a seat in the room.

"I'm really glad you came in," Tommy said, holding out his hand to Syd. "These things are going to help us tremendously. And speaking of evidence, Gale, we'll be taking a trip out to Brooklyn."

"Bevins?"

"She's located several boxes in the building that was flooded, so she's taking us up on our gracious offer to come in and help them excavate."

"*Your* gracious offer." She sighed. "Of course. We'll go."

"I gotta run an errand first, over to the hardware store. Gimme five minutes."

"Oh," Drew interrupted. "Can I join you? I need to pick up a couple of things."

Syd looked at him curiously. "After the Home Depot?"

"I need longer screws for the grab bar next to the toilet."

Syd rolled her eyes. "He's old-farting my bathroom."

"Good," Gale said. "Better to be prepared. I did that for my dad ten years ago. He protested, but now it's the reason he's still in the house at ninety-one and not in some facility."

"Ninety-one, wow. And you installed them? Yourself? I'm impressed."

Tommy hiked his thumb toward Gale. "She's got a toolbox that puts me to shame, and I was raised by a guy who owned a construction company."

"You are a woman of many talents, Detective," Syd said once Tommy and Drew were gone. Her voice fell to a low teasing lilt.

"I have been told, yes." Gale couldn't believe her own reaction, the blush spreading up her neck as Syd reassessed her. It was the second time Syd had elicited that reaction in her. She hooked her thumb into her belt next to her badge and cleared her throat, now suddenly dry. "The do-it-yourself route was, uh, self-preservation. My wife didn't care for my haberdashery spending, so, to keep the financial peace, I learned how to repair anything and everything in-house." Gale saw Syd deflate a little.

"I did notice that about you." Syd tipped her head toward Gale's ensemble, a fine-grade Harris tweed suit. "So—" Syd sighed. "Your lucky wife gets a sharp dresser *and* a jack-of-all-trades."

"Got."

Syd looked at her questioningly.

"Kate died a few years ago."

"Ohhh, I'm so sorry…" Syd's reaction, the sorrow and sympathy immediate in her eyes, caught Gale off guard.

"That's, uh—"

"Please don't say it's okay. It never is. And yet we mitigate it by dismissing the seriousness of it. For social sake."

"Because life goes on. 'Yesterday the sun went hence and yet is here today.'"

"John Donne."

Gale fixed Syd in her gaze, but her eyes wandered over to the white board again. "And those of us left behind live with the loss."

This time, Gale knew she had to address the elephant. "We're still working with the photos, as you can see."

"Were you able to learn anything from them?"

"Yes and no." She wasn't about to tell Syd that she'd called in a forensic spatter specialist. Some things a person didn't need to hear.

"What does that mean?"

"Don't go there, Syd," Gale said gently. "There's no reason to think about them again."

"Unfortunately, they live in my head."

Gale hesitated, not wanting to let Syd leave on that note. "Let's take a walk around the block."

Out on the street, Gale followed the prescribed route she and Tommy always took. "I'll tell you what I can when I can. I know you want more, but you have to trust my instincts. I've been doing this a long time." She watched Syd mulling this over.

"Can I ask you a personal question?"

Gale cocked her head.

"You're speaking from experience, not as a cop, aren't you? Somewhere along the way, you were touched personally."

Gale turned her attention down the street and breathed in a healthy lungful of spring air. She wanted to answer the question, but she wanted to do it carefully.

"I only ask because, well, you've been kind. And you're attentive and in tune. I think that's unusual. And I'm very glad because right now, I'm feeling lost and out of control."

Gale nodded. "That's normal. You've carried Wyatt's murder all these years. And it was extremely traumatic. I'm not sure how you got through it, or how you did what you did. But that's a testament to who you are." And, Gale thought, *I like that about you.* "And now it's all being raked up again, which has to be terrifying."

Syd nodded, looking down.

"When I was a kid, I'd sometimes overhear my dad telling my mother about certain murder cases he worked. He's a tough guy but some of what he saw was beyond the pale. It could get to him. How my mother was strong enough to be the place where he could unburden himself, I'll never know. Eavesdropping on those moments, well, those were first-hand lessons in the brutal side of life. But they went hand in hand with how we care for each other."

When Syd focused those ice blue eyes on her again, there was the barest hint of tears in them. "Thank you for that."

Gale looked away for a moment. "I promise you're in good hands. But I want to ask you again about those young men Lucas told you were all dead."

"Okay," Syd said tentatively.

Gale started walking again. "Tommy and I think maybe some of them weren't. Aren't." Gale saw the look of alarm skitter across Syd's face. "So I've been running down obituaries on them." She omitted that there were a couple of them she couldn't find obituaries for, which might simply mean she had to dig deeper to find out where they'd come from before landing in the city, or where they'd gone when they left. Young people with terminal illness often went home to parents to die. "Anything you can tell me?"

"Yes. Maybe. I'm not sure."

"Would you like to deconstruct that for me?"

Syd told her about Duane Valchek, his supposed death from AIDS early in 1983, and of her futile online search for anything about an obituary or funeral. "It's as though he disappeared—and then reappeared for that one moment in the photo in Lucas's apartment."

"You're certain the photograph was taken after his death?"

"Yes. They all went to New Orleans for Lucas's birthday that year, nineteen eighty-five, for Mardi Gras. One of the boys—I don't remember who—sent me a postcard."

"I see." Gale made a note in a small, lined pad she took from her suit jacket breast pocket. "Do you still have the post card?" She hadn't been able to find Duane's obit last night or this morning, either. She'd put it on the list she'd given Tommy to see if he'd have better success. If he didn't, they'd have to begin tracking him as a living person, find his birthdate, hometown, where he'd gone when he'd left New York.

"No, I don't. And why did I believe Lucas at first? Of course he could be lying. This just gets more complicated, doesn't it?"

"Many of these cold cases do. Another question—how well did you know Ned Rossiter?"

"I didn't. I didn't really want to—he wasn't trustworthy. He was a bully."

Gale had suspected that. "I'm looking for links. Were any of these boys involved in Ned's business life, I mean, with men Ned knew on a corporate level?"

"I don't know."

"What about the other way around? Was anyone Ned did business with ever in his company at the gay clubs?"

"As a matter of fact, yes. Lucas would know all of that, of course. And probably Theo Hall."

Gale already had a page of notes dedicated to Theo, Wyatt's lover at the time of the murder. Because of his past, she and Tommy had done extensive research in preparation for their eventual interview with him.

"Why—what are you getting at?"

"You've said more than once that you don't think Wyatt embezzled on his own. Or that it was even his idea."

"I don't. He was a good person."

"Good people can be thieves, Syd. But if Ned was behind it, we have to look at everyone in his life at the time, too, see if anyone other than Ned was driving this."

"Will you be able to do a forensic examination of his finances at the time? All these years later?"

"As much as we can, yes. And of Wyatt's."

"Oh, God…"

"What?" Syd's reaction worried Gale.

"You know he gave me the money for graduate school. And he left me his house on Fire Island as well as a substantial trust fund to keep that house so that Drew could spend summers there when he was young."

Gale made more notes in the little pad. "That's good to know."

"It didn't occur to me until I spoke with Lucas that all of that could've been from embezzled funds."

"I'm sure we'll find that out. Money can leave remarkably long trails in some cases. Or it can burn and be gone in a flash. Either way, Tommy's like a bloodhound with that."

They had arrived back at the front steps of the station. Tommy and Drew were crossing the street toward them.

"Do you think I could see you once a week?" Syd asked, shifting, an eye on the men. "Or talk to you? About all this? Get an update?" She put her hands in her suit jacket pockets. "Maybe take a walk like this, get a cup of coffee. I think I'd feel less at sea."

The relief on Syd's face once the question was out was evident, almost as if she'd felt awkward about asking Gale on a date, and now that she'd jumped that hurdle she could exhale. But not knowing Syd's orientation, Gale's option was to keep things professional. However, she did think the weekly meetings might be good for both of them.

"It would depend on my schedule, but yes."

Syd bit her bottom lip and then let it go, so quickly Gale might've missed it had she not been looking. The resultant smile, small and short-lived, Gale definitely saw.

"Okay, we have banged around the hardware store and I, for one, feel better," Tommy said. "I'm about ready for a messy, moldy evidence warehouse."

"Let me go get my gear. Syd, next week." Gale shook Syd's hand and went into the station house.

Fifteen minutes later, they were stopped at a light on Second Avenue. Tommy glanced at Gale. "What's next week with Syd?"

"She wanted to meet now and then so I can brief her on the case as we work. She's feeling—out of sorts."

Tommy nodded, his eyes on the road.

Gale adjusted the seat belt. "It's, uh, a way of—keeping in touch, keeping Syd in the loop. You know."

"You want me there for these?"

"Oh no—not necessary. It'll just be, you know, a walk or a cup of coffee in the break room."

"Meet her at the diner. The break room's not conducive."

"It's not a date, you know."

"And yet you look a little bit happy."

Tommy's remark surprised her. "Shut. Up." She landed a quick light punch on his bicep.

"Owww!" Tommy exaggeratedly feigned pain. "I'm driving here!"

"Then pay attention to the road."

"I'm gonna have to report you for abuse in the workplace."

Gale glared at him, and they both laughed.

He turned on the radio and found the city news station. "But just so you know, she plays for your team." He looked sideways at Gale, a smile beginning.

"What?" Gale asked warily.

"Drew had some questions in the hardware store—he's so concerned about the threat to Izzy, but I talked him down. And then I asked him about Syd."

"You didn't! Thanks a lot, Detective Blunder."

"Keep your shirt on, Detective Fumble. I was 'Mr. Smooth-and-Casual' about it." He hit the button to roll the windows partway down. "Turns out Aunt Syd is quite the catch that no woman has been able to keep."

Gale studied the traffic and the road ahead.

"Drew's not sure why that is, that nothing lasts longer than a year, maybe three. He's always worried about that. Wishes Syd would find a happily ever after."

"Hmm."

"Just—be careful on the playing field. It's still a case."

"It's against regulations. I will not be on the playing field."

"Didn't say you would be. But you two *do* seem to be circling each other. Even if she's on the fifty-yard line and you're in the end zone."

"Get out."

"Hey—I'm trained in this sort of thing. You haven't always been privy to her looking at you. But I've seen every glance and moment of study on her part."

Gale did her best to keep her face as passive as she did when she was questioning a suspect. "This is merely a professional courtesy. Nothing more. She's feeling vulnerable, I'd be doing it anyway."

"Mmm-hmm."

Gale looked out the passenger window. She'd already mentally begun going through her closet for the right suit for next week's meeting with Syd. And she also wondered why Syd didn't have a long-term lover. Or wife. But more than that—*had* Syd been assessing her all this time?

CHAPTER ELEVEN

As Syd carefully applied her mascara, her hand shook a little. She stopped and put both hands on the counter to steady herself for a moment. "You are an idiot," she said to her mirrored self.

Makeup hadn't mattered the first several times she'd gone to the precinct. Of course, she always wore lip gloss, a little eyeliner, and a touch of mascara, but that was a daily regimen if she was going out. She never wanted a fellow New Yorker to summon the police after looking at her on the Lexington local and deciding she'd died the night before and ridden unnoticed all through rush hour.

But then she'd gone and done it last week—asked Sterling if she could see her on a weekly basis to talk about the case. She'd told her she was feeling insecure, at sea (but not that she was terrified). That was all true (including the "terrified"). Also true, that she wanted to be kept informed about what the detectives were doing, what they came across, because she knew she could help, could fill in things that they missed or wouldn't even know they were missing.

The truth she finally had to admit to herself, though, was that she simply wanted to see Detective Sterling. The seed of that admission was planted the moment she'd walked in the wake of her perfume the first day they'd met. She knew it was a purely physical attraction, easy enough to put away. She'd certainly done that enough times in her life. But then she began to get to know the handsome detective. It had dawned on her slowly—she liked the woman behind the shield. More than she'd liked anyone in a long time.

Asking Sterling was a painfully comic moment for Syd, bringing her right back to the tenth grade when she'd agonized over approaching pretty, dark-haired Elizabeth Keegan to be her science lab partner: she'd planned it to look like a casual request; instead, it had been an excruciating performance for her. But it had worked; she and Elizabeth had taken apart a frog and come together to explore each other. Syd wasn't sure what would happen this time. Because it wasn't a schoolgirl crush, and there would be no frogs to act as icebreakers. Sterling had once had a wife; all Syd had was an abysmal record. Eventually, she would have to come clean about her romantic past. And hope that maybe at this point in their lives, some things mattered less. First, though, Syd had to determine if Sterling even thought of her as anything other than part of the case.

Syd had described Lucas Rose's apartment to the detectives, and now here they were, that magnificent view of Central Park in the near distance. But it was Lucas Rose's face that Gale was studying. When she'd called to tell him of the newly launched investigation into Wyatt's murder, requesting an interview, she'd heard the sonic thunder wrapped in the quietude of his reaction. Now she regarded a blank canvas as she and Tommy sat in front of cups of coffee. No fruit plate, bread or cheeses for them. Just coffee, a pitcher of milk, and a sugar bowl. And Lucas Rose's carefully curated face.

"This is like a bombshell to me," he said. His voice modulated enough to indicate surprise. Gale doubted he was—Syd's visit would have seen to that. Gale's fear that this visit further amplified her already-growing concern for Syd's safety slowly blossomed in the pit of her stomach. She and Tommy had agreed to proceed cautiously so, with some difficulty, she turned her attention back to the interview in time to hear Lucas ask who had received the threat.

"We're not at liberty to say." Tommy was using his gravelly voice, the theatrical one he pulled out of his diaphragm when he wanted to intimidate without getting out of his chair or approaching the suspect. It was working—Lucas shifted in his seat.

"Well, then, I should tell you right up front that Sydney Hansen visited me not long ago. She used to work for Wyatt—at the Academy of the Divine Heart School. But you probably already knew that."

"Yes," Gale said. She watched Lucas pick up his coffee cup and take a sip. Left-handed.

"I hadn't seen her in forty years, although I had occasion to call her the night Ned Rossiter died in March because it came to my attention that she'd visited him that very day, out of the blue. I found that curious. Ned..." Lucas hesitated, but Gale didn't sense that it was for effect; it almost seemed like he was struggling. "Ned was...the board treasurer at the school for years. He was the one who discovered that Wyatt was embezzling—after the fact, of course—somehow Wyatt managed to hide that from Ned. But again, you know all this, I'm sure."

Gale was intrigued at Lucas's offering up so much right away, and at his use of the phrase "after the fact." It was a distancing tool. It spared him from using the word "murder." "Do you know why Sydney Hansen visited Ned that day?"

"You haven't spoken to her yet? I'd have thought she'd be the first one you talked to since she was so close to Wyatt."

Gale listened for hints of anger, even fear, in his voice, but didn't hear them. "We did, yes."

"And that led us to you," Tommy said.

Lucas's eyes darted over to Tommy, then back to Gale.

"How did you and Wyatt first meet?" Gale asked.

With the faintest smile, Lucas replied, "Nineteen seventy-one, two boys fresh off the farm in a gay bar."

The visual was amusing but Gale didn't smile—she needed to maintain a neutral distance. "And how did you each meet Ned?"

Lucas chuckled. "That was Wyatt. He needed a job so we took to crashing society events where he thought he'd meet the right people and he could talk himself into one. With good money and benefits. And by God, he did. Charmed the pants right off Ned at the Met Gala. Of course, the theme that year was 'untailored garments,' so that made it easy."

Gale wanted to look at Tommy but knew she couldn't—this answered the question they'd asked each other days ago: who was in Wyatt's bed? They knew Ned was; she'd assumed Lucas was, too. But these liaisons preceded Theo Hall showing up in Wyatt's life in 1981. Had Theo's presence tipped jealousies among these men into something deeper?

"And everyone having fun between the sheets, right? Any green-eyed monsters in your game of musical beds?"

Of course, Gale thought, Tommy's voice registering even lower than it already had and reverberating in her chest, of course we're on the same page, but what happened to "proceeding cautiously?"

Lucas's eyes went wide, and then he laughed. "Are you kidding? We were gay men living in one of the biggest cities in the world. We were all playing, and we thought the music would never stop. It *was* raining men—jealousy was never an issue."

And there was the hint of condescension Gale had been listening for. She stepped back into her role of "good cop" before either man did any more damage. "Mr. Rose, do you remember where you were the night Wyatt was murdered?"

His answer about having dinner with Ned before Ned went to the governor's ball came without hesitation, the scent of rehearsal all over it. "We were supposed to meet Wyatt at Bareback afterwards, but—we didn't."

"Why not?" Gale asked.

"Ned called me around ten to say Wyatt left the ball early so he wanted to go to the Saint."

"What was the governor's ball?" Tommy asked.

In her recent research on Ned, Gale had come across articles about the gilded fundraising gala in all the society pages of that era, the governor seeking an unprecedented fourth term filling his war chest by tapping all the city's political deep pockets. Lucas's explanation matched what she'd read.

"And after you tripped the light fandango?" Tommy asked.

"We went back to my apartment."

"How long were you there?"

Once again, at the sound of Tommy's voice, Lucas repositioned himself. "Almost all night. We didn't want Wyatt to know because, well, he might've gotten jealous. We didn't want him asking to join us." He glanced at Gale. "Anyway, Ned always left before dawn."

The implication of the threesome was clear to Gale, along with the intimation that it wasn't unusual.

"So let's get this straight," Tommy said, leaning forward and tapping his left palm with his right index finger for emphasis. "Wyatt was killed somewhere between ten p.m. and two a.m., and you and Ned were each other's alibis? And of course now Ned is dead. I don't suppose there's anyone you knew back then who could corroborate your whereabouts that night?"

Lucas looked at Tommy, a half-smirk appearing. "You don't seriously think I had anything to do with Wyatt's murder? Or that Ned did?"

"Or that you both did?" Tommy asked.

Lucas stilled. While Lucas's question was a classic, the kind of moment Gale had seen in every police procedural show, always making her laugh, she wished Tommy had held off with *his* dueling question.

Gale went into clean-up mode, not something she often had to do. "What Detective D'Angelo means is that we're simply doing our due diligence, Mr. Rose, questioning everyone still alive who knew Wyatt at the time."

"No, he's accusing me," Lucas said quietly, looking directly at Tommy, the tiniest piece of fury a tic at the corner of his right eye. "And how do you know who those people are, who are still alive?"

"We have a very credible source in the person who was threatened," Tommy said, the rasp in his voice answering Lucas's challenge.

For once, Gale was not enjoying their usual tag-team questioning. Tommy was coming at Lucas too hard too early, having the unintended effect of making her more uncomfortable than it did their quarry.

Then, a tiny fissure showed up in Lucas's facade. "You know he picked up a guy at Bareback that night. A stranger." He paused, for effect; the crack was calculated. "He was always picking up scrubs, that one."

"How do you mean?" Gale knew exactly what he meant. And Lucas knew she did. But she wanted to catch him in his trap of pointing the detectives away from himself. If he was egotistical enough, she would.

"Strays. Puppies. Another toy for Ned's circle. He'd sample the goods and pass them on to Ned. Or not. If they were halfway intelligent, they'd become part of Ned's never-ending club coterie."

"Club coterie?"

Lucas smiled. "All the glittering boys that Ned could never get enough of."

Gale was surprised by Lucas's admission. But then, she supposed it was easy enough to throw a dead man under the bus.

"And what did he do with his coterie?"

"Danced. Fucked. And did drugs."

As she calmly held Lucas's gaze, Gale wondered if Syd was right, that Ned leveraged the boys to do his bidding, selling drugs. Did that also include the prostitution Syd had intimated she'd been privy to on several occasions? And had Lucas acted as the "madame" to distance Ned from any of it, assuming that's what was going on then? Gale continued circling. "Was Wyatt jealous of any of the boys? Or vice versa?"

"Any of them consider Wyatt an obstacle?" Tommy asked.

Lucas didn't blink but disdain pulled at the corners of his mouth. "I wouldn't know, Detective. I was too busy partying at the time to care about Wyatt's feelings."

Cold, Gale thought. In that moment, she knew the interview was over, too. That last question of Tommy's left her no room to work her way through scenarios she'd mapped out about any struggle between Wyatt and Lucas for control of the reins where Ned was concerned, if control was to be had. Gale's understanding was that Wyatt was the queen bee regardless of what Syd had told her about Lucas's involvement selling drugs at clubs and his incessant use of Ned's credit cards. She'd wanted to draw Lucas out about Ned's money problems, which Tommy was only beginning to uncover. Were they the driving factor behind Wyatt's embezzlement, and is that what had gotten him killed? Or had Wyatt acted alone? Did Lucas know about the financial theft? Or was it petty jealousies among these men that had driven that knife into him? They had no real proof of anything either way. Not yet. So she'd hoped to poke and prod Lucas enough, goad him into revealing himself. That was out of the question now. The guarded face that greeted them at the door was firmly in place, and it had become hard. Gale slid one of her NYPD cards across the table. "If you think of anything—"

"Or remember anything," Tommy's voice, and the insinuation, scraped right through to the cement floor.

Lucas stood, but he left the card on the table. "I'll be sure to call."

She and Tommy both heard the insolence.

"Oh." Gale took an index card and a pen out of her pocket and slid it across the table. "Would you give me the name and address of the place in Connecticut where Ned was, in case we need it for any reason?"

Annoyed, Lucas wrote something on the card and shoved it back across the table. "Let me see you out."

Gale glanced at the neat writing. "May I use your powder room first?" She hated that term but knew Lucas would respond to it.

He pointed her in the direction of the bathroom. It would take her past the photo of Duane Valchek, according to Syd's descriptions of the place.

As he unlocked the front door, Lucas turned to Gale. "You know, someone said that the guy Wyatt picked up that night was military."

"How so?" That was nowhere in the notes of the detectives on the case back then.

"Buzz cut. Uniform. Shiny boots. Ramrod straight. And uncomfortable in the bar."

"What kind of uniform? And do you recall who told you?"

"I'm not sure about the uniform—blues were in it. And it came from several sources, through the grapevine."

Gale cocked her head inquisitively.

"We had to protect ourselves from predators like that. So word traveled fast. From every direction."

"Anyone remember seeing him before? Or after?"

Genuine thoughtfulness creased Lucas's brow. "No."

"But the description was the same all around?"

"From every boy who was there to every boy who needed to know. I'm sure most of them are dead now, though. So many of them are dead."

Lucas's eyes, as empty as his tone, almost frightened Gale.

"One more question, if I may." Gale knew it was a Hail Mary, but she threw it anyway, despite the look of animosity that greeted her. "When you went to work for Ned, were there any signs that any of the funds embezzled from the Academy had reached Rossiter Enterprises?"

The tic that Gale had seen at the corner of his right eye before jumped again. "I don't know anything about the embezzlement." His voice was cold, haughty. "What I do know is that, ironically, as a hedge fund manager, Ned was a mess. There was money everywhere but not where it should've been. Client portfolios were a nightmare, missing funds, dividends, and quarterly reports. He still owed auction houses for the artwork on the walls and pieces of period furniture. I spent almost two years cleaning it up, straightening out his personal and business accounts, cleaning up the back paperwork and overseeing investments."

"What do you mean, there was money everywhere?" Gale asked.

"Millions, Detective. He was leaving millions unattended in accounts."

"And it didn't occur to you that these might be the embezzled funds?"

The tic appeared again, answering Gale's question.

In the car, Tommy put the all-news radio station on, and they drove to the precinct in silence listening to the weather, traffic reports and the mundane mayhem of the city's daily life. He slipped the car into one of the angled slots in front of the building and they both stared straight ahead. He unsnapped his seat belt. It landed with a thunk. "I blew it, didn't I?"

"I believe you might have, Detective Blunder."

He sighed. "Shouldn't have accused him. Shouldn't have asked about Wyatt being an obstacle, either."

"Nope."

He gently hit the steering wheel with the palm of his hand several times.

"Not the first time one of us did that." Gale looked at him, an exoneration.

"Yeah." He nodded and looked away. "So maybe we go get into some of the stuff from those wet boxes of evidence. Stuff I been hangin' up's gotta be dry by now."

That was one of the many things she liked about Tommy: he didn't beat himself up past the first punch; he simply moved on to something productive.

He opened the car door. Gale stopped him, a hand on his arm. "Did you notice anything out of the ordinary when I asked Lucas for Ned's address?"

"Yeah. Pen in his right hand after drinking his coffee with his left hand. Switch-hitter. I didn't miss that. I knew what you were doing."

She showed him the index card. "Look familiar?"

"Looks kinda like…Syd's red ledger. But not."

"I'm confused, too. More than one ledger keeper?"

"Keeping tabs on more than one thing, why not?"

An hour later, her hands gloved and a mask over her nose and mouth, Gale was carefully prying apart pages of a slim hard-bound book that had been affected by the flood, trying to preserve what was on them. They looked like charts. Graphs. Lists. The further she got into the book, the easier it became to separate the pages and the clearer the contents became. Each page was labeled by month and year, charts and graphs on one side of the page, some kind of list on the other. She still had the card with Ned's address on it in her pocket and took it out to compare: definitely Lucas's neat handwriting on the page with the lists. But she couldn't make heads or tails of anything. And the smell of the book itself was getting to her even with a mask. She flipped it closed and looked at the cover.

In fact, the smell of mold in the large storage room was more prevalent today than it had been a few days ago. Gale made a mental note to get a dehumidifier and some air fresheners. She absently wondered if they'd work at cross purposes. Anything to keep the odor at a minimum since the captain had been good enough to let them use the room. They didn't want to piss off the whole precinct. She glanced around at all the papers and files they'd spread out on all the folding tables. Most were crinkly, yellowed, and faded from the damage inflicted on them in two separate floods, one that had happened only last month. The barrels they'd been in had the misfortune of getting shoved into leaky old warehouses years ago where cases prior to the department's transfer to computerization were housed. Gale nearly groaned at the thought that there were two more barrels they were going to have to pull out and bring here. Tommy was so certain they'd be able to decipher the papers and find something that, to speed the process, he'd strung up a series of clotheslines around the room and clipped the wet papers to it. He'd set up an oscillating fan in the corner. Every so often, he came in to check on things and switch out dry pages for wet ones. Gale didn't have his confidence, but she couldn't put a pin in his balloon, either.

Careful not to break her glove, Gale used her index fingernail to scrape at the mold that covered the book. Slowly she reached the fine pebbly finish and red peeked out. She sat back. It was exactly like the one in Syd's box, still locked in the closet in her office. That one had contained a series of changing numbers with decimal points listed in columns with seemingly random numbers at the top, but those random numbers were the same across the top of every page. This ledger was entirely different, including the handwriting that might be Lucas's. She opened the ledger again and looked at one of the charts. It contained that same set of random numbers across the top of the chart as Syd's ledger. Not so random, then? Down the side were the same letters as were on the first page. Gale's crossword puzzle instincts kicked in, pushing aside her confusion.

Tommy turned off the blow dryer he was using. "Hey, not for nothin' but you been sittin' there for fifteen minutes like a statue with that book."

"Come look at this."

He joined her at the table. She closed the book to show him the bit of red she'd flaked the mold from. "Soap and water will take the rest of this off."

"Another red ledger?"

Gale opened it and showed him both sides of a couple of pages. "Yeah, but not like Syd's. So at the top of this page, the month. It starts with January of eighty. Across the columns, these letters. X, B, R, H. Down the side, more letters, LR, DV, BH, etc. Thirteen in all. Numbers with decimals in the boxes, same as the other ledger. I'm going to guess this is money." She delicately scratched her nose trying to avoid a sneeze. "Here," She pointed to the graph below. "Same month, now the double letters are at the top of the columns, nothing down the side, more numbers, smaller." She turned the page.

"Here, those same random numbers from Syd's ledger across the top of the page. Now the X, B, R and H run down the side of the page, and further down, those double letters, different handwriting." She held up the index card.

"Lucas's handwriting."

"Mm-hmm." She flipped the pages back and forth a few times.

"Wait. Go back to the first page." Tommy took out his cell phone. "I got a hunch on some o' this." He put the phone on speaker when it was answered. "Hey, Doug, I'm here with Gale and we got a question."

"Nice to hear from the refrigerated unit. What can I do ya?"

"You narcos are good with the alphabet. The letters X, B, R, H—what do they bring to mind? Mean anything to you?"

"Ecstasy, bennies…probably Ritalin and heroin. You catch an old drug murder?"

"Complete with embezzlement, maybe some prostitution thrown in for fun. Livin' the dream, man. Thanks for the decode—next beer's on me." He ended the call.

They looked at each other. Gale flipped back to the first page. "LR."

"Lucas Rose," Tommy answered. "DV, Duane Valchek."

Gale ran her finger down the page. "BH, Billy Highsmith. These other initials are going to match up with Syd's list."

"This," Tommy said, "is a goddam sales chart. Although what is this, then?" Tommy flipped the page. "Money, but what? And Lucas in charge of it? And am I wrong to think it looks a bit like the writing in Syd's ledger?"

"We're going to have to compare. Something's off. Don't you think Syd would've said that it was Wyatt's handwriting in the ledger she had?"

"Whoever it is, it looks a helluva lot like Lucas's."

"Could it be Ned's?" Gale asked. "Financial guy. Expensive taste. And these ledgers were high end."

"Ned wouldn't have been the bookkeeping type, c'mon. His secretary would've done that." Tommy looked at Gale. "Or Syd. She's the bookkeeping type. We didn't think to get a writing sample from her."

Gale drew in a breath and let it out slowly. Tommy was only doing his job. "We have on occasion been taken before. My gut says Syd's not involved. The picture she's painted of Wyatt—he wouldn't have pulled her into this. *If* this is him, because look—" She ran a finger down the page. "No WR."

"You seein' her this afternoon? First date?"

"Yes, Yentl." Gale chose to ignore the broad smile on Tommy's face. But not the implication about Syd's handwriting.

"And here I was thinkin' that blue suit was for Lucas Rose. Nice day for a walk, though. And some interrogation in the form of casual questions."

"Just what I was thinking."

"You gonna tell her we saw Lucas this morning?"

"In the interest of her safety, yes." Gale got up from her chair, pressed her fingers against the nearest wall and stretched her throbbing back. Too many hours of sitting.

Tommy nodded. "While you're out, I'll call Mike Avery and Billy Highsmith, set up interviews. Although I'm sure Lucas has beaten us to that. And we'd best get to Theo Hall sooner rather than later. I know that's a trip upstate, though."

"While you're at it, Mr. Finance, put your brain to work on what these numbers could mean."

"Fine." He flipped to a random page. "You think this is more than a drug sales ledger?"

"Let's dry this book out and find out. And clean the cover while you're at it, Jeeves."

Tommy bowed at the waist. "Yes, madam."

❖

The desk officer told Syd she could make her way to the cold case division. Sterling must've left word with him. When she reached the doorway of the office, Syd hesitated, watching her write something in a notebook. She rather liked that Sterling was both old school and new school. She rather liked the suit she was wearing, too, an unusual Delft blue. Beneath it was a pale pink shell. A suit of that color had to have come from a tailor and a bolt of imported cloth. It fit her closely, accentuating her shoulders. Syd smiled. This woman looked good in anything she wore. The white board caught her attention: the sheet covering it was gone, but so were the photos of Wyatt's apartment. In their place hung a large chart, the kind of organizational thing Syd was used to seeing in annual reports or corporate restructuring announcements.

"Are you going to stand there all day?"

Sterling's bemused expression caught Syd by surprise. "I thought we might take a walk. It's a beautiful day out and I'm guessing you're stuck in here for most of it."

"We are."

Sterling stood, but Syd nodded toward the chart.

"May I?" She walked over to it. Sterling joined her and Syd was at once aware of that perfume that had enchanted her at their first meeting. For a moment, it stole her attention.

With difficulty, Syd's eyes traveled from the top of the chart, where Wyatt's and Ned's photos were pinned next to each other, to the bottom where a blank square with a question mark in it stood by itself. It was a "Who's Who" of everyone in Wyatt's life at the time. Sterling had found high school or college photos of every lost boy. As she looked at them, memories of her youth in their company with Wyatt at dinners, dancing with them until dawn at after-hours clubs, and lazy Sundays spent in Central Park came swirling back. They brought with them the haunting sense that one of them could've killed Wyatt.

Some photos were paired with a second one: what the boy looked like now if he was alive. Sterling had done the same for the major donor parents from the Academy of the Divine Heart—official corporate photos from 1982 linked with today's photos. Laid over all of them and secured with push pins were three sets of colored threads: red fanning out from Wyatt's photo, Kelly green from Ned's, and black from the business associates of Ned's that were also pinned to the board. That black thread ran to some of the lost boys. Syd should've been surprised, but she wasn't. The detectives were piecing things together. Many of the different colored threads crossed and met at many of the same young men.

"This is extensive."

"It's an unwieldy and complicated case."

Syd ran a finger over the black threads.

"Seems some of our illustrious bluebloods liked a little on the side," Gale said quietly.

"Smart to research Ned's background. Impressive that you found things."

"The *Times* and *Wall Street Journal* archives are vast. So are the *Post,* the *Daily News, Vogue,* and a whole host of past media sources. The more we know about everyone, dead or alive, the easier it will be to assign motive or eliminate."

"I don't suppose that's happened yet. Anyone being eliminated."

"Possibly." Gale returned to her desk. "Would you do one favor for me before we head out?" Sterling had a lined pad on her desk. "Would you copy the things I've written on this page?" She handed her a pen.

Syd looked at the letters and figures. "What is this?"

"Please?"

Syd sat in the chair next to the detective's desk and copied everything. Sterling casually slid the water-damaged ledger she'd recently found from beneath some papers on her desk. It was open and encased in plastic.

Syd glanced at it, and became alarmed. "What happened to Wyatt's book?"

"This is a different book."

"Where did you get it?"

"Evidence warehouse in Brooklyn."

Syd handed Sterling the piece of paper and her pen and took a closer look at the ledger—it was quite different from the one from Wyatt's desk. In the same moment, Syd understood: Sterling had a job to do—she was testing her handwriting. And that gave Syd the answer to how Sterling saw her. She was nothing more than part of the case. She shouldn't have gotten her hopes up.

"That's Wyatt's handwriting," Syd said, pointing to the chart on the open page. "The one in the ledger that I have is not."

"Had you ever seen this one before?" Sterling asked.

"No. I never saw the other one, either, until Ned pulled it out of Wyatt's desk that day. Like I told you, I took it from Ned's briefcase before he left. I wasn't in the habit of going through his desk unless he needed me to find something if he was out, but I went through it after Ned found that ledger. I wanted to make sure there was nothing there to hang Wyatt. I also wanted to get Wyatt's personal things out of there to send to his father."

"And did you? Find things?" Tommy had been busy with papers when she'd first come into the office, but now he seemed interested in the conversation.

"Ohhh—the photo of Drew, some Academy yearbooks, there were letters from his dad, a college tie that he wore to alumnae events—"

"Where is that stuff now—did his dad keep it?"

"I'm not sure. I'll ask Drew. The letters had a beautiful blue-and-white striped ribbon tied around them, almost like a seersucker blue, so they'd be easy to remember if he came across them when he was cleaning out the house."

"Did you look inside the ledger that day?" Sterling asked.

"Very quickly. There was so much I needed to photocopy if I was going to try to clear Wyatt, once I knew what was going on, and I had to get to it whenever Ned wasn't at the desk. It was full of numbers, so I took it. But this"—she pulled it toward her—"this has nothing to do with the school." Syd ran her hand over the plastic bag covering the page. "Nothing at all."

Tommy nodded. "Can you ask Drew if he came across those letters?"

"Of course." Syd studied the ledger. "What is this anyway?"

"Come on, this spring day is wasting."

Sterling's voice was gentle, but Syd was wary. She'd reconciled herself to the fact that these detectives would uncover things she wasn't going to like or didn't want to hear. But how would they affect her in light of her burgeoning feelings for Detective Sterling? Of course, now that she knew Sterling merely thought of her as a piece of the case, it might be a good time to bury those feelings. That, Syd thought, is something I'm good at.

As she turned to pick up her canvas bag, a photo on the chart caught her eye. She walked over to it and touched it. "Schuyler was such a nice guy. Everyone at school loved him."

Sterling came back over to the chart to get a closer look at the photo.

"Do you know, after he was killed in that mugging in December, all Ned could think about was that he wouldn't get the money from his widow for the endowment." Syd shook her head. "What a dick."

"Schuyler Tilden was part of the three big donors."

"Uh-huh. And he was dead less than two months after Wyatt. One of those senseless killings, when angel dust was king." She put her bag on her shoulder. "Ned got his precious money. Schuyler's wife honored the pledge even after the embezzlement came to light. But I guess you knew that, didn't you?"

Sterling nodded. "We did."

Syd cocked her head toward the door. "Tell me what else you learned while we walk."

Sterling retrieved her gun from her desk and followed Syd out the door.

CHAPTER TWELVE

It was an unusually cool and breezy afternoon for late April, the temperature more autumn than spring. Out on the sidewalk, Syd threw her jacket around her shoulders and gathered it to her. Gale had always found a sensuousness in that act, in the way a woman hugged herself in whatever she pulled close around her shoulders to ward off the cold, the way her body drew into itself protecting the inner core of her warmth, shielding her breasts with folded arms. Gale pushed those thoughts away as she caught up to Syd.

Obviously, their interview with Lucas Rose was paramount, if only to remind Syd to be careful. Tommy wanted Syd to know about the old public records pertaining to Ned's hedge fund that he'd uncovered in the business library on Fifth Avenue. He was also excavating records at the archives of the bank the Academy had used in 1982.

"I have no idea why the bank kept this stuff," he said excitedly when he called Gale on his second afternoon from the storage room to tell her about the trove.

"Does it have 'Destroy By' dates on it?"

"No dates on any of these boxes. I mean, it's sheer luck I even found them. Only because they're shelved by year and I'm diggin' around 1981. Some corporate drone musta forgot about it. My fuckin' lucky day!"

When Gale questioned his need for Syd to know about these papers, Tommy had looked at her, surprised.

"She's an accountant. I could use a little help here."

One thing she wasn't going to tell Syd: that neither she nor Tommy had been able to unearth an obit for Duane Valchek.

"Thanks," she said, when Tommy handed her the five obituaries. "I couldn't find him either."

"Wait—" And then he threw his head back and laughed. "You gave him to me after you couldn't find him?"

"Sometimes you succeed where I run into a wall." Gale shrugged.

In fact, Gale had nothing since his high school yearbook photo. Being unable to find information on the baby boomers' activities before the late nineties wasn't unusual. Internet service providers hadn't emerged until 1989 in the US, and then it wasn't until fiber optic cables changed the game in the mid-nineties that it really took off. Such technology proved a boon for the cold case division, and it was part of the reason Gale had joined it—catching a killer by tracking his online life was the kind of cat-and-mouse game she liked. People loved their Instagram, Facebook, and TikTok. And no one could hide from the cameras on city streets now. But Duane Valchek had simply vanished and not left a grave behind. If he wasn't dead, then he was a master at avoiding current social media—or else he'd changed his name. However, anything she picked up online prior to 1990 on any of Syd's lost boys would be refracted through the rearview mirror of time, only of relevance if she could tie it to the case. Finding Duane that way would be needle-in-a-haystack work, although she'd done it before.

"So, game plan?" Tommy asked, the obits still in his hand.

"I begin haunting Malone, New York, online. His parents are gone. I'm going to call the cemetery where they were buried, see if Duane happens to be there with them. Also going to call the Catholic church. It's a guess, I know," she said when Tommy raised an eyebrow. "Pardon me for profiling—if he was Polish, he was Catholic. I'll see if there's a record of a funeral for him. I've got the high school yearbook, I'll check old classmates. The trail has to start somewhere if he's still alive."

"So," Syd said, pulling Gale into the present, "I'm glad this is okay, my coming to see you like this."

"It benefits us, so I am, too. Tommy has some financial stuff he'd like you to look at and—we saw Lucas Rose this morning."

Syd stopped in the middle of the sidewalk. "And?"

"Nothing much this time that we didn't already know." She withheld that he'd given them a bit of description of the stranger Wyatt had picked up that night.

"This time?" Syd said, falling in beside Gale again.

"Oh, we'll have another go at him."

"And what does Detective D'Angelo want me to look at?"

"Honestly, I just gave it a quick once-over. That's really his domain. I can't even do my own taxes."

Syd's laugh was gentle, sympathetic. "Numbers scare a lot of people, Detective Sterling, but you know, all they are is a different language—well, for most people, anyway."

"Hm, I have enough trouble navigating this one. And please, call me Gale." It was out before she'd thought about it. But she'd been contemplating it for days. She glanced at Syd whose shy smile told Gale she liked the idea. "Listen, I don't want to sound like a broken record, but now that we've approached Lucas, I want you to be careful, vigilant, even. And if he calls you…" Gale hesitated. "We'd like you to engage him. But only on the phone. Don't go see him again." Gale didn't like the wary expression that settled on Syd's face. "We're not sure he knows who came to us. We told him we talked to you as a matter of course when he brought you up. So he may contact you, sniffing around. Be as vague as you can, but not suspicious. Play stupid. And let us know what he asks."

"So—I'm bait."

Gale realized her mistake too late—she should have put it in terms of Syd aiding them, not being used by them. "Only if he calls. He's a very cool customer. I don't expect him to do anything stupid."

"You think he did it."

"We're still following evidence. There's a lot of it and it leads in any number of directions. We're setting up interviews, Tommy's combing through old financial records, I'm piecing together Ned's life." Gale ran her fingers through her hair as they waited to cross the avenue at the light. "And we have to look at all the boys, dead and alive—were any of them angry with Wyatt, jealous of something, or was Ned backed into a corner of some kind, can we find proof that he hired one of them to kill Wyatt? Or that he hired someone only he knew." They crossed the avenue and continued walking east. "The questions and scenarios are endless. It's proving to be a complicated case, and forty years of time passing is hampering it. I almost don't wonder that the detectives back then didn't solve it and basically walked away from it." Gale sighed in frustration.

Syd had stopped walking. When Gale turned to face her, Syd looked puzzled; there was a crease between her eyebrows she'd never seen before.

"What—if Wyatt had been straight it would've been easier to solve? If he'd been screwing girls instead of boys, if it had been female prostitutes, if Lucas had been a woman they shared? Things would've miraculously fallen into place? Those detectives walked away because Wyatt was gay."

Gale had hit a button she should've remembered was there. "That's not what I meant and those detectives were wrong. You follow a case no matter who it is, what they've done, or where it leads. They didn't do that. I think the condition of Wyatt's apartment told them that it was a crime of passion, and they took the easiest route. And yes, they were biased, but worse than that, they were lazy."

They looked at each other in the middle of the sidewalk, a stand-off.

"You think it's that simple."

"My thinking out loud was—a moment of frustration. I think those detectives would've acted the same way no matter who was involved. What Tommy and I are doing now would've been a lot of work back then, too, chasing down all those young men, looking at finances once they found out about the embezzlement, trying to figure out who the stranger was. It was easier to walk away from the dead faggot." With a loud sigh, Gale ran both hands through her hair. "I'm not making excuses for them—"

"I think you are," Syd interrupted. "They wouldn't have walked away from a straight man lying in that bed because they would've seen themselves there."

"I'm not so sure. This would've been a complex case back then, and these weren't complex detectives, if you get my drift." Gale thought Syd might be reconsidering—her brow furrowed again. "Reconstruction of this case is painfully slow. But we're sifting through evidence very carefully, letting it speak. Lucas was quite a challenge. I have no idea what we'll find with Billy Highsmith. And frankly, I'm not looking forward to talking with Theo Hall." Gale usually didn't unload like this with anyone but Tommy. But something in the expression on Syd's face that had slowly metamorphosed from wary anger to sympathy opened a door. It was almost like Kate was standing there listening.

"Look." Syd put a hand on Gale's arm. "It was a moment of anger. The wrong moment. And the wrong anger. And I'm frustrated, too."

Gale nodded. "I'm kind of glad you are. I need someone to be frustrated with." She started walking again, and Syd followed.

"Well, but Tommy must—"

"Nope, not in his vocabulary. He allows himself about ten seconds of it. Then he moves on."

"And you bake muffins."

Gale looked away. Syd's remark made her smile. "And what does Sydney Hansen do when she gets frustrated? Or doesn't she?"

"Golf. I play golf."

Gale cocked her head questioningly.

"Nothing like whacking a tiny white ball a hundred and fifty yards with a titanium club to get out all your frustrations *and* work out your anger issues."

Gale laughed. "And here I was thinking it was a sedately polite game for old duffers."

"I beg your pardon—"

"No, no, I didn't mean—" Gale, still laughing, held up her hands defensively.

"It's a highly competitive sport that requires a unique set of strategy skills. Plus, there's the hitting the daylights out of that little white ball. *So* satisfying."

Gale collected herself. "You do surprise me every time we get together."

"Do I?"

Gale heard the fully intended teasing note in Syd's voice and figured she must've won that battle. Syd was shifting gears. She felt the blush on her neck. Again. It was a recurring pattern every time the two of them got together: argue, flirt, blush. She wanted to ask Syd if *she* ever managed to surprise *her*. She absently touched her badge and cleared her throat. "Did Drew find those letters of Joe's that you took from Wyatt's desk?" *Was that a look of regret crossing Syd's features?*

"I'm glad you brought that up."

Gale was sure she wasn't, really.

"He thinks he did, and he sent them to me. I should have them any day now."

"Bring them in next week? How's he doing, by the way?"

"The issue was more how is Izzy doing." Syd shook her head. "She wasn't going to cooperate and stay home. He didn't want to leave me, but he didn't want her out of his sight, even with the Alma police there."

"You became quite a part of his life, didn't you? Anyone can see he's devoted to you."

"That was all Joe. He made sure I spent every holiday with them so I'd have the connection during the year in anticipation of the summers. They were such good people, Wyatt's parents. I miss them."

"Your parents were okay with you being with Wyatt's family so much?"

"Please. Jack Frost and the Snow Queen?"

"Ouch."

"Let's talk about *your* family."

That's how Syd was introduced to the infallible Sullivan Sterling. Gale had her laughing with tales of working side by side with her father renovating the brownstone where she'd grown up after her mother died, turning it into two separate residences so she and Kate could move in.

"He was the worst project manager, oh my God. He fired me dozens of times. But then he'd bring a lasagna by my apartment, and I'd put on my hard hat again. And Kate was right—this was the only way we were going to own property. And he'd have built-in care if and when the time came. But you know that saying—" Gale concentrated on the middle distance ahead. "We make plans and God laughs. Nothing turned out the way we thought it would. And now, I'm not sure if I'm taking care of my dad or he's taking care of me."

She shrugged. "At this point in my life, he's my best friend. And of course now in retirement he *loves* to give advice on my cases."

"You became a cop because of him?"

"There was no other career for me to consider. I'm the sixth generation of Sterlings in the long blue line."

Syd stopped walking. "I'm impressed. That's a serious legacy."

Once again, they stood looking at each other in the middle of the sidewalk, but this time it wasn't a stand-off. Gale noticed Syd's eyes were a deeper color than the cloudless sky today. She wondered if she'd find the name of it among the paint chips at the hardware store. As much as she wanted more of this, of Syd, she knew she had to pick up the professional tenor she'd dropped.

"Listen, uh—" They were a block from the precinct house and Gale nodded toward it. "We should get back if you want to take a look at what Tommy has before you leave."

"Oh—yes, I do."

They walked in silence for a moment.

"You know—" "Maybe we should—" They spoke at the same time.

Gale put her hand on the small of Syd's back, wanting the connection. "You go first."

This time, a hand where Ned used to touch her felt right. "I was going to say, maybe we should play a game of golf one day. We'd have two hours to talk, if we played nine holes."

Gale thought about it. "I've never played."

"I'll teach you. Believe me, if I could master it, you could. Think about it. What were you going to say?"

"There's a lot of rain forecast for next week. I wondered how you felt about lunch instead of walking under umbrellas. There's a diner a couple blocks away."

"On one condition. I buy."

"Hmmm…All right, I guess so. You drive a hard bargain, Sydney Hansen."

"I do not. You folded like a lawn chair."

Gale laughed and they walked up the steps of the precinct.

❖

Syd couldn't believe she'd asked Gale to play golf with her, and she worked hard to banish the mental picture of Gale teeing off, her body torquing as the ball arced up and away. A bit of unexpected warmth spread inside, and she fought the blush she was sure was creeping up her chest. Gale hadn't seemed to notice as they walked up the steps to the precinct.

"Where the hell did you get all this?" Syd asked Tommy once she was settled in the chair next to him concentrating on his computer screen. He'd walked her through Rossiter Enterprises income statements from 1981, annual reports and foundations of corporate accounting from 1979 to 1983, and then he'd switched to files that contained letters of complaint from investors; from there he'd brought up credit card reports and mortgages. "Who even *had* this stuff? I mean, this should all have been gone decades ago."

"I know, right? It's like God is takin' care of business. Karma comin' around again. This—" he pointed to the Rossiter Enterprises folder on his desktop. "This all came from the business library in midtown. They got a research collection you wouldn't believe. These," he said, moving his cursor to the file marked *Ned $*, "these came from the bank archives the school did business with."

"How did you even gain access? I thought you needed a subpoena for records like these, and an attorney who's prosecuting a crime to get that."

"I am. An attorney. But no, even you could get a subpoena. You go to the Civil Court Clerk's office and pay the fee."

"Oh." Syd looked at Tommy as though seeing him for the first time, and then she looked over at Gale who was locked into something on her computer. "I'm surrounded by surprising people."

"Everybody's blessed with something. We'll find yours." Tommy pulled up the *Ned $* folder and clicked on an Excel chart called Personal Finances. "Here—" Tommy pointed to the first of several pages of his chart. "Nineteen seventy-nine. Some credit cards maxed out." He opened page two of the chart. "Nineteen eighty, second mortgage on the co-op. More cards." He clicked the next page. "Nineteen eighty-one, second mortgage on the Hamptons."

"More credit cards. Oh my God," Syd murmured. Ned's debts were breathtaking.

"So now he's millions in the hole." For effect, he clicked on page four, which contained the three previous charts overlaid.

"Now here—" He opened several documents in quick succession in the Rossiter Enterprises folder. "I found some other files pertaining to Ned's business in the bank archives. I don't know why they were there, but look—they had letters of complaint, too: 'My statements aren't reflecting growth,' 'where are my returns, you promised twenty per cent, I've seen nothing for six quarters,' et cetera."

Please tell me he wasn't running a Ponzi scheme. "The banks would have wanted this after the embezzlement was discovered." *And that is why Ned was so desperate to hang it on Wyatt.* "They would have kept it until that was sorted out by the police and in the courts, if it went that far, plus the requisite seven years."

"I think they lost track in the multiple mergers. Now," he opened a folder Syd hadn't seen in the bottom corner of his screen. It was marked *Divine Heart*. "This is where I may need help from you." He pointed the cursor at three files: one was titled *Operations*, a second was labeled *Tuition*, and the third was *Endowment*. He clicked on document after document, photocopies of bank accounts from 1982 appearing on the screen. "I went over to the Academy yesterday. Lovely headmistress, she wasn't thrilled to see me or my badge. Wasn't inclined to let me in to look around, either. But I wasn't born yesterday, did my research before I knocked on their door. It turns out she's a Fontbonne Hall girl, Bay Ridge. And I am a Xavier Prep boy, same neighborhood. We grew up ten blocks from each other." He shrugged. "She gave me access to this stuff which they hung onto as a reminder that history shouldn't repeat itself."

Syd sat back. "The 'Small World' department."

Tommy fished a thin gold chain from inside his shirt collar. A gold cross dangled from it. "Maybe we're just getting a little help." He nodded at the similar cross around Syd's neck, and her hand went to it.

"So, if I think I'm seein' what I think I'm seein'," Tommy said, "Each of these accounts began to lose money little by little in nineteen eighty-one. Small. Slowly. Regularly. Wouldn't have caused alarm bells to go off. In some cases, it was moved from one account to the other. Then, it disappeared. But I'd like you to double-check me." He placed a file folder in front of her on the desk. "Because in nineteen eighty-two, it takes off. So I printed a year's worth of the statements from each account. Because—" He clicked on a tab in the Excel chart from the *Ned $* folder. "Late nineteen eighty-one, infusions of cash. Small. Slowly. Regularly. Wouldn't have caused alarm bells to go off. But eighty-two—"

Syd deflated inside. Tommy had pulled the salient information from all the documents he'd found so far to create a picture of a man in deep financial trouble and a story was falling into place behind it. This was Tommy's forte, teasing out the financial bits and weaving them together to create that picture. Her stomach churned as she looked at the incriminating line of growth in the 1982 chart that symbolized more than the losses at the Academy that didn't quite match the growth in Ned's bank accounts and at Rossiter Enterprises. Obviously, money was coming in from somewhere other than the school. Tommy wanted her to put two and two together. And he wanted to see her reaction as he unfolded it to her. She was under scrutiny. She only had one card to play, and that was her truth. "He was getting money from somewhere else, too."

"Had to be. And a lot of it. Unless he was wringin' that little private school in places I don't know yet."

"Then from where else?" Could this mean an exoneration of Wyatt?

"My guess—the answer's somewhere in the red ledgers."

Syd thought for a moment. "Setting that aside, how do you suppose Ned accounted for the cash infusions?"

"Ah." Tommy opened another document. "First, he paid off cards and a mortgage. Then, existing clients got the supposed returns they'd originally been promised on their investments, so there goes a lot of it." Tommy touched the screen at various points with a pencil tip, at the charts showing growth in certain client accounts. "But as the spigot opened wider, he linked new clients to the new cash infusions. Only problem, I could only find some of them. They were dead, of course. Paper. So he was effectively parking dough."

"They weren't real?" Syd felt a little dizzy.

"Tracked 'em. Some of the Social Security numbers led me to numbered plots in Green-Wood Cemetery. From the nineteen forties.

Sent my great-nephew and a couple o' his friends out there the other afternoon to look. They thought it was great fun for the price of a couple o' pizzas and six-packs. They located the actual headstones. With help from the main office."

Syd sat back. "So, he *was* running a Ponzi scheme."

"And he couldn't do it alone. He needed to clean up the missing investments he used to maintain his very expensive lifestyle. That called for a lot of money, and for those funds to be close at hand. Which is why I'm beginning to look for Wyatt's old bank accounts. They couldn't funnel everything through Ned's accounts, they could only take so much out of the Academy and through vendor accounts, so they'd obviously turned to a third source. There was another bank's account in the Academy's boxes that had nothing to do with the embezzlement, or so one might think. If I can track the account down, there might be something there, because I think it might've been Wyatt's. Name on it was Joe Reid."

Syd looked at him, astounded.

"Headmistress thought it might've been personal, Wyatt taking care of some of his father's finances in a local bank, had the statement in his drawer, it got pulled into the embezzlement stuff, nothing came of it. But it was a helluva lot of money."

"But you don't believe that."

"No such thing as coincidence in my line of work."

And there it is. Even Tommy thinks Wyatt's guilty. She suddenly felt very tired. She needed to leave before she betrayed her emotions. "I've got errands to run. I'll look at these and tell you what I think." She put Tommy's file folder into her bag and turned to Gale. "I'll see you next week."

"I'll walk you out."

"No, that's okay." Syd held her hand out defensively. "I, uh—I have to go."

Out on the sidewalk, Syd made her way toward Fifth Avenue. She wanted to pause, let the sunshine wash over her, heal her a little, but she was afraid Gale might be right behind her and her emotions were too close to the surface. There was only one place to go when she needed to shore up her defenses.

Half an hour later, she sat in front of Monet's paintings in the European Gallery at the Metropolitan Museum. The spartan beauty of *The Four Trees* always restored a sense of order to her when things were stressful. The rooms weren't overly crowded, giving her a nearly unobstructed view for most of the hour that she sat there. Her eye wandered to *Haystacks (Effect of Snow and Sun)* and *Morning on the Seine near Giverny.* But always she came back to the trees. Four spindly poplars that stood on a riverbank at exact distances from each other and from the inside edges of the frame itself. Their orderliness brought the kind of peace to her that numbers did. The wild undergrowth on the banks was cloaked in the purples and blues of late afternoon shade cast by the setting sun. The same shadows infused the sparse leaves of the trees with a deep cornflower blue. Behind the poplars was a field, and sun spilled across it from its heightened angle splashing the trees in a distant grove a muted yellow. The sky was that pale blue barely spattered with the purple of the coming night. Syd had been here many times before contemplating the scene, wrapping herself in its solitude. It always reminded her of Wyatt. He used to tease her when he came in slightly hung over some mornings and found her bent over her clean and minimally adorned desk transcribing his notes from a donor visit. *"You are entirely too neat and tidy."* He tossed his coat on a chair. *"It's not good to be so uptight."*

"I'm not uptight." She never looked up. *"I appreciate the orderly. I think it's why you hired me. Because* you *are louche. You needed a buttoned-up someone to clean everything up and make you look good."* She smiled at the notes, and he laughed at her industriousness.

"I'll loosen you up yet. I'll teach you how to live life like it should be lived."

It wasn't until he was gone that she realized he'd done just that in the time they'd spent together. He'd taught her the art of fine dining, of choosing topflight wines. He'd shown her how to listen to jazz, and where the best cabarets and clubs were. Most importantly, he'd taught her who the kinds of solid, down-to-earth people were with whom she should surround herself, the ones who would have her back. That went hand in hand with the difference between generosity and buying people, and when you needed to do which; and how to drive a deal, when to compromise, and where it might be wise to lose gracefully so that next time, you could win. The inference had been that if she applied those tenets to every aspect of her life, she would become "that woman that everyone wanted to be or to be with."

She had to prove to Tommy that there was one thing Wyatt hadn't taught her, and that was how to defraud. And how to do it right under everyone's noses. Tommy had studied the documents he was able to uncover, and that was where the evidence led him. It was a knife to her gut. She didn't want to believe that Wyatt had been willingly involved. But now, sitting in front of Monet's poplars, the shadows engulfing them, she had to find a way to reconcile who he'd been to her with what he'd done. She was losing him a second time.

She wished she could walk into the painting and let that long-ago sunset wash over her.

Chapter Thirteen

S yd didn't want dinner, or even a glass of wine when she got home from the Met. Price and Waterhouse greeted her at the door and then Price promptly walked back to the living room as though he needed to pick up the thread of something terribly important that he'd left. Waterhouse chirped at her until she picked him up. After a much-needed squeeze, which he protested only gently, she put him down. He trotted toward the kitchen, turning back to make sure she was following. He never missed an opportunity to tell her it was time to eat, even if it wasn't. But it was, so she made their dinners, hung up the jacket she'd dropped on a chair, and went to the bedroom thinking a long hot bubble bath would be heaven. The message light on her phone blinked. Another robocaller. She hit Play and a voice from long ago surprised her. It was deeper with age but nevertheless recognizable.

"If this is Sydney Hansen who once worked at the Academy of the Divine Heart, this is Billy Highsmith—well, I go by Bill now. We knew each other back then. I was hoping to connect with you on a— personal matter. If you could call me." He left a 212 number.

Syd called Gale.

"This is good. We just set a meeting with him for the day after tomorrow. If he's reaching out to you—"

"He's panicking," Tommy said, loud enough for Syd to hear. "We've flushed someone out we didn't think was guilty of anything."

"What guilt? You said he never left the city." Syd waited for a response. "Are you two rolling your eyes at me?"

"Anyone finding you that fast after we call is feeling guilty about something, Syd. Call him back. On your cell phone," Gale said. "Take notes. And again, sound like you're as baffled and surprised as he is. You know nothing. And no, we weren't rolling our eyes at you. We were shaking our heads."

"Very funny, Detective. Look, I know you think my computer's been hacked. But my home phone, bugged? Oh shit—"

"What?"

"There was a telephone repairman here the day I got the blue envelope. I completely forgot to tell you that when I came in to see you!" Gale said something to Tommy, although Syd couldn't make it out. "What?"

"Maybe now we can request the tech team to look at your phone and computer. Homicide doesn't like to share them with cold case. It's a financial thing—we're the ugly stepchild."

"That's just wrong."

"You'd think, but no."

"Wait, on second thought," Tommy interrupted Gale. "Let's have her call on her land line. If someone *is* listening in, maybe whatever she and Billy talk about might draw them out."

Tommy's plan made Syd feel like a worm on a hook.

"Can you do that, Syd? And call me right back?"

Kissing the bubble bath good-bye, Syd dialed the number.

"Syd, I hoped you were the right person," Billy said.

I'm the only one in the phone book, she thought.

"Thanks so much for calling me back, and it's really, really good to hear from you."

"You, too," she said, picking up a too-smooth melting caramel tone in his voice. "This is a surprise. How are you?" *Knowing nothing...*

"Good, Syd, good, thanks. I was hoping we could catch up in person, get together, say, over an ice cream at Emack and Bolio's, maybe tonight, even? The one near you? It's such a beautiful spring night. You know the place?"

Billy hadn't taken a breath, and Syd was caught off guard.

"Oh, hell, I'm gonna come clean, This is more than a social call. I reached out because the police called me, Syd. They've reopened Wyatt's murder case."

"Yes, I know. They spoke to me last week."

"Did they? Well, now they want to talk to me. You gave them my name? Would you have any insight into what's going on? Why they're looking into it? That's why I looked you up."

"I don't know any more than you do, Bill. I answered some questions for them, told them who I remembered from those days, no idea who might still be around, and that was it."

"Would you mind meeting me anyway? I'm feeling a little at odds. And it would be nice to see you and catch up. How's nine o'clock?"

Syd wasn't sure she could handle one more thing today, but she couldn't say no to this, either. Billy was afraid of something and must think she could be his conduit to answers. She thought the same of him. The plans in place, she called Gale back.

"Shit. I didn't expect this. We're going to have to wire you."

"I'm not sure I like that." Definitely a worm on a hook.

"It's really quite easy. It's small. Looks like a Fitbit. I'm going to bring it by your place right now, if that's okay."

Half an hour later, Syd opened her apartment door. She stared at the vison before her. If Mattel had made older versions of Barbara Millicent Roberts, Gale could've been the model for Gold Shield Barbie in her black cowboy boots, black slacks, and button-down, and the thin gray leather jacket with the short stand-up collar. Her Ray Bans were tucked into the top of her shirt. The gun and badge on her hip were visible. Her silver hair was windblown.

"Are you sure you're okay to do this?" Gale said as they stood in the living room. "You left awfully abruptly this afternoon."

To Syd's surprise, the cats, who never wanted to meet anyone, came into the room. Waterhouse occupied a patch of sunshine on the rug, looking Gale over like a rotund Sydney Greenstreet measuring Bogart in *The Maltese Falcon*. Price circled her warily.

Syd wanted to touch the leather jacket to see if it was as soft as it looked. Instead, she gazed out the window. The waning sunlight cast an ethereal blue glow over the glass apartment buildings on the water's edge of Long Island City, their windows reflective balls of fire. "There are demons I'm wrestling with, Gale," she said, so quietly she wasn't sure she'd voiced it. "Seeing these men after so many years…"

"I'm here if you want to talk…but I won't push." She took Syd's hand and gently wrapped the listening device around her wrist. Her touch, feather light, brought on in Syd that sense of just being on the edge of drunk, of floating off. She had to concentrate closely when Gale walked her through how it worked. She was right—it was going to be easy enough, especially since all Syd had to do was wear it. "I'll be parked on Second Avenue right outside the shop."

Gale's pronouncement snapped Syd out of her ethereal moment. "You can't guarantee you'll get a parking space there."

"Tommy went over after your call. He's sitting on a space waiting for me. This call of Billy's could be the key to something, so I'll be listening in."

Syd suddenly felt better, safer, even. "Wait—don't you need a truck for that sort of thing?"

Gale laughed. Syd liked the melody of it. "This isn't *Blue Bloods*. I can listen with a device almost as small as yours." Gale held up an earpiece about the size of a hearing aid. "The other thing I want you to wear—" She took a small gadget out of her other pocket. It looked like a shirt button with a wire attached to it. "Is this. It's a tiny camera in a button. May I?" She indicated the placket of Syd's polo shirt, and Syd nodded. Gale unbuttoned the middle button and threaded the wire through the buttonhole, snapping the cover into place. Syd watched Gale's hands as she worked, felt the backs of her fingers rest gently on the rise of her breast for the leverage she needed, tried to keep her breathing even. Syd had noticed those hands at their first meeting, too. They were a little bit rough and there were callouses in a couple of places on both of her palms. They looked strong, obviously used to the manual labor Gale had told her she did. But Syd also noticed the gliding birds they became, gracefully underpinning the points she was making when she talked. Now they felt like silk against her skin. The sensation was all too brief. For an instant, Syd let her mind wander to the possibility of those hands elsewhere on her body. "You need to match." Gale's voice pulled her back. "One odd button will stand out." She fished two more button covers out of her pocket. There were no wires dangling from them. She snapped them into place. "This camera is keyed to Tommy's computer. He'll be watching you."

"Okay."

"Now, if at any time something's not right, is there a word or a phrase you'd feel comfortable using that would let me know, and we'd get you out of there?"

Syd thought for a moment. "Iceberg."

Gale looked bewildered.

"It's spring. Who talks about icebergs in the spring?" Syd asked.

"Climate scientists. But we'll use it."

"What will happen if I say it?"

"I'll have a young undercover detective in the shop. She'll pretend she recognizes you from somewhere and she'll get you out of there. Billy seems to be a solid citizen with a career he'd like to retire from in five minutes, but we take nothing at face value. Especially considering his reaction to our call was so quick."

Syd was startled by the intensity of Gale's gaze. The gold flecks were like tiny fires against the hazel.

"Thank you for doing this, Syd. I'm not taking it lightly. Please be careful."

Syd nodded. She wondered if there might be something more than concern for her safety behind Gale's worry.

"All right, I'm going to relieve Tommy."

"Now?" Syd looked at the clock on her mantel. It was just seven.

"This is the glamorous side of police work, Syd. Undercover stake-outs." Gale leaned in closer to her. "Maybe I'll take you on a ride-along sometime," she said intimately, but then, the flicker of a smile that had come, went.

Syd bit her bottom lip. "If you ask me, I just might say yes." Her flirtation was met with that blush that she found so enchanting. She liked that she could cause it so easily, and that Gale reached for her badge every time.

Gale cleared her throat. "Okay, I'm just, uh, going to—" She cocked her head toward the door.

"Right. Okay." Syd saw her to the door. "I'll see you later. Or—or not. I won't see you later."

Gale smiled. "Actually, you will. My undercover is going to tail you partway home to make sure Billy's not following you for any reason. I'll take over from her at Sutton Place Park. I figured we could sit there while you give me your impressions ahead of our interview with Billy."

Syd liked that idea. A lot.

After Gale left, Syd stretched out on the settee and watched the sky over the East River as it faded from the pastel blue of late afternoon to the muted blue of dusk. The clouds slipped from white to smudged blue-gray, lit from below by the angle of the setting sun. Close to nine, she headed out to the ice cream shop.

As she neared Emack & Bolio's, Syd scanned the cars looking for Gale. Then she saw a tall white-haired gentleman standing by the outdoor tables of the shop. He matched the photo on the white board at the precinct. He wore dark green shorts, a butter-yellow polo shirt, and a color-block sweater tied about his shoulders. It was that rolling gait of his that she recognized, though, as he walked toward her, the shoulders dropping as he swung his arms. She'd always thought it an odd gait, half hurry, half stroll.

"Syd. I'd have recognized you anywhere."

"Bill, you look terrific."

"So do you. So…" He gestured toward the door. "Shall we?"

Syd hadn't considered the noise factor for Gale, but she eyed the tiled décor of the shop and knew sound would bounce off those walls. She was right. Most of the eight tables were taken and the din of chatter was almost overpowering. Looking around at the people, Syd wondered which woman was the undercover cop.

Once they had their ice cream, she suggested sitting outside, the traffic on Second Avenue negligible at this hour. Several folding wood chairs and lattice-topped wrought iron tables abutted the shop's picture window. Syd glanced at the cars parked nearby as she settled at one. Still no silhouettes resembling Gale.

Billy was nervous. Needing to put him at ease for her own sake, she peppered him with questions and listened intently as he spoke about how he'd managed to move on from the lost boys, confirming Syd's suspicion that Ned didn't let them go once he'd latched onto them. But Billy had been a smart boy, destined for more than being a gold-painted cage dancer at night clubs. And he was: City University of New York, and then Wall Street, followed by several major banking houses.

He'd acquired a husband along the way, a doctor who worked at the hospital near the apartment where they lived, and a home on the shore in Connecticut. "We even got married about five years ago." A little smile appeared. Then he asked about her life, and she was succinct, suspecting he was being polite but wanted to get to the reason for their meeting. There was something she wanted, too, and she sprang it on him right away, closely watching his reaction.

"Wow. Ned—hadn't thought about him in years and then yes, I saw the obituary. Too late for the service, though." Billy had been playing with his plastic spoon, spinning it on the table. His head still bent over the task, he peered up at her. "Did you go?"

Syd saw and felt that sense of being measured as he studied her. "No. Unfortunately I had to be out of town that day." It wasn't entirely a lie. She'd had a doctor's appointment below Houston Street. That constituted "out of town" for her. "Would you have gone?" Syd needed to poke the bear.

"If I'd seen the obit in time? I doubt it."

"Lucas Rose told me it was a big affair." *Poke.*

Billy sat up. "You talked to him?"

"Briefly, a couple of weeks ago. He called me when Ned died." She could almost hear Gale saying, "Play stupid!"

"I had no use for Ned." Billy's face reflected disdain as he looked down Second Avenue. "Acchh." He brushed a hand at the air. "It was a long time ago. I wouldn't even think twice except that now…" He leaned conspiratorially forward. "There's this police investigation. Are you at all worried? I mean, why is it happening? Who would open it now?" He sat back. "I'm not still in touch with anyone—are you?"

Billy's yo-yoing made Syd nervous. "No, it's been years. And you dropped out of sight before I did." Syd was startled by her own observation, suddenly remembering that Billy had been there one day and gone the next. And no one ever spoke of him after that.

"I was so overwhelmed, Syd." Billy had been fidgeting with the spoon and dropped it into his empty cup as if he'd already said too much.

"By?"

"The attention I was getting, the other guys quibbling, and then lashing out at me. Ned demanding favors, Wyatt expecting them, too, but at least he gave me things, and I still wasn't sure I was gay—" He clapped his hand over his mouth, such an unexpected move in a man his age and of his bearing.

Syd wondered what that next train of thought he'd derailed would've been.

"Oh, Syd, I'm sorry, I know how close you were to Wyatt."

She knew her smile was tight and short, and she was sure that wasn't the train. "Wyatt wasn't one for keeping secrets. I knew he was fond of you." She studied his face trying to calculate what this was all about. She desperately wanted to find out, and what better way than to wiggle on the proverbial hook. "What I only suspected Ned was up to back then, Lucas verified for me when I saw him recently."

Billy's mouth fell slightly open.

"We got together in mid-April. He originally called me because I went to see Ned after I spotted an article in the *Post* about Edward Junior parking him in that Connecticut home." Billy's eyes seemed to become iridescent in the light. "I—needed to see him, I had a bit of unfinished business." Syd could only imagine that Gale had her head in her hands in the car.

"What kind of business?"

"I was angry about so many things in the days after." Syd looked at the happy people in the shop. Ice cream was such a delightful thing—why weren't they sitting in a bar? "Ned was treating me like I was a doormat, so I said some very spiteful things to him. And I—I hid some documents that he might've needed for the embezzlement investigation because I was sure Wyatt would never steal, at least not of his own accord."

"What—documents?"

Billy's voice, quiet, indicated she might've poked the right spot this time.

"It doesn't matter. Ned told me they were inconsequential." The lie came easily, the skill honed from years of Catholic school education, facing nuns with rulers in their hands.

Billy sat back, an arm casually slung over the back of the chair. There was something menacing in the act, the posture. His face seemed very hard. Syd wanted to attribute it to the shop's harsh fluorescent light piercing the darkness around them, but she instinctively knew it was more. She leaned back so the button camera would get his face.

"You already knew about the investigation by then. By the time you saw Lucas."

"No." Syd lied again. "I got a call from the detectives much later."

Billy's face got stonier. "You said you learned some things about Ned from Lucas."

"Oh." Syd gingerly picked her way through this mine field. "There were things I was aware of, Bill, like the drug dealing. He corroborated it."

Billy sat forward and dangled his hands between his knees. "You have no idea how much I hated that. The pressure was tremendous."

"Then why didn't you say no?"

"Syd." Billy regarded her like a small granddaughter he was very fond of. "You didn't say no to Ned. Not to the drugs, not to the prostitution—" Billy's eyes widened and he looked away.

"Yes, there was that." Syd went right along with Billy's confession.

"You knew."

"I guessed." As an accountant, Syd had been very good at taking calculated risks when it came to the people around her. She decided to take one now—if Tommy wanted to flush Billy out, this might be the best chance. "I came across a ledger in Wyatt's desk drawer once. It was self-explanatory."

They looked at each other over the table, a deep red flooding Billy's face. Syd had told Gale she didn't know what that ledger she'd found meant, but Billy's reaction now told her what it was: it had to do with the prostitution ring that she'd never wanted to believe Ned ran, possibly with Wyatt's help.

"I don't care, Bill. I didn't then, I don't now."

"Do you know what happened to that record book?"

"No idea. I'm assuming the police took it as evidence back then." Syd let that sink in as Billy studied her. "What Lucas told me led me to believe Ned was either in on the embezzlement at Divine Heart or that he was behind it. He said that Ned put many of the boys through college, even grad school."

Billy let out a short laugh and looked at the sky. "I didn't know anything about that embezzlement until I read about it in the papers, but did Lucas also tell you that Ned's 'generosity' came with a heavy price tag? Ned was insatiable. And so were his friends."

Syd remembered the photos Gale had found of Ned and his financier pals at galas, some of the lost boys with them, and puzzle pieces began fitting into place.

"Do you remember who any of those friends were?" She sensed she was in dangerous territory now by the anger and melancholy that settled on Billy's face. For a moment, anger won the battle before he banished both, tipping his head back.

"Ahhh. No, I don't. Wall Street guys." He looked at her again, pointed a finger. "Some parents from your school, yeah."

"No." It wasn't disbelief. She was certain. He was wrong.

"Coupla guys, young money men, and the wife of one of them— she was into some kinky stuff and the boys obliged."

Syd couldn't even entertain the thought of that wife, much less any other parent. "I'm not sure I believe you."

"Suit yourself." Billy shifted. "Tall blond guy, pretty blond wife. Can't remember their names."

How convenient. "That describes half the parents back then."

Billy shrugged. "I was there one night because Ned knew I could entertain the wife *and* keep the husband happy."

A cold fear ran through her followed by a burning hot question. Maybe she just wanted to hurt Billy with it. Maybe she wanted to knock his legs out from under him. "Bill, what would you say if I told you I spotted Duane Valchek in a photo in Lucas Rose's apartment that was taken in nineteen eighty-five?"

The alarm on Billy's face was fleeting "Not possible. He died of AIDS, before we really knew what it was, right after the new year in eighty-three. I went to the funeral in Malone, Syd."

His agitation and anger were clear, so Syd sat back hoping the move would calm him.

"You remember his uncle came with me? He was a cop in the Tenth Precinct, Duane was always bragging about him getting us out of trouble. He took us in when we first came to the city."

She nodded contritely, even though she had no such recollection. "I'm sorry, Bill. That was such a hard time. I didn't mean…"

"We never mean, Syd, and still we ask." Billy's face had become an inscrutable mask. "Maybe you were mistaken. Those photos of us back in the day, they all looked alike, and we looked alike in them." He shifted, focused his attention up Second Avenue. "I just want to know who went to the cops to open this case again." He picked up the plastic spoon again and drummed it on the table, looking right at Syd.

"That makes two of us."

"Whoever killed Wyatt might not even be alive today—have the cops thought of that?" Billy's voice was tinged with anger. "I'm sympathetic to whoever's reopened this case, but I don't want to be tarred with that brush. Wyatt's killer obviously had a lot to lose, but it wasn't me."

Syd scrutinized Billy's face. Why would he go there? Had Gale been right? Or had Syd just spent half an hour with a cold and calculating murderer? "We all lost a lot that night, Bill." She picked up his dish and walked it to the trash with hers. When she turned back to the table, Billy had her in his crosshairs, an odd look on his face.

"Did you mention anything we've spoken about to the police? The ledger, the drugs, the prostitution?"

It was more than a simple question. The tone of his voice caused the hairs on the back of her neck to stand up. "They didn't ask." Frozen in his gaze, Syd clawed for a way out that wasn't "iceberg." "Will you call me later to tell me how your interview with the police goes?"

As Billy hugged her good-bye, Syd stole a glance at the parked cars again. About half a block away, she turned to see if she could identify the undercover cop following her and instead, spotted Billy watching her. She waved to cover up the move. He waved back and she turned away.

When Syd crossed the street near Sutton Place Park, she saw Gale leaning against a black SUV not far from the park entrance and felt a flood of relief. But it was quickly infused with anger. She didn't know where it was coming from, but it gripped her. "How is that possible? I saw that car, but you weren't in it." She regretted her tone instantly, watching Gale fold her arms across her chest to confront her.

"Of course I was in it. I'm an expert at shrinking. And how is it possible that I asked you to play stupid, but you handed Billy Highsmith everything he's going to need to evade our questioning tomorrow?"

The anger drained right out of Syd.

"And even that aside, how am I supposed to protect you when you keep poking lions in their dens? First it was Lucas Rose. Now Billy Highsmith! Asking leading questions, bringing up evidence-related information?"

"*You* sent me into this one!" Syd felt the anger flash through her, and it wasn't only from tonight.

"With the caveat that you be careful and act like you knew nothing."

"You can't catch a killer with nothing!"

"He's not the killer."

"I wouldn't be too sure about that!"

"What do you mean?"

"He's frightened and angry and he wants something. And I think he thinks I have it." Syd put her hands on her hips and took a big breath. A small panic was creeping in. "You know, I always thought someone was looking for something in Wyatt's apartment that night—the destruction was so catastrophic."

"You don't mean the ledger? That doesn't make him the killer."

"I don't know. All I know is I have a target on my back and Lucas and Billy are looking right at it."

Gale reached to hug Syd. "I'm so sorry. I never should have asked you to meet him."

"And I never saw your undercover following me." Syd let Gale enfold her, put her arms around Gale, like she'd wanted to before this night. The panic receded.

"That's the whole point."

She heard the gruff scowl in Gale's voice as she breathed in the leather of her jacket. It was mixed with the jasmine and thyme of the scent she wore. The jacket was as soft as it had looked. Gale's physical warmth slowly pierced the tension that she didn't even realize had been pervading her body; it began to ebb. Reluctantly, Syd pulled away from the safety. They were standing beneath a streetlight, and the gold flecks in Gale's hazel eyes shone bright as stars against the darker color. Syd wanted to touch her, wanted to kiss her to find out if there was a promise of something more within those eyes, but they were impenetrable. She sensed the possibility that she wasn't simply one more case to Gale. A soft electric current carrying desire shot through her. She was confused, though: was it want, or a need based on their circumstances?

"Thank you for finding out that the ledger had to do with the prostitution," Gale said gently. "But you have to let us ask the questions, Syd."

"If you're going to send me out as bait, don't you think I should decide how big a worm I should be on that hook?" Syd knew she shouldn't take her anger out on Gale; it wasn't fair.

"Maybe we won't send you out anymore."

Syd heard the sharp answering tone, turned away, and walked into the park.

"What?" Gale asked.

Syd settled on one of the low brick benches that sat back from the fence overlooking the East River. The waters surged noisily by even on a warm night like this when there were no breezes, it wasn't a full moon, and no storms were forecast. Gale sat next to her.

"I know." Syd sighed. "You've done this so many times you could probably run a cold case in your sleep. I have no idea what I'm doing, and I'm afraid, but I want answers. And I can ask questions that you can't."

"I tell you to play stupid because there are procedures and protocols we follow so that we get answers we need. It's a cat and mouse game."

Syd heard the anger in Gale's voice, but now she didn't care. She knew how to play cat and mouse, too. She was pretty sure after talking to Billy tonight, her mouse had drawn his cat out of its lair.

"You're running roughshod over things, Syd."

She looked away. *I should've known she'd think that...*

"But I'm at fault for putting you in harm's way."

Syd continued to peer out at the river, miffed.

"I can't actually run cold cases in my sleep. And right now, I'm afraid, too."

Syd looked back at Gale, who was concentrating on her hands in her lap. She seemed vulnerable for the first time since Syd had met her, and she reached over and covered Gale's hands. They'd been frustrated together; they'd been mad at each other. Now they could be afraid together. The perfect trifecta.

Gale searched the sky. "You're not going to like this. I can't put any manpower on sitting outside your building, so I want you to text me whenever you go anywhere, when you get there, when you leave to go back home, and when you get home."

"You're kidding." Syd withdrew her hand.

"I can't hazard anything happening to you on this case."

"Because I'm bait?" Syd rose. "I've got to get home." She started to walk down the brick path toward the front gate, but then she felt Gale's hand on her shoulder. Strong. Insistent. Pulling her back.

"Because I can't—because we can't lose you."

There was a trace of fear on Gale's face. Syd's anger dissipated.

"Who else is left to interview? After Billy?"

"Well, Theo Hall. And Ned's son."

"Theo won't know anything. He was a basket case for months. And Edward Junior is all hat and no cattle. Besides which, he was ten at the time."

"Thank you for those insights."

Neither of them moved.

"If you need me to run roughshod with either interview..."

Gale closed her eyes. "I'd better get you home. I need my wire, my camera, and all my button covers."

"I can walk from here, you know."

"No." Gale popped the fake button covers off Syd's polo shirt and a second later, her two fingers were inside the shirt working the little wire out. Syd shivered.

"Are you cold? I can give you my jacket.".

"No." Syd unclipped the device from her wrist and handed it to Gale. She'd thought from the first day they'd met that Gale's shield lent her an authority and a gravitas that was comforting, but now she realized it wasn't the shield at all.

There were things about Gale that Syd hadn't expected, so much that she'd paid little attention to at first, when Gale was still "detective" and Syd was so focused on the threat and all the old fears being raised. Now something was pulling her inexorably toward this woman—was it Gale herself, was it her own fear bound up in this case, or was it something deeper Syd needed that had walked out the door behind Marie all those years ago? Gale had said "I can't" before amending it to "we can't lose you." She wasn't sure now how she would do it, but she needed to find out if Gale was afraid for her or the case. Because for Syd, Gale was becoming as important as the case.

CHAPTER FOURTEEN

The interview with Billy Highsmith on Wednesday morning had gone about as well as Gale and Tommy thought it would, which is to say it garnered as little information as the interview with Mike Avery the previous afternoon. They'd sat in Billy's big corner office at the international bank headquarters where he worked downtown and looked at Lady Liberty through the floor-to-ceiling windows behind him while he intoned "I honestly don't remember" and "I couldn't say" to most of their questions, just as Mike had while they'd sat in the beautifully appointed office of his funeral home. Would Billy have stonewalled them anyway, Gale wondered, or had Syd influenced the outcome with her pointed questions and deliberate information last night? Or, had Mike contacted him?

"He's lying," Gale said, once they were out on the street. "He might've divorced himself from those lost boys back then, but somehow that separation paid dividends to Ned that we don't even know about. Otherwise, why would he let Billy go?"

"We got nothin' to come at him with, Gale. Same as Mike yesterday. Billy at least admitted to the drugs and prostitution, so now we're certain that's what the ledger was about. But there's no statute, he was eighteen, a hayseed from upstate, and he cleaned up his life."

"Something's wrong with this picture. All my instincts tell me so."

"Mine don't. He never fled. And that kind of chutzpah would take big brass ones. What else can we look for with him?"

They watched the early lunchtime foot traffic emerge from buildings all around them.

"Phone records. Bank records. He owns a car. Maybe since Syd's visit to Ned, he's driven places he ordinarily wouldn't go. Bridge and tunnel receipts or an EZ Pass record might tell us something."

"Okay, I can dig. But I think we're pissin' into the ocean here."

"Maybe Billy wasn't involved in the embezzlement. But he knows something about the murder, Tommy—he makes the hairs on the back of my neck stand up."

Hands in his jacket pockets, Tommy shrugged. "All right, I'll put in for those. And there's more evidence to dig through in those boxes."

"We've been looking at a one-thread, one-person scenario. But this case is about more than one thing."

"Our two favorite demons. Jealousy and money."

"But whose jealousy and whose money?"

"I don't follow." Tommy's brow furrowed.

"I don't think they're linked. Why would Ned kill the golden goose?"

"Only way he could silence Wyatt. By my research, Ned had made up his losses and was even ahead. I think he wanted more—the man had a very expensive lifestyle. And I think he thought he was gonna buy boys until the day he died. If Syd's right, and Wyatt was being coerced, maybe there was a fight there."

"So, money, not jealousy."

"You're gonna owe me ten big ones."

"But Lucas intimated they were sleeping together. All three of them. I wonder if Ned was the prize they both wanted." Gale slid her hands into her pockets and jingled the change there.

"That doesn't work for me because we know from Syd that Lucas began shacking up with his Fire Island Pines sugar daddy eight months after Wyatt's murder, and he stayed with him for thirty years. Would you kill to keep a certain woman and then walk away from the relationship less than a year later?"

"I wouldn't. But I know some women who would."

"You don't do dyke drama, thank God for small favors. You're too practical."

"So I've been told. You're married to Syd's theory that Ned was behind the murder. We still have to fit Billy Highsmith into the story.

And I'm not done with Duane Valchek. Especially after connecting with one of his classmates who didn't remember him dying in eighty-three. And this guy's never left Malone, knows everything and everyone. Even went to his parents' funerals." She looked at Tommy. "What is it with small-town America? Why don't they ever go see the world?"

"We like our small towns."

"You're a city boy."

"Brooklyn's a small town, Gale. Only reason I even go to the Bronx is to see the Yankees with you."

Gale chuckled. "Someday we'll have to go to Queens and see the Mets."

"Not gonna happen."

"Promise me—no tunnel vision."

"I will carefully consider all the evidence we dig up." Tommy crossed his heart and then held the two fingers up.

Gale nodded. The lunchtime crowds had grown.

"You wouldn't kill for a woman, either, would you?"

"Are you kidding?" Tommy snorted. "What I'd kill for right now? Is a meatball parm hero from that food truck over there."

Gale turned her attention to the red, white, and green truck a few feet away, and the aroma hit her. "Me, too. Let's go."

❖

Gale sat at her father's kitchen table staring at her laptop screen in disbelief. It had been a long shot contacting the San Francisco Police Department. She and Tommy figured the city would be the perfect place to move to in 1983 if you were a young gay man wanting to hide in plain sight. And if you were stupid enough, you might get yourself arrested. Duane Valchek had been stupid enough.

Dammit, why couldn't we have had these this morning when we went to see Billy?

Gale slowly scrolled through the three arrest records the SFPD sent: breaking and entering, a minor drug sale, and lewd behavior in public. All between 1983 and 1990. Then she reread the email from Detective Rawlings: "Between 1989 and 2000, this gentleman's name was flagged for many arrests in other parts of the state of California—Sacramento, San Diego, Los Angeles. Please contact those departments for the records." *God bless technology. And the digital footprints we leave.*

"Whatcha workin' on, kid?" Sullivan put a small glass of Macallan single malt next to her laptop. "Dinner was good tonight, by the way. Thanks for helping me give Celia the night off."

"Never a problem, Dad. We've got a good care team in place, I like to keep them happy."

"This your forty-year-old murder or something else?" He sat across from Gale and took a healthy sip of scotch from his own glass.

"Info from the San Francisco police on that case. They had arrest records on one of our suspects, as do three other Cali cities. Dating back eighty-three to two thousand. We were told the guy was dead. I'd like to call Tommy but it's late."

"How did you figure out he wasn't dead?"

"Sydney Hansen, the woman who brought us the case. She found a picture of him in the apartment of another suspect, taken well after he was supposed to have died."

"What was she doing there?"

"Some sleuthing." Gale peered at him over her bifocals. "Which we have discouraged her from doing any more of."

"Mmmm. You don't want her turning up dead, too." Sullivan ran his thumb over the bristles of his white brush moustache.

"No, I very much do not." What her father supposed, and Gale's real reason for not wanting Syd dead, weren't one and the same. She pictured Syd sitting next to Tommy at his computer, her hands steepled under her chin, a studiousness about her as he took her through all the financials. Gale realized she'd never seen Syd in professional corporate accounting mode, and she had to admit she'd been intimidating firing all her questions at Tommy, as intimidating as she'd been last night challenging Gale when she got angry at her about the way she'd handled the meeting with Billy. Syd had given as good as she'd gotten, standing up to Gale like Kate used to do.

"San Francisco was a damn good guess. Lucky, too. What cities will you try now?"

"How do you mean?"

"He obviously left California, nothing in the last two decades there. Which way did he go? I'm sure you've already targeted the big cities he'd find large gay havens in so you can tap those police departments next."

Gale sat back, a smile emerging. "You never cease to amaze me, Dad."

"Well, you have, haven't you?"

"I wouldn't be Sullivan Sterling's daughter if I wasn't already six steps ahead."

He rotated his glass on the tabletop. "Why didn't you contact them all at the same time? And did you check the NYPD's records?"

It was a direct hit to Gale's solar plexus. The NYPD records hadn't occurred to her. "Not something you do for a dead guy." She tried to recover what was left of her shredded shield. "You know, in the 'Dead Men Don't Make Threats' department."

"Touché." He drummed his fingers on the table. "Are you still having your weekly meetings with her?"

"We are. I am." She took a sip of her scotch. "You don't approve." She wasn't going to let him beat her twice.

"It's unorthodox, but I see what you're doing, including her, getting information from her."

"She knows things that we don't. It's like working with a live research compendium." Gale looked back down at her screen, knowing he was scrutinizing her, knowing he read her as only a father could.

"Why don't you have Sydney Hansen to dinner soon?"

She looked back up at him, caught the solemnity and compassion on his face. Of course he knew.

"How about a couple of weekends from now. I'll fire up the barbecue—it's getting to be grilling season."

Gale snorted. "Grilling season's all year for you."

He shrugged. "Flavor doesn't abide by a calendar. I'd like to meet this woman. Hell, invite Tommy over, too."

Gale rolled her eyes. "Yes, your lordship."

"He seein' anybody lately?"

Gale smirked. "You know Tommy. He'll still be playing the field in the nursing home."

Sullivan shook his head and raised his glass. "Why have one woman when you can have 'em all, eh? Well…" He stood and stretched. "I'm going to watch the Mets game. Join me when you can."

"The only time I'll join you for a Mets game is during the subway series."

"How did I raise a child who bleeds pinstripe blue?" Sullivan put a hand on her shoulder and left the kitchen.

Gale checked the calendar on her laptop. Two Saturdays from now was May 21st. She forwarded Detective Rawlings's email to Tommy and followed it with a text.

Gale: *Hate to say it, but I told you so. Open yr email. We're going back to see Billy Highsmith.*

Minutes later, her phone dinged.

Tommy: *Did u just get this??*

Gale: *Yes. Timing is everything. You question him next time. You're more frightening."*

Tommy sent a laughing emoji. *Bklyn tomorrow, last two barrels of evidence. I'll pick you up 8am. Searching billy's ez pass now, phone records. Current bank records don't show anything out of the ordinary. Zach & Billy live 15 mi. from each other ct. V. interesting, no?*

Gale: *Told you something was wrong. He left everything out of the interview incl. the kitchen sink. Come to dinner 2 wks Sat*

Tommy sent back a thumb's up.

Gale: *Sullivan wants to meet Syd. He's grilling. Steaks. But probably her, too.*

Tommy sent back a wide-eyed emoji.

Gale: *Yeah, me, too.*

Tommy: *He never misses a trick.*

❖

Gale was stunned, but she didn't know if it was because she should have seen it coming, or because she never saw it coming. Before she could react and give free rein to her anger, Tommy was in Officer Bevins's face.

"What do you mean, there's evidence missing?" In disbelief, Tommy glared through the property room window at Officer Bevins. "Who else is in here besides you?"

"You do know there's a whole property division, right?"

"Yeah, but who works this one with you?"

"They're all online, Tommy," Gale said, trying to mitigate the confrontation and contain Tommy. "We can look this up."

"I don't want to look it up. You got a regular shift, so does the guy in front of you and the one behind you."

"Franklin four to midnight, Ahern midnight to eight, but he's a minute away from retirement. I always catch him sleeping when I come in."

"I want to see the security tape and what the hell went missing? Son of a bitch!"

Bevins picked up a typed list and retrieved a pencil from behind her ear. "There were twelve items listed. There were five in there when we discovered the broken tape."

"What. Went. Missing," Tommy growled. His face turned a deep red. Gale stopped pacing long enough to put a hand on his arm.

"Shirt. Pair of pants. Socks."

"Fuck!"

Bevins glanced up at Tommy. "Belt, shoes, underwear."

"I'm a fucking idiot!"

"No, we're not," Gale said. "They couldn't get to this stuff when we requisitioned it. The less-flooded boxes were the only ones accessible."

"What's the God damn seventh item?"

"Seven-inch butcher knife," Bevins said quietly.

Tommy swung around and punched the five-gallon bottle on the water cooler, nearly knocking it off the stand, letting out a string of expletives that rang through the cavernous space. "I wanna see the boxes!"

Bevins pointed behind her to two regulation brown boxes, the red and white seals broken on them. The boxes looked like they'd been through a very bad day in the back of a filthy delivery truck.

"And the security tape."

"I already looked at it. Nothing."

"I want to see it, Officer. Now."

Bevins unlocked the storage room gate and led them to a desk near a window about twenty feet away. She sat at the computer, brought up the security tape, and hit Play.

"Boxes came in Monday, here."

"What the fuck, you didn't call us until yesterday?!"

"We get very busy with court cases, Detective."

They watched a police officer bring a hand truck into the room and unload the secured boxes. He left, and Bevins lifted the boxes onto a bottom shelf next to the door, just out of camera range.

"Why'd you put them there?" Tommy asked.

"Because that's where outgoing boxes go. Look, I had a ton of stuff going out for court this week, so yours got the bottom shelf." She turned back to the computer. "You know how this works, forward, rewind. I gotta get back."

"You couldn't make one phone call."

"We were buried in the Russian mob racketeering case. I had thousands of boxes to locate and move. A lot of 'em by myself." Bevins went back to the window.

Tommy sat down and began advancing slowly through the tape. "Coulda called me on your lunch hour," he muttered.

Gale put a hand on his shoulder. "Tommy, first of all, we have to go through this in real time. We can't sit here now and do this."

"I know." He stopped and sat back. "I'm so freakin' mad."

"I am, too, but railing at Bevins isn't the answer."

"She shoulda called us, Gale."

"Yes, she should've, and I intend to report her, much as I hate doing that. But we have a much bigger problem here."

"What?"

Gale lowered her voice to a near-whisper. "I don't know if it's a mole or a bug, but if those boxes were broken into, we've got an insider up in our business."

Tommy's face drained of color and when it returned, it was bright red again.

"No, don't. We are detectives, we work *this*"—Gale indicated the tape and the boxes—"like any case, but we keep it between us."

Tommy nodded once.

"Have Bevins voucher the tape to your email. We need to get department IDs on these property clerks because I don't know what they look like. Neither do you. I was going to get everyone in homicide to go over tape with us since we have four days' worth of it, but now I think it's you and me at my dining room table this weekend with a pot of coffee. We can order in."

"Bevins," Tommy called.

The property clerk came over to the desk.

"Send this to us."

"Yeah, okay."

"No. Now. I want to watch so I know it gets done right and right now."

Bevins glared at him but sat down at the desk.

While she worked, Gale pointed at the window and rubbed the fingertips of her right hand together: the dust on the ledge was undisturbed. She quietly walked down the aisle toward the back of the warehouse looking for more windows. As she did, she called Syd to tell her that something had come up and she couldn't meet with her for their rainy afternoon lunch. Gale had been looking forward to it.

Bevins finished her task.

"Thank you. I'll be right back." Tommy walked after Gale.

"Only five other windows, dust untouched. This was inside," she said when he found her walking toward him along the back hall. "We're officially fucked. I want to go to Esposito when we get back to the station house."

"The captain ain't gonna like this."

"Neither do I."

❖

Syd had spent half the evening spinning. She knew Billy Highsmith lied to her the other night. He'd been truthful about the lost boys being involved in drug sales and prostitution; that's what the red ledgers meant. But then he'd insisted Duane Valchek was dead since 1983. The photo on Lucas Rose's wall said otherwise.

Gale was right—so much evidence leading in so many different directions, it was hard to make sense of it. And everyone claimed they weren't involved. Syd could've laughed out loud at the absurdity of it. It was like an Agatha Christie novel—everyone *was* involved somehow. She sat back. Maybe that wasn't so absurd. Lucas hadn't been forthcoming. Billy was still hiding something. And Duane Valchek was—hiding. Jealousies had been hidden; money had certainly been hidden. Could everyone have had a role in Wyatt's murder, each unknown to the other? She'd been looking at this through the wrong lens. Had Gale and Tommy considered this?

She wanted to call Gale and ask, but it was late, and she was still mad at her about the sharp words they'd had in the park the other night. If she was being honest with herself, though, she also wanted more than a half hour walk around the block to talk about it. Gale had proposed lunch, but Syd wondered if their tiff meant that it wasn't going to happen. At all. She'd canceled it today. Something had come up, she'd said. Granted, this wasn't the only case she was working on. But selfishly she wanted Gale's attention on *this* case. And maybe if they were away from the precinct and beyond the constraints time put on them there, they could be themselves and they wouldn't get so short with each other. Taking a chance that Gale would still be up, Syd texted her: *Missed seeing you today. But still a little mad at you. Want to move Tues. mtg.* A moment later, her phone rang.

"I'm sorry about today. I was stuck in Brooklyn. And—I guess I was a little insensitive the other night."

Syd thought the hug had been anything but insensitive. "Yes, you were. But so was I."

"You were, a little bit."

Syd was taken aback, but she let out a short laugh. "Well, you didn't have to agree with me."

"Syd, you can count on two things with me. I will always be where I say I'm going. And I'll always say what I feel."

Syd took the statement in quietly, as quietly as Gale had offered it, wondering if Gale lent it more than just the surface meaning. "I'll hold you to that."

"I hope you do. So, your text said you needed to move Tuesday's meeting?"

"Yes. No. Not the day. The time. And the place."

"That's a lot of moving."

"Bear with me here—after all, I went to Sutton Place Park for you at nine o'clock at night." Syd drew in a breath and let the next sentence out on the exhale. "Let's meet in Central Park after you leave work and talk there."

"Because we did so well in the park the other night."

Gale's voice had softened, and Syd laughed. "I thought we'd tendered a truce of sorts at the top of this call."

"Is that what that was? Go on."

"I've had some thoughts I'd like to run by you. I figured a bottle of wine, cheese, and a quiet place in the park would make it easier to sift through things together."

In the silence that followed, Syd wondered if she'd set herself up for disappointment again despite how open Gale had been from the beginning, and how generous with her time.

"I think that sounds like a good idea. I'll meet you outside the precinct around six. And I'll bring my best trained sensitive manner with me."

Syd sighed. "We're bound to lose patience now and then. Look, I was extremely agitated after the meeting with Billy."

"I was mad about a few things then, too, but we seem to have gotten through it."

"Yes." Syd saw herself standing in Gale's embrace in the park— it had been solid and warm and had conveyed more than the "I'm sorry" it had started with.

"Okay, then."

When Gale hung up, Syd felt an absence that had nothing to do with the case.

CHAPTER FIFTEEN

I need lunch," Tommy said. "My eyes are bleary from fast-forwarding."

"I've got turkey, roast beef, cheese. And for you, mozzarella, tomatoes, and basil. Heroes, rye, and pumpernickel from the Italian bakery."

"Oh, yeah, the tomato mozzarella sounds good, on a hero." Tommy stood up and stretched.

Gale took several packages in deli paper from the refrigerator. "It still doesn't make sense to me that Esposito thinks our boxes were accidentally opened by cops mistaking them for the Russian mob case."

Tommy rubbed his eyes. "I hate to say, it did to me. But when he said the stuff coulda been taken before the boxes were even sealed in eighty-two? Which means they've been gone all this time? How would we ever know now?" He shook his head. "And I almost murdered Bevins over it."

"We've got to go through these tapes anyway—due diligence. And this isn't like you to still be beating yourself up."

"Gale, c'mon, I was horrible to Bevins. I gotta apologize."

"Tommy, it was a serious infraction. She didn't call to tell us the boxes had come in *or* that they'd been compromised. I wrote her up."

"Yeah, okay. Still. I'm not that jerk."

"She's lucky it was you going after her. I'd have cut her shorter than you did. You want a little oil, balsamic vinegar?" Gale held an open bottle over Tommy's sandwich.

"Yeah, thanks. You got any beer?"

"Bottom shelf."

"Sullivan gonna come up and see how we're doing?" Tommy took a Sam Adams from the refrigerator and pulled the magnetized bottle opener off the side.

"The elevator's working. But he was pretty angry when I told him what happened and why we're sitting at my dining room table this weekend."

"Bet this never happened in his day." Tommy opened the beer and took a swig.

"Bet it did. I think that's why he got so mad. Some things never change." Gale put their plates on the table and took two small salads out of the refrigerator.

Tommy sat down. "Salad—yer killin' me."

"It's good for you."

"When they bottle a dressing with my mother's marinara, I'll think about it."

"She does make good sauce."

Tommy raised his beer.

"Listen, Sullivan wanted to know if there's anyone in your life right now. Do you want to bring her to dinner next week?"

Tommy raised an eyebrow. "Yes, a very cute flight attendant, but she won't be in town. Makes it easier to see the other gal in Hook and Ladder Twenty-one."

Gale shook her head. "You're incorrigible. So bring her."

"Sullivan wouldn't approve. I think she's maybe thirty."

Gale smirked.

"Hey, don't judge. And you should have a maybe thirty in your bed, my friend. I'm not the only good-lookin' detective—I see those young gender-fluid gals checkin' you out when we hit McNulty's after work."

Gale snorted. "Gender fluid." She'd finished her salad and stabbed a forkful from Tommy's plate. "By the way—I contacted the Sacramento, San Diego, and LAPD, asked them to send Valchek's arrest records. I also put in requests with Miami and DC police."

"Oh, sure, go all 'cold case' on me now, avoid the dating questions. Fine."

"Tommy, we need to check the NYPD records."

"No, no way Valchek comes back here."

"Might be a nice way to start the week on Monday if we find something."

"If we find something, it's gonna piss me off that it never occurred to us."

"He was dead."

"Evidently not, Detective Fumble, and we were stupid for believing it without so much as a second thought."

"Our initial mistake on this case was thinking that anything was what it seemed."

The elevator gears kicked in.

"And here comes himself to tell us what else we might've missed," Tommy said, laying on an Irish accent. He finished his beer and opened two more, putting one at the empty chair for Gale's father.

Tuesday morning, Syd sat down with her second cup of coffee and her laptop. She wanted to be on the golf course—a stress-relieving morning like that would be nice. Instead, she'd substituted a workout of stretches with her weights because more than she wanted to play golf, she wanted to research something that had been nagging her for days after she'd first talked to Gale. Wyatt's nocturnal habits had been legendary among the lost boys: he knew every bar, every cabaret, every hole-in the-wall, and a retinue of the boys always followed him every night like a trail of stardust. He was never alone. But that night, he had been. So she wanted to put a list together for Gale and Tommy of all the places he used to frequent. Maybe there was a link between Bareback and the other bars she'd heard him talk about, bars so well known that she'd heard about them long before she passed them on the street when she'd finally made her way down to the Village to explore: the Eagle, Ramrod, Rawhide, the Anvil, and so many more. There had to be a history of them online, articles memorializing the ones lost to the AIDS era or unintentionally lost in the homogenization of the gay rights movement itself. She wasn't sure what she was trying to articulate with the list, but maybe as she looked around online it would become clearer to her.

She wrote down the names of the places she remembered him mentioning when he sometimes told her about his conquests Monday mornings, which he did because her utter boredom made him laugh. *"I'll only be interested in your story if there's a handsome butch involved,"* Syd always said.

"Darling," he always answered, *"if there's ever a handsome butch involved, it means I'm in the wrong bar."*

To her surprise, several articles came up right away. The first one, a *Times* article from over a decade ago, was short. The next one, a 2013 *Village Voice* article titled, "Where Did All the Gay Bars Go?" wasn't much of an article, either. She didn't want to despair, but she wasn't hopeful about the remaining handful of articles.

The third piece was from an online magazine she'd never heard of, but it turned out to be a gold mine. The title was lengthy: "RIP to All the Gay Bars I've Known in New York City," and the inventory was just as protracted. It was a quirky, funny description of every bar the author had been to in the 1980s and 1990s, and he'd been to all of them, even if he'd walked in and walked out five minutes later. She added more bars to her list as she read familiar names. At the end of the article, and she sat back when she saw it, was a message board that catalogued remarks and conversations that had gone on for nearly three years after the author posted it four years prior. She scrolled through them, reading the discussions that went back and forth. A post caught her eye. *"I remember Bareback well because I was the gatekeeper to the second floor in the 80s!"* Syd felt like the breath had been sucked right out of her. The post was signed "tinydancer80" but there was no email address, like there were with other posts. There had to be a way to find out who he was. She couldn't get this close and let it go.

She picked up her cell phone. "Hello, sweetiedahling. I need your help."

"Sydney!" Elisa said. "I'd like to tell you I'm in a meeting and I can't take your call right now but we both know I'm not that important. What's up?"

"Could you talk Frank into sending his best IT guy on a house call?"

"I can go down to the bullpen and ask."

"Bring a bottle of Johnnie Walker Black with you. I'll reimburse."

"When do you want him?"

"Soon as possible."

"What do I tell him?"

"I think I've got a hacker, someone who's tracking me. I also need to find someone but all I have is an online name."

"Syd, this sounds—serious."

"Please?"

"Does it have to do with this police investigation?"

"I think I was hacked before I went to the police. I told you someone didn't like my visiting Ned."

"Syd—you know I worry about you."

"I'm in good hands, Elisa. No need to worry." A vivid image of Gale, and the sensation of her hand on the small of Syd's back, came to her mind.

"All right. And the other? This name thing?"

"That has to do with the investigation."

"Should you bring it to the cops?"

"Probably, but they don't have the IT support."

"Seriously? The police?"

"Apparently, the cold case division is the ugly stepchild when it comes to support."

In the silence that followed Elisa's sigh, Syd crossed her fingers waiting for her friend's consent. She didn't want to get her into trouble. They'd done this many times before, prior to Syd's retirement, borrowing people from the firm to do things for them like rebuilding a hard drive on their personal computers or moving furniture too big for them to handle. Of course, they'd paid them well. Now, though, it would be Elisa acting on her own. On Syd's behalf. While doing something that wasn't so kosher.

"All right. I'll see what he says."

Syd let out a breath of relief. "Thank you."

"Now you have to indulge me. How is your handsome detective?"

"Still handsome."

"Syd."

"I told you I'm remaining professional. Although I took your advice and told her I was feeling vulnerable."

"And? Reaction?"

"She very professionally told me that was normal."

Elisa made a sound that was half exasperation, whole disappointment.

"But I did ask her to Central Park for our meeting next week. We usually walk around the block in the afternoon, but I thought maybe a bench at sunset with wine and cheese."

"Perfect. Baby steps, sweetiedahling. So I'm getting a fifth of scotch?"

"Yes. And I'll take you out to dinner next week."

"Good. You can tell me what happens in Central Park."

Syd stared at the computer screen for a few more minutes after Elisa hung up. Shock, elation, and fear had caught her by surprise when she'd read tinydancer80's posts. Someone who might know something *was* out there. But where? And what if he didn't know anything? But what if he did? She knew how frustrating the one would be. But how frightening would the other prove?

"I'm going to find you, tinydancer80."

Gale stood behind Tommy's chair looking at his computer. A 2019 arrest record for Duane Valchek for loitering and harassment in the Port Authority stared back at them. The arresting officer had found nothing on him. And of course, not only had he skipped the court date, but the charge had been dismissed. Gale would've laughed at the information on the desk ticket, but she was too angry with herself. The phone number listed was for his childhood home in Malone, he'd knocked ten years off his age, and she was sure the cell phone number listed was fake. She dialed it from Tommy's desk phone and got that recorded three-beep signal followed by the automated "We're sorry—" She hung up before it even finished.

"I wonder…" Tommy opened the police database.

"What?"

"Webcam footage will be long gone, but maybe this Officer Rodriguez remembers something, anything."

"Get out. Do you even remember half the people we interviewed six months ago?"

"If I saw their names, maybe." He pulled up Officer Rodriguez's information and called the cell number. She didn't recollect the arrest.

"If I sent you a photo of this guy from 1983? He's wanted for murder. You can maybe age him in your mind?" The phone cradled to his ear, Tommy pulled up the photo Gale had surreptitiously taken of the photo in Lucas Rose's apartment when she'd used the bathroom. "Okay, Rodriguez, sending it now. He's right in the center. Let me know." He hung up and turned to Gale. "Long shot, but that seems to be our MO. I'll tell ya." He pointed at the screen. "We go back to Highsmith and threaten him with obstruction of justice. Valchek in New York in nineteen? He can't tell us he didn't know. Those two were tighter than Velcro."

"Fuck threaten. I want to bring him in." Gale spat the words out.

"Whoa, I'm usually the bull in the china shop. Let's talk to him first."

"He's going to lawyer up. You know that."

"Maybe we catch him off guard. Let's just show up at his office tomorrow at, say, eleven."

Tommy's phone rang. "Jesus, this is Rodriguez already." He put the call on speaker.

"I think the guy you sent me is him. I remember him because he was a dirt bag and had that 'vampires don't age' thing goin' on. He was targeting lone teenage boys—couldn't tell if it was for drugs or sex, but he made my skin crawl. I wanted to shut him down."

"Thanks, Rodriguez. Huge help."

"All right," Gale said. "Billy Highsmith in the morning, Lucas Rose tomorrow afternoon. Let's scare the shit out of them. And it's time to see Theo Hall." Gale felt that energy that always hit her when they were about to kick a door open on one of these cases. She also felt vindication: she'd be able to give Syd something positive on Tuesday. More than that, it would put them a step closer to solving this case, or maybe Duane *was* the solution and had been all along. Maybe this dead man *would* talk. Of course there was that nagging doubt that nothing was as it seemed with this case.

And then there was the equally nagging thought about what would happen between her and Syd once it was solved.

CHAPTER SIXTEEN

Syd's desktop computer with its two screens sat in the corner of her living room. It was a purposefully compact office: Syd had never wanted to slide into that ditch of work overtaking her personal life. If bringing work home meant confining herself to that space, it wouldn't be worth it, even if it came with a good bottle of wine and a river view. Now she sat quietly on the couch with a novel in her lap watching the tall, angular young woman named Kaylee, who'd folded herself into Syd's Aileron chair like a stork, run diagnostics on her computer and laptop. Tools unidentifiable to Syd were spread out on the desk. Cables ran everywhere. Kaylee's long straight brown hair shrouded her face from Syd's view, making it impossible to measure how things were going.

The cell phone ringing at eight this morning had surprised her, as had the number coming up from her old firm—it wasn't Elisa's. It was Kaylee telling her she'd be there in half an hour. Elisa had worked quickly, and Syd texted her a brief thank you.

She'd joked with the young string bean of a girl when she'd opened her door. "Why don't I think you're a scotch drinker?"

"Frank kept the bottle. I wanted the job."

"Oh?"

"Corporate hacking isn't challenging anymore. This is—it's why I got into this line of work. Frank knows how good I am. He said to say hi, by the way."

Minutes after sitting down, Kaylee confirmed Syd's fears: someone had downloaded spyware. Her stomach roiled.

"This'll take me some time, but I'll clean everything up. Then, I can install better fire walls, and set up end-to-end encryption on your laptop and your desktop, including email. No third parties can decode your data that way."

"No—you can't." Syd quickly walked over to her. "They can't know that I know."

"I don't understand."

"I'm sorry, I know you came thinking you were going to fix something bad, but you've already been an enormous help. You can't touch it. What I really need to know is, can you identify the hacker—or where it came from?"

Kaylee opened the list of files and scrolled down them, stopping at one that Syd had never seen. "This is them. Bananacreampie.exe. They kept sending you bogus emails from places they thought you bought from online like Amazon, which is an easy guess, New Balance—" Kaylee looked at Syd's sneakers. "And Samsung."

Syd remembered the incessant Samsung emails last winter only because she was going to need a new phone soon and wondered how they knew. "It wasn't random, was it?"

"No."

Syd got an uneasy feeling—had someone been as close to her as they'd been to Izzy, close enough to see the brand of sneakers she wore and know what phone she used?

"Whoever it is has been looking through emails, some files but not others, and your calendar. This is sophisticated stuff, Syd. I can try and track the IP address, the next step to finding out who it is."

"When did the spyware come in?"

"Mid-March. That's when I see some files you don't usually use being opened."

"What files?"

"Old company files." Kaylee looked up at her. "You really should delete those." She went back to the screen. "They combed through your email in one night, and you have thousands of them, which means they employed a word-search bot." She glanced up at Syd. "They went through your trash, too. And there was a lot of activity in your photo file that night—but none since."

Nauseated, Syd sank onto the chaise. All the photos of Isabella were there, everything from her birth photo to the latest Goth phase. "Kaylee, can anyone figure out where an online photo was taken?"

"Sure, if it has exif data. You right-click on it, select properties or information, and the GPS coordinates will appear."

"Can you—" Syd vaguely indicated the screen with her index finger and Kaylee opened the photo file. "The photo would say 'March Goth.'" It was the file where all her recent photos from Izzy were stored.

Kaylee located it, opened a photo and the coordinates came up with it. "There. You just need to be good in math and geography to find it."

"Thank you. Excuse me." Syd went to the bathroom, flipped up the toilet seat and was on her knees just in time. Waterhouse joined her, alarmed. She sat back and petted the cat to comfort him as much as herself. Lucas. Lucas knew she'd been to visit Ned that day in March. If there was a Kaylee at her old company, there were three at Rossiter Enterprises who could've found Izzy through that photo. She made her way back out to the living room.

"Here's a list of all the files used since mid-March. That should help you figure out what they're trying to find."

"They already found it. If I gave you an address, a physical address where someone lives, would that help you track the IP address?"

"For sure—well, unless this is routed through so many countries that it can't be traced. But I'm pretty damn good at that." Kaylee wrote down the Park Avenue address Syd gave her, Lucas's address, and got to work.

"What else has the spyware been looking at?"

"Every night at midnight, your calendar."

"Oh, fuck." Gale had figured it out very early on, but she'd never told her how. Or had she been erring on the side of caution? Either way, Gale was in that calendar.

"You could plant false information to throw them. I had a nasty ex once, a serious hacker, so I fooled him with old school stuff like changing names, dates, and places on the calendar. He bought it so hard he went to the decoy restaurant one night. I had a friend there watching. He got the message."

"This is more serious than that."

"Oh." Kaylee looked momentarily perturbed.

"And you're too young to have nasty exes."

"Not really. I had my first one at fourteen. Social media's a tricky thing." Kaylee went back to work.

Syd watched her for a moment and then realized she needed to flag Gale. A text would be the safest. *Brought in tech support from my old co. She found spyware. Certain it's how they ID'd Izzy.*

About five minutes later, her phone vibrated.

Gale: *Don't remove it! Can't let hacker know you know.*

Syd: *I know.*

Gale: *You shd hv let us do that.*

Syd: *Said the ugly stepchild.*

Gale sent back a scowling face emoji. *Fine. See you 6p.*

The tension Syd was carrying across her shoulders dissipated at the thought of this evening, and she went to the kitchen. The small canvas picnic bag was already on the counter. She packed it with the bottle of red wine, the corkscrew, paper plates, napkins, crackers, and a cheese knife. The list of the cheeses she'd pick up on her way to the precinct went into her pocket. Then she put the packet of Wyatt's old letters to his father that had finally come in the mail from Drew into her jacket pocket so she wouldn't forget them.

Kaylee appeared in the kitchen doorway. "Listen, this trace could take time. You want to show me where the Verizon and AT&T ION boxes are?"

Syd wasn't sure what she meant.

"The main boxes the phone companies use in this building."

"Oh, right. I found them yesterday in a basement workroom. Hold on." Syd went to the bedroom and returned with a small laundry bag and bottle of detergent. "In case we run into anyone—we're not supposed to be in that room."

In the elevator, Kaylee asked about security cameras.

"There's one when we get off, but I think we can avoid it."

Down the hall, Syd pointed to the door marked "Employees Only," and Kaylee gently tried the handle. It opened, she turned the light on in the small room and closed the door behind them. With a flat-head screwdriver she'd put in her back pocket, Kaylee opened the box.

"Hello," she said, and pointed to the wire attached to a bundle of them in the corner of the box. "Inductive tap. And it's being monitored remotely." She took a picture of it.

"What does that mean?"

Kaylee secured the phone box, quietly opened the door, and peeked into the hall. "I'll explain upstairs."

"I'm a little worried about your safety, Syd." Kaylee finally broke the silence in the elevator. "Should you maybe go to the police?"

"That's why this is happening—because I went to the police on a—very old matter, and someone isn't happy about that. In fact, it was the cold case police who thought I might've been compromised, but they didn't have a technician available who could do what you've done for me today, so, thank you."

"That sounds a little messed up, but when you're ready, call me and I'll fix you up. I can kill the tap then, too."

"I will. So—" Syd unlocked her apartment door. "How does this tap work?"

Kaylee opened the photo on her phone and explained the splitter on the fiber optic wire draining a bit of the flow of light—which were Syd's calls—to a monitoring port. "This means someone got into your building, gained access to this box and clipped the wire to your phone."

Syd knew immediately it was the repairman from several weeks ago.

Kaylee went over to the computer and peered at the screen. "You know what—the IP address this hacker used bounces all over the place. Russia, Zimbabwe, Scotland, you name it. I'm gonna work on this at home later. I have a friend who's even better at this than I am. He'll help me." She packed up her tools. "We'll find this tinydancer guy for you, too."

"Listen, let me pay you—" Syd pressed two bills into Kaylee's hand.

"Oh, no, Frank would kill me."

"Buy yourself lunch—he doesn't need to know."

Kaylee looked at the bills. "This'll buy me lunch for, like, two months!"

"Good. Because Frank's got scotch for, like, two months." Syd winked at her.

After she left, Syd texted Elisa. *It was worse than I thought. You're a life saver.*

Elisa: *Call me tonight. xo*

❖

When Gale appeared on the steps of the precinct, Syd stood at the bottom unable to take her eyes off her. The suit she wore, a denim blue so deep, shaded to purple overtones. NYPD cufflinks were in place on the lilac-on-white pinstripe shirt. The favored boots were navy blue as well. *She looks like a million bucks.* Syd's only thought as they walked toward Fifth Avenue was that they belonged together this way.

"Where are we going?" Gale asked when they passed through the entrance in the park's stone wall.

"Shakespeare. He's got his own corner, big ring of benches and trees They'll be that beautiful spring green right now." Syd closed her eyes and inhaled. "Do you smell that? That's the earth waking up after winter."

Gale inhaled. "I guess I don't always notice it." She nodded. "So are you okay with the phone tap, by the way? We can get a search warrant and pull that."

The question stopped Syd, the joy draining from her. "You said we can't let them know that we know." She took Gale's hand, the terror she'd felt earlier in the day returning to fill the space vacated by the joy. "If it's Lucas, I was screwed before I went to see him with Drew. He probably hacked my computer right after I visited Ned, and it wasn't enough, so he sent the guy to tap my phone and leave the blue envelope. Which means he knows I went to the police because you and Tommy have been in my calendar since the second time I came to see you. The spyware looks at it every night." She glanced down at their entwined hands, ran her thumb over the back of Gale's hand. It felt soft. Gale's grasp tightened the tiniest bit. "It's how they found Izzy. It scares me that someone went to Nebraska to take that picture for him."

"Or someone knew someone in Nebraska who would do that for him. Who else besides Lucas knew you well enough?"

"That's what's baffling me. I've had no contact with any of these men in nearly forty years." Syd reluctantly dropped Gale's hand and put hers in her jacket pockets to stop from reaching for her again. She felt the packet of letters there and pulled them out. "Here—for Tommy."

Gale tucked them into her pocket.

"It all comes back to my visiting Ned the day he died. If I'd gone to see him—even three days earlier, would Lucas ever have seen my name in the visitor's register?" Syd shaded her eyes against the setting sun. "What scares me more is that this spyware came in on an ad for Samsung phones. The hacker sent ads from places like Amazon and New Balance, which means they could've been standing right next to me somewhere looking at my clothes, watching me on my phone, and I didn't know it." She looked at Gale. "I'm wondering if they want to kill *me* now. They've proven they could get close enough."

"They could've taken long-range photos to see your sneakers and your phone, like they did with Izzy." Gale put her arm around Syd's shoulders. "We'll keep you safe." It was a small gesture, but the protective feeling it gave Syd contained a whole world. They walked down the sidewalk.

"If we look at it as 'they' being Lucas, he doesn't want to kill you, Syd. A fresh murder would call attention. He wants your silence."

"But I don't know anything."

"Your visit to Ned says otherwise. Whoever it is, they're holding their breath hoping we don't figure this out. So you understand why I need to know where you are all the time."

Syd nodded. She'd thought she was going to hate texting Gale every time she went out; instead, it was a relief, as though Gale's arm was always protectively around her like this.

They came to the clearing where Shakespeare's statue stood on an enormous pedestal, and sat on a bench facing it. "Is there any chance Zach Feinberg and Billy Highsmith still know each other, since Billy has a house in Connecticut?"

"I have no idea." When Syd sat back, she noticed the Bard, and the trepidation melted away. Someone had climbed up and placed a wreath of late spring flowers over the folios in his hand. Gale followed her gaze and smiled. Syd reached for the bottle of wine and the corkscrew, finally able to put her anguish away for a moment and revel in the display of colors around them. The new leaves billowing in the breeze were a delicate green, deep yellow daffodils planted at their bases. Purple, white, and pink lilac bushes dotted the area, too, pushing spring into early summer. But all too quickly, Syd felt her world pressing in on her again as Gale spoke.

"We're going back to see Billy again tomorrow and we'll be asking about Zach, among other things."

Syd wrestled the bottle of red wine open, two glasses on the bench between them. "I thought I ruined the possibility that Billy had anything of value. Why are you seeing him again?"

"You didn't. He didn't. He probably would've been that wary without anything from you. No. We found something else we think he could help us with."

Syd handed Gale a half-full glass, looking at her expectantly. Gale stared at the glass.

"I can't believe I agreed to this. It's illegal to have any open alcohol outside in the city."

Syd closed her eyes. "It never crossed my mind."

"And I wasn't putting two and two together when we spoke." She reached over and clinked Syd's glass. "Let's hope there are no patrols in the area."

Syd breathed a sigh of relief. "You said you found something?"

Gale put her glass down and took Syd's hand. "Arrest records for Duane Valchek from twenty nineteen, here in New York. Our facial recognition software ID'd him. He's still alive, Syd."

For the second time that day, Syd was shaken to her core. Her hand trembled, but Gale held fast as she recounted contacting the San Francisco Police Department on a one-in-a-billion guess, and how the payoff led to her finding a lifetime of petty arrests in California and cities up and down the East Coast.

"We've a mind to arrest Billy for obstruction of justice tomorrow but we're going to lean on him for Duane instead, and then Duane can give us Lucas."

A pain laced with sadness overtook Syd. "You think Lucas did kill Wyatt?"

"We're still focused on the stranger. We think he was known to one of these three men, and to Ned, so not actually a stranger. Perhaps he was someone they all knew, maybe a lost boy."

"No, I can't think Ned would do that. And—Wyatt picked men up all the time."

"Perfect cover for Ned, if Wyatt was going to go to the FBI about the embezzlement, or for Lucas if the jealous showdown going on between them erupted. Any of those boys seemed to need money. If the payout was big enough—"

"No."

"But you always thought it was murder for hire."

Syd finally set her glass down and looked away—what she thought and what she could face were two different things. Duane Valchek—she never thought. Could Ned have been that underhanded? The anger began to build in her again.

"Are you okay?"

"No." Syd stood up, walked around, and then came back to the bench. "The ironic thing is, I wanted to talk to you about jealousy the other night. I began to wonder if that wasn't the real motivation behind Wyatt's murder. There was such a merry-go-round of the same men in his life—Ned, Lucas, Theo, even Billy, apparently. But then it occurred to me. Wyatt went to that bar alone that night. And he never went anywhere alone." She gazed up at Shakespeare again. "I wonder if he was set up."

"He could've been."

"I don't think those detectives ever went to that bar to talk to anyone to see if they'd seen something."

"No, they didn't. I don't think they even knew about it. But, Syd, no one would've talked to them if they had."

"I'm sure you're right." Syd looked up at the passing clouds. They were all fluffy and white today. "I did some research the other day, online, about all those bars back then."

"We did that the first week. Thought something might jump out at us. It was a long shot, but as Tommy pointed out, this case seems to rest on them. But that theory was too long of a shot."

Syd pulled the article out of her bag and gave it to Gale.

Gale's eyebrows rose as she scanned the pages.

"Something jumped out at *me*." She opened the article to the third page and pointed to the message board at the bottom. "I found the bouncer from Bareback. From back in the eighties."

Gale's mouth fell open.

"I don't have a name yet. He goes by 'tinydancer80.' But the tech gal from my old company said she can find him, but it'll take time."

"You should let us do that."

"Ugly stepchild, remember?"

"Our tech guys live for this kind of stuff. Do I remember you saying you were bringing cheese? I'm starving."

Syd reached into the picnic bag and unpacked things. She wasn't hungry now, not in the face of all the information Gale had just given her about Duane. It swam in her mind, made her angry, sickened her, and she felt betrayed. She wanted to get into her bed and pull the covers over her head. But she put together a plate of cheese and sausage slices with a handful of crackers for Gale as she perused the article.

"I'll be damned," Gale said, her eyes on the article as she took a napkin from Syd. She bit into a piece of cheese sitting on a piece of salami and her eyelids closed. "Oh, this is so good. What is it?"

"Stilton and a soppressata salami. I have a Double Gloucester and a white sharp, too." Syd reached into the bag for them, trying hard to keep it together. How much had Lucas and Billy known all these years? When she'd questioned Billy about Duane's photo on Lucas's wall, she'd known something was wrong. Duane Valchek—alive. He'd been involved, hadn't he? With Lucas. Who'd lied right to her face. It had been him pulling her into this chaos with Izzy's photo and the threat, even though anything she'd known back then was all conjecture, all based on the things she'd seen and heard. She'd wanted it to add up, and so it had.

She was the only one who'd really loved Wyatt at a time when everyone around him wanted to destroy him. The lost boys had hated her for being someone in his life that they never could be. Ned had hated her very existence; it challenged his, somehow. And what was this going to mean for her safety? As tears began to blur everything, Gale's hand moved into her line of vision. She took Syd's hand again.

"This is hard. I know it is. But I also know how strong you are."

Syd nearly crumbled and Gale swung over behind her on the bench, embracing her from behind. Syd held her breath—she wouldn't cry.

"This is a lot coming at you on top of what you're already dealing with. What can I do to make it better?"

Syd shook her head. "You're already doing everything you can." She quirked around to look at Gale. "How close are you?"

"We'll know more tomorrow. When we talk to Billy. I knew he was stonewalling us. I'm hanging my shield on him knowing everything, especially since we found Duane. And if Billy gives us his whereabouts, then we can arrest them both to scare the shit out of them."

"But you don't actually have anything."

"We have outstanding warrants on Duane, and we'd have obstruction on Billy's part. It's a solid beginning. And they'd both be off the street, so I'd worry less about you."

"Me, or the case?"

Gale drew back to look at her. "You. It's always been about you."

The blush creeped up Gale's neck and Syd ran her finger over it. "Has it?"

Gale closed her eyes for a moment. "You received a threat concerning an unsolved cold case, so, yes. You might try my patience every time we get together, Sydney Hansen, but you're a very smart woman and your input on this case has been invaluable."

Gale's voice had wavered, and Syd raised an eyebrow. "Is that all?"

"No. But it will have to do for now. I have to solve this case first."

"And then?" Syd let her finger wander down Gale's throat to that sweet spot above her collarbone and was pleased to hear Gale's breathing become a little uneven.

"I've been thinking about that."

"Oh?"

"I—haven't reached a conclusion about how to get there from here."

"Should we work on that together?"

Gale cleared her throat. "We seem to be working on everything else together."

Syd felt a warmth flooding her, and she wanted to kiss Gale. Instead, she reached for their wine glasses and settled into Gale's embrace. They sipped in silence.

"We could maybe start by you coming to dinner on Saturday night."

Syd angled herself in Gale's arms to see her face. "Coming to dinner?"

"At my place. My father's been following this case, giving me a little advice here and there and he'd like to meet you."

"Giving you advice or meddling?"

Gale laughed. "I painted a really clear picture of him with you, didn't I?"

"I'd love to. What can I bring?"

"Yourself."

It wasn't until a few hours later when she texted Tommy to ask him if he could suggest something she could bring to the dinner since she knew he'd be there, too, that she found out that Gale's father wasn't just a retired detective; he was a legend. Bringing Sullivan the bottle of Macallan would be easy. Keeping him from sensing her growing feelings for his daughter would be another thing altogether.

CHAPTER SEVENTEEN

Gale felt guilty, not telling Syd about the evidence stolen from the boxes in the warehouse. She could've done it when Syd was taking in the scent of the earth and the flowers in Central Park, Gale's hand in hers. She could've mentioned it when Syd was opening the bottle of wine or slicing the cheese. And she certainly could've brought it up when she had Syd in her arms trying to allay her fears about so many things this case was raising for her. That would've kept Syd closer longer, and having Syd so close was heaven. But she hadn't. She wanted to shield Syd from everything, even though she knew she couldn't keep it all from her. Tommy had told her she was experiencing "white knight" syndrome. She'd both hated and loved that diagnosis.

As she came down the hall toward the office now, Gale noticed that the door was closed, the lights off. Odd. She'd never been one of those bosses who felt the need to be the first one in every morning; most of the guys were there by a quarter to eight anyway because that's when fresh coffee was brewing in the break room for the new shift. Had she missed something? She reached for the handle of the door only to find it locked. She jerked it several times.

"Hey, yeah, who's there?" Tommy called.

"It's me. What the hell?"

The door opened a sliver and Miller peeked out. He motioned her inside.

Gale did as she was told, inching through the slightly larger wedge that Miller allowed.

With the blinds drawn, it took a moment for her eyes to adjust to the darkness and the figures of Tommy and another detective bent over something on his desk. It was a pair of gold-rimmed aviator glasses, twisted out of shape, one arm broken off. A small, crumpled manila envelope and wrinkled, black-smudged plastic evidence bag sat nearby. She knew immediately that these were Wyatt's glasses. "What's going on?"

"That last flooded box we brought in? The one so badly damaged I didn't think it was gonna be worth going through after I saw the mold?" He held up a pair of latex gloves, the fingers black with the stuff. "Christmas came early this morning."

Gale looked at him, stupefied.

"I couldn't sleep so I came in to unload it, and this"—he held up the evidence bag—"was buried near the bottom. I brought it in here to work with because—"

"I keep Luminol at my desk," Miller interrupted.

"We know, Miller," the other cop said.

"Come look." Tommy motioned to Gale.

She put her bag and coat on her chair.

"Someone cleaned up the glasses somewhere along the way, but—" He held them up for her to see.

"Son of a bitch."

There was a splash of bright white light on the minute Phillips-head screw still attaching the one arm to the glasses, and a larger one visible around the thin curled arm that held the remaining nose pad in place. It was all they would need for the lab. Tommy gently poked at the nose pad with the tip of a pencil.

"This should move. It doesn't. So maybe there's dried blood under there."

"Let's hope it's not just Wyatt's blood," Gale said.

"We always said there was too much of it in that apartment for it to have been only his."

"Yeah, but on glasses?" Gale watched Tommy deflate and pivoted. "Okay, yeah, the guy could've been leaning over him. I get it."

"Or the glasses were the first thing to go, and his blood dripped on them later when he was tossing the place."

"Yup." One in a million chance, Gale thought, in a case that seems to be resting on them.

"That'd be why he cleaned them up, dontcha think? Let's drop this off at the lab on the way downtown. Maybe Christmas comes twice when we confront Billy."

"And maybe—" Gale took the packet of letters Syd had given her out of her briefcase. "Santa leaves something in the stocking."

"All right!" Tommy took the letters from her. "I been waitin' for this."

Gale glanced around the room. Was one of these detectives their mole? "Let's lock them up for now."

Tommy placed them in the evidence closet, and since no one else had anything in it, she pocketed the key.

"Hey, I got a strange call this morning," Tommy said as they headed out the door. "Some Fed lookin' to see did we have information on Billy Highsmith. Think he said his name was McCarthy."

"What for?"

"Wouldn't say, other than that he was working that old mob case that just blew, the one tied to the current administration, they're calling it LaundryGate—happened in the eighties, with the money laundering and the prostitutes?"

"Wait—was he intimating Billy was involved with that? How?"

"Dunno. He wouldn't give an inch so neither did I."

Gale stopped him. "We'd better figure this out fast, if their case is somehow tied to ours."

"The call did give me pause."

"Crap. No one said the prostitutes weren't women. We just assumed. I'm not losing this case to the Feds." Gale thought of what would happen to Syd if they did.

"So, we don't talk to them."

The first time Gale and Tommy came to the bank headquarters to talk to Billy, visitor IDs were waiting for them at the front desk. This time, they had their badges out. The guard on the desk phoned upstairs, then took his time printing their building IDs. But when the elevator doors opened on the executive floor, Helen was once again waiting for them, the same no-nonsense look on her face. A gray suit, white shell, pearls, and sensible black pumps completed her armor. Billy had told them during their first visit that she'd been at the assistant's desk when he arrived twenty-five years ago. Gale wondered if she'd come with the building. As they crossed the large Oriental rugs whose hues of rose, cream, and deep sand set off the opulent cherry wood furniture, Gale was aware once again of the thick pile meant to muffle the sound of footsteps. Helen nodded and lead them through the ornately carved archway and toward Billy's office.

The dark sand wall-to-wall carpeting of the beautifully appointed open area where the assistants sat at desks of cherry wood absorbed every noise as Gale and Tommy passed, but she suspected these women had sonar hearing developed over years of working in environments like this. She felt the eyes of every one of them on her even though no one acknowledged them.

As they neared the corner office with the magnificent view of Upper New York Bay and the Statue of Liberty, Gale deftly removed her handcuffs from her belt and curled the fingers of her left hand around them. Even as a child handling Sullivan's cuffs on the rare occasion he let her, she'd loved the shape of them, their heaviness, the cold steel. They didn't fit into the palm of her hand then, but there was still that finality about them, that sense of judgment. Obviously, Billy wasn't going to make a run for it; she simply wanted him to see that judgment in her hand as Tommy talked. She had the regulation zip-tie cuffs in her back pocket, but she'd kept the old metal ones because they made a statement that plastic never would.

Billy was standing at the window, behind his chair, his arms wrapped around his chest. He was in a bespoke banker's gray suit, which Gale admired. He turned to greet them, his starched white shirt accented by a club tie of grays, black, and white.

"Before you say anything, Detectives, I've called my attorney. He'll be here soon. He's advised me not to say anything."

He wasted no time, Gale thought.

"Not a problem We'll do the talking. You listen," Tommy said, dropping Duane Valchek's many arrest records on Billy's desk.

Helen noiselessly stepped out of the room, the door hushing shut behind her.

"Look familiar?"

Billy picked them up, perused them and slowly became a shade paler than his shirt.

"So much for that funeral in Malone, eh? We also bet you knew your old pal had a penchant for larceny and petty drug charges. So our first question is, where is he? Our second question is did you willfully obstruct justice?"

Gale let the handcuffs unloop from her palm. They made a clinking sound in the stillness of the room.

Billy looked at them dangling there. Gale was afraid he might vomit so she eyed the space for his trash can.

"Our third question? How much time do you want to do? The answers to the first two questions may go a long way toward determining that."

"Look, I—"

A series of emotions flickered over Billy's face so quickly that Gale was reminded of the way people looked in strobe lighting. She caught the fear and the shock, but she also thought she saw a deep abiding anger.

"I don't know where he is now."

Gale let out a slow, quiet breath. Duane Valchek *was* alive.

"When was he here last and did you see him?"

"I always see him. Briefly. He hasn't been here since twenty nineteen."

The office door opened. Gale and Tommy turned to see a dapper gentleman of about eighty walk in, a briefcase in his hand. He hadn't stopped long enough to give Helen either the homburg still on his head or the coat over his arm. His bright blue eyes were trained on Billy like twin gun barrels, and the Van Dyke beard and moustache framed an amused smile that Gale was sure hid a steel trap.

"All talking stops now, please, Detectives. My name is Adrian Schnabel. I'm Mr. Highsmith's attorney. If you want anything further from him, we'll discuss immunity first."

"Immunity?" Tommy asked.

Gale smiled. "Means our Mr. Highsmith has information that's valuable to this investigation. But we'd have to talk to the DA first."

"You don't even have an ADA yet," Adrian said. "I checked."

"Doesn't mean we won't in—" Gale glanced at her watch. "An hour."

"I doubt it."

Gale cocked her head at Adrian like he'd been a misbehaving boy. "We found a missing piece of evidence this morning. It's at the lab now being tested for DNA. Should be enough to identify our murderer. That's something a DA would be very interested in. Along with other evidence we've uncovered, should be enough."

"I'm going to guess it's all circumstantial, but what piece of evidence, may I ask?"

"You may not." Gale swung the handcuffs around her finger and back into her palm. "In the meantime, we'll take Mr. Highsmith in for questioning on the obstruction of justice charge and hold him for the requisite forty-eight hours." Gale looked Billy up and down. "Prison jumpsuits come in orange, not banker's gray."

"Adrian—" Billy's voice held a note of pleading.

"Why don't we all sit down here and see what agreement we can come to?" Adrian motioned to the overstuffed chairs and coffee table. Gale and Tommy looked at one another and made their way to the chairs. Adrian opened Billy's office door.

"Helen, coffee, please, and perhaps a few croissants."

"I'm not interested in croissants," Tommy grumbled. "I want to know why you stonewalled us, where Valchek is now, what he's been doing all these years and where, and why he comes to New York."

Adrian held up his hand, sat down, snapped his briefcase open and took out a legal pad. He brought a fountain pen from his breast pocket and uncapped it. "Stonewalling, Duane's whereabouts now and—past forty years, you said?" He continued writing. "Trips to New York. Let's see."

"Add obstruction to that list," Tommy snapped.

The steel trap smiled at him. "I'm not sure we're going to answer any of these questions because they go to the heart of your accusation—"

"Not an accusation, counselor, a reality. There was no funeral in Malone, so for decades your client has been harboring a fugitive."

"From murder? No. From some parking tickets and pot sales. Knock yourself out."

At the precise moment that Gale held up her finger, cuffs dangling, Helen walked into the room with a tray of coffees and a plate of croissants. "We can take him in for obstruction and aiding and abetting a criminal we are seeking in a murder investigation."

Helen set the tray down, her glance at Billy inscrutable, and left.

"Like I said," Gale continued. "Requisite forty-eight hours. Won't look good when we walk him out of here even if we drape his suit coat over these cuffs."

Billy dropped his head into his hands. "Please, Adrian."

"You don't have evidence of that murder, but tell them where he's been for the last forty years, Billy."

Gale was curious that Adrian seemed to know everything about everything they were about to discuss. When had Billy called him?

"They already know. They have his arrest records."

"Tell us why he's been on the run," Tommy said.

"I honestly don't know. He left the city in a hurry that December after Wyatt's death. He wouldn't tell me why. He only said that he didn't murder Wyatt, that he did something else. He comes to New York every three years to see Lucas. It used to be Ned he'd see. He's here and gone." Billy rubbed his eyes with his thumb and forefinger. "Obviously he's lived all over, staying out of sight."

Like a bolt of lightning and a clap of thunder, it hit Gale that Duane could've been behind the photograph of Izzy that was sent to Syd.

"Ned made me lie about Duane's death. He concocted the story, then sent me to his place in the Hamptons that January with Duane's uncle, like we went to a funeral, and told me to never let anyone know. I've had to stay quiet all these years to protect myself."

"Until the internet caught up with you," Gale said. "Your Franklin Academy classmate Sam Stokes says to say hi to you, by the way. He was most helpful in debunking the rumors of Duane's funeral."

A look of disgust crossed Billy's face.

"Duane had an uncle in New York," Tommy said. "He still around? Where can we find him?"

"Retired NYPD. Moved out to Long Island years ago."

Gale went cold. She looked at Tommy, but he was already taking his notebook out.

"You got a name and address?"

"No. I mean, I lost track of him. Pete Nowak."

"Will that suffice for now, Detectives?" Adrian asked. "According to my client, all Duane's business seems to be with Lucas Rose, so that would make him your man of the hour."

"No, it won't suffice," Tommy said. "When is Duane's next visit?"

"Umm—" Billy shook his head as if to clear cobwebs. "Soon."

"Is this a rock-solid schedule? Does he call Lucas, or does Lucas call him?"

"Duane calls me. I call Lucas."

"Which means Lucas is at a remove from Duane."

"Yes."

"Which also means you know how to reach Duane."

Billy looked at Tommy, incredulity stamped on his face.

"Call him. Tell him Lucas isn't waiting for his call because he needs to see him."

"I don't like this, Detective," Adrian said, standing.

Without moving from her relaxed position, Gale held up the handcuffs and he sat back down.

"Where do you usually meet with Duane?" Tommy asked.

"I don't. He meets Lucas somewhere and leaves the city again almost immediately."

"Okay. Set up the next meeting."

"Now?"

"We'll all be very quiet while you talk to him. Won't we, counselor?"

Adrian nodded. "Bill, I'll see to it that giving up Duane goes a long way toward any charges against you being dismissed."

Billy looked like he might cry, but he got up, took his cell phone out of his pocket, and walked to the window. Tommy followed him. Billy seemed angry about this, but he placed the call.

"Now what, Detective?" Adrian quietly asked Gale.

She thought for a moment. "You're not Lucas's attorney, too, are you?"

Adrian's smile came and went, and he shook his head. "I would never have thrown Mr. Rose to you wolves if I was."

"I'm not sure we should be giving you our game plan, but since it's ever-changing. Lucas Rose is our next visit. We'd best not find out Billy called him." She cleared her throat. "We'd like to convince him that it will be in his best interests to cooperate with us in Duane's visit as well. You will keep your client available to us, of course, or we'll move heaven and earth to bring him in."

"Understood."

Tommy returned to his chair, Billy behind him. "Our man Duane isn't the low-level drug dealer we thought he was. He's more mid-level. He's currently at the Cannes Film Festival to supply certain clients, but he's graciously agreed to fly back week after next."

"You're kidding me," Gale said.

Tommy held up a piece of paper. "We can't bring him in, but we've got his number. We can run a check, see if that's where he really is, and if anything goes amiss—" He turned to Billy. "You'll be on the hook for Duane."

"Oh, I don't know about that," Adrian said.

"Oh, I do, counselor. My JD from NYU and my lengthy police career tell me so."

"You're a lawyer?" Adrian was genuinely amused.

"And an expert courtroom witness in the psychology of sociopathic murderers," he said, looking at Billy. "Nice meeting you, counselor." Tommy walked to the door, Gale behind him. She turned around.

"Bill, are you still friends with Zach Feinberg?"

The expression on Billy's face became that of a deer caught in headlights.

"I know you knew him back in the day. He lives in Connecticut now, not far from you, has a practice in plastic surgery."

"Does he? No, I had no idea."

Gale nodded. "I see. I hope you're not obstructing again, are you? Wouldn't be smart on your part."

Billy looked at Adrian and he nodded. "I see him now and then at parties, maybe we run into each other at the gardening store in the spring. Stephen and I don't socialize with him, if that's what you mean."

Gale clipped the handcuffs back onto her belt. "That was exactly what I meant." She walked out the door where Helen stood next to Tommy waiting to escort them back to the elevator.

"Did you tell Syd that Duane's still alive?" Tommy asked in the elevator.

"Yes."

"And?"

"She was overwhelmed."

They listened to the quiet of the elevator as it floated down the thirty-two floors.

"Duane Valchek has an uncle in the NYPD," Tommy mused.

"Retired. How did we miss that?"

"Duane was dead, remember? And the uncle's not Valchek. We need to call him in."

"We can't. We can't let anyone know we know Duane's alive." Gale let out a big sigh. "And I know we were going to interview Zach Feinberg anyway, but now we need to see him sooner rather than later," Gale said. "Billy admitted knowing him."

"I already set up the interview for tomorrow. Figured we could use a nice spring drive to Connecticut, look around both towns, have lunch. They got nice clam chowder in that state."

Gale smiled.

CHAPTER EIGHTEEN

Gale loved the art of surprise. Laying out everything for Lucas just as they'd done for Billy a mere two hours ago, Gale half expected to see an attorney walk through the door, but none appeared. Lucas recovered his arrogance quickly. Gale listed the charges they could bring against him, and it was breathtaking to watch him wave them off like they were so much detritus that didn't concern him. But handcuffs have a way of kicking the legs right out from under arrogance. A moment later, Lucas knew where Duane was, that he was coming to New York soon, and he was offering him up in lieu of those charges. Gale put her handcuffs away, saying nothing about dropping anything, urging him to go on instead, interested to see how far into the hole he would dig himself. She hadn't told Billy or his attorney that they didn't need Lucas to be part of the trap to pick up Duane—they only needed Billy. And his silence, which he'd already broken if Lucas knew Duane would be back in the city soon. Things went as deep between Billy and Lucas as she'd suspected. She'd asked Billy's attorney to keep his client muzzled. Adrian Schnabel hadn't kept his word. But they weren't going to keep theirs, either. They weren't going to turn around and arrest Billy. They needed him to get to Duane. So for now they'd let both Billy and Lucas think they were off the hook. Until they had Duane.

Like Billy, Lucas swore that Duane hadn't killed Wyatt, that he'd done something else that led him to leave the city for good in 1982, but Ned kept him in the dark about what that was.

"Ned paid Duane to disappear. And then he set him up with a bank account in San Francisco so he could wire funds to him. You know, until he got on his feet, found a place to live, got a job."

Gale was stunned. This was more than the smoking gun they'd been looking for—it was a bomb that went right to the heart of motive. But she had to hide her reaction. "And did he? Get a job?"

"If you call drug dealing a job," Lucas said sarcastically. "He's made a career out of it, and of living off Ned's largesse." Lucas looked out the window. "Stupid son of a bitch."

"No love lost, I see."

It had been threatening to rain all morning and now lightning flashed on the other side of the Hudson, followed seconds later by distant thunder.

"I never liked the little shit. He was a petty criminal and a thief then, still is, and you can add 'blackmailer' to that list."

"Ah, now we're getting somewhere," Tommy said. "So you can see how we think you might've been obstructing by not telling us all this the first time we questioned you? Enlighten us about the blackmailing."

Gale wondered why it was so simple for Lucas to roll on Duane now. She also wondered if there was a scheme afoot involving Billy.

"He's lived off Ned for forty years, man!" Lucas scowled at Tommy. "Ned was so frightened of him he made me set up a trust in perpetuity years ago. But that spigot will be turned off after his next visit. No more money. Ned's dead, this is not my problem."

"And you're not frightened?" Tommy asked. "You think this 'little shit' will walk away from—how much money are we talkin' here?"

"He comes to New York to pick up a hundred fifty thousand in cash every three years."

Jesus, maybe I need Lucas to be looking after my *investments.*

"And no, I'm not frightened. Duane is a gnat in my world." Lucas folded his arms. "There's not much left in the fund anyway. I stopped reinvesting it right after Ned went into the old fart's home two years ago."

Gale almost laughed at the irony since Lucas was seventy-five, but then a light bulb clicked on. "So you never intended to continue with these payments once Ned was gone."

"No." Lucas's face was hard, his eyes dark pools, and for the first time, Gale saw in them that he couldn't have killed Wyatt: he was too confident about turning Duane out, stopping payments that were surely hush money, and handing him over to the law. Duane was coming more sharply into focus as Wyatt's murderer, probably the one hired by Ned. But fifty thousand a year for life—was that enough to buy someone's silence? Although if he was flying to a film festival in Europe to sell his "wares," he was probably doing just fine and Ned's money was counter-insurance for both of them. A heavy rain began pelting the windows.

"Tell us about Zach Feinberg. You're friends with him."

"Not really. The last time I saw him, Billy and I were having drinks at Le Rivage in the theater district. Maybe two years ago. Zach and his husband walked in. They'd been to see a show. Of course we had to ask them to join us. But it was so boring—all the three of them talked about was what to do with aging parents. I don't have any, so I ordered a double whiskey."

Gale almost felt sorry for Lucas—no parents, even if they were a challenge in their old age; no husband, his sugar daddy having died over a decade ago. Maybe he had a radiant circle of friends, but if you were left with an empty bed at night… She turned away from a thought that was too close for comfort.

When Gale brought up the red ledgers, Lucas's demeanor changed—he sat up straight and pulled his body in. "What ledgers?"

Gale was having none of it. If Billy knew about them, and got equally nervous, then Lucas was stonewalling. "Don't. We have them both."

Lucas paled to the point that Gale wondered if he'd pass out right in his chair. "I'm sorry, Detective—I don't know—"

"I can finish reading you your rights," Gale said, "and take you in."

Lucas focused on a spot well beyond Gale, a spot that could've been 1982. "I thought they were gone."

"What made you think that?"

"Ned told me."

Lucas's breathing was shallow, thready—Gale could hear it. What was it about the ledgers that was setting off both Billy and

Lucas? Along with everything in Syd's box of evidence that she and Tommy had combed through so carefully in the past weeks, they'd studied both of the ledgers until she felt like a human scanner. They'd broken the code on the waterlogged drug sales ledger relatively easily, the exception being the flip side of each page; it seemed so much like Syd's ledger, which they hadn't been able to puzzle out.

Gale was tired of the obfuscation. She confronted Lucas, dropping her voice into the low gravelly register Tommy used. "Billy was very interested in those ledgers, too."

"No, I—"

Gale laid the handcuffs on Lucas's desk. "I know it's your handwriting in one of the ledgers. Along with Wyatt's. We're going to want you to decode them for us. Maybe you come down to the station and do that now, hmm?"

Lucas shook his head, almost imperceptibly.

"Well, then," Gale stood. "You have the right to remain silent—"

Lucas opened a desk drawer and at the same time, Tommy stood, his gun drawn. Lucas threw both hands up.

"No, I need to show you something—please!"

Gale came around the desk and peered into the drawer. She kept her emotions in check as she took a pair of latex gloves out of her pocket, put them on, and picked up the pale blue envelope sitting on top of everything in the drawer. It matched the one Syd had handed her that first day at the station. "This?"

Lucas nodded. Tommy holstered his gun.

"I got it right before you came to see me. The first time."

Gale opened the envelope carefully. It contained the same *New York Times* obituary for Ned Rossiter. Scrawled across the bottom of the article in the same black ink were the words "I want the red ledger or one of you is dead." She showed it to Tommy and turned to Lucas for an explanation.

By now, the storm had ramped up, thunder and lightning dazzling and loud, right overhead, the rain driving hard against the windows. The fluorescent lighting was all the brighter for the darkness blanketing the city, and in its illumination, Lucas looked haggard.

"One of you?" Gale asked.

"You've reopened a can of worms with Wyatt's case. Those ledgers implicate very powerful people who were at the top of their professions and New York society."

"It was forty years ago," Tommy said. "They're dead. These came from someone very much alive who knows what's going on now. One of you who?"

Lucas shook his head. "They're connected to that FBI case, LaundryGate." Lucas looked at Gale plaintively. "I am afraid for my life. I don't know who it is and I don't know what they mean by 'one of you.'"

In the moment it took Gale to calculate what to do with Lucas's confession, Tommy pointed the way.

"Then Wyatt's murder hinges on those ledgers, not the embezzlement. What do you know about the ledgers, Lucas?"

"We were the prostitution ring. Those red ledgers were the accounts and they contained powerful people."

Gale was taken aback. This was big. FBI big. But nothing in anything the media was reporting on this burgeoning scandal indicated a male prostitution ring had been at the center of it. Why hadn't that come to light?

"That's why the FBI called you last week," Gale said to Tommy. "Lucas, I'm assuming Ned ran the ring?"

"No. I did. But the money went to Ned."

"Who used your services?" Gale asked.

He reeled off names, men and women both who were at the top of their game in that era, who either had or were busy amassing millions: bluebloods, politicians, socialites, athletes. And the mob. Gale grabbed her notepad and wrote as quickly as he spoke, recognizing some of New York's and DC's best, brightest, and lowest.

"These were Ned's people, big spenders, the Forbes four hundred. And those don't come without mob ties. We showed 'em a real good time and then we picked their pockets."

"What makes you think one of them is behind this?" Tommy asked.

"Who else would want those ledgers gone? Especially if the FBI is closing in?"

Until they had the code from the ledger that had been in Wyatt's desk, there was no way to know. Gale had researched Ned's circle, at least everyone they found in the media from that era, and they knew who was still alive, where they were, and who might stand to lose something. She'd wondered for days if their mole was that someone who had figured out how to get an ear inside the precinct. But she couldn't lose sight of this opportunity now with Lucas. "You know so many of the people involved that you could probably help us unravel the code."

"It's in one of the ledgers."

"The code? No way. We been over 'em with everything but a laser," Tommy said.

"Wyatt told me—he put the code in one of the ledgers."

Tommy looked at Gale, puzzled.

"What about Sydney Hansen?" Lucas asked.

"What about her?" Gale felt suddenly protective.

"She wanted something when she showed up at my door. I'm not stupid. What did she tell you about the ledgers?"

"She didn't know anything about them."

"And you believed her? The girl Wyatt groomed to take his place when he knew it was all coming to an end?"

Gale's stomach plummeted several stories. "When what was coming to an end?"

"C'mon, you must've figured out Wyatt was going to the police about the embezzlement. He thought it would be like a whistleblower thing and he'd get off easy. But he was still afraid, so he was pouring everything he knew into Syd because he never wrote anything down and she was an organized machine."

Gale felt a clenching in her stomach. She got hot and then cold. Could Tommy have been right several weeks ago, that Syd knew more than she'd told them?

"So Ned had him killed," Tommy said.

Lucas looked at his hands in his lap. He shook his head and said "Jesus" so quietly, Gale almost missed it.

"Ned said he forgot something at Wyatt's apartment that night. I got angry, I told him not to come back to me if he was going to him. But he called me later from Ben Ford's apartment, said he'd gone there instead, asked me to forgive him. There was something in his voice that scared me, though." He looked up, surprised. "But what I heard wasn't psychobabble 'I just killed someone' nerves."

"How do you know?' Tommy asked. "You ever killed anyone?"

"I don't appreciate the attitude, Detective, especially when I'm cooperating." He brushed away a tear. "Ned never asked anyone for forgiveness. It was out of character. I think he was at a loss to be at that juncture with me."

Gale, still standing behind Lucas, shook her head at Tommy. Ben Ford was a major puzzle piece, but for the life of her, she didn't know how it fit. Yet. "Ben Ford, the attorney? You're sure he called you from his place?"

The question stopped Lucas. Gale recalled the unsigned second will of Wyatt's—Syd had shown it to her, the one that left everything to Ned and Ben. Lucas had been a witness. How else might Ben have been involved? And what else might Syd have taken? Did Syd, in fact, know more than she was telling them? Tommy suspected she did—he'd made that clear to her.

"Well, it was quiet in the background, but Ben sounded steady, like he always did."

"They could have been calling you from his office. They could've been gaslighting you. How well did you know him?" Gale asked.

"He was the first one to take me under his wing. I'd have known if he was covering anything up for Ned. I'd have heard it in his voice." Lucas sighed. "He's long gone now, AIDS. Ned put him through law school, the first of us he did that for. If Ned had killed Wyatt, Ben would've been the person to turn to. But you couldn't walk into that posh Park Avenue building where he lived with blood all over you."

But you could walk into a deserted office building, Gale thought.

"Even if you had a coat on the doorman would've seen it. And it was way downtown from Wyatt's. Ned didn't walk anywhere. And he couldn't have taken a cab covered in blood."

Gale saw tears in Lucas's eyes. "What?"

"Ned couldn't have done it. He loved Wyatt. It was a real problem for me." He brushed at his eyes, a small laugh escaping him. "And for Theo. Because I loved Wyatt, too." Lucas took a tissue from a box behind his desk and wiped his nose. "So did Syd. It was the most fucked-up relationship I've ever been in. And it still hurts all these years later." Lucas reached for a second tissue as the tears he'd held at bay a moment ago slowly spilled over and down his cheeks. "I should've hated Wyatt for leaving me so easily. I tried to hate Ned, but you couldn't hate Ned. As screwed up as he was, he was—magic. It was an awful merry-go-round but I didn't want to get off."

Lucas's words brought Syd to Gale's mind again—it was the same reference Syd had used the evening they'd talked in Central Park when she'd intimated that jealousy could've been behind Wyatt's murder instead of the embezzlement. *Should I be worried? Was Syd dropping a crumb?* It sparked that anger in her again, anger at Syd for being where she shouldn't, even in Gale's head; for the possibility that she might be guilty, but of what, Gale wasn't sure; and at herself for even having feelings for Syd.

"But you did get off, didn't you? You and Ned didn't last long," Tommy said, his tone sarcastic.

"Wyatt's death put a pall over everything. It broke us all," Lucas said, his sarcasm and arrogance gone.

"All who? Who else was on the merry-go-round with the three of you? Duane? Theo?" Maybe, Gale thought, we haven't paid enough attention to Theo.

Confusion played out across Lucas's face.

Gale leaned forward. "Wyatt's apartment looked like a slaughter-house, Lucas." Kicking a man while he was down had always been a tried-and-true way for Gale to get a confession in these cases.

"No, don't."

"It was crime of passion."

"I don't know, okay? I don't know. Oh God." Lucas stood up and went to the window.

Gale looked at Tommy, whose eyes had gone wide.

"I think I should consult my lawyer," Lucas said.

"One more question."

Lucas whirled around. "No!"

"Did you boys party with any parents at the school?"

His eyebrows rose in surprise. "Who told you that?"

"I'll take that as a yes."

"Leave my office, please. Now."

"Your attorney?"

"Get his number from my assistant."

Gale followed Tommy out of the office, but she turned in the doorway and held up the evidence bag continuing the blue envelope. "One of you is dead. You might want to think about that and talk to us since we have the ledgers. Maybe we can help you stay alive." Lucas's face fell. Gale left.

Five minutes later, Gale and Tommy sat in the parked car, the rain tattooing the roof as they stared up Eighth Avenue, traffic hissing past on the wet pavement.

"Jesus," Tommy said, his hands gripping the steering wheel.

"Yeah." Gale held up the blue envelope in the evidence bag. "I sure didn't see this coming."

"We're gonna have to find out if Billy got one."

"I'll deck that asshole if we see him again. I'm running out of patience."

"But he walked right into our trap, Gale. It was a gift."

"Yeah, I know." She tossed the evidence bag into the glove compartment. "We have to comb that list we put together of everyone in Ned's life. Someone there is the key."

"We're definitely pivoting to the ledgers?"

"I don't know." She rubbed the back of her neck. Her whole body ached. "I keep going back to Wyatt's apartment. It was a crime of passion. And not about names in a book."

"What if everything's connected? Jealousy to the money, the money to jealousy? But—to the embezzlement or the ring?"

Gale ran her hands through her hair and looked at Tommy ruefully. "I'm beginning to wonder. And Ned and Wyatt seem to be at the nexus in both cases."

"Do we need a new Venn diagram?"

"I'm hampered without knowing the code to that ledger. Let's take a good look at that book when we get back, maybe take it apart at the seams."

"I gotta ask. Especially after this interview. Should Syd be on our list?"

Gale studied him for a moment, and then concentrated on the rain strafing the windshield.

"We have to look at her, Gale. And you wouldn't be the first detective who—"

"I know."

"Okay. Just sayin'. And I thought Friday we should go up to Beacon, see Theo Hall. But he's savin' us gas, called to say he'll be in the city and can come to us, eleven o'clock."

Gale nodded. "I think we should go see Judge Albrecht, get a tap-and-trace and a pen register on Lucas's phones, cover our bases."

"Agreed. Let's see who he calls and who calls him while we're waiting on Duane."

"And I want Syd in the station house on Friday at the same time as Theo. We can use the ledgers as an excuse, tell her we need her to look at something in them again."

"You want me to call her?"

"No. I will. She'll know something's up if you call. But I want you to sit with her that morning. I'll interview Theo."

"You're sure?"

No, I'm not, Gale thought. I want to look into those ice-blue eyes and know that she's the woman of integrity I thought she was from the beginning. "You're better at those small talk questions than I am." Her throat suddenly dry, she took a swig from the water bottle in the cup holder.

Tommy pulled out into traffic. "Okay, let's call on Albrecht."

On the drive downtown, all Gale saw through the curtain of rain dappling brilliant colors in the headlights was Sydney Hansen.

The menus sat on the table unopened, a half-full bottle of sauvignon blanc next to them.

"It's been a long time since I've felt like this," Syd said after recounting for Elisa the events that transpired in Central Park between her and Gale. "We obviously can't get involved while the case is open. At least she won't."

"Would you, if she did?"

"Apparently, I try her patience. I need to change that."

"Didn't answer my question."

Syd looked at the traffic snaking along East Sixty-Fourth Street. The night was mild, perfect for outdoor tables on the sidewalk. "I want this to be different. To go right."

"You're invested in her."

Elisa could always read her. "Yes. We might clash, but she makes me feel like I'm the only woman in the world when I'm with her."

"Then you've finally put down the torch you've been carrying for Marie."

"I doused that a long time ago. It just left a very deep scar."

"A revolving door scar."

"I never wanted to get hurt like that again."

"Syd, it happens to everyone. It's part of the package."

"Not if you choose not to sign for the package."

"And yet, I sense your pen is poised."

"We still haven't had our 'getting to know you' period."

Elisa laughed. "Oh, sweetiedahling, what do you think you've been doing on your weekly walks with your handsome detective? And now she's invited you to have dinner at her place, to meet her father. I didn't even bring Ari home to *my* parents until we were engaged."

"Not necessarily to meet her father. This is just one of our weekly meetings. And her father told *her* he wanted to meet *me*."

Elisa crumpled into a fit of quiet giggles.

"Okay, fine, thank you for pointing out how totally ridiculous that sounded." Syd tossed the wine cork at her.

"Ohhhh, sweetiedahling, what are friends for?" She picked up the menu and fanned herself. "Oh! Wait, before I forget—all this talk about your detective just reminded me." Elisa opened her purse and pulled out an envelope. "Kaylee came up to my office with this today, asked me to give it to you."

Syd tore the envelope open, took out the piece of paper, and scanned the slanted penmanship. Everything inside her juddered— Kaylee had found tinydancer80. "George Oakley, 380 West 95th St. 4R." The phone number had a 212 area code. That meant George Oakley was a long-time resident of the city, here before the needed addition of other area codes. So he could be who he said he was, the bouncer at Bareback in the '80s. Kaylee had also found his cell phone number.

Elisa was recounting some office gossip that ordinarily would've made Syd laugh, but her mind had already begun to race. She wanted to get up from the table, hail a cab, and ring George Oakley's doorbell.

Syd had to concentrate hard for the next hour to telescope her world down to what was in front of her and pay attention to Elisa. The envelope in her pocket was practically burning a hole there. She knew what she wanted to do with it.

❖

Gale stretched out, put her feet on the ottoman, and stuffed a handful of popcorn into her mouth. She hadn't felt this relaxed in weeks. Sullivan changed the channel to the Mets game.

"We don't care about the Oriole at-bat against the Yankees, do we?"

"No, I'm happy to watch the Met lineup go down one, two, three."

Sullivan chuckled.

As she picked up the small bottle of Coca Cola she'd been nursing, her cell phone vibrated on the coffee table with an incoming text. She picked it up.

Syd: *I found tinydancer80.*

Gale was astonished. In the same moment, she knew what Syd was going to do. Her persistence and resolve were at once an albatross and a gift: she was truly Ahab pursuing Moby Dick. Gale quickly texted back: *Do not, repeat do not go see him!*

A moment went by, then another. Gale's agitation hit seven on a scale of one to ten. *I know you want to, but don't. I need to handle this—he might have a description of our murderer.*

Another moment ticked by. Gale stared at her phone.

"Everything okay?"

Reluctantly, she told her father what was going on.

"Well, you know what they say. If you can't fight 'em, join 'em."

"What do you mean?"

"Go with her. Tell her you'll meet her at this guy's place. Because you know that's where she's headed."

Gale stared at him. How did *he* know Syd so well? Or was it that he knew her better? "Is this something in your book of crime solving?"

"No, but it's in hers because this is a very personal thing for her, and you don't seem to be able to corral her. If she's the walking compendium you say she is, then harness that. She's already gotten you places you wouldn't have gone without her, right? So if she's found a guy says he was there, I'd be halfway to wherever she says he is right now."

Gale let out a low, exasperated growl and texted Syd: *Give me the address, I'll meet you there.* A moment later, Syd sent it. Gale shoved her feet into her sneakers, took the stairs to her apartment two at a time, grabbed her coat, car keys, and a file from her briefcase, and slammed out the door that led to the fire escape staircase on the side of the townhouse.

This woman is going to be the death of me!

CHAPTER NINETEEN

George Oakley's brownstone had wide white cement steps. Their broad waist-high white walls swept down and curved outward to meet the sidewalk, an encompassing welcome. The polished wooden front doors inset with large oval windows gave the building a ghostly feel at this hour of someone watching, even with lights shining in various white-framed windows against the blue-gray facade. It didn't help that the streetlights cast ethereal shadows outside their circles of illumination. Syd paced part-way up and down the block, her hands in her pockets.

Gale would be mad. Syd was once again breaking procedure, crossing a line. Again. Syd thought her defense, "why wait," was a rock-solid argument. Because George Oakley was important, break-policy important. She'd had a feeling that if she texted her, Gale would come—it was that promise of protection as well as that sense of duty. They'd butted heads over and over, but this time Syd was right: this interview required her eyes, ears, and knowledge of Wyatt's life against George's answers. What purpose would waiting serve?

A lone car turned onto the street, stopped in front of George's building, and double-parked. Syd walked toward it as Gale put her NYPD placard on the dashboard.

"You look a little discombobulated," Syd said tentatively when Gale stood in front of her.

"I was watching baseball with my dad. I had a nice bowl of hot buttered popcorn in my lap, a bottle of Coke, and I was enjoying being a little less worried than I have been in days. The Yankees were winning. The Mets were losing."

Syd knew that look of calm on Gale's face; it preceded the controlled anger Gale let peek out if its cage but rarely unleashed. She braced herself.

"You know what's most amazing to me? How you manage to show up when I least expect it. And upend whatever I had planned."

"I know, I'm—"

"And you know what else amazes me? That I tell you something and you listen and nod and agree, usually begrudgingly, and yet here we are in front of the apartment of someone I know nothing about because I didn't have the time to do a background check on him."

"Oh, I never thought—"

"And here—*here* is the most amazing thing of all. Even with all your fears, you had to do this. *And* you knew I would come. I gave you that card and you played it."

"You're right. I had to."

Gale ran her hands through her hair, exasperated. "I didn't give you carte blanche to chase this kind of lead and invite *me* to join *you*. *I* invited *you* into the investigation because you're *my* library of information. I am not *your* ride-along."

Gale was standing at the edge of the halo of light from a nearby streetlamp. The gold flecks in her hazel eyes seemed bright. The light glinted off the silver of her hair. Syd wanted to touch it, put her hand on Gale's shoulder. *My instincts are right,* she wanted to say. *You have to trust me.* And then that anger bubbled up again, not nearly as hot as when she carried it into Ned's room at White Willows, but still there, the catalyst that was keeping her going.

"I brought you Duane. I brought you Lucas. I brought you Billy. And now George Oakley. Carpe diem, Detective." Syd hated putting that distance back between them, but she needed to make a point.

"No." Gale stepped closer. "We would have—"

"I found the spyware, but only because you knew it was there. And now I've brought you the one person who might've seen what happened that night to one of the few people in this world that I ever truly loved."

The words hit home. Gale stilled, her eyes on the sidewalk. "I'm—sorry."

Syd hadn't meant to remind her of Kate, not in the middle of all this. She wanted to take her into her arms, but she couldn't.

Gale cleared her throat and put her hands on her hips. "Do we even know if this guy is home?"

"I called him from the restaurant and pretended I had a wrong number. That was—"

"Forty-five minutes ago." She held her hand out toward the steps.

"What do we say after we ring the bell?" Syd asked as they reached the landing.

Gale took out her badge. "This does a lot of talking for me."

They waited for a response from George's buzzer.

"And by the way, if he lets us in, I talk, you listen politely."

George Oakley's deep voice came crisply through the intercom, and then he asked Gale to hold up her badge to the camera over the front door. He asked to see it again when he opened his apartment door, the chain still in place. Gale had one of her business cards under her thumb on the badge, and he took it, closed the door to unlatch the chain, and let them into an apartment that was half-museum, half-homage to the disco era of the late '70s and '80s. Syd was astounded by the number of framed mementos from clubs and cabarets that were long gone. Surrounding them were photos of beautiful young men with a handsome younger George; she suspected they were as long gone as the clubs. Gale made introductions. Syd studied George. He was an imposing man, his face marred only by the remnant of a broken nose. The word "gay" would never have come to her mind if she'd passed him on the street.

The apartment itself looked like it hadn't undergone any renovation since that disco era, either. Its kitchen floor of large black-and-white tiles echoed the '60s. The planked living room floor worn beneath its shine of cleaner was probably an upgrade from the '40s. But the rooms were spotless, lovingly cared for and tastefully appointed. Syd guessed it was rent controlled, and that George had been here for close to fifty years.

"This is an unusually late hour for police work, Detective. Can I offer you coffee? Something stronger?" George gestured toward his open kitchen.

"I apologize for the hour, Mr. Oakley. I'd like to have waited until tomorrow, but due to some recent developments in this case, time is of the essence. Syd found you online, and we have reason to believe you could be helpful to us, so we thought, well, sooner rather than later."

Syd couldn't believe what she was hearing. *We'll have to talk about* that *later.*

"A murder from nineteen eighty-two, that got my attention, yes. Only reason I let you in. That, and you look like a cute couple."

"Oh, no, we're not a—Syd's a civilian. She brought the case to us, but she's been very helpful in the research department."

Syd thought a blush bloomed on Gale's cheeks; Gale's thumb hooking over her belt next to her badge was all the confirmation Syd needed.

"Yeah, I figured you were something else—never pulled out a badge."

Syd spotted a small poster hanging on the wall touting George as a 1980 heavyweight Golden Gloves winner. No wonder he was still in such good form for a man who looked to be in his mid-eighties. It would also explain his bouncer status back then.

"So, nothing? Coffee, water, tea?"

"No, thank you, and we won't stay long at all. We only have a few questions."

"Please, sit."

Gale and Syd sat on the couch. George settled into an easy chair. He'd muted the television, but left it on, tuned in to the Yankees game, which Gale glanced at from time to time.

She laid out the case for him, showing him photographs of Wyatt, Lucas, Billy, and Duane. If Gale happened to have those photos with her coming from her home, Syd realized she must be working on this case after hours, and it gave her pause. She also felt chagrined for her "carpe diem" remark.

George pointed to Duane's photo. "Him I seen a lot. And then I didn't. And I seen those two—" George indicated Wyatt and Lucas. "Yeah, came in together all the time, sometimes left together, sometimes with other guys. Then," George tapped Wyatt's photo. "He stopped coming in. Of course, word got around, it always did back then. Is he the dead one?"

Gale nodded.

George shook his head sadly. "Happened more than you'd think." He picked up Billy's photo. "Never seen him."

Syd put her hand on Gale's arm. "How do you remember all this?" Gale tensed up under her touch.

George chuckled. "Same way we all do at this age, I guess. I might not recall what I had for dinner last night, but things I did in my twenties and thirties, they're burned here in my memory." He tapped his forehead. "All the guys at Bareback wanted the big scary bouncer. I haven't forgotten any of it."

Gale picked up Duane's photo. "So, you said you saw him a lot and then you didn't? Do you know what happened?"

"He was there a lot maybe—eighty to eighty-two, and then he was gone, never came back. I thought he moved or something."

"Did you ever ask anybody where he'd gone?"

"No. Didn't like him. Didn't care."

"Why didn't you like him?"

"Something off about him. The kinda guy who would've loaded his gloves if he'd been a boxer."

Gale nodded. "And he hung around with these two?"

"No. I spent time inside the club, too, and you could tell they didn't like him, either."

Gale picked up Wyatt's photo again. "October thirtieth of eighty-two. It was a Friday night. We think he picked someone up in Bareback that night, a stranger no one remembers seeing before. It would be a chance in a million, but that's why we're here—would you recall a stranger that fall that men at any of the bars like the Anvil or the Eagle would've talked about, someone they had cause to be afraid of? Maybe you heard something from other bouncers?"

George shook his head. "The regulars I remember. Strangers, we got a lot of those. Men from out of town, guys lived on Long Island, Jersey, Connecticut." He smiled broadly. "One guy from Philly told his wife he was away on business, stayed with me all weekend. Never saw him again. Sure haven't forgotten him, though." His smile disappeared. "I'd only recall someone if there was a fight and I threw him out. Didn't happen a lot, gay bar and all, but I carried those faces just in case." He tapped his forehead again. "I'd have to see a photo, though, if you've got one.

"Is there a day you'd be able to come to the station? I have photos there of other men considered suspects. I could reimburse your cab or Uber."

This was news to Syd and she looked pointedly at Gale.

"Any day next week. I have doctor's appointments the next couple of days. I'm better in the morning when I'm fresh and have more energy. Let me call you on Monday, see how I feel."

Gale stood and shook his hand; Syd followed suit.

"What other suspects?" Syd asked before they'd gone four steps down toward the third floor.

"Every man on our chart is a suspect."

"But most of them are dead. I didn't get a threat from a dead man."

Gale stopped on the stairs. "Your threat might not have come from the killer. Certainly not if he's dead. And possibly not if he's alive."

"That doesn't make sense."

Gale continued down the stairs. "Wyatt's killer might be dead himself. But if George recognizes a face, it'll help us build a scenario of that night." Gale turned to Syd. "Someone adjacent to the murder may be worried about other revelations surfacing, and that could be where your threat came from." Gale took the next flight down.

Syd followed, the conversation she'd hoped to keep a little more private than this echoing off the walls. "What revelations? Adjacent how?"

"The drugs, the prostitution. According to Lucas, there were some very prominent people involved with Ned's lost boys. And for a steep price."

"You saw Lucas again?"

"Yes, and he said you might have the key to the red ledger from Wyatt's desk."

They reached the lobby. Gale held the door open.

"Me?"

"Wyatt was preparing you to step in if anything happened to him, wasn't he? If he was arrested when he blew the whistle, or if he had to disappear."

Syd was stupefied. Had Lucas told her this? What was he playing at? "Lucas and Wyatt were estranged before the murder. How did Lucas even know about that ledger? I'd never seen it before the day Ned found it."

"He was involved in the prostitution, and that's what that ledger was about. Obviously, it was a known entity. Billy was very interested in it, it scares Lucas, and it seems to be a big threat to whoever sent you Izzy's photo because Lucas got a similar threat. Why don't we finish this discussion in the car?"

Syd felt like she'd been sucker-punched: suddenly Gale was Detective Sterling again. She followed her and got in the passenger seat of the car.

"This isn't just about Wyatt's murder anymore," Gale said.

Syd could only stare out the windshield as Gale took her through the interview with Billy that led to the impromptu visit to Lucas's office. At one point, so much information coming at her, she shifted her focus to the sideview mirror trying to comprehend it all. Or get away from it. She noticed a tall rangy man walking down the far side of the street, in the street itself. Something about his lope was familiar, but her mind was in so many places, making concentration impossible. Before she could fully disengage from what Gale was saying to think about him, he went down the basement steps of a building.

"That's why we want you to come in on Friday and go over that ledger carefully."

"What was in Lucas's threat?"

"It was very similar to yours."

"Does he know I got one?"

"Not unless you told him. We would never divulge that."

Syd looked at Gale plaintively. "I thought *he* was behind the envelope sent to me."

"I don't think so. He's terrified."

Syd looked out the window. "So am I."

"I'm beginning to think we're dealing with someone who was involved with the prostitution who's hell-bent on making sure nothing surfaces, so he's trying to shut down this case. My guess: he thinks you and Lucas know something he needs kept quiet."

"What about Billy?"

"We've left him a message asking if he's gotten an envelope." Gale looked at Syd. "*Was* Wyatt getting you ready to take over his position? Did he give you some kind of key to the ledger?"

"No. No to both. I mean, suddenly he was bombarding me with information. He just up and said one day that I needed to know everything. But that ledger—it had never been there, and I went through that drawer all the time because that's where he tossed the donor information for me to file. I'd never seen it until the day Ned pulled it out." Syd put her head in her hands. "I am so tired."

Gale reached over and rubbed her shoulder. "Let me get you home."

In truth, Syd didn't want to go home. She sank back, glad that Detective Sterling had disappeared. She felt Gale's fingers in her hair. The stroking calmed her down.

"I promise you we're going to get to the bottom of all of this."

Syd could've stayed like this all night.

❖

What about Billy, Gale thought as she drove home after dropping Syd off. Had he gotten an envelope threatening his life? Then why did betraying Duane take precedence over a threat on his life—unless they were one and the same: give Duane up, save your life. She wished Tommy was in the passenger seat. It was so much easier to puzzle this sort of thing out with his sounding board skills.

And what about that involuntary noise she'd heard Syd make when George admitted he might not remember a stranger at Bareback unless they'd caused a fight? Gale had glanced at her, seen defeat written all over her and wondered if this was what Ahab had experienced every time the great whale disappeared beneath the waves. But she couldn't worry about Syd's feelings. Not now. Billy was too important, and now she had to admit that he was an altogether different entity—she didn't understand him. He was beginning to bother her, like a Sunday *Times* crossword whose theme she couldn't crack. He concealed facts, he misled them, purposefully muddied the waters, and he'd been blatant with Syd about wanting the red ledger. There was more to him than Gale had originally thought. She'd underestimated him, thinking he didn't have very much to lose in all this. He could simply quietly retire to Connecticut no matter what broke in the news. No one would care. Unless Billy knew otherwise.

Like, if he was tied to LaundryGate. The Feds had come calling, after all. But they hadn't come back. Did it all still come back to those red ledgers?

Gale focused on the road; it was as straight as a timeline. Red ledgers and blue envelopes. Syd's had come first, after her visit to Ned. Lucas must've gotten their conversation out of Ned. And then he got an envelope. Did Billy have one? Or was Billy giving them out? The other day, he'd showed his hand in terms of the closeness of his relationship with Lucas, warning him that Gale and Tommy were coming. So it would be safe to say that Lucas had shared Syd's visit to Ned with Billy. Who outside of the three of them knew about the red ledger? Theo Hall? Zach Feinberg? They didn't seem likely candidates to threaten murder. *Although we haven't talked to them yet.*

"Call Tommy," Gale said, and her phone connected. She told him about the visit to George Oakley.

"Did you happen to mention to Syd that they don't pay us overtime for this sorta thing?"

Gale snorted. "When did anything I told Syd make a difference?"

"She's a handful, but ya gotta admit—her bull-in-a-china-shop's brought us a helluva lot of stuff pretty quickly. Makes me look like an amateur."

"Your bull has an NYPD shield. She doesn't. So what happened tonight?"

"You were smart to have me work on that new case tonight while the squad were all leaving. A, no one suspected I was staying late on purpose, and B, several of the neighbors you called in to talk coughed up a suspect."

"Who?"

"Apparently, our vic owed a loan shark."

"A what?" Gale shouldn't have been surprised, but she was.

"Everyone in that neighborhood's scared o' this guy, but six years and one pandemic out, maybe not so much. According to our pious churchgoers at St. Joe's, the dead handyman was into him big for the ponies. Now we gotta build the case."

"Always easier from the back end. And the tech guys? What time did they show up?"

"Eight o'clock, like I asked 'em. No spyware anywhere, nothin' on anyone's phones."

"Doesn't mean our mole wasn't sitting right there listening to our conversations."

"He was, Gale, but he wasn't one of us. Tech guys brought a bug hunting device with them, said it was just for kicks, but then they found a mike under the lip of your desk."

Gale was shocked. Someone had gotten that close, and they didn't know it.

"Obviously, they took it with them, wanted to see what they could learn. So we're not outta the woods yet in terms of our own guys." Tommy's momentary silence spoke volumes, but then the pain in his voice caught her off guard. "I sure hated bringin' in the tech division on our own team. It's killin' me that it could be one of them."

"Don't go there. That was Esposito's call, not ours. Let's see what the tech guys find out."

Tommy sighed heavily.

"And, Tommy, when they're through with it and if it's still in one piece? I want it back. Doesn't matter what they find. Let's stick it on a lamp post somewhere downtown."

Tommy chuckled. "I like that. Oh, and before I forget—after the tech guys cleared our computers, I used the database, found Duane's uncle, Pete Nowak. Long Island. We need to see this guy, Gale, at least let him give us his version of Duane's death, maybe he lets out enough rope to hang himself and we get proof Duane's guilty. This uncle woulda protected him if he'd killed Wyatt."

Gale's mounting frustrations with this case seemed to know no bounds. "I don't like it. We can't just show up on his doorstep. We'd have to give him the courtesy of a phone call. I think he'd freak out and contact Duane."

"And what if Billy already gave him a head's up. Or Duane?"

"Or both of them? We don't have anything in the phone records between Billy's and Pete's phones, do we? And I know, doesn't mean he's not using a burner." Gale ran her hand through her hair. "My bet is he called Duane back after we left. And Duane called his uncle. This case is like cats in a bag."

"My bet," Tommy said with a growl, "is that Billy's the conduit between Lucas and Duane for a lot more than he's tellin' us."

Gale almost laughed out loud. Tommy *had* been in the passenger seat after all.

"All right, no Nowak. Lemme see what else," he continued. "Oh—Billy's EZ Pass records came today, I don't think they'll be much help except maybe with the frequency of trips, like, is there a pattern, did he ever break it. And I think we should go see Billy's place on Shippan Point."

"Nice day for a spring drive, right? What else?"

"In that packet of letters Drew sent back to Syd, the one she'd sent to Joe from Wyatt's desk that she thought were all letters from Joe to Wyatt? There was a love letter to Wyatt from Schuyler Tilden."

Gale had just put the car in park in the driveway or she might've rear-ended Sullivan's Range Rover. "That parent who was murdered in the mugging?" Her skin ran to goose bumps.

"It's a scorcher, Gale. We might got us a new ball game."

She was glad she was sitting down because now she felt light-headed. "Jesus. You were right about the blue ribbon."

"No one ties up a bunch of letters with ribbon unless there's something romantically sentimental in there. Learned that from my sisters."

"Send me a photo of the letter. I'll pick you up tomorrow morning at the precinct, eight o'clock, we should be at Feinberg's office by ten."

Gale sat in her car after disconnecting the call. Schuyler Tilden. She'd never seen him coming. And suddenly there he was, smack dab in the middle of her Venn diagram with the money, the jealousy, and the other dead.

She wanted to call Syd and ask her about him. But it would have to wait. Gale sighed. So much about Syd would have to wait.

CHAPTER TWENTY

Gale thought Zach Feinberg was a nice enough guy, right up until the moment his husband interrupted the interview to tell Zach that White Willows was calling to let them know his father had fallen out of bed. Again. And Zach curtly told his husband to tell them to put him back *into* his bed.

Gale shifted uncomfortably in her chair and even broke her rule to glance at Tommy who was focused on her, his eyebrows asking the question he couldn't. "Oh—White Willows. I hear it's a nice place." Nothing, Tommy always said, is a coincidence.

"You know it?" Zach seemed surprised.

Gale scrambled. "I came across it when I was researching places for my father. He's ninety-one and reaching that point. But I discovered he's better off at home with in-house help."

"I wouldn't be able to handle that." Zach's voice was weary. "White Willows is top-notch. He's been there over five years now."

"A long time," Gale said sympathetically.

"Yeah. He's eighty-six." Zach took off his glasses and rubbed at his eyes. "Dementia hit him seven years ago. God forgive me, I don't know why he's hanging on. I couldn't deal with him anymore, though. That seemed like the best place. They take good care of him." A wan smile appeared. "I recommended it to Lucas when he mentioned Ned's son was looking for a place."

"So you're there on a regular basis?" Gale wanted to know how often Zach saw Ned and Lucas there.

Zach peered up at her as he polished his glasses. "Please don't think me callous, Detective. My father stopped recognizing me a long time ago. I haven't been there since we moved him in. The emotional tank was empty long before then, I saw no reason to tax it further."

Gale was stunned silent. Tommy finished up the questioning and they left.

"Dementia's about as hard as it gets, but how do you let a parent go like that?" Gale asked as she turned the key in the ignition. "I'd like to think that if Sullivan went that route, I'd see him all the time anyway. I'd miss him like hell but I'd be there."

"Not everyone is as lucky as we are, lookin' after parents still in good shape. My mother oughtta be beatified."

Gale stared straight ahead. "There's something else I didn't like about him. He said he was rarely in touch with Lucas or Billy. Yet he recommended White Willows to Lucas." She glanced at Tommy and then back at the modern glass building that housed Zach's practice. "These guys have stayed in touch."

"We're goin' to White Willows, aren't we?" Tommy asked as he clicked his seat belt into place.

Fifteen minutes later, Gale pulled into the parking lot of the elegant facility.

"Wow," Tommy said, scanning the grounds. "Can you imagine having the money for a place like this?"

"I can, but I think I'd rather die at home. These places can be stuffy."

"Says you."

"Money turns you into an asshole."

"I'd still be me if you gave me a million bucks."

Gale laughed. "I believe you would."

"So, what are we doin'?"

"No idea. Looking for some kind of connection."

Gale took out her badge as the front doors slid open. They were greeted by a well-dressed chipper woman Gale gauged to be in her seventies. She admired the woman's tailored spring green suit—it matched the season blooming outside—and wondered if having a receptionist the same age as the residents was calculated. It was certainly a comfortable plus that the woman fit in so perfectly with the monied surroundings. Gale approached her, reading the nametag. "Good morning, Miriam. I wonder if you could help us?" Gale held up her shield and then flipped it to reveal her ID.

Miriam fumbled with the glasses on a chain around her neck, peered at the ID, and then at Gale. "You're an awfully long way from home."

"We are. I'm Detective Sterling, NYPD, my partner, Detective D'Angelo. We're working an old case. We're here following up on an interview with a Dr. Zach Feinberg nearby in Norwalk. I understand his father's here, has been for about five years?"

"You've seen Dr. Feinberg? Is he all right?"

"Uh, yes, he's fine." Gale hid her surprise.

"Acchh, good! I was worried about him! Such a sweet man. I haven't seen him for weeks, thought he might've gotten Covid and was thinking I should call him."

"So he does come to see his father." Gale glanced at Tommy, who appeared as puzzled as she was.

Miriam changed gears. "Oh, I'm afraid I can't—I'd have to get the manager."

"Ah, of course, privacy laws, I understand. Not a problem." Gale aimed her arrow. "I imagine you're the kind of person who runs a ship-shape front desk. They're lucky to have you."

Miriam's reluctance thawed into preening. "We're careful about everything."

Gale had hit her target. "I bet. You'd recognize a photo of Dr. Feinberg, if we showed you? That wouldn't violate any policy, would it?"

Tommy held up his cell phone before Miriam could process that thought, and she scrutinized the photo on the screen. "That's not him."

"What about him?" Tommy asked, flashing Lucas's photo at Gale before showing Miriam.

"Why, that's Lucas Rose. Wonderful fellow. He used to visit Ned Rossiter every Monday night, from the week Ned moved in here two years ago until the night he died in March." Miriam tutted. "When his own son never came."

Gale was inwardly amused at Miriam's sudden disregard for policy.

"And him?" Tommy presented another photo.

"There, that's Dr. Feinberg. I don't know that first man."

Tommy showed the phone to Gale—he'd pulled up the shot of Billy Highsmith and not for the first time in this investigation, her skin ran to goose bumps. "Apologies. I accidentally showed you the wrong person first." Tommy mouthed the word "Zach" to Gale.

"How often does Dr. Feinberg visit?" Gale asked.

"Oh, I really shouldn't say."

"Oh, darn, my fault—" Tommy fumbled with his notebook. "Forgot to write that down when we were with him. Every other week?"

"Every Sunday like clockwork, nine thirty. Oh, but he hasn't been now in weeks. That's why I was so worried about the Covid."

"And has he always come on such a regular basis since moving his father in?"

"Oh, no, only since January. His sister promised him she was coming to see their dad, but he'd only recently found out she wasn't, and he felt awful. He's so busy with his practice, you know." Miriam put an elbow on the counter, confidentiality written all over her face. "Said he'd give me a free consult even though he didn't think I needed any work done." She smiled broadly. "But I wasn't born yesterday."

Gale stifled a laugh.

Tommy held up one more photo for Miriam. "This is Dr. Feinberg's brother, Duane. Did he ever come in with him?"

"No, I don't believe so." Miriam straightened up. "The doctor's not in trouble, I hope?"

"No, we're dotting our i's and crossing our t's before closing the case," Gale said. "Do you remember when he was here last?"

Miriam crossed her arms and tapped a perfectly manicured nail against her sleeve. "Late March. I didn't see him at all in April. Covid can be so dangerous, and such a long recovery at our age."

Tommy took the lid off the big candy jar sitting on the counter and fished out a piece wrapped in shiny red foil.

"Miriam, you've been a big help," Gale said. "Thank you."

Tommy tipped the jar toward Gale. She set her cell phone down and took two pieces.

"Oh, one more question," Tommy said, putting the lid on the jar. "Who has the best clam chowder around here?"

Back out in the parking lot, Gale started the car but left it in park. "Oops. Left my phone in there."

"What—by the candy jar? You never leave your—ohhh, the old 'forgot my phone' ploy. Nice move, Detective Fumble."

The doors glided open once again, and sure enough, there was Miriam chatting on the desk phone. She waved her fingers when Gale held up her cell phone.

Gale turned off the recording app and was halfway to the door when something in Miriam's conversation stopped her. Her instincts had been spot-on—Miriam was talking to "Dr. Feinberg." She picked up a brochure from the table near the front door, then pretended to read it as she listened to Miriam tell him that it was those two nice detectives from New York who'd let her know he didn't have Covid. Fuck.

Gale flung herself behind the steering wheel.

"I'd put all the money I'd need to end up in this five-star waiting room to Heaven that Billy was seeing Ned Rossiter here every week. What did you pick up in there besides your phone?"

"She was talking to 'Dr. Feinberg.'" Gale made air quotes.

"Oh, crap. You called it—you always do."

"Yeah, huge pile of crap." Gale sat back, depleted. "Dammit! Now Billy knows what we've stumbled on."

"All right, don't let's lose it here. Nothin' some good strategizing can't overcome."

"What strategizing? We can't even see the chess board! Billy's lied to us so many times, what's he hiding? He asked for immunity, so it's got to be big." Gale ran both hands through her hair and growled.

"Why don't we get outta here. It's pushin' on noon, I think we find this place Miriam recommended and have lunch. It's right on the water. I'm gonna—" He pecked at his cell phone. "Okay, directions to this place. Not too far off."

Gale nosed the car toward the front gate. "Billy was desperately interested in that ledger." One finger rose off the steering wheel. "He lied to Syd about Duane." Another finger. "About walking away from the lost boys, about seeing Ned." Two more fingers, leaving her thumb hooked there. "About Lucas." Gale dropped her fingers back down. Passing cars stalled their exit. "About every last shred of it."

Grumbling that he wished the NYPD would upgrade their cars for Bluetooth, Tommy plugged his cell phone into the USB port and a female voice issued directions to turn left.

"But he never left the city." Gale drummed her fingers on the steering wheel. "Duane did. To the tune of a lot of money."

The Waze voice repeated her instructions to turn left.

"Are you okay to drive?" Tommy asked.

"I'm pissed off, I'm not deaf."

Tommy held up both hands.

"I'm fine. I won't cause a road rage incident." Both lanes finally clear, Gale made the turn. "I'd like to arrest Billy now."

"Can't. We need him. Let's put a timeline to this, see if anything new pops." Tommy took out his notebook, and Gale was grateful he was moving on from her anger as quickly as he always did from his own. "One: Miriam says Feinberg, aka Billy, has been comin' to White Willows since January to see his 'father.' Obviously, he's got ID says he's Feinberg. Then, he stops visiting when Ned dies. Two: we know Lucas visited Ned every Monday since he'd been in the joint. Three: Syd visits Ned in March, gets a threat in April. So timeline question number one is, why does Billy start comin' in January? What's so damned important after forty years, and after Ned let him go when he kept Duane?"

"Duane is a very expensive insurance policy. Why was Billy so expendable?"

"His silence for his freedom? Could it be that simple?"

"Nothing in this case has been simple. And silence about what? There are so many secrets with this case that the secrets have secrets." Traffic had slowed in another picturesque small-town business district. Like the towns before this one, one store window sported a sailing motif, another a golfing theme, and the hardware store windows were pushing barbecues and beach gear. They'd only left New York four hours ago, but Gale couldn't wait to get back. Suburbia gave her hives. Her mind worked on the problem of Billy Highsmith while she window-shopped came to a standstill. What *would* cause Billy to break his silence after forty years?

As if she'd said it out loud, Tommy said, "Something—or someone—happened to Billy in January."

"That's where it began," Gale said, clouds clearing.

"What?"

"We've been thinking that ground zero is Syd's blue envelope after her visit to Ned."

"But it's Billy," Tommy said, picking up the thread.

"He needed something from Ned. So he went in as Feinberg. He was either working his way into Ned's good graces or bullying him. Syd was the fly in the ointment."

"Timing is everything, right? Syd goes to see Ned after Drew finds out how Wyatt really died. Ya know, she never told us what they talked about. And he's dead that night?"

"And since it was a Monday, Lucas was there," Gale said.

"I don't see Lucas being the architect of that," Tommy said. "Not sure the autopsy would prove anything, either."

"No, but would Ned have told Lucas about Billy and Syd?"

"Of course he would. Lucas saved Rossiter Enterprises, the old man owed him his life."

"So Lucas must've confronted Billy during a Feinberg visit. That might not have gone so well." Like words that would come to her on Thursday after returning to the Sunday *Times* crossword every night, Gale was seeing things she hadn't last week. "But it would've been before Lucas got his blue envelope."

"Obviously, they kissed and made up."

"Billy must've told him what was going on, and Lucas must've gotten involved—that's the reference in Lucas's note to 'one of you—'"

"They were both looking for the red ledger, then. He just didn't tell us."

Traffic, which had finally begun to flow for several miles, slowed again. Gale couldn't see the cause and rolled the window down, craning her head out. "I hate small-town traffic."

"Ya know, there's no timeline. In Lucas's note. Just 'find it.'"

"I noticed. So, did Billy get a blue envelope in January? And why did whoever is behind this go to him and not Lucas or Ned?"

Up ahead, the clanging of arms descending at a railroad crossing sounded and a dilapidated freight train rumbled by. Its whistle hung in the air long after the red lights ceased blinking and the arm rose. "Sweet Jesus, we're going to be stopping for sheep next. This clam chowder had better be good."

"Why *didn't* they go to Ned?"

"They must not have thought he had the ledgers," Gale said.

"So Billy was targeted—he musta gotten a blue envelope."

"And we have the red ledger. Which now they know thanks to the mole."

Tommy looked at Gale. "We have to break Billy or Lucas," he said quietly. "Or, we have to lean on Syd about the ledger since Lucas thinks she holds the key."

Gale could feel Tommy's eyes on her. "Fine. I'll talk to her tonight."

"And?"

"We'll see how she acts around that ledger when you sit down with her tomorrow."

"You gonna be okay with that?"

"I'll be fine." But Gale knew she wouldn't. It had already occurred to her that the woman flirting with her, the woman she was beginning to have feelings for, could have a finger in this pie.

"Rose-colored glasses don't look good on you." It was Tommy's quiet reminder voice.

"I know." Gale found a '60s station on Sirius. She kept the volume low. The song playing was Creedence Clearwater Revival's "Bad Moon Rising." Gale sighed.

"Are you ready for Theo Hall tomorrow?" Tommy asked.

She nodded.

The automated Waze voice interrupted. "Turn left in one-quarter mile."

Gale pulled into the parking lot of Clams Ahoy. Miriam told them they were open year-round, and the best no matter what the season. There were a few parking spaces left. Gale found one and cut the car.

"You know what's still bothering me?" Gale asked.

"Are we free-associating now?"

"Syd said Wyatt never went anywhere alone, but he went to Bareback solo that night." She looked at Tommy. "Kind of a red flag for me."

"You think he was set up?"

Gale shrugged. "Isn't it odd that the one night he breaks an old habit, he's murdered."

"What is my mantra, Gale?"

"There are no coincidences."

"C'mon. Let's puzzle this over chowder and a lobster roll."

As she'd been instructed, Gale gave the hostess Miriam's name and suddenly the last open table on the deck was theirs. They settled against the weathered shingles in the sunshine. Gale opened a package of oyster crackers while they waited for their server. "I keep thinking there's someone in this picture we're not seeing. If Syd's right and someone else killed Wyatt, the question remains: at Ned's behest or on his own? And was he conveniently at Bareback?"

"I still like Duane for it. He could've murdered Wyatt for Ned and torn the place apart looking for whatever it was Ned wanted. I'm convinced it was the ledgers."

"It could've been the owner of the blue envelopes. What if he was around back then—Syd received a threat then, after all."

"Shit. We never thought of that."

"We're thinking of it now," Gale said.

"You know we have to close this before the FBI calls us again and takes this case from us. Because they won't care about Wyatt's murder."

"Unless it's tied in. Duane's flight lands next Thursday at six a.m. He's not on it, we wake up Billy and Lucas and solve it that way."

"Yeah? Let's hope they don't clam up."

The waitress arrived at their table.

"See what I did there?" Tommy asked Gale.

"How y'all doin' today?" the waitress asked.

"If you don't get this man a cup of clam chowder right away, I'm probably going to kill him."

"How long y'all been married?"

Gale and Tommy looked at each other and burst out laughing.

It was only 6:15, but everyone was gone. That was another reason Gale like cold case: you could leave at a decent hour. But tonight, she had other plans. She took the red ledger out of the evidence locker. She turned it over and over, studied the cover, front and back, opened it and peered up the spine. There was a Maglite in her desk drawer.

She elongated it to get the bright concentrated pin spot and shone it up the dark tube of the spine. Nothing. A close inspection with the light on the cover as she ran her hands over every inch turned up nothing. Just like before. She opened the ledger, went over every page, shining the light at the bindings. Again, nothing. That just left the insides of the covers. The light didn't illuminate any unevenness, but Gale didn't trust that: she took the razor blade out of her box cutter and went to work, carefully guiding the blade under the endpaper of the front cover. Halfway around the top and the outer side, she could lift it. Nothing. She repeated the task on the back cover's endpaper and before she'd reached the outer corner to move down the side, she could see it, the piece of paper within. The endpaper had been tampered with before, evident in the neat layers of glue along the top.

How had she not felt that under her fingertips before? After opening the entire top and some of both sides, she slid the piece of paper out. The Holy Grail. She sat back and read the numbered names next to all the letters of the alphabet. She recognized every one. They matched some of the names Lucas had reeled off the afternoon of the interview in his office, and many of the names she'd found while researching Ned's network. Most of them were long dead. But among the ones still alive, she was certain someone had a penchant for blue envelopes.

She turned the paper over looking for the identities of the fourteen boys. It was blank. She peered back into the endpaper with the Maglite. Empty. Fuck.

Gale took the list to the copier down the hall. Then she sealed the original back into the endpaper with the bottle of craft glue that Miller kept in his desk, using the barest sheen on her fingertip so that it looked undisturbed. The book went back into the locker, along with her hope that Syd still wouldn't know anything, even under the harsh barrels Tommy could aim when questioning people he didn't think were telling the truth.

CHAPTER TWENTY-ONE

Syd was nervous. Gale's call last night had been unsettling: she'd gone straight to business, asking her to come in this morning to look at the ledger from Wyatt's desk yet again. She'd also wanted an accounting of her conversation with Ned the day she visited. Syd went over it, admitting that she was less than gracious, that Ned cried, that he hadn't uttered a word. "In fact," she said, "later I wondered if he'd suffered an ischemic attack and I didn't know it." Gale's silence frightened her. It made her feel like she'd been a monster with Ned. And that wasn't who she was. That's what surfaced in the circumstance, that rage Ned had helped to create. It had sat dormant in her until she needed it. Or so she'd thought. She'd given it haven for so long that maybe she never saw the things it did to her, the relationships it cost her. She didn't want it to cost the possibility she might have with Gale.

Their small talk afterward was awkward. Syd stared out the window after they'd hung up, thinking that possible future could be setting with the sun.

Gale wasn't at her desk when Syd arrived. Tommy took her to an interview room. She'd never been in one before. It made her feel guilty, its austerity off-putting, bright overhead light annoying, and that big window—everyone knew it was a two-way mirror. Was Gale there, listening?

Tommy sat next to her so that they could both look at every page of Wyatt's ledger as she turned each one slowly, the book sidelong to accommodate the width of the chart. At the top of the first page,

January 1980 was printed neatly in black ink. The days of the month were underneath, serving as column headings. Down the side were numbers one through fourteen. The alphabet ran along the bottom of the page. The boxes contained a letter from the bottom of the page and a number from the side of the page next to a three- or four-digit number. Some boxes contained more than one such combination. One box in particular, number five, listed at least four combinations more than once a week.

"I'd long thought these were dollar amounts. You don't need decimal points to figure that out," Syd said. "And then Billy locked that in for me when he admitted to the prostitution." Syd ran her finger down the numbered side of the page. "Fourteen. Just like the drug ledger."

"But we can't figure out who's who like we could with the drug accounting. Whoever concocted this switched to numbers."

"So that no one could ever identify the boys."

"And the alphanumerics in the boxes hide the identities of the johns."

Syd slowly flipped pages. "Box number five was particularly active every month, sometimes four entries in a day."

"So who among the boys was suddenly flashing cash back then, do you recall? Ned had to give them a cut of their own action. Because this here is a lot of money. For instance." Tommy took a piece of paper out of a file he'd tossed on the desk. "If you add up all the numbers for this month alone, you get a tidy sum."

Syd took the piece of paper from him and studied it. The document held totals for each month of the year. "Tidy" was an understatement.

"Now multiply by twelve," Tommy said.

Fast with numbers, Syd already had the total in her head. Tommy's eyes were on her, and it wasn't a casual glance. "Wouldn't Lucas know, since he seemed to be the one doling the boys out in the clubs?"

"He didn't keep the books. And we don't think these boys were just workin' the clubs, by the way. He said he doesn't know what any of this means. But he thinks you do. You kept the books for Wyatt at Divine Heart—gifts, pledges, donations, payments, bank accounts. So let's look at December of eighty-two here. Because suddenly, we're missing two numbers. Five and six drop off the grid. You know who they were?"

Syd's stomach was beginning to roil like it did when Tommy talked about Wyatt's involvement in the embezzlement. He'd just implicated her in that. And now he was trying to place her at the center of Ned's illicit business. Was Gale complicit in this line of questioning? Her head felt light. Her breath slowed, and then her pulse ramped up so that she was quietly fighting for air. A panic attack. She couldn't let him see it. Or Gale, if she was behind the mirror.

"It's why we need the code, Syd. And now would be a good time to come clean if Wyatt gave it to you."

Syd curled her fingers around the ledger's cover and hung onto it, blocking everything out, willing Aunt Ingrid's voice to reach her. She had to stop the panic attack. *Breathe, Sydney. You're panicking. I do it, too. Three deep breaths will kill it.* She needed four just to push it back an inch, but when she spoke, it was slow, and deliberate, as though each word was a knot that she could use to pull herself back up the thick rope to breathable air. "I didn't know about the embezzlement until Wyatt was dead. And I never knew the drugs and the prostitution were a business until I saw the head of one of the crime families at a club one night with Ned. That could only mean one thing. I left the club immediately."

Tommy took out his phone. "Could you identify him?" He showed her a photo.

She nodded.

Gale wanted to rap on the glass, find out if it was the same crime family involved in LaundryGate, but Theo Hall would be sitting at a table in the room next door by now. Gale left hoping that Tommy wouldn't squeeze Syd much longer. She didn't look good. And years of experience told Gale she didn't have anything to do with the ledger.

Theo Hall was tall and thin, his skin as smooth and youthful as it looked in all the photographs, unchanged since dropping out of the limelight ten years ago. Except for the crinkles around his eyes, and his hair gone salt-and-pepper, he looked much younger than his seventy-five years.

Gale dropped a folder onto the table. Theo's entire career was in it: decades as decorator to the stars and private wealth set, the *Times* article on his marriage to Giovanni Martoli, a then-young dancer with the American Ballet Theater, and the story she'd stumbled across in *Saveur's* farm-to-table issue. She never would've thought to look for him there, so it was kismet, really, when she'd recently come across an old issue Kate must've squirreled away in a kitchen cupboard, thumbed through it, and found the article highlighting Theo's vegetable kingdom in Beacon, New York. It was on twenty acres where he'd built a drop-dead gorgeous home surrounded by breathtaking English gardens, and beyond those were the sizeable vegetable gardens that now supplied local restaurateurs. He'd brought in sheep to roam many other acres and won awards for the cheeses made from their milk. The photo of him standing among rows of staked tomatoes with Giovanni, now of an age where dancing was no longer viable, was charming. Giovanni held an adorable floppy-eared lamb in his arms, and a sheep dog leaned against Theo. When Tommy read the article, he said he could envision himself in Theo's life. Minus Giovanni.

"No offense," Tommy had said.

"None taken," Gale replied. "I'd want to be minus Giovanni, too. But I'd need more than the sheep."

Gale introduced herself to Theo and sat down. "What have we here?"

A small plastic bag sat in front of him, inside it a pocket square the color of autumn marigolds spattered across the four tips with blood. The initials "WCR" were embroidered there in a darker orange, beneath the spray.

"I thought you'd want this."

Theo's voice was soft, vulnerable. Gale looked at him expectantly; he was struggling with his emotions. "Sydney Hansen gave this to me when she came over to my apartment that night to tell me Wyatt was…gone."

Gale was shocked. Why would Syd have removed it, and why hadn't she mentioned it to her in the myriad of things they'd talked about? DNA evidence hadn't yet been solidified as a courtroom tool then, but laboratories were working with it. "Tell me how it happened."

The story poured out as if he'd been wanting to tell it for some time—he had so many regrets. Three weeks in LA refurbishing poolside cabanas for a movie star had left him too tired to see Wyatt when he got back to New York that Wednesday. He needed to collect himself for the governor's pre-election black-tie fundraiser Thursday night, which was why he'd come back to New York in the first place—he could land countless commissions that would keep him busy all year at such a gala.

"I was running late, of course," Theo said. "I was always late in those days. I told Wyatt I'd meet him there."

When he found him, Wyatt was flirting with someone at the party, someone Theo was certain he was having an affair with, and he'd tried gamely but failed.

"I'm not a second fiddle, Detective. Never have been. I took a cab home. He called, several times that night, but I didn't pick up. I thought the pounding on my door Friday night was him finally coming around, begging me to take him back. Again."

Instead, Theo had seen Sydney and Marie through the peephole, the pocket square in Syd's hand, and he knew there would be no taking Wyatt back ever again. He pushed the plastic bag to Gale.

"I embroidered that for him."

Gale recalled the jacket from one of the photos, carefully folded over the back of the couch. Had Syd done that, or had she found it that way? Only someone who loved Wyatt would take the time to do that.

"I didn't know what to do with it. I didn't want it. So I put it away in this bag. Far away. But now, I'm wondering if it can be of use, for DNA."

"Thank you." Gale would certainly have something to say to Syd later. She opened the file, apologizing for taking him through the same events with her questions, closely watching his face as he answered. He grappled with deep emotions, and was hazy on some points in the days after Wyatt's murder, but Gale didn't sense that he was hiding anything. Not even when she inquired about Lucas and Ned—the bitterness was real, but so was his love for Wyatt.

Tommy would look at the tape later, but she was sure he'd agree that Theo's body language didn't exhibit telltale signs of a long-ago murderous rage. Although the surprise they were about to spring on him might tell a different story.

Her cell phone buzzed with a text—Tommy letting her know that he and Syd would be at his desk in five minutes. The other detectives were out on cases, so the room was theirs. Gale asked Theo if he'd mind looking at some photos back in the homicide division office.

Syd's astonishment when she saw Theo was palpable. Gale had wondered if it might be a moment of panic on Syd's part. Instead, Theo stopped when he saw her, and Syd stood as he put down the bag he was carrying, came around the desk, and hugged him.

"Oh my God, how are you?"

"Good. I'm good."

"And you're married now. I saw the announcement in the *Times*."

Theo laughed and sniffled against her shirt collar. "Yes, twenty years."

"Good. You're happy? Growing tomatoes up there in Beacon?"

Theo nodded. "We grow so much more, you know," he said, wiping at a tear. "I don't miss any of the rat race."

"I know. I read an article online a while ago."

"Beacon is like Mars for you, isn't it?"

"Anything outside the city is another galaxy, darling, you know that. And I didn't think you ever wanted to see me again after the funeral anyway."

"I didn't. I didn't want to see anyone. But you could've called. Like, two years later."

"Would you have picked up?"

"Absolutely. Wyatt loved you. I—have missed you." Theo smiled tentatively. "And you—you're happy? Married? Cats?"

Syd shook her head. "I never married. I still have cats—Scrooge and Marley are long gone, though. Happy? Relatively."

"And this—" Theo gestured around the room. "What is this really about?"

Syd looked at Gale, who nodded. "I initiated it, Theo. I'm so sorry. I got a threat."

Theo's whole body jerked, his eyes widening. "What?"

"Someone left it at my apartment door after Ned died in March—"

"I had no idea he was dead until Detective D'Angelo told me on the phone—but why would anyone threaten you over that?"

"I visited him the day he died. They may have thought he said something to me about—"

"Wyatt's murder." Theo looked at Gale and Tommy, and back to Syd. "Did he?"

"No. I supposed I hoped he would when I went up there, but he didn't. I went because Drew finally found out the truth about Wyatt's death when he was cleaning out Joe's house—"

Theo's surprise was evident again.

"I'm sorry, Theo—he died in November. Covid. Drew found things Joe kept all these years in a notebook, and he wanted me to go to the police. But I went to see Ned instead."

"Who sent the note?"

"We don't know yet who it was," Gale said. "The investigation is ongoing—"

"Who put that prick's photo up there?" Theo interrupted. He strode over to the whiteboard and snapped Schuyler Tilden's photo off, the push pin flying.

Tommy was next to him in three paces. "Easy does it, Theo. Do you want to tell us about him?"

"He was having an affair with Wyatt! He was the one!" He turned to Gale.

"Yes, we know," she said quietly.

All the air seemed to leave Theo's body and he let Tommy take the photo and pin it back on the board. "What does it matter…it was forty years ago."

"It matters a great deal," Gale said. "Schuyler was killed just over a month later which might indicate he was involved in the murder."

"He was mugged. Tell them, Syd."

"She already did," Gale said. She glanced at Syd, saw the stricken look on her face, and knew she was trying to deal with what she'd just heard. "Syd has told us a lot about what went on back then. But we're trying to reconstruct that night because Lucas Rose also received a threat. His seems to be related to the red ledgers, though. You know." Gale crossed her fingers, hoping her next step paid off. "The ones Wyatt kept about Ned's drug sales, the prostitution, and the embezzlement."

Theo's eyes widened. "They weren't about the embezzlement. They were about the drugs and prostitution."

"How do you know?" Tommy asked.

"He told me. I kept finding him working on them whenever I came over, and it drove me nuts because he wouldn't put them away. So I took one from him one night. He got mad at me, so I made him tell me what they were before I gave it back. When he spilled everything, I got angry—my God, embezzling—that wasn't who he was, that was Ned. I wouldn't see him for a couple of weeks after that, until he called and said he'd given the books to Lucas and told Ned he was done with all of it."

"And was he?" Gale asked.

"Yes. We were going to go to the FBI when I got back from a job in Miami, but I got pulled out to LA, so it had to wait. And then *that* asshole—" Theo pointed emphatically at the board, his finger poking each word. "Schuyler fucking Tilden, who I knew was sleeping with him for almost a year—tried to get him to go to the Maldives with him! Said he was going to divorce his wife, wanted Wyatt to take the money and flee. Because they don't have extradition with the US."

Gale had her eye on an ashen Syd as she had sat down at her desk.

"But part of that money was Schuyler's, wasn't it?" Tommy asked.

"Tilden didn't have any money—he had a hard chest full of medals from the Marines and a smokin' body to match. It was his wife's money. Wyatt told me Schuyler thought it would be the perfect solution to disappear with her money from the capital campaign, but Wyatt couldn't do that because he was already in so deep with Ned. If he was going to do that, he said he wanted to do it with me."

"Did you kill Wyatt when all this came out? Were you angry or jealous?" Gale asked, seeing Syd in her peripheral vision come out of the chair.

"I loved him. I'm the one who urged him to go to the police. I wanted to get him away from Ned, from everything, before it was too late, but running away wasn't the answer. I'd sooner have killed Ned."

"Or Schuyler fucking Tilden?" Tommy asked, the rasp in his voice an attempt to push Theo.

Theo tipped his head back and laughed, but he was incensed. "This is like a bad Ionesco play. We'd have to start in the second grade with Cara Dunleavey if we were going to talk about people I might've killed because I was jealous or angry. She stole my black crayon to cross out Stuart Whitman's name in the valentine heart I made and wrote in her own. And last week, I was angry at Giovanni for forgetting our anniversary. Both still alive! Oh my God!" He pointed to Lucas's photo on the white board. "Did you ask Lucas, that lying sack of shit? Because, Syd, you told me Wyatt's apartment had been torn apart that night, that someone was looking for something. He knew more than he was telling anyone back then."

Tommy handed the red ledger to Theo.

"This? This is what Wyatt's murderer was looking for?" Theo asked, incredulous.

"We think so, but we can't be sure until we can decode it."

"Then color him Ned," Theo said with disgust. "The code was his, the business was his." He sat down at Gale's desk, opened the ledger to the back, took a Swiss army knife from his pocket and gently picked at the end paper. Slowly, the glue across the top of the paper gave way to the flat of the knife, and Theo slipped a piece of lined notebook paper out with the tweezer tool embedded in the army knife's handle.

Syd gasped. Gale was glad to hear the noise.

"I used to watch him glue it back in here. He thought I was asleep." He held the paper out.

Tommy took it from Theo. Gale joined him in the thick silence that enveloped the room, looking at it with him. She'd tell him later that she'd discovered it last night. Tommy laid it on Gale's desk.

"Wait. Am I allowed to see it?" Syd asked.

"No," Gale said. "Theo, do you know who's on this list? Did you ever look at it?"

"I saw it one night when he left it out while he was on the phone. It's why I got so mad."

"Did anyone from the list try and contact you after Wyatt's death?"

"Why would they? No one knew about me. Except Lucas, Ned, and Schuyler. And Syd. I was still closeted."

"One more question. The ledgers weren't about the embezzlement, but there had to be paperwork somewhere. Where did Wyatt keep it?"

"He didn't. But he spent enough time at Ned's apartment for me to think it had to be there."

"So, long gone…" Tommy sighed.

Gale shook Theo's hand. "Thank you for coming in. We'd never have found that code otherwise. I have your number, if we need anything else."

Theo picked up his bag. He turned to look at Syd, and then walked out, Tommy behind him.

"I'd like to walk you out, Syd, but let's give them a moment," Gale said.

Syd sat down and closed her eyes.

"Are you okay?" Gale kneaded her shoulder muscles. Syd looked wrung out. But Gale had a job to do. "You never told me about Wyatt's pocket square. The one you gave to Theo that Friday night?"

Syd opened her eyes, and Gale felt her tense.

"Theo brought it in today. Where did you find it?"

Syd looked up at her. "It was in Wyatt's jacket pocket that morning."

"And where was the jacket?"

"On the back of the couch."

"Folded like we saw it in the photos?"

"Yes."

"Are there any other things you've not told me about?"

"I don't understand."

"Nicholas's photos gave us a very clear idea that the murderer had feelings for Wyatt—that folded jacket, the shoes so carefully placed by the closet afterward. And you said you found Wyatt tucked in his bed. If it was you and not the murderer who had arranged things—" Syd's shoulders became hard under Gale' manipulations.

"I could barely function after I walked into that apartment that morning. I haven't kept things from you—I buried them so I could function. They're so far away in some cases that until someone brings them up, I don't remember them."

Gale trod carefully, the sharpness in Syd's tone warning her. "As long as you're not picking and choosing. You can't do that to us."

"Why would you think I'd do that? No—don't answer that." Syd held up a hand. "I understand that you have to consider me a suspect, but at some point, you have to clear me, or this—" she indicated a link between them. "—doesn't work. We have to trust each other."

"Yes, we do."

"So, do we?"

Gale took a piece of paper out of her jacket pocket and handed it to Syd.

She opened it. "What is this?"

"The code from the back of the ledger. I found it last night. You fought back when Tommy questioned you earlier—you really didn't know where this was. That went a long way toward finally establishing your innocence. I had to ask about the pocket square."

"Wow. So you've considered me up until now?"

Gale was upset by the flash of anger in Syd's eyes. "Bear with me—this is not a straightforward investigation. There are ramifications forty years down the road, it may be linked to a federal investigation, and every day, Tommy and I feel like we're playing whack-a-mole."

"Do you think I would've come to you if I was guilty of something?" Syd, angry, picked up her bag.

"People do fantastic things when it comes to murder, Syd. We have to be sure."

"Well, here's something I'm sure of. There isn't much trust here." Syd headed for the door.

"This isn't how I wanted this to go," Gale said, following her.

Syd whirled around. "Then why didn't *you* talk to me, *you*, not Tommy? We've seen each other every week, you could have asked me anything. Why didn't you?"

"I did. Indirectly. I couldn't show my hand, though, if you were somehow involved."

"Sleeping with the enemy."

"What?"

"You've been sleeping with the enemy all these weeks."

Gale felt like she'd been slapped. "If anything, I've been—" She ran her hand through her hair. "Working with you has made it more difficult to do my job." She wanted to tell Syd that she *did* want to sleep with the enemy.

Syd frowned. "Really? Well, let me be on my way, make your day a little easier."

"Syd, this isn't about my suspecting you of anything."

She turned back again. "Then what? Because you're not exactly exonerating me."

"Please come to dinner tomorrow night like we planned."

"Why? There's nothing here."

Gale walked up to her. "There is, and you know there is."

Syd blinked. "What time?"

"Seven."

"You want the enemy on your home turf?"

Gale took her hand. "You're not the enemy."

"Well, that was both interesting and informative," Tommy said, as he came into the office.

Gale let Syd's hand go.

"Syd, you're comin' to dinner tomorrow night, right?"

Syd kept her eyes on Gale's. "Yes. Yes I am."

❖

Gale and Tommy sat at their desks, Tommy tipped back in his chair.

"I knew we needed to take that book apart."

"Sorry I did it without you. It was spur-of-the-moment, nobody was here, so no possibility of our mole."

Tommy looked at the photocopied list. "A prominent publisher. With a family of seven. I mean, how do guys even—?"

"And we've got the crime boss and the labor official." Gale swiveled back and forth eying all the photos on the white board. "You know, they used to be linked in the news, those two. Kickbacks and whatnot. Now I wonder if it was more. That labor guy's still alive. And still linked to the mob."

"If not for the threat to Syd in eighty-two, I'd be wonderin' if he wasn't behind the blue envelopes."

"I doubt it. But we're dangerously close to LaundryGate here and I don't want the Feds knowing about the list until we solve Wyatt's murder."

Tommy chuckled and pointed to a name on the list. "I didn't even see her, this society doyenne."

"That one I could understand," Gale mused. "Did you see who else was there? Schuyler-fucking-Tilden's wife." She looked over at Tommy. "And guess who she spent all her time and money with?"

Tommy looked at the page Gale had photocopied from the other red ledger, the one with the drug sales. She'd surmised the fourteen names would be in the same order in both ledgers, that Lucas would keep things easy that way. "Shit."

"Your favorite and mine, number five, Billy Highsmith."

Tommy squared the chair, opened his bottom drawer, and took out a bottle of Jack Daniel's and two glasses. "I know it's only one thirty, but I need this." He handed off a pour to Gale, who took it and went back to staring at the board.

Gale shook her head. "Billy Highsmith serviced more people on that list than anyone else. But I'm most especially interested in how often he was with Margaret-fucking-Tilden."

"Please—let's not denigrate—of the old-money Winthrops. I think she married Schuyler for his family name."

"He certainly had the right pedigree, didn't he? Military. Budding political career. And he sure had the looks."

"And the wife's money. I bet she thought she'd ride him right to the White House."

"You think?" Gale walked over to the board. "Military." She unpinned the photo. *Shit, that was in my research—why didn't I see this before?* "Hey—" She turned to Tommy, holding up the photo. "Didn't Lucas say the guy Wyatt picked up that night had a military haircut? That he was clean-cut, stood ramrod straight, had shiny boots?"

"Yeah?"

"What if he wasn't a stranger? What if he'd just never been to Bareback before?"

Tommy, slouched in his chair, sat up. Gale pulled out her cell phone and called George Oakley.

"Mr. Oakley, it's Detective Sterling. We spoke the other night, remember? Your cell phone can receive text messages with photos attached, right?"

Tommy stood and took a tight shot of Schuyler's photo with his cell phone.

"Okay, I'm about to text you a photo of a man we hope you might recognize. You call me right back?...Yes, thank you."

Gale leaned against the window waiting, phone in hand. The late spring breeze smelled fresh and carried the promise of a warm afternoon. A moment later, the scent of the doughnut shop around the corner reached her, and Gale realized how hungry she was, but it was for more than food. Her phone rang. "Mr. Oakley?" As Gale listened, the blood pounded through her. "You're absolutely clear-as-a-bell certain?" She nodded. "Okay, yes—No, no need for you to come in. I'd like to stop by and get a video testimony from you, though. Around four today? And thank you. So much!" Gale held the phone up and drew in a big breath. "He'd been in twice that month. Only times George ever saw him. Said he only remembered him because both times he was loaded for bear, and the second time, he caused a big fight. Both times he went right for Wyatt." Gale drained off her whiskey. "The second time George remembers distinctly because it was Halloween and he thought Schuyler was in a military costume. Of course the guys at the bar were all over him because who doesn't love a man in uniform, and he ended up punching a guy, knocking him out, grabbing Wyatt, and leaving."

"I don't get it."

"Schuyler Tilden was a Marine—he served in Viet Nam during the last days. That wasn't a costume—he was in full dress uniform that night because he'd been to the governor's fundraiser. Theo told me in his interview."

Gale grabbed a file off her desk and shuffled through photocopies, pulling out a *Times* article with a photo of Schuyler and his wife standing with the governor and his wife at the ball.

"*He* was the man Theo found flirting with Wyatt at the ball."

Tommy took the photocopy from her. "Oh shit."

"I think Wyatt went after Theo when he left. He didn't go to his apartment, though—he called him but Theo wouldn't pick up. I think he ended up at Bareback. Didn't Lucas say they were supposed to meet there that night? Schuyler must've tracked him down."

"Son of a bitch. It *was* jealous rage."

"I don't know how we'll prove that they went back to Wyatt's apartment. Then we have to find out who killed Schuyler." Gale pinned Schuyler's photo back on the board. "Because that wasn't a random mugging. There are still three men in my Venn diagram, a second threat, and too many payoffs floating around that tell me that was a hit." She turned back to Tommy. "And not a word to Syd. This stays under wraps until we have Duane Valchek in custody." Gale grabbed a tube of toothpaste and a toothbrush out of her top drawer.

"Schuyler's wife still lives on Park Avenue," Tommy said.

"I know. Call her, make sure she's home. I don't want to smell like we just walked out of a bar when we ring her doorbell."

"Right." Tommy took a stick of gum out of his jacket pocket.

CHAPTER TWENTY-TWO

The mid-May night was still warm when Syd stepped out of the cab in the West Village. She gazed up and down the tree-lined street, the old brick townhouses with their wrought-iron fencing transporting her to Edith Wharton's nineteenth-century New York. Each one was charmingly different—window boxes here, black shutters there, and every front door a hint as to who might live there. The wide black steps of Gale's house led up to a plain black entry over which hung an old-fashioned carriage house lamp. Two potted spruces sat on the top step overlooking planters of pansies running down the steps in bursts of yellow, apricot, and orange.

The break in the row of houses on the side of the street where she stood had allowed for a driveway next to Gale's. Syd recognized her car parked there.

The front door opened, and Tommy stepped out, grinning at her. "I'm glad you came, Syd. C'mon in."

"I am, too." She'd thought more than once about calling Gale and canceling, but then she'd be drawn back to the conversation they'd had in Central Park. Despite their many arguments over the case, and even Gale's confession that she was still suspected of involvement as late as yesterday, there was a promise there. And there was Gale's unspoken plea yesterday before she left. She needed to find out if it was real.

Tommy spotted the gift bag in her hand, the white bow on the liquor box nosing out the top. "Perfect—you should give that to him yourself." Tommy cocked his head. "He's out back on grill duty."

Standing in the foyer, Syd heard Gale on the phone in the kitchen. She was pulled toward the room, but Tommy led the way toward the back of the house.

Out on the deck, Sullivan was at the grill piling blackened tomatoes, mushrooms, onions, and asparagus onto a platter. The sound of a baseball game floated over from a small radio balanced on the railing.

"Sullivan," Tommy called.

Syd hadn't heard her, but Gale was right there to take the platter from him as he turned. She and Gale looked at each other before Gale covered the platter with a piece of tin foil in her hand, put it on the table, and went back into the house before Syd could say anything.

"The inimitable Sydney Hansen. A pleasure to meet you." He held out his hand.

Syd smiled and shook it. She'd dealt with men of all sizes during her career, both egotistically and physically, and was impressed that at ninety-one, Sullivan could still hold a candle to them. In his prime, he must've seemed fearsome in his NYPD uniform. And he had those chiseled features that he'd passed on to his daughter. But Syd was aware that he was a father first, Gale's father, so she wanted to navigate this evening with utmost care. "I'll take that as a compliment," she said.

"Anyone who calls my daughter's bluff and wins is one of a kind, and most welcome at my table."

Syd held up the bag with the bottle of Macallan in it. "For your table, for after dinner."

A broad smile creased his craggy face. "I knew I was going to like you." He put the bag down next to the grill, an impressive thing on wheels that sat on a fire-proofing platform of what looked like worn cobblestones sunk into cement. "What can we get you to drink?"

Syd nodded at Sullivan's glass. "I'll have what you're having."

"I'll get that—Sullivan, you need a refill?" Tommy asked. "You want a chair?"

He shook his head. "I can stand all day now on these titanium knees."

Tommy disappeared, leaving the two of them alone.

"My golf clubs are titanium. That's high-strength stuff."

"Whatever it is, I feel about fifty years younger since I got 'em." Sullivan leaned against the railing. "I'm glad you came tonight. I've been looking forward to meeting you." Sullivan sipped his scotch, his eyes narrowing. "I've sensed that this case is a difficult and driving force for you, and that's lit a fire under her. I know how she's doing. But how are you holding up?"

Syd was taken by surprise at Sullivan's concern, and unexpectedly touched. "I'm—all right. She's taking good care of me." She was, even if they'd had another one of their arguments yesterday.

Sullivan nodded. "She's good at that. I'm glad she chose to partner with you on this investigation. She rarely does that, but I think you both needed it."

Syd read between the lines, but she still wondered how much he knew, how much Gale confided in him. Before she could respond, Gale returned with a plate of steaks and Syd's scotch. Still nothing was said. Syd looked around the deck and the backyard. The weathered octagonal oak table sitting under a canvas umbrella was already set for dinner. A centerpiece held the same orange, apricot, and yellow pansies. They bent gently to the evening breeze. Syd spotted more of the pansies in the garden that ringed the small yard. The beds held greenery, small trees, and many other flowers. "Who's the gardener?"

Syd was focused on Gale, but Sullivan answered. "You're looking at him. When we first moved in here almost fifty years ago, Rita was the one wielding the bandsaw and hammer to refurbish this place. I don't have those skills. But I figured I'd better develop one or she might throw me out, so I went to the local nurseries and learned a thing or two." Sullivan opened the grill. "I found I liked having my hands in dirt and nurturing things other than my daughter. I'll give you the tour after dinner. I've got some beautiful milkweed come in for the monarchs." Sullivan pointed the tongs to large patches of tall orange flowers in the corners of the yard before flipping the steaks. "How does everyone want their steaks done?"

Syd smiled. A man who cared about butterflies—unusual.

When everything was ready, Syd sat next to Gale at the table, acutely aware that they'd exchanged no words so far. She'd wanted to follow her into the kitchen at one point and apologize, until she remembered what their argument had been about. Gale had been there for her every step of the way—why couldn't she let it go? Platters were passed. The occasional breeze carried Gale's perfume. Syd breathed it in, getting lost in the expressions on her face as they all talked, the pinpoints of gold flecks shining in her eyes in the candlelight now that darkness had fallen.

Sullivan prodded Gale and Tommy to recount some of their old cases. That took Syd's mind off the current frost shadowing her and Gale. When Tommy urged Sullivan to tell about the night he and half the precinct dismantled one of the Village's cobblestone streets the night before the city was going to pave it over back in the '80s, Syd realized she was hearing a part of city lore.

Sullivan pointed to the platform the grill sat on, and the bricks that formed the garden's edging. "They were beautiful old cobblestones the city had no intention of reclaiming. We couldn't let them go to waste. And the mayor's office tried to call it theft!"

"You certainly caused quite an uproar with City Hall," Gale said, a note of sarcasm in her voice.

Sullivan rumbled a growl. "That's because it highlighted the mayor's myopia. *And* because no one would talk, not even the people who lived on the street who even helped us that night." Sullivan's laugh was deep and hearty. "There are still numerous Long Island homes with cobblestone patios and pool decks courtesy of that evening. But I always look at it as responsible citizenship: we recycled."

When Sullivan's home health aide Ray arrived at ten o'clock, Syd realized she hadn't looked at her watch once since she'd arrived. Sullivan was reluctant to break up the evening, but anyone could see he was tired. "Gale, show Sydney the garden," Sullivan said before disappearing inside.

"I've had the tour," Tommy said. "I'll clean up here."

Gale and Syd descended the steps to the yard.

"Kind of hard to see the garden in the dark even with porch lights on," Syd said.

"It's not about the garden. He wants me to apologize to you."

"For what?"

"For being so callous yesterday."

"You told him about our argument?"

"He's a good sounding board."

Syd felt a momentary flash of jealousy. She'd never had such a parental yardstick. Nor did she have Gale's perspective on liking your parents well enough to stay with them into their old age or trusting them with your problems. When she'd boarded the train in St. Paul for New York City over forty years ago, she'd never looked back. "What was the consensus?"

"That I should've been more honest, and you could've been more transparent."

As Syd considered Sullivan's wisdom, Tommy emerged from the house. "Kitchen's in good shape, I'm heading out." He raised his hand. "Thanks for a terrific evening, and I'll see you Monday, Gale."

"You're the best, Tommy."

"I know."

Gale shook her head as she watched him go. "He really is the best."

"You two have a very special relationship. I admire that." An unexpected breeze blew over the yards and Syd shivered.

"We should go inside. You haven't really seen the house. Would you like to?"

Walking from room to room, Syd admired the craftsmanship she saw everywhere—flooring, cabinets and shelves, door and window frames. "This woodwork alone is exquisite." Syd ran her hand up the carved mahogany archway of the kitchen, grapes, pears, apples, and other fruit coming alive under her palm.

"She was an artisan."

"I'd like to have met her." Syd leaned against the counter. "I should have been more transparent with you. Sullivan was right."

"I should have put you through the battery of questions right up front."

"Why didn't you? And why did you keep things from me like Wyatt's affair with Schuyler?"

Gale hesitated. "Would you like to come up to my apartment for a drink?"

"Only if that drink is seltzer or water and comes with answers. Two glasses of wine were more than enough for me."

"Me, too."

Gale led the way to the hallway elevator and hit the "up" button.

"Was this your mother, too?" Syd asked. "Rather prescient."

"Yes, she was ahead of her time. Every hall and doorway can accommodate a wheelchair, as can Sullivan's shower downstairs. She meant to stay here as long as she could, but breast cancer got her first."

Syd put her hand comfortingly on Gale's arm. "I'm sorry."

Gale put her hand over Syd's.

When they stepped onto the third floor, a lamp illuminated the apartment.

"Make yourself at home," Gale said, moving into the kitchen and taking two glasses out of the cupboard.

Syd realized from the blueprint of the rooms she'd walked through downstairs that walls had been knocked out to achieve a light airy space on this floor. And instead of bookcases, the shelves in the living room had been built to order for a large record collection and a stereo console. Syd was fascinated—she'd never seen such an accumulation of albums in one person's possession. "May I?" she asked, a hand on one of the shelves. Gale nodded and she slid out a record. Frank Sinatra. Another shelf garnered classical works, and a third, country artists. There were albums from every rock era, soundtracks, spoken word discs, jazz, ragtime, international artists. "This is amazing." She continued to pull out and peek at albums.

"I never liked the sound quality of CDs," Gale said.

"You've been collecting all your life, haven't you?"

No response was needed. A Lena Horne record in her hands, Syd watched Gale breaking the old-fashioned handled silver ice tray over the sink, filling their glasses. The kitchen was modern, outfitted with gleaming silver Viking appliances. Against that backdrop, Gale's silvery hair glinted in the light thrown off by the lamp. She looked beautiful working industriously behind the counter. Syd sensed the kitchen had been Kate's territory, and for a moment, she saw Gale in *her* kitchen, which she'd modeled on her mother's airy farmhouse kitchen with its wide-plank pine floors and glass-fronted cabinets trimmed in white. That seemed more Gale's style. Or maybe it was just wishful thinking.

Gale set the glasses of ice water on the coffee table, took the record from Syd, put it on the turntable, and dropped the needle.

Lena Horne's rich voice quietly surrounded them. They settled on the couch.

"When we first found out about Wyatt's affair with Schuyler, we didn't think it had any bearing on the circumstances surrounding the red ledger, which we've now come to believe is at the heart of this case. So, no, I didn't tell you about it. I think I was half afraid you'd go see Margaret Tilden without telling me."

Syd sighed. "I suppose I deserve that. Although I wonder if I could get more out of her than you will."

"She told us everything she knew yesterday afternoon. Wasn't much."

"So where does that leave you?" Syd sensed a hesitation in Gale. What had Margaret told her?

"Waiting for Duane Valchek on Thursday."

"I'd like to come with you."

"Oh, no."

"Why not? I think I've earned that ride-along considering that you wouldn't even know about him if it wasn't for me. I want to see his face, I want to know if he's guilty."

"Never mind that it's against department policy—"

The gold flecks in Gale's eyes seemed to flash. "I think you could get Esposito to waive that," Syd challenged.

"Maybe I don't want to. Maybe I don't want to endanger your life, which both of us have already foolishly done. More than once."

Syd heard the bite in Gale's words and nipped back. "How would that be endangering my life? I'll stand off to one side—"

"And what if something goes wrong?"

"What could go wrong picking up someone getting off a plane?"

"If he knows we're meeting him, which I'm certain he does—plenty. No one looks for guns when people are getting off a plane, Syd. Only when they're getting on. It's feasible someone could've planted a gun on the plane for him and he could wreak havoc in the airport and escape. I'm not having you in the middle of that. You've been in the middle of just about everything else."

"I've involved myself because this is important to me, a lifetime of important. I had to make sure you got it right." Syd hadn't intended for things to get out of hand like this.

"And who was talking about the trust not working between us yesterday?"

"Because you were still seeing me as a suspect!"

"And now you're intimating that I'm incompetent, so *you* don't trust *me*." Gale got up and walked to the kitchen to refill her glass. Syd followed her.

"That's not what I meant and you know it."

"You have involved yourself every step of the way," Gale said. "You didn't trust us to handle Lucas, you didn't trust me about George Oakley—"

"I did trust you—I texted you because I knew you would come. Because I needed you. I've trusted you with everything from the beginning. I need you, Gale." It wasn't the case she was talking about anymore, and she kissed Gale. She was tentative at first, but that went out the window when Gale kissed her back. Hard. Syd heard a button hit the floor, and her reasoning followed it. She pulled at the buttons on Gale's jeans as Gale lifted her polo shirt off by the hem. She unbuttoned Gale's shirt as Gale pulled down the zipper on her shorts.

"Hold my hands," Syd commanded as she shucked her sneakers and stepped out of her shorts. If she fell, she'd surely break something. The gold flecks in Gale's eyes seemed to suddenly glitter as Syd looked at her. That scent of jasmine, thyme, and leather teased at Syd's senses, stoking the desire that had suddenly imploded. She wanted Gale right now. "Get out of those pants."

Gale stepped out of her sneakers, her pants pooled around them, and into her arms, removing Syd's bra in the process. Syd hadn't been this naked in front of anyone in a couple of years and was suddenly self-conscious, especially standing in the kitchen. But Gale's hands were running down her back, into her panties, sliding them down, and she was going to her knees to take them off. Syd held onto the counter, and when Gale rose again, Syd buried her fingers in Gale's hair as she kissed her.

"I can't make love on kitchen floors or counters anymore," she whispered in Syd's ear. "Come upstairs."

The bed was big, a down featherbed beneath them. Gale pushed several books to the floor, quickly shed her panties and bra, and took Syd into her arms, kissing her. They were long, slow kisses despite

Syd's impatience, and she fell into the rhythm of them, riding the thigh Gale had pushed between her legs. Over the next few hours, Gale was relentless, and she responded, her back arching into her, fingers and tongue finding her, mouths together in the kind of communion she hadn't felt in a long time. There were moments she hadn't expected, and her infectious laughter had Gale laughing along with her after Syd got a charley horse in the middle of an orgasm. Gale needing to come up for air at an inopportune moment sent them into fits of giggles. But then Gale would be between her legs again, and she couldn't be sure where Gale ended and she began as they savored each other, scents and sounds and tastes filling her, then leaving her wanting more. Gale's hands, as strong as they looked, took charge of her body. She gave Gale everything she had, and when she thought she was empty, Gale found more. Things she didn't know she'd been holding onto left her mind and her body under Gale's ministrations and she realized she was crying at one point. Gale wrapped herself around Syd and rocked her, telling her to let it all go. Then they melted into one another again with the kind of heat that hadn't stoked Syd in years.

Toward dawn, Gale lay next to Syd tracing a finger over her face. "Yesterday, you told Theo you were only relatively happy."

Syd looked at her.

"I'd like to make you more than relatively happy."

Syd rolled into her arms. By the time they were finally sated, a pointillistic gray had overtaken the black of night, and Gale pulled the quilt around them and curled around Syd.

CHAPTER TWENTY-THREE

Gale was still in a deep sleep when Syd left her bed far earlier than she'd intended. Ray, preparing Sullivan's breakfast, let her out the front door. She sent Gale a text from the cab: *I had to leave. I can't put my finger on why. But I still want our Tues. mtg.*

She knew why she'd left, though. Except for telling Syd she wanted to make her more than relatively happy, Gale hadn't wanted to talk about where this was going. Perhaps the promise she'd alluded to in Central Park was nothing more than dandelion seeds floating on the breeze.

Syd couldn't sit through Mass. Pushing out the door into the sunshine, she felt Father Moore's eyes on her. He hadn't yet delivered the sermon.

Price and Waterhouse were curled up in the sunlight on the living room floor when she got home. Not having experienced her overnight absence in a long time, they chose to ignore her. She wasn't above buying love, though. Before she'd even taken the catnip out of the kitchen cupboard, they were beside her, stretching up and reaching for the countertop, snuffling excitedly. Within a minute, a serene Price's paws were contentedly curled around his plate. Waterhouse rolled around on his back, his big head on his little plate as he pushed it about the kitchen on his back legs, alternately stopping to twist over and kiss it. Syd left them to their drug high and went to the bedroom. Fighting fatigue, she texted Gale again since it had been over five hours since she'd sent the first message: *R u okay?*

Bleary-eyed, Syd read a few paragraphs of the novel on her nightstand while waiting for a reply. Nothing came back. She slid under the covers and floated toward sleep trying not to attach any significance to Gale's online absence.

When she awoke, the day was nearly gone. She looked at her phone and found a message from Gale. *I shouldn't have broken department policy and let last night happen. I apologize. No need for Tues. since we're picking up Duane on Thurs.*

With twenty-four words, Gale had erased her and their night together. Syd dropped back onto the pillows. The phone fell to the floor. How could she? They'd shared so many things in those hours: in her arms, Gale told her about her life with Kate and what that loss had cost her, and Syd had offered up what the years with Marie and her subsequent departure when she needed her most had done to her. Gale made it safe for her to let go of it, to cry for Marie, for Wyatt, for Nicholas, for herself, holding her in return, a vessel to be filled, until Syd was empty. Where had she misjudged?

She was disconsolate. Those words had taken the fight out of her, finally. No Tuesday meeting, no going to the airport. No Gale. How could she have been so stupid?

And, if Duane didn't comply, or fold, no murderer.

She wouldn't get to measure the sense of guilt on Duane's face. Or an innocence that would point them in another direction. She rolled over and let the tears she thought were gone come again.

Tommy was right behind Gale as she stopped in the break room with a shopping bag, grabbed some plates, and started unloading muffins.

"Oh no—Sullivan try and solve the case at breakfast yesterday?" He picked up a blueberry muffin.

"No." She continued unloading cranberry and banana walnut muffins.

"Wait—I'm confused."

Gale paused, a muffin in her hand. "Remember when you slept with that woman from the basement murder case a couple years ago?"

"Yeah. Sylvia. The gal whose aunt was walled up for thirty years. She was nice."

"And I made you shut it down?"

"Oh. Yeah. Department policy."

"How did you tell her that you couldn't see her again?"

"Like you just said, can't see you, I'm on a case that involves you, that's our policy." Tommy made short work of the muffin he'd picked up.

Gale mulled it over, then put more muffins on the plate.

"You wanna tell me what's goin' on?" He picked up a cranberry muffin.

"I did something stupid Saturday night. I slept with Syd and now I've had to walk it back. But there's really no walking something like that back, is there?"

"Say what now?" Tommy had the paper halfway off the muffin. His eyebrows rose.

"I couldn't just shove these feelings away until we solved the case. Dammit." Gale reached for another plate. "Now I'm sorry I made you stop seeing Sylvia. I didn't have to be such a hall monitor."

Tommy hadn't blinked or breathed. Now he did both.

Gale sighed. "I shut her down. After we spent the most incredible night together. And I don't know what to do."

"Call her."

She looked at Tommy. He couldn't be serious. "It's not that easy."

"Yeah, Gale, it is. You women complicate things with all your feelings and your shoulds and shouldn'ts. Pick up the phone. Tell her you're worried about policy but that we're right at the finish line. If Duane's not our man, we arrest Billy and Lucas. One of them knows something, one of them will break, and then you're free and clear. You gotta get out of your own way. Or is this about something else?"

Gale raised an eyebrow.

"Kate?"

She ran a hand through her hair.

"And you don't have to tell me. Tell her. Whatever you did or didn't say Saturday night or Sunday morning, finish saying it. Because you don't shut a woman down after you've been intimate with her. And I don't think you want to shut Syd down at all."

Gale was always surprised by the things that went on inside Tommy's head. He was right, part of it was Kate. Grief, that ethereal thing, kept showing up on her doorstep. But part of it were these inexplicable insistent feelings for Syd. She was infuriating and intelligent. Beautiful, complicated, and down-to-earth. And Gale *was* hiding behind department policy because she was afraid. She'd spent her adult life with Kate, and then she'd put her heart away. Sydney Hansen was never supposed to happen, never supposed to show up and awaken things in her mind and her heart. But here she was, challenging her at every juncture, about herself, about the case, and about her ability to love again.

"So," Tommy said, folding Gale's shopping bag. "This was your Sunday, huh?"

"I detailed the cars, too."

"Jeez. Basket case."

Gale put her head in her hand. "You have no idea."

"I've been where you are, my friend. Call her. So—no chocolate chip?"

"I only made six. I ate two of them last night, Sullivan took two and the other two I ate on the way in this morning."

"Wow. Well, usually I'd tell ya we should work on the case, take your mind off everything, but I got something of my own to confess. I called Pete Nowak in for questioning, sent a coupla uniforms to get him. And before you go ballistic—"

Gale had opened her mouth to speak.

"He was already involved since he helped Duane fake the funeral. He's gotta know more. And if we present it to him as the best way to help his nephew before everything goes down on Thursday, then maybe he cooperates and we get it all without anyone getting hurt, and maybe even some reduced sentences. I can't sit on him anymore, Gale."

"But we agreed not to—"

"I know, but if Billy called him, considering the unknown numbers I still have to track down on Billy's call list that look like burner phones, and considering how many days it took me to get Pete on the phone, I think he knows everything."

"How many days? And why didn't you tell me you were doing this?"

"Ten. I insubordinated because I knew you'd say no, but I got a strong feeling about him. He's been dodgin' my calls. I even drove out to his house yesterday after church, dialed his number watchin' him through his living room window, and he looked at the number on his cell and didn't answer, like the other hundred times. I'd already left a buncha messages that we were lookin' into an old case he worked and needed his take on a coupla things. Obviously, he didn't believe me, which says he's known for years."

Gale inhaled but didn't let it out.

"He'll be here in about fifteen minutes."

The breath came out as a complaining moan. "This early? We haven't prepared!"

"Our guys wanted to avoid traffic on the LIE. And of course I'm prepared."

Tommy's desk phone rang. He picked up. "Got it." He quirked his head toward the door. "They got him here early."

They walked out to meet Pete Nowak. At the front desk, several older cops were gathered around him laughing at a story he was telling. Tommy joined them. Gale watched and listened from beneath the archway, looking Pete over, finding him so average with his mouse-brown hair, ordinary face, medium height and build, and a Yankees baseball cap, that no one except his wife would ever pick him out in a crowd for any reason. He could rob a bank without using a mask and not be caught because the descriptions of him would be so bland.

A moment later, the desk sergeant held up the phone and called Gale over.

"Yes, sir, that's Pete Nowak...Yes, sir." She hung up the phone, returned to her self-appointed post by the archway and texted Tommy: *Esposito said to "get that piece of shit" out of his house and report to him.*

Tommy looked at his phone, pulled Pete aside, and Gale watched him make an explanation and walk him out of the precinct.

She went back to the desk sergeant. "What do you know about that retired cop and why the captain threw him out?"

"Nowak? Yeah, he's on the captain's shit list, somethin' from back in the day. He had me toss the guy out about three weeks ago."

"What was he doing here?"

"He came in to see you. I let him back there, didn't check to see you were out. Captain saw him leaving, told me he didn't ever want to see him here again, that if he came back, I should let him know ASAP."

"Wait—you never told me he came to see me. And you'd let someone into our office without calling me? What did he say he wanted?"

"Just said he had something, I completely forgot, Gale, sorry. He was in and out in ten, and being retired NYPD, I let him in."

Twenty minutes later, Gale and Tommy walked out of Esposito's office.

"Jesus," Tommy said, chagrined. "Why isn't there some kind of database we can check for "cop non grata by your captain?" I sent him to the coffee shop because I think we still oughtta talk to him, so why don't we go over?"

"Not yet. When I asked the sarge what this was all about, he told me Nowak was here three weeks ago to see me. He let him in, but we were out."

"Yer kiddin'!"

"Are you thinking what I'm thinking?"

Tommy broke into a trot. Several of the detectives were at their desks when they reached the office.

"Any of you see a Pete Nowak in here three weeks ago, retired NYPD?" he asked.

"Yeah," Miller said as the others nodded. "He was looking for you, Gale. Sat at your desk to write you a note and then left."

"I didn't get any note."

"Maybe he decided not to leave it."

Tommy pulled Gale out of the office. "But he left the bug under your desk instead. So he's in on it. He knew we were out, too."

"This isn't good for Syd." Gale went to her desk and dialed Syd. "Tommy, send those uniforms to the diner to see if Pete's still there. C'mon, c'mon, Syd, pick up." When there was no answer, she grabbed her car keys. "I've got to get to her." She unlocked her drawer and holstered her gun.

"Not without me you don't. Put those keys away—we're taking our precinct car. And I'm drivin'—don't even think of arguing."

Tommy had the lights and siren going before Gale had her seat belt on.

Gale kept redialing her phone. "Dammit, where is she?"

Tommy threaded through traffic with the practiced ease of a driver at Le Mans. When they reached Syd's apartment building, Gale barely waited for him to stop the car. She heard Pete yelling, and surprised him as she came through the door, gun trained on him, her badge in her other hand crossed over it. Pete had a badge in his hand; the doorman held the desk phone.

"Pete Nowak, police—step away from the desk."

"You gotta be kidding me!"

"Does she look like she's kidding?" Tommy emerged through the revolving door. He kicked the chair sitting next to it into the door, blocking it, and circled around Gale to the other side of Pete.

"Detective D'Angelo, what's going on here?"

With her gun, Gale motioned to the doorman to move away from the desk.

"We're taking you in is what's happening," Tommy said. "We want to talk to you, but you knew it wasn't about an old case of yours, didn't you?"

"No idea what you're talking about."

"And yet here you are in Sydney Hansen's lobby. You know it's about our cold case," Gale said, drawing his attention away from Tommy. "We know you're Duane Valchek's uncle. And I'm betting you're in this up to your neck, so why don't you make this easier and put your hands over your head."

"You have nothing to hold me with."

"Let's start with that duplicate shield you're holding which violates department policy. And then let's move on to Sydney Hansen, who you wouldn't know if you weren't privy to this case. Who called you? Billy? Your dead nephew Duane?"

"I want my lawyer."

"You'll get him. Hands." Tommy, who'd been inching closer to Pete as Gale talked, pushed his head to the desk to secure his hands.

Keeping her gun trained on Pete, Gale unblocked the door. "I need to go upstairs, see if Syd is all right."

"I know."

She watched him walk Pete to the car and asked the doorman to call Syd to tell her that Detective Sterling was on her way up. Syd was in her open doorway when she got there. Her hair was wet, and Gale smelled the soap and shampoo that had been on her skin Saturday night. "You were in the shower. I've been calling and texting."

"I see that now. And then *you* didn't answer. What's going on?"

Gale explained the morning's events. Syd was astonished, and then frightened. "How did he know where I lived?"

"We're not sure. Listen, I'm very worried for your safety, but I still can't put a uniform here. I need you to stay home until we have Duane. I'll tell your doorman no one comes upstairs for any reason. If you get any deliveries, the guy leaves it and then you go downstairs for it, okay? Nobody but the doorman has access to you. I'll tell the one on duty that goes for all your doormen, police orders."

"Well, I appreciate that you're worried for my safety." Syd retreated into the apartment and closed the door, but Gale's hand stopped it.

"Wait." Syd had every right to be mad at her, but instead of the wrath that she was expecting when Syd focused those ice blue eyes on her, there was a blankness in her face that Gale had never seen. Was Syd covering her emotions, or was she done with her? "I owed you more than a texted apology. I'm sorry I did that to you. Could we— take a walk in the park Wednesday night? And talk?"

"Why?"

"So I can tell you Saturday night wasn't a mistake." Gale pulled her in for a kiss. "I've got to go. I'll call you from the precinct around six on Wednesday." She didn't look back as she walked to the elevator, but she didn't hear Syd's door close either.

CHAPTER TWENTY-FOUR

Rain threatened, but Syd and Gale sat in the park watching the rays of the setting sun struggle to light up the eastern sky through low scudding clouds.

"I wanted to straighten this out before we pick up Duane tomorrow. I'm an exacting boss in all respects," Gale said. "So for me to break department policy with you during an ongoing case—"

"You should've said something."

Gale caressed her face. "That was a four-alarm fire Saturday night. I didn't want to stop it or give you any ammunition to either."

A few fat spatters of rain hit the sidewalk. They both looked up to see the sky darkening.

"I really have driven you crazy during this investigation," Syd said.

"In *so* many ways."

"You understand why, though."

"I do, yes. But that's not going to get you to the airport."

"I wasn't going to ask again—you made it abundantly clear on Saturday night."

"I can't risk it, Syd. He could be like a cornered rat, and now that you and I have arrived here, I don't want to risk losing you for any reason."

Syd put a finger to Gale's lips. "No more arguing. Let's go back to talking about Sunday morning."

Gale kissed her finger. "You know the two of us are still going to argue over everything even when this case is over."

The spatters became a sprinkle. Gale took off her coat to shield Syd. "We should probably get to the car."

They began walking and the rain changed to drumming drops. Suddenly it was like nightfall. They ran to the car, ducking inside the front seat seconds before the cloudburst came down in sheets. The windows fogged up. Gale cracked hers and the crisp air dissipated the vapor. In the violence of the downpour, rain shimmered on the pavement in the streetlights.

Syd shook out her hair. It was damp despite the protection of Gale's jacket. "I'm only argumentative when there's a reason, Detective Sterling. But you have won this last battle and therefore the war. I'm trusting your instinct that Duane Valchek holds the key to everything."

"It only makes sense since he disappeared for forty years. And stayed disappeared while collecting a major payoff from Ned."

"Yes, it does. I would rather talk about Sunday morning, now, anyway. I wish you'd told me in your text what was going on. You know, I'd always meant for Saturday night to happen in my apartment because I was afraid of how wrong things could go for us if you had a reaction to my being in the bed you shared with Kate."

"Did you now? You planned to sleep with me? I'd love to know how long ago that was."

Syd blushed.

Gale took her hand. "It was always going to hit me the first time, wherever it happened. But I'm glad it happened where it did. Because I missed you after you left. That's what scared me. All I knew was that I wanted you back in my bed. And—in my life. And I was paralyzed, not knowing what to do. So—I hid behind that text. You deserved better than that. But I'll also point out that you left well before I was awake."

Syd was hoping Gale wouldn't bring that up, but, good for the goose... She wasn't sure how she was going to explain her abrupt departure to her.

The downpour was over as quickly as it began. They watched the sky trade black for gray and then white, the rain merely water on the street now, its iridescence gone. Gale rolled her window down. Everything smelled of wet pavement and spring. "You ran away from me, Sydney Hansen. I think—" She pulled Syd across the console between the seats for a kiss. "We need to find out what made you run."

Syd couldn't form a coherent word, the ones she wanted to say being "our future" as she looked into Gale's eyes, the gold flecks against the hazel as splendent as the rain had been on the street.

"Come on, it's turning into a beautiful night," Gale said. Let's take a walk." Gale put the windows up and got out of the car.

Syd was off the hook. She let out a sigh. Zipping her jacket up, she glanced at her side mirror. There was a tall man coming up the sidewalk by the park's stone wall. He had that same familiar loping gait as the man she'd seen the night she and Gale sat outside George Oakley's apartment in her car. His face was hidden by the same kind of hoodie. This time it came to her—that height and the way he dropped his shoulders and swung his arms, half hurry, half stroll. She was about to get out and greet him, but Gale was there, opening the door for her.

"Gale, it's Billy—" Before she could finish the sentence, what felt like a fire-tipped arrow ripped across the top of her right shoulder, the windshield shattered, and she heard the gun report. She tried to cover her eyes against the flying shards of glass but her arm was limp and the pain buzzed loud in her ears. She gripped the top of the car door with her left hand, struggling to get out as another shot sounded and Gale fell, gun in hand. She didn't move. Syd slid down to the ground. All she could think about was protecting Gale, and she forced herself on top of her, covering her as best she could. Another gunshot rang out. Syd braced for death even as she prayed for God to spare Gale. But she didn't feel anything. Where was the blackness? Why could she still hear things? Didn't sound disappear when you lay dying? An unmistakable voice called in a frantic "officer down!" dispatch. Then, Tommy was in her ear.

"Syd, can you hear me? Can you move?"

Tommy was a hallucination. She was too shocked to move. There were sirens in the distance. *I'm not dead.*

"Syd, I'm going to move you onto the sidewalk. It's gonna hurt like hell but I need to see Gale's injury."

The pain as he gently moved her told her she was very much alive. So did the sound of people's voices. The last thing she thought before blackness overtook her was—where was Billy?

When she came to, paramedics were bent over her. One was shining a light in her eye, asking her questions she couldn't answer. She turned her head, pain shooting everywhere, and saw more paramedics with Gale. She tried to reach for her, but nothing moved. "Is she alive?"

"Yes," he answered as he applied a pressure bandage to her shoulder. "Look at the light. Tell him your name."

She answered. "Where is Billy Highsmith?" she asked.

"Who?"

The man who shot us."

"He's behind us."

Syd peered over, but all she saw was Tommy standing near another group of EMTs.

"Is he alive?"

"No."

Syd closed her eyes.

"Hey, don't go anywhere, we need you to stay with us," the paramedic said as he slipped an oxygen mask on her. "Can you take a big breath for me so I can hear your lungs?" But she couldn't stay.

❖

Syd felt the shaking but no pain. Her inner eyelids had turned to sandpaper. She couldn't open her eyes.

"Syd, they're going to prep you for surgery."

Last thing to go, first thing to come back, hearing. Still not dead. What was Tommy doing here? And where was "here?" She raised her hand to rub at her eyes, but nothing happened.

"Syd, they need your permission to operate. Those were hollow point bullets that hit you and Gale. They did some damage. They're gonna put your collarbone back together with plates and screws, okay?"

Syd tried unsuccessfully to move her shoulder. "Yes."

"Gale's already in an OR. Punctured lung, but she's gonna be okay. I'll be here when you wake up." He grasped Syd's hand. "You did good."

"Billy's dead?"

"Yeah."

"How?"

"Gale got a bullet off, and so did I."

Several nurses moved in, and Tommy backed away.

"Wait—my cats."

"Where are your keys?"

"My coat pocket."

"I'll put a uniform on them."

Everything seemed black. *Now I must be dead.* She heard murmurs. For all the times she'd wondered what angels' voices would sound like, she'd never imagined they'd be low and gravelly like—"Tommy?" Syd barely heard her own voice.

"Yes, Syd, I'm here. Sullivan is with me." He stepped over to her side.

Gale. Where was Gale?

Sullivan joined him, and as if he'd heard her unspoken question, he took her hand. "Gale is next door. She's okay. Hooked up to a lot of tubes, but okay."

Miller came into the room with two coffees in a cardboard holder. "Detective Sterling, I brought coffee. They told me you were in here."

Sullivan waved him off. "Thank you, son."

"It's been hours, Sullivan," Tommy said. "You have to have something."

For the first time, Syd wondered how many hours, what time was it?

"Miller, you bring the sandwiches?" Tommy asked.

"In the other room. If you need anything at all, sir, please don't hesitate to ask. That's what I'm here for." Miller produced a pint of Macallan from his coat pocket. "A shot in your coffee, sir?"

Sullivan smiled at the bottle as if at an old friend. He nodded.

Miller handed him the cup of coffee, deposited a splash, and capped the bottle. "You need to eat, too, Tommy. We leave in about an hour." Miller looked at Syd. "Hey, nice to have you back with us. Thank you for protecting Gale." He left the room.

"Where are you going?" Syd asked as Sullivan returned to his chair.

"Airport. Duane lands in two hours."

"Where were you?"

"I've been right here. Or in Gale's room."

"No, I mean when it happened. You were there. Where did you come from?"

"I tailed you and Gale. I was parked about five cars behind you. She'll hate me when she finds out, but I had a real bad feelin' after Pete Nowak. He never shoulda known where you lived."

"How did he know?" Gale hadn't answered the question when she'd asked it, and it was the last thing Syd had wanted to talk about with her last night. Now she sensed that Tommy's big brown eyes, trained on her, were making a calculation.

"We found a bug in the office, you had one in your computer and phone. So, hard to say. You get some rest now. I'll come see you before we leave." He patted her hand, and he and Sullivan left.

She saw the clock on the wall. It was close to four in the morning. How long had her surgery been? How long had Gale's been? When could she possibly see her? Right next door but it might as well be Mars. She was very grateful, though—had Tommy not tailed them, Syd knew she'd be in a morgue right now, on a table next to Gale instead of in the hospital room next door, albeit Mars. She closed her eyes to say a prayer for Tommy.

Low voices filtered into Gale's dawning consciousness. Wherever she was, it was getting dark and cooling down. And it was very soft. A cloud? Was this how they moved? It felt good, like the teacup ride at the state fair, only in incredibly slow motion. She struggled to open her eyes—she wanted to see the other teacups, see who was in them because she swore Syd had drifted by in one and she'd reached out and seen that her gun was in her hand, but that didn't make sense. When she finally succeeded in prying her eyes open, ceiling tiles came into focus. There was a water stain on one of them. Sunlight invaded the room through partially closed blinds on a window. Was that her father in a big chair?

"Welcome back," Sullivan said.

"From where?" She didn't recognize the croak of her own voice and looked down at her body in the bed. She saw tubes everywhere and was instantly nauseated. She didn't mind dead or maimed bodies, gunshot wounds or mummified remains—over the years she'd gotten used to that. But hospital tubes? That meant her mother, Kate, holes in the body that shouldn't be there, invasive medical procedures, things coming out that belonged inside. And death.

"Do you remember anything?" Sullivan asked.

Gale tried to shake her head. It wasn't clouds but painkillers she'd been experiencing. She was so relaxed that nothing moved when she willed it.

"You were shot. Left lung. But you're a tough one. You're going to make it. Doctors put a new titanium one in there."

Gale would've laughed if she could've—Sullivan loved his titanium knees. She closed her eyes but this time they popped open. "Dad! Where's Syd? She was with me!"

"In the room next door. Doctors had to patch up her collarbone with screws and plates. She's fine, Tommy checked."

A vague memory of Syd on top of her after she was shot began forming. But that couldn't be right. Syd was on the ground herself. Everything happened so fast—Gale thought Syd was dead, pulled out her gun, fired at Billy with intent to kill, and then her chest felt like it was blown up and everything went black.

Billy. Her eyes must have closed but she jumped, wide awake now. "What day is it?!"

"It's Thursday morning."

Gale reached over the tubes for the covers.

"What do you think you're doing?" Sullivan demanded.

"Airport."

"Oh no you don't—" He was out of his chair, the officer on duty right behind him.

"Tommy." She tried unsuccessfully to fight Sullivan's gentle hold.

"He's got capable backup."

A nurse came into the room. "We're seeing activity on the monitors at our station."

"She's trying to join her partner."

"Thinks she's leaving, does she? We see it all the time. You can't leave, Detective Sterling. You've had major surgery. Come on, back under the covers." The nurse smoothed out Gale's sheets. "I'll add a little more sedative to her drip."

Gale lay back. "He needs me," she whispered, her eyes closing.

Sullivan leaned down. "So do I. And I believe Sydney Hansen does, too. So, Detective Sterling, are you listening?"

Gale recognized that particular timbre of her father's voice through the fog that was creeping in. "Sir?"

"You are officially off duty and on medical leave until such time as your commanding officer deems you fit and ready again. You will stand down."

The nurse returned and added the sedative to the mix dripping into Gale. "That'll take care of her for a while."

Gale's energy was already sapped, but one thought remained. *Sydney Hansen needs me.* Her eyelids closed on their own.

CHAPTER TWENTY-FIVE

Syd was cranky. The nurses kept waking her up to give her medicine. She wanted to sleep. No, she wanted to be in the room next door. The television was on, muted, to the noon news. Billy Highsmith's corporate bank photo front and center shocked her. She turned the sound up and listened to the story of what she'd lived through with Gale in the park, the anchor delving into the link to the LaundryGate scandal, which was breaking wide open everywhere. An FBI agent and his monotonous government tone filled the screen,, drawing a line between a city government in bed with the mob forty years ago straight to the current City Hall, a trail involving city unions and money-laundering then and now, resting on the history of a male prostitution ring, of which Billy and several other lost boys had been members. Syd was stupefied at the breadth of the scandal—had Wyatt been part of it? Nor did she understand how Billy could have thought shooting her and Gale was the answer to protecting his identity. Photos of Lucas Rose and Zach Feinberg flashed on the screen as the agent identified other men, now in FBI custody, who had ties to both eras, Wall Street, and the mob, and Syd felt sick to her stomach. What had Gale and Tommy known? *My God, they've been protecting me from so much.*

Syd wanted to be furious with Gale for hiding this aspect of the investigation, but she couldn't. Instead, she laughed at the absurdity, but the resultant sharp pain in her shoulder stopped her. She'd been fortunate that Gale had shared anything. She never had to, but she did. *And in return she got information she'd never have been able to find on her own.* She'd also gotten Syd's heart in the bargain.

The anchor's follow-up story drew Syd back to the screen.

"In a connected investigation, the NYPD picked up a man at JFK this morning wanted in a cold case murder that occurred in nineteen eighty-two here in the city. He'd been thought to be dead for the last forty years."

Syd watched as Tommy and several police officers walked Duane Valchek out of the Air France terminal, a coat over his handcuffs. He was the small, trim elf he'd always been, his hair still brown. Syd was sure he dyed it, and that he'd had a facelift along the way. The sadness that settled on her as she watched Tommy push Duane into a waiting police car burrowed its own deep hole, as if it expected to stay a long time. A reporter thrust a microphone at him demanding a comment.

"Not as dead as we thought he was," Tommy replied before getting into the back seat with Duane.

Syd shook her head. Nothing fazed Tommy. She loved that about him. That and a million other things, chief among them that he cared so much for Gale and looked out for her.

So that was it. It had been Duane after all. Syd thought back to the blue envelope in her door in April. A major part of her past had changed within a whirlwind of events in a little over two months. There was an absurdity to it, wasn't there? Not so absurd, a gift, in fact, was that it had brought Gale into her life.

Tommy breezed through the door with an orderly and a wheelchair. "Oh, good, you're awake! You saw my fifteen minutes of fame? More like two. I'm hijacking you to go next door."

Syd half-expected her heart monitor to ramp up. "Is Gale awake?"

"She is, and I got permission to wheel you over so I can fill you both in at the same time on what happened this morning."

Syd grimaced as the orderly helped her into the chair. The pain wasn't going to defeat her, though—she'd have walked across the Sahara to make this trip.

Gale was propped up in bed looking peaked but alert. Everything in Syd vibrated at the sight of her. Gale reached out a hand and the orderly parked her wheelchair close enough to the bed that they could hold hands.

"So." Tommy pulled up a chair and cracked his knuckles. "Everything did not go according to plan this morning. But then, why would it? Like we been sayin' from the beginning, nothing was what it seemed with this case."

Syd had been holding her breath. "*What* didn't go according to plan?" The sentence spilled out as one word.

"Musical chairs with Duane, Lucas, and Pete Nowak. I had those two in interrogation rooms at the precinct, doors open, from six thirty this mornin', waitin' on me to walk by with Duane right into the room next to them. Ghost of Christmas past and all, figured that'd scare the bejesus out of one of them and we'd get our confessions. Nothin' like thinkin' your old buddy is rolling over on you to get you to talk faster than him for a chance at parole over life."

"But?" Gale asked.

"FBI broke up my party. Came in and hauled Lucas outta there before I even got going."

"Because of that LaundryGate case. Which neither of you told me had anything to do with Wyatt's case." Syd looked pointedly at Tommy as she squeezed Gale's hand.

"We only just figured it out ourselves, and we were trying to keep everything we had out of the FBI's hands," Gale said. "How did the FBI know you were picking up Duane?"

"When I figure that out, I'll let ya know. I'm just glad they didn't take him or Pete."

"Yet," Gale said.

"Pete's nothin' to them. Duane, maybe. So tell her what we know, Gale—what we've known for several days."

For all the years she'd wanted answers, Syd had to steel herself now to hear them.

"Billy wasn't involved in Wyatt's murder. Not the way we thought he was, anyway. But he was tangled up in that original money-laundering. Do you remember those boxes in the red ledger that had four or five entries more than once a week?" Gale asked.

Syd nodded.

"Billy. It turns out he was servicing a lot of highly placed gentlemen. And carrying messages back and forth between City

Hall and the mob. The Feds figured it out through a back door, with evidence they had that we didn't, and they've been waiting for us to lead them to the answers they still needed."

"This couldn't have been Wyatt. This was Ned," Syd said.

"We're not sure if Wyatt had a hand in this. An Agent McCarthy got in touch with me lookin' for info on Billy a while ago," Tommy said, "but I stonewalled him. He was stand-up enough with me this morning to share that Ned was laundering money for the mob through his prostitution ring. It was gonna break in the news today anyway, no skin off his nose. Ned did it as a favor for a Wall Street friend, against his will, until he saw how much he could skim off the top to cover what his embezzlement at Divine Heart wasn't covering with his hedge fund clients. Only McCarthy told me it wasn't just the mob's money. They were in bed with city union officials who were playing with members' union dues. Ned didn't know that part at first."

"And this is connected to Wyatt's murder how?" Syd asked, fear seeping in that the red ledger she'd taken might have been at the heart of Wyatt's murder, for which she'd never forgive herself.

"Through Wyatt himself," Gale said, so softly that Syd nearly missed it. "He went to the FBI. He didn't wait for Theo to get back from Miami. He didn't want the mob to catch up with Ned. So, he had some degree of involvement." Gale squeezed Syd's hand when she saw the dumbfounded look on her face. "The Feds were ready to move on all of it when he got himself killed and the ledgers went missing. They had written testimony from him, but without the ledger and the codes, all they had were some wire taps, but not enough to make a case. When Ned found the ledger in Wyatt's desk, he must've thought Wyatt was planning on going to the Feds. He didn't know he already had."

Syd put her head in her hands and Gale reached out to rub her back. "And then I took the ledger from Ned's briefcase."

"Ned obviously had friends in high places who kept him safe."

"Wait—so the mob killed Wyatt?"

"No," Gale said.

Syd looked at her, frustrated. "You know, don't you?"

"We're not a hundred percent sure," Gale said gently.

"We're not any percent sure." Tommy sighed in frustration. "But we know Duane holds the key."

"No, we're close to being sure. We're missing one small link. Where is Duane now?" Gale asked Tommy.

"Precinct holding. I gotta talk to the DA. FBI wasn't interested in him this morning, but if what we think is true, once Lucas talks, they will be. I need to put him into protective custody away from them."

Gale sighed. "How possible will that be? We just can't disappear him from the FBI."

"Yeah, I think we can."

"Long enough for me to get out of here? I think I can swing it in a couple of days. I want a crack at him."

"You work on gettin' outta here, I'll stash him." Tommy stood.

"Wait!" Syd was angry. "Who killed Wyatt? Why can't you tell me what you know?"

"Because we don't know," Tommy said. "It's not the same as what we surmise. And surmising's not enough. We gotta get it from Duane on a recording. Because we're pretty sure he knows." Tommy stretched. "I am really beat. Gale, I figure we got three days at the most. And by the way, Duane knows Billy is dead."

Gale nodded.

Tommy's departure left a silence in the room, and Gale turned to Syd with an apology on her mind but was met with a look she recognized, and it meant only one thing: trouble.

"*You* will not be ready to leave here in a few days, first of all. And second, whatever you and Tommy thought you knew about Wyatt's murderer almost got us killed last night!"

Gale put her hand to her chest. "I didn't see it coming, what happened Wednesday. But Tommy did. I never would've put you in such danger."

"Then why couldn't you tell me what you and Tommy put together?"

"Because I couldn't have you following leads on your own that might trigger something or be a dead end or worse, end up with you dead." Gale could practically see the smoke coming out of Syd's nose and took her hand. "You mean far too much to me now. And I *will* be ready in a few days."

Syd opened her mouth to protest but Gale held up a finger.

"I just need to be able to sit at a table and talk to Duane."

"Then I want to be there with you."

Gale put her head back and let out a loud sigh.

"No. Listen to me. My being there will matter. Duane having to look me in the eyes will make a difference."

Gale considered her. "You might have a point."

Even with a whole painkiller in her system, Syd felt a dull ache in her neck and shoulder. Her arm was still in the sling, and now she rested it on the kitchen table of the safe house where Tommy had driven her and Gale. Duane Valchek sat across from them. He was slouched on a kitchen chair, a hand of solitaire on the table as though he couldn't have cared less that Syd was there or that Gale was about to offer him a deal. Either way, Syd wished him decades of solitaire behind bars.

Tommy leaned against the wall by the front door, one eye on Syd and Gale, and one eye on the front lawn and driveway of the house. In the kitchen, Detective Miller, who'd accompanied them, periodically moved from the kitchen window to the windows along the back of the house. "I don't trust the mob," Tommy had said when Gale questioned the need for a second set of eyes with Miller's presence. The uniforms who'd been babysitting Duane were posted at windows on the second floor. Syd felt completely safe and at the same time totally exposed.

"I don't get how this is going to help me," Duane said, the edge to his voice scraping at Syd's nerves.

"Somebody killed Wyatt Reid. I don't think the state cares at this point who goes away for it," Gale said. "But we can make sure you get parole if you tell us what you know. You want to die in a supermax instead, I can arrange it." Gale turned on the recording app on her phone and set it on the table. "Interview with Duane Valchek in the Wyatt Reid cold case murder of nineteen eighty-two." She stated the day's date.

Duane rubbed his mouth and chin like a child who knew he'd misbehaved and was trying to decide if he could still have the cookie if he lied. It was taking every ounce of willpower for Syd not to kick him under the table, but Gale had said if she didn't sit quietly, Tommy would take her home.

Duane slumped back in his chair. "I didn't kill Wyatt. Schuyler Tilden did."

"How do you know?" Gale asked.

"Because Ned called me after. To come over and help him. I lived right around the corner." Duane concentrated on a card on the table, and then flipped it over. "Ned said he was coming up the stairs because the elevator was out, and Schuyler came tearing out of Wyatt's apartment covered in blood, said Schuyler freaked when he saw him and ran up to the roof."

Nausea rolled over Syd like a rogue wave.

"When did Ned tell you that?"

"When we were looking for the ledgers. He wanted two red ledgers that Wyatt was supposed to have. And he wanted them real bad. But hell, everything in there was red, and I knew we weren't going to find them because it looked like Schuyler ransacked the place already. If he didn't find them, we sure weren't going to."

Syd hugged her stomach with her free arm.

Gale pressed on. "How do you know Ned didn't kill him and blame it on Schuyler?"

"Because when I got there, there wasn't a drop of blood on Ned."

Gale nodded. "Why did Schuyler kill Wyatt?"

"Everyone knew they were having an affair and that Schuyler wanted out of his marriage. It was for show anyway. She wanted his name. She was busy shagging anything that walked, mostly Billy. Schuyler wanted to take the money she'd given that stupid school and leave the country with Wyatt. But by then, Theo was in the picture. He wasn't gonna leave him—we all knew that, too. Man, they had some screaming match outside Bareback that night when he told Schuyler. Bouncer had to break it up."

"George Oakley," Syd said.

Gale nodded. "We corroborated it with him."

Syd couldn't hide her distress, and under the table, Gale took her hand. It was a lifeline.

"Were you there?" Gale asked. "How did you know about the fight at Bareback?"

"Everyone was there. It was Halloween. The whole block saw that fight. It spilled outside. The bouncer didn't want the police called so he shoved Wyatt into a cab and decked Schuyler. He got up all bloody in his Marine uniform and hailed a cab. I went home about a half hour later with Rhett Butler and Scarlett O'Hara. I wasn't home twenty minutes when Ned called."

"What happened?"

"Like I said, we looked everywhere, couldn't find the ledgers. I wanted to go after Schuyler. I knew where he lived. But Ned wouldn't let me. So we just—left and closed the door. I'm sorry, Syd. I wanted to call the police, tip them off, but Ned said no. I'm sorry you walked in on that. We figured it'd be Theo who found him."

Syd looked away, fighting bitter tears. Behind her, Tommy cleared his throat. She almost reached for his hand.

"Tell me about Schuyler. Because you did go after him, didn't you?"

"Yeah, I did. Ned needed him gone. I saw the opportunity there. I told him that for a price, I'd take care of it if he'd let Billy go." Duane gathered the cards into a pile. "Billy was my best friend from when we were seven. He hated what he'd become, this machine, Ned's biggest earner. He'd take on five guys in a day and then he'd do two more on the side that Ned didn't know about, like those mob boys. The money was real good. But he was hurting and he wanted out of Ned's world. Only nobody walked out of Ned's world. So I made a trade. Billy's life for Schuyler's. And some annual spending money for me to become a ghost. Ned said I knew too much anyway. So I made us all disappear."

"How?"

"Once Ned agreed, I told Billy he had to off Schuyler, make it look accidental, and get outta Dodge."

"So you didn't kill him?"

"No, man, I don't kill people."

"No, you give that job to your best friend." Gale let the silence hang for a moment. "How did he do it?"

Duane shuffled the cards. Syd wanted to slap them out of his hands. "Bought a piece in Times Square. Ambushed him three blocks from his home, under some scaffolding, made it look like a mugging gone wrong. Used gloves, tossed the gun in the East River, burned his clothes and shoes. Then he rented a room off the books from some guy way out in Red Hook for six years, changed his appearance, went to Brooklyn College using his middle name, Frank. No one knew who he was. Except for me." Duane's laughter was soft. "After college, he landed a bank job, moved back to Manhattan, and began his new life. And no one knew that, either, except for me. And Lucas. He lived blocks from Ned, blocks from you, Syd. No one knew. You gotta love New York."

Syd wanted to hurl something at him, but even something as light as an epithet might've gotten her thrown out, and she wanted to hear the whole story. She bit her tongue.

"So Billy calls one day in January, says some mob guy and his gun contacted him about working for Ned back in the day, wanted Ned's books before the Feds got them in this LaundryGate thing. I came. Like I always do. I called the guy, told him the books were long gone. He said his old man was in touch with Ned in some nursing home, and Ned told him I'd know where the books were, said his old man wanted to talk to me. I figured Ned was fucking with me. Next thing I know, this guy is driving me out to the Pine Barrens. You have a lot of time to think when you're digging your own grave in the middle of nowhere, so I told him I'd bring 'em to him. I sent Lucas the blue envelope and waited."

By now Syd had her head in her hands. "What was in that envelope?"

"Death threat. Just like yours, Syd," Tommy said.

"Not quite like Syd's," Gale mused. "You didn't send a child's picture to either of them, did you?"

Duane shifted in his chair.

"What did it say, Duane?"

"Find the red ledger or one of you dies."

"And then you left. Left them both holding the bag, didn't you?" Gale asked. "Nice friend. And then Syd showed up at White Willows and all bets were off."

Duane's demeanor changed, his face taking on a bored look of disgust. "I had nothin' to lose. Send another note to Sydney. The first one shut her up. Maybe the second one would lead to that fucking ledger."

Syd's mouth opened in astonishment. "*You* planted the first one!"

"I wrote it. Ned put it there. It worked, didn't it?"

Syd stiffened so Gale ran interference. "Too bad for you the second threat didn't work. None of it worked. It'll take time to prove Rossiter Enterprises hackers were responsible for your computer bug and phone tap, Syd, but we'll do it." She turned back to Duane. "You thought it would be so simple, that once we got the red ledger from Syd, your uncle Pete could break into the evidence room again and steal it, right? Just like he did in eighty-two when he stole Wyatt's bloody clothes for Ned."

Duane shrugged.

"We figured out it was your uncle who put the bug under my desk."

Duane shrugged again. "He kept us out of a lot of trouble back then. And I did what Lucas and Billy told me to do over the years. I wasn't going to jail for any of that."

Syd was enraged. "That wasn't 'trouble!' You took a life!"

"Syd, I didn't take nobody's life. Schuyler killed Wyatt. I arranged for Schuyler to pay for that. You should be grateful."

The look of hubris on Duane's face slipped into confusion when Syd scraped her chair back and leaned over the table, seething. She felt Tommy's hand cupping her good shoulder, although the entire collarbone was now throbbing. "You have *no* idea what you did, do you?"

"I don't understand," Duane said to Gale. He looked at Tommy who now had an arm around Syd's waist restraining her. "I just gave you everything. Syd, an eye for an eye."

"And what about your life?" Syd spat at him. "What about all of your lives, lived as though nothing happened? But something *did* happen. And you all walked away from it."

"Syd, Wyatt made his own choices. We just cleaned up the mess. If anything, it was Ned. But he was Wyatt's choice, too."

It was as though Syd had been smacked in the face. She sat back down, all the fight in her gone. She wanted to cry. But Duane was right, there was no way around that. Wyatt had choices, and he'd made them, not the least of which had been Ned Rossiter.

She let Gale finish the questioning. If she could have leaned on her for support, she would have.

There was no sleep for Syd that night. There was only one man for whom nothing was enough so many years ago. Ned had been a chimera for everyone in his orbit. His genius was twofold. He so easily became the conduit for what you wished or hoped for—he had a gift for reading people. At the same time, he let you in on the illusion. Of course you would pay the price for that moment of grace—to be the someone you always wanted to be in that reflection; to receive the desired invitation beyond the velvet rope. For many, however, it was the veritable road to perdition. For Wyatt, it had proved a dead end.

She rested her head on the bed pillows and closed her eyes. There was one ray of light for her to hang on to: Wyatt had gone to the FBI. He had finally been who she thought he was.

EPILOGUE

Syd put two peach daiquiris and a small bottle of Coca Cola on the table between the chairs on the deck, sank into one, and breathed in the briny sea air. Her shoulder ached. Physical therapy was taking its toll on her; her therapist had warned her the months of it would be hard. Waterhouse meowed from his seat on a living room window. "No cats outdoors. You know the rule."

She shaded her eyes and looked toward the surf. A laughing Isabella ran out of the whitecaps with a football, turned around, lined up the laces, and threw it to Gale. She had to jump to grab it, splashing down beneath the waves when she secured it. Syd winced. It had been three months since the shooting, but it still made her nervous whenever Gale overexerted herself. Then again, maybe it was good for her. Izzy was certainly a balm for both of them.

Drew had brought her to New York the moment school let out and stayed most of the summer to help Syd get back on her feet with the physical therapy. He and Izzy went to museums, shows, and other tourist spots in the afternoons, leaving Syd and Gale to meet in various parks to walk, talk, and mend. Drew even went out to Fire Island one weekend to open the house with Izzy, and then he flew back to Nebraska. He told Syd to keep Izzy until school started.

What remained of their beach summer was idyllic. Days in the saltwater were restorative. In the evening, Syd and Gale cooked, teaching Izzy how to butterfly, sauté, julienne, and blanch. After dinner, a fire going against the cool August nights, Izzy taught them a thing or two about buying, selling, and banking with Monopoly.

Looking a little waterlogged now, Gale and Izzy trotted up the beach. Gale was tan from working in the rose gardens around the house. Wyatt had planted them the first summer. Syd always had to get a local landscaper to look after them to make sure she didn't kill them, but Gale knew exactly how to handle them, and loved spending time in the gardens. She had Sullivan's green thumb after all.

A sigh escaped her—Gale looked spectacular in her one-piece black suit and Syd felt a quickening tingle everywhere. She'd have to wait until later to take care of that, though.

Izzy stepped back as if to throw her the football.

"Don't you dare, Isabella Reid! There's glass on the deck."

Gale grabbed the ball from her and ran the rest of the way, Izzy pounding up the ramp behind her in pursuit. She dropped into the chair across from Syd and put the ball between her feet. "Izzy, you're gonna do me in—I am so out of shape!"

Syd thought otherwise as she glanced at Gale's lithe figure.

"Mmm, is that what I think it is?" Gale picked up the drink and took a long draught.

Izzy grabbed the Coke and a handful of walnuts from the bowl on the table and sprawled on the chaise. "I love it here, Aunt Syd. I could stay forever."

"I'm surprised—there's not a whole lot to do here. Or any kids your age."

"That's what I like about it. It's just you and Gale. And the drag queens next door. I like them. There's nobody here I have to do stuff for to seem cool. I can download books and work on the quilt—it's heaven. I'm not gonna dye my hair anymore, either."

Oh, thank God, Syd thought, noticing in late July that she hadn't been keeping it up, and the blond was slowly reappearing. "Won't Snipe be surprised if you're a blonde again? That is his name, right, Snipe?"

"That's his punk rock name, for his band. His real name is Connor. We broke up. I don't like punk music." Izzy took another handful of walnuts and finished her Coke. "I'm going to go take a shower."

"The insouciance of the young," Gale said, watching her go.

"It's hard finding yourself when you're that age."

"You're really good with her."

Syd waited to hear the screen door slam and Izzy thump upstairs. "I found life hard at many junctures. That was one of them. I was lucky—I had Aunt Ingrid. There's more daiquiri mix in the blender."

"Right now," Gale moved to the chaise Izzy had vacated, "what I'd like is you." She patted the space next to her.

Syd cast an envious eye at the traces of salt forming in certain places on Gale's suit, the water droplets still clinging to her, and the damp tendrils of hair she'd tried to slick back. "You're all wet."

"You're telling me." A sly teasing smile crossed Gale's face.

"I meant your suit. The other will have to wait." Syd lay down next to her, thrilled to have Gale's body next to hers in any form.

Gale chuckled. "I know. Good thing I like making love to you by moonlight. Or at dawn."

Syd kissed her. They were still at the long, slow kisses stage. She liked tasting the peach daiquiri on Gale's tongue, and the saltwater on her lips. "Are you okay with Izzy staying a couple more weeks? I can send her home whenever."

"Oh no—I think she's a lot of fun. She wants to learn how to garden, says she likes knowing this is her grandfather's legacy." Gale looked around at the roses climbing the banisters of the deck. "And I'm kind of interested in how quilts are made."

"You? Big tough city detective taking up quilting?"

"We strong and silent types can surprise you. She showed me how to make a wedding ring yesterday out of some strikingly beautiful patches. Who knows—maybe there's a quilt in our future. Besides, since I'm going to retire, I need new outlets. So you'll finally get to teach me how to play golf."

While they both lay in the hospital, Syd fantasized hearing those words. With everything they'd talked about during their walks in the park, now that Gale was saying when and not if, she realized what they portended.

"You're sure?" Syd said.

Gale nodded. "Now that I've had this summer with you. It's what I kept coming back to in that hospital bed when I was wrestling with what could have happened. The time we wouldn't have had if it had gone the other way. I want that. Time. And you. And you've made it abundantly clear that you want it, too." Gale kissed the top of her head.

Syd nestled against her. "I would like to be with you for the rest of my life, my love."

"September, then. I'll turn in my papers."

That night, as she watched Gale sleeping after they'd made love, she thought about how much she'd wrestled with after the shocking confession from Duane. It was the NYPD therapist Gale was required to work with who'd helped her when he'd invited her to one of Gale's sessions.

"Whether you know it or not, you've been on a quest most of your adult life, chasing something you might not even have realized you were chasing. Until it came seeking you." He'd been sympathetic, but emphatic. "That's a lot to sort through and let go of, and maybe an independent eye, or ear, would help. I can recommend someone."

She was left with a lot of baggage and no tools after Wyatt's murder was solved. She was building trust in Cara, her new therapist, with each Zoom session. A younger woman, she had ideas Syd sometimes needed the week to think about, but she pushed Syd to look at things through a different lens, and she'd been smart enough to liken the work they did together to moving items from the debit column to the credit column, earning Syd's respect.

Wyatt had broken her heart twice in a lifetime, but he'd mended it, too, in the end. She looked down at Gale stirring in her sleep and realized this woman was one last gift from Wyatt. She gazed out at the darkness, heard the waves gently washing up on the beach, and thanked him.

About the Author

Mary Burns is a long-time resident of New York City where she shares a wonderful life with her wife of over twenty years. She received a master of fine arts in playwriting from Columbia University in 1991. After a career as an executive assistant, she took a sabbatical to write a play and came out with a novel instead, *Forging a Desire Line*, published by Bold Strokes Books in 2020. That was followed by *Suspecting Her* in 2021.

She has also published short stories in Sinclair Sexsmith's 2019 award-winning *Best Lesbian Erotica, Volume 4* under the pen name Catherine Collinsworth, and *Volume 5* (Dec. 2020 / Cleis Press).

When she's not busy writing, which is most of the time following a 20-year bout of writer's block, she enjoys reading what everyone else is writing.

Books Available from Bold Strokes Books

An Independent Woman by Kit Meredith. Alex and Rebecca's attraction won't stop smoldering, despite their reluctance to act on it and incompatible poly relationship styles. (978-1-63679-553-9)

Cherish by Kris Bryant. Josie and Olivia cherish the time spent together, but when the summer ends and their temporary romance melts into the real deal, reality gets complicated. (978-1-63679-567-6)

Cold Case Heat by Mary P. Burns. Sydney Hansen receives a threat in a very cold murder case that sends her to the police for help where she finds more than justice with Detective Gale Sterling. (978-1-63679-374-0)

Proximity by Jordan Meadows. Joan really likes Ellie, but being alone with her could turn deadly unless she can keep her dangerous powers under control. (978-1-63679-476-1)

Sweet Spot by Kimberly Cooper Griffin. Pro surfer Shia Turning will have to take a chance if she wants to find the sweet spot. (978-1-63679-418-1)

The Haunting of Oak Springs by Crin Claxton. Ghosts and the past haunt the supernatural detective in a race to save the lesbians of Oak Springs farm. (978-1-63679-432-7)

Transitory by J.M. Redmann. The cops blow it off as a customer surprised by what was under the dress, but PI Micky Knight knows they're wrong—she either makes it her case or lets a murderer go free to kill again. (978-1-63679-251-4)

Unexpectedly Yours by Toni Logan. A private resort on a tropical island, a feisty old chief, and a kleptomaniac pet pig bring Suzanne and Allie together for unexpected love. (978-1-63679-160-9)

Bones of Boothbay Harbor by Michelle Larkin. Small-town police chief Frankie Stone and FBI Special Agent Eve Huxley must set aside their differences and combine their skills to find a killer after a burial site is discovered in Boothbay Harbor, Maine. (978-1-63679-267-5)

Crush by Ana Hartnett Reichardt. Josie Sanchez worked for years for the opportunity to create her own wine label, and nothing will stand in her way. Not even Mac, the owner's annoyingly beautiful niece Josie's forced to hire as her harvest intern. (978-1-63679-330-6)

Decadence by Ronica Black, Renee Roman, and Piper Jordan. You are cordially invited to Decadence, Las Vegas's most talked about invitation-only Masquerade Ball. Come for the entertainment and stay for the erotic indulgence. We guarantee it'll be a party that lives up to its name. (978-1-63679-361-0)

Gimmicks and Glamour by Lauren Melissa Ellzey. Ashly has learned to hide her Sight, but as she speeds toward high school graduation she must protect the classmates she claims to hate from an evil that no one else sees. (978-1-63679-401-3)

Heart of Stone by Sam Ledel. Princess Keeva Glantor meets Maeve, a gorgon forced to live alone thanks to a decades-old lie, and together the two women battle forces they formerly thought to be good in the hopes of leading lives they can finally call their own. (978-1-63679-407-5)

Murder at the Oasis by David S. Pederson. Palm trees, sunshine, and murder await Mason Adler and his friend Walter as they travel from Phoenix to Palm Springs for what was supposed to be a relaxing vacation but ends up being a trip of mystery and intrigue. (978-1-63679-416-7)

Peaches and Cream by Georgia Beers. Adley Purcell is living her dreams owning Get the Scoop ice cream shop until national dessert chain Sweet Heaven opens less than two blocks away and Adley has to compete with the far too heavenly Sabrina James. (978-1-63679-412-9)

The Only Fish in the Sea by Angie Williams. Will love overcome years of bitter rivalry for the daughters of two crab fishing families in this queer modern-day spin on Romeo and Juliet? (978-1-63679-444-0)

Wildflower by Cathleen Collins. When a plane crash leaves eleven-year-old Lily Andrews stranded in the vast wilderness of Arkansas, will she be able to overcome the odds and make it back to civilization and the one person who holds the key to her future? (978-1-63679-621-5)

Witch Finder by Sheri Lewis Wohl. Tamsin, the Keeper of the Book of Darkness, is in terrible danger, and as a Witch Finder, Morrigan must protect her and the secrets she guards even if it costs Morrigan her life. (978-1-63679-335-1)

A Second Chance at Life by Genevieve McCluer. Vampires Dinah and Rachel reconnect, but a string of vampire killings begin and evidence seems to be pointing at Dinah. They must prove her innocence while finding out if the two of them are still compatible after all these years. (978-1-63679-459-4)

Digging for Heaven by Jenna Jarvis. Litz lives for dragons. Kella lives to kill them. The last thing they expect is to find each other attractive. (978-1-63679-453-2)

Forever's Promise by Missouri Vaun. Wesley Holden migrated west disguised as a man for the hope of a better life and with no designs to take a wife, but Charlotte Rose has other ideas. (978-1-63679-221-7)

Here For You by D. Jackson Leigh. A horse trainer must make a difficult business decision that could save her father's ranch from foreclosure but destroy her chance to win the heart of a feisty barrel racer vying for a spot in the National Rodeo Finals. (978-1-63679-299-6)

I Do, I Don't by Joy Argento. Creator of the romance algorithm, Nicole Hart doesn't expect to be starring in her own reality TV dating show, and falling for the show's executive producer Annie Jackson could ruin everything. (978-1-63679-420-4)

It's All in the Details by Dena Blake. Makeup artist Lane Donnelly and wedding planner Helen Trent can't stand each other, but they must set aside their differences to ensure Darcy gets the wedding of her dreams, and make a few of their own dreams come true. (978-1-63679-430-3)

Marigold by Melissa Brayden. Marigold Lavender vows to take down Alexis Wakefield, the harsh food critic who blasts her younger sister's restaurant. If only she wasn't as sexy as she is mean. (978-1-63679-436-5)

The Town that Built Us by Jesse J. Thoma. When her father dies, Grace Cook returns to her hometown and tries to avoid Bonnie Whitlock, the woman who pulverized her heart, only to discover her father's estate has been left to them jointly. (978-1-63679-439-6)

A Degree to Die For by Karis Walsh. A murder at the University of Washington's Classics Department brings Professor Antigone Weston and Sergeant Adriana Kent together—first as opposing forces, and then allies as they fight together to protect their campus from a killer. (978-1-63679-365-8)

A Talent Within by Suzanne Lenoir. Evelyne, born into nobility, and Annika, a peasant girl with a deadly secret, struggle to change their destinies in Valmora, a medieval world controlled by religion, magic, and men. (978-1-63679-423-5)

Finders Keepers by Radclyffe. Roman Ashcroft's past, it seems, is not so easily forgotten when fate brings her and Tally Dewilde together— along with an attraction neither welcomes. (978-1-63679-428-0)

Homeland by Kristin Keppler and Allisa Bahney. Dani and Kate have finally found themselves on the same side of the war, but a new threat from the inside jeopardizes the future of the wasteland. (978-1-63679-405-1)

Just One Dance by Jenny Frame. Will Taylor Spark and her new business to make dating special—the Regency Romance Club—bring sparkle back to Jaq Bailey's lonely world? (978-1-63679-457-0)

On My Way There by Jaycie Morrison. As Max traverses the open road, her journey of impossible love, loss, and courage mirrors her voyage of self-discovery leading to the ultimate question: If she can't have the woman of her dreams, will the woman of real life be enough? (978-1-63679-392-4)

Transitioning Home by Heather K O'Malley. An injured soldier realizes they need to transition to really heal. (978-1-63679-424-2)

Truly Enough by JJ Hale. Chasing the spark of creativity may ignite a burning romance or send a friendship up in flames. (978-1-63679-442-6)

Vintage and Vogue by Kelly and Tana Fireside. When tech whiz Sena Abrigo marches into small-town Owen Station, she turns librarian Hazel Butler's life upside down in the most wonderful of ways, setting off an explosive series of events, threatening their chance at love…and their very lives. (978-1-63679-448-8)